Foreword to the Paperback Edition

I cannot yet believe that the first hardcover edition of my novel sold out before a copy was available in the book-stores. Or that a second and a third edition should have to be printed within a fortnight of the first. It is enough to turn the head of any writer. It has mine.

It took me twenty-five years to piece together this story spanning several centuries of history. I put in it all I had in me as a writer: love, lust, sex, hate, vendetta and violence — and above all, tears. I did not write this novel with any audience in mind. All I wanted to do was tell my readers what I learnt about the city roaming among its ancient ruins, its congested bazaars, its diplomatic corps and its cocktail parties. My only aim was to get them to know Delhi and love it as much as I do. The readers' response has been most gratifying and gives me hope that I may achieve my object.

New Delhi   *Khushwant Singh*
July 1990

A Note from the Author

In this novel I have tried to tell the story of Delhi from its earliest beginnings to the present times. I constructed it from records chronicled by eye-witnesses. Hence most of it is told in the first person. History provided me with the skeleton. I covered it with flesh and injected blood and a lot of seminal fluid into it. It took me twenty-five years to do so. I am not sure whether I have succeeded in my venture.

Some chapters in an earlier draft were published in *Evergreen Review* of New York and *The Illustrated Weekly of India*.

New Delhi   *Khushwant Singh*
15 September 1989

PENGUIN BOOKS
DELHI: A NOVEL

Khushwant Singh was born in 1915 in Hadali, Punjab. He was educated at Government College, Lahore and at King's College and the Inner Temple in London. He practised at the Lahore High Court for several years before joining the Indian Ministry of External Affairs in 1947. He began a distinguished career as a journalist with All India Radio in 1951. Since then he has been founder-editor of *Yojna* (1951-1953), editor of the *Illustrated Weekly of India* (1979-1980), and editor of the *Hindustan Times* (1980-1983). Today he is India's best-known columnist and journalist.

Khushwant Singh has also had an extremely successful career as a writer. Among the works he has published are a classic two-volume history of the Sikhs, several novels (the best-known of which are *Train to Pakistan*, *The Company of Women* and *Delhi*), and a number of translated works and non-fiction books on Delhi, nature and current affairs.

Khushwant Singh was Member of Parliament from 1980 to 1986. Among other honours he was awarded the Padma Bhushan in 1974 by the President of India (he returned the decoration in 1984 in protest against the Union Government's siege of the Golden Temple, Amritsar).

Delhi

a novel

KHUSHWANT SINGH

PENGUIN BOOKS

PENGUIN BOOKS
Published by the Penguin Group
Penguin Books India Pvt Ltd, 11 Community Centre, Panchsheel Park, New Delhi
110 017, India
Penguin Group (USA) Inc., 375 Hudson Street, New York, New York 10014, USA
Penguin Group (Canada), 90 Eglinton Avenue East, Suite 700, Toronto, Ontario,
M4P 2Y3, Canada (a division of Pearson Penguin Canada Inc.)
Penguin Books Ltd, 80 Strand, London WC2R 0RL, England
Penguin Ireland, 25 St Stephen's Green, Dublin 2, Ireland (a division of Penguin Books Ltd)
Penguin Group (Australia), 250 Camberwell Road, Camberwell, Victoria 3124,
Australia (a division of Pearson Australia Group Pty Ltd)
Penguin Group (NZ), cnr Airborne and Rosedale Roads, Albany, Auckland 1310,
New Zealand (a division of Pearson New Zealand Ltd)
Penguin Group (South Africa) (Pty) Ltd, 24 Sturdee Avenue, Rosebank, Johannesburg
2196, South Africa

Penguin Books Ltd, Registered Offices: 80 Strand, London WC2R 0RL, England

First published by Penguin Books India 1990

Copyright © Khushwant Singh 1990
Page vi is an extension of the copyright page

20 19

Printed at Chaman Offset Printers, New Delhi

This novel, which took me over twenty years to write, I dedicate to my son Rahul
Singh and his friend Niloufer Billimoria.

Contents

I asked my soul: What is Delhi?
She replied: The world is the body and Delhi its life.

Mirza Asadullah Khan Ghalib

1

Delhi

I return to Delhi as I return to my mistress Bhagmati when I have had my fill of whoring in foreign lands. Delhi and Bhagmati have a lot in common. Having been long misused by rough people they have learnt to conceal their seductive charms under a mask of repulsive ugliness. It is only to their lovers, among whom I count myself, that they reveal their true selves.

To the stranger Delhi may appear like a gangrenous accretion of noisy bazaars and mean-looking hovels growing round a few tumble-down forts and mosques along a dead river. If he ventures into its narrow, winding lanes, the stench of raw sewage may bring vomit to his throat. The citizens of Delhi do little to endear themselves to anyone. They spit phlegm and bloody *betel*-juice everywhere; they urinate and defecate whenever and wherever the urge overtakes them; they are loud-mouthed, express familiarity with incestuous abuse and scratch their privates while they talk.

It is the same with Bhagmati. Those who do not know her find her unattractive. She is dark and has pock-marks on her face. She is short and squat; her teeth are uneven and yellowed as a result of chewing tobacco and smoking *beedis*. Her clothes are loud, her voice louder; her speech bawdy and her manners worse.

This is, as I say, only on the surface—like the evil-smelling oil people smear on their skins to repel mosquitoes, midges and other blood-sucking vermin. What you have to do for things to appear different is to cultivate a sense of belonging to Delhi and an attachment to someone like Bhagmati. Then the skies over Delhi's marbled palaces turn an aquamarine blue; its domed mosques and pencil-like minarets are span-ned by rainbows, the earth exudes the earthy aroma of *khas*, of jasmine and of *maulsari*. Then the dusky Bhagmati glides towards you swaying her ample hips like a temple dancer; her mouth smells of fresh cloves and she speaks like her Imperial Majesty the Empress of Hindustan. Only when making love does she behave, as every woman should, like a lusty harlot. It is a simple formula: use your heart not your head, your emotion not your reason.

I make Delhi and Bhagmati sound very mysterious. The truth is that I am somewhat confused in my thoughts. What I am trying to say is that although I detest living in Delhi and am ashamed of my liaison with Bhagmati, I cannot keep away from either for too long. In these pages I will explain the strange paradox of my lifelong, love-hate affair with the city and the woman. It may read like a *Fucking Man's Guide to Delhi: Past and Present* but that is not what I mean it to be.

*

The plane touches down at Palam at 2100 hours, one hour behind schedule. 'Air-India planes used to arrive on the dot till the government took it over,' says someone. A voice over the speaker system orders us to remain seated. 'Why?' I demand of an air hostess gliding past me. She confides in my ear: 'Health!' India, mother of most diseases known to mankind, does not want to add any more to her list. We sit encapsuled in light, talking in whispers and preventing our newspapers from rustling.

Someone slaps the plane with a heavy hand: thump, thump. The steward yanks open the door. Two men in medical white waft in with a gust of hot air. They go down the aisle distributing printed forms. We busy ourselves filling in the answers: Where did you spend the last ten days? Nine days? Yesterday? One man takes a canister out of his pocket and strides up the aisle spraying us with hospital smell. We can disembark.

We file out. Near the base of the ramp attached to the first class exit stands an enormous grey Rolls-Royce bearing the

President's three-faced lion insignia on its numberplate.
Beside the car, stand the President's ADC and an orderly with
an armful of flowers. Behind them are half-a-dozen
photographers with cameras raised to their noses. A white
woman carrying a fur coat on one arm and a hat-box in the
other comes down the steps. Flash bulbs explode. The ADC
clicks his heels and salutes. He takes the white woman's fur
coat and hat-box and hands them to the orderly. He garlands
the woman, presents her with the bouquets and salutes her
again. She flashes her teeth at him. They get into the Rolls-
Royce. The Rolls-Royce purrs away into the dark.

Who is she?

We are herded together and directed to follow an Air-India
official. We shade our eyes against the glare of airport lights
and showers of moths. We skirt past long-snouted bandicoots
skating on their bellies and enter a door marked 'International.' A large poster with a picture of Pandit Nehru bids us
Welcome to India.

A police sergeant scrutinizes our health forms and stacks
them in the 'out' basket on his table. A sub-inspector inspects
our passports, stamps them and hands them back to us. A
customs officer gives us sheafs of forms to fill in triplicate.
Three each for what we have bought abroad; three each for
what we have in foreign currency. We spend half-an-hour
filling them. Customs men eye us to see if our expressions
betray undeclared items. We look bored; our expressions
betray nothing.

Forty minutes later trollies rattle into the customs shed.
Coolies offload cases on the floor. I locate my valise and grab
a customs inspector. I have bought nothing and have no
foreign currency. He does not believe me. He examines my
declaration forms and my passport. He opens my valise and
fires a stream of questions as he digs into my clothes.

'Any whisky-shisky?'

'No.'

'No tape recorder?'

'No.'

'Transistor-shranzistor?'

'No.'

'Camera-shamera?'

'No.'

'Watch-shotch?'

'No.'

He grabs my hand and examines the shiny new Vulcan alarm watch on my wrist. I bought it at Beirut's duty-free shop in the airport store for £35.

'How much?'

I produce a receipt for the watch I bought for my cook which is tucked in my hip-pocket. 'Seven pounds.'

He is a bad loser. He chalks my valise as if he were writing 'Fuck off.' One takes a lot from these customs bastards.

A porter grabs my valise. We pierce through a wall of clamorous taxi-drivers and find a cab. The porter dumps my valise on the rear seat and exclaims: 'Okay sir, *salaam!*' Airport rules say don't tip porters. He takes five rupees off me.

The Sikh cab-driver has a Sikh friend in the front seat. Twenty minutes later we arrive at my destination. The cab-driver lights a match and reads the meter, 'Eighteen fifty plus two for the luggage. Twenty fifty.'

'Eighteen fifty?' I pack as much disbelief as I can into my voice. It is more than double what I paid on my way out to Palam airport a few weeks ago.

'Eighteen fifty,' repeats the cabbie. His friend lights another match and reads: 'Eighteen fifty. See meter.'

One Sikh may argue with one Sikh. One Sikh must never argue with two Sikhs—certainly not after dark. I pay twenty rupees fifty paise plus another two rupees as tip.

The night-watchman of our block of apartments is also a Sikh. When I go out of Delhi, I leave the key of my flat with him. He is an honest fellow but a little soft under his turban. He was discharged from the army for his eccentricities. Although he was only a truck-driver he never forgets he once wore a soldier's uniform. He jumps up from his *charpoy* and orders himself: 'Salute!' And salutes me as if I were the colonel of his regiment. 'How was His Majesty the King of England?' he asks me in English.

'England now has a Queen.'

He thinks that a matter of small detail. 'Very well, sir. Did you ask His—beg pardon—Her Majesty, why he/she did not answer my letters?'

'Budh Singh, how long have you been like this?' I enquire very gently. Budh (knowledge) Singh gets this way three times in the year; then he becomes a Budhoo (simpleton) Singh. One has to be very gentle with Budhoo Singh.

His eyes burn. 'You think I mad?' he screams. 'You want dismiss me?' I do not answer. He unlocks the door, switches on the light and lets me in. He carries my valise to the unlit bedroom mumbling to himself. He comes back and presents me the key of the apartment with both his hands like a vanquished general surrendering his sword. 'Sir, here is your key and here is your job!'

'Budh Singh, I only asked you how long you have been like this,' I say taking the key.

'Yes, but I know truth,' says he peering into my eyes. 'Public say Budh is Budhoo again. Sahib sack him when he back from foreign. I say *Hunooz Dilli Door Ast*: you know what that mean? It is a long way to Delhi.'

'But I am back in Delhi,' I remind him. He looks at me more intensely. 'Okay! Forgive and forget.'

He assures me the apartment has been swept, furniture dusted. 'All okay. Cold machine okay, air-condition okay. Come and look,' he commands. I follow him to the bedroom and press the switch. *Click*. No result. *Click, clock, click, clock*. No result. 'Excuse me, bulb fooze,' explains Budh Singh. He presses another switch. The burst of light gives him a shock. He leaps in the air and pirouettes like a dancing *dervish*.

He puts a finger to his turban and explains. 'Springtime something happen here. Don't mind, salute!'

'It will pass,' I reassure him. He comes close to me till his beard almost touches mine. He says in a conspiratorial whisper, 'Excuse me! Your *hijda* come many time to enquire if you back.'

Budh Singh does not like my mistress Bhagmati because she called him Pagal (mad) Singh. Budh Singh has never forgiven her. He calls her a him or a *hijda* (hermaphrodite). Bhagmati has a small bosom and a heavy voice. 'Excuse me,' he confides to my beard, 'everyone is talking about it. They say, take woman, take boy—okay! But a *hijda*! That's not nice. Don't mind my saying so!'

I say nothing. Budh Singh takes it as a reprimand. He stands stiffly to attention, salutes for the umpteenth time and orders himself: 'Right turn!' He turns right. 'By the left, quick march.' And marches out with measured steps.

Hah!

I peel off my clothes and go into the bathroom. I turn on the tap. A muddy ooze trickles down into the bucket. It is followed by a little muddy water. Then a fart. No water. I give up.

I go to my study, pick up the phone and dial the number of the caretaker on night duty. Two girls are on the line yakking away about their Daddyji and Uncleji. I put down the receiver, slap a mosquito against my paunch and try again. They are still at it; this time about their Mummyji and Auntyji. I put down the receiver, extract fluff out of my navel, inhale its shitty smell and try a third time. They are exulting over the piquancy of the *chaat* in Bengali Market: 'Yum! Yum!' I lose my temper and tell them that it is almost midnight and they should be doing what their Mummyjis are doing to their Daddyjis. 'Some dirty fellow on our line,' says one. 'Will buzz you later. Ta-ta.'

I dial my number. Engaged. Three minutes later I dial again. Engaged. I dial Complaints. The man at the other end tells me to dial Assistance. I dial Assistance. This operator tells me: 'Number out of order please, dial Complaints.' I give up.

I go to my bedroom to let the air-conditioner cool my naked flesh and raw temper. It welcomes me with a distinct lowering of tone, but soon its drone lulls me to slumber. In a short while, however, it resents my indifference and goes off in a sulk. The bedroom becomes like the Black Hole of Calcutta.

Power cut. No light, no fan. I come out into my patch of garden and flop into a canechair. It's hot, humid, dark and still. There are a few stars, but they are very very far away. And there are too many mosquitoes. I think angry thoughts. I will write letters to the papers about delays at the airport, the manners of customs inspectors, cheating by cab-drivers, the inefficiency of the electricity company, Delhi telephones, Delhi water supply.... Then I think of Bhagmati. I wonder how much whoring she has done while I have been away. She likes to tell me of her exploits because she knows it rouses my desire for her. I sit in the dark many hours. I am angry, I am wanton. Then less angry, more wanton. A pale, old moon wanders into the sky. A light goes up in the temple behind my apartment. The electricity is back when it is not needed. I get up and drag my feet into the sitting-room.

I switch on the table-lamp. 5.15 a.m. I throw open the window. The curtains flutter. A cool breeze fragrant with the *madhumalati* which covers the outside wall drives away the dank fuzz of yesterday's dead air. I sink into my armchair and gaze out of the window. Streetlights go off with a silent bang. Through the foliage of the mulberry tree appears the grey dawn.

Flying foxes wing their soundless way back to perch on massive *arjun* trees. The old lady who lives in the apartment above mine slish-sloshes along the road. She stops by my hibiscus hedge, looks around to see if anyone is looking, quickly plucks some flowers, thrusts them in her *dupatta* and slish-sloshes on towards the temple. Her old man follows her. He also stops by my hedge, looks around to see if anyone is listening, presses his paunch, and lets out a long, painful fart. He walks on with a lighter step and a 'who did that?' look on his face. A light goes on in the opposite block. A woman draws the curtains, ties her untidy hair into a bun and stretches her arms towards me. More lights are switched on and off. The morning star is barely visible in the pink sky. Crows begin cawing to each other. Sparrows start quarrelling in the mulberry tree. The muezzin's voice rises to the heavens. Temple bells peal to awaken the gods from their slumbers. The milkman cycles round the block with a noisy clanging of milkcans. Another cyclist follows tinkling his bell and shouting *'Paperwalla! Ishtaitman, Taim of India, Hindustan Taim, Express, Herald, paperwalla!'* I hear the shush of papers being pushed under my door. I stay in my armchair. The morning breeze wafts the light of dawn into the room. It is cool, fragrant, pregnant with sadness and longing; it is the *bad-i-*

saba—the morning breeze—sacred to lovers. And I am back in my beloved city.

*

I settle down to the *Hindustan Times*. The front page has a picture of the white woman who came off the plane last night. 'Lady Hoity-Toity says it's great to be back home in Delhi.' So that's who she is! She has come to collect material for a book on archaeology. She is staying with the President at Rashtrapati Bhavan.

I glance over the headlines and look at the pictures.

My cook-bearer enters with a welcoming grin. I give him the Japanese watch I bought for him. His grin changes into a smile. He gives me a mug of black coffee and asks me if I will be in for lunch. No. Dinner? Yes, but I may be late, so leave it on the table. What would I like? I know he's thinking of Bhagmati because she eats only Indian food and I eat Anglo-Indian *ishtoo* or *sawset* with *kashtar* for a *putteen*. I do not know how, when or where I will find Bhagmati. But I am not going to tell him, so I reply 'Anything.' He goes away constipated with curiosity.

It is time to catch up with Delhi. A quick shower and I am off in my Hindustan Ambassador. More roads and round-abouts have had their names changed. The Windsors, Yorks, Cannings and Hardinges have been replaced by the Tilaks, Patels, Azads and Nehrus. There are red flags outside a petrol station with three men chanting 'Death to petrol-stationwalla.' Red flags outside Dr Sen's nursing home. Six men yelling, 'Death to Doctors.' Red flags outside Food and Agriculture Ministry building. Four men in garlands sit cross-legged on the lawn. A placard in front of them says *Third Day of Relay Hunger Strike*. A procession with saffron flags goes along Parliament Street chanting 'Our religion and our country are one. The cow is our mother. Death to cow-eaters.' On the lawns of Connaught Circus there is a political meeting. The speaker yells into the mike: 'All together cry —*Jai Hind*.' The crowd obeys: '*Jai Hind*.' The man at the mike is not happy. 'That's not good enough. We cannot fight those Chinese pigs with such feeble voices, can we? Let your voices be heard as far as Peking. All together *Jai Hind.*'

'JAI HIND.'

Pekinese pigs piss in your pants. With enemies like Indians you've nothing to lose except your piddle.

I park my car beside the stalls of the Tibetan 'antique' dealers on Janpath (once Queensway). The same brand of American tourists bargain for the same kind of brass and stone bric-à-brac. The same set of Sikh fortune-tellers mumble the same kind of romances and travel to foreigners. One fellow spots my Marks-and-Sparks T-shirt. 'You come from *phoren*, you go *phoren* again,' he assures me. 'One minute you give me and I tell you love-affairs. Rich, white lady passioning for you. I tell you name. I tell you how to make her and her much fortune your own.' I speak to him in Punjabi. 'Tell these things to the *Amreekans*, I have no money.' He knows his victim. 'Money?' he sneers indignantly, 'Money is dirt on back of hand. You great future. Much riches. Much love-affairs with *phoren* ladies. One evil star stopping you. Close palm.' Without thinking I clench my fist. 'Now open.' I unclench my hand. There is a black spot in the middle of my palm. 'See!' he says triumphantly, 'Black star! You give rupee one only. From *Amreekans* I take rupees ten. I tell you how conquer black star.' I give him a rupee and am instructed in the art of seducing foreign women. 'Sardarji, your lady love name begin with J.H.T. Yes?' I know no woman with the initials J.H.T. He goes on: 'When you get white lady with J.H.T. in name you remember Natha Singh, world-famous palmist-astrologer.'

I arrive at the All India Cooperative Coffee House. More red flags. One banner says *Give us our demands.* A man hands me a leaflet listing the demands. I roll it up and return it to him with an obscene gesture. He returns the compliment. Nasty man!

I cast my eyes over the noisy throng. Can't see anyone I'd care to be with. I buy a copy of *Delhi Underworld* from the news-stand, grab a table just as it is vacated and tilt three chairs against it. I plunge into my weekly ration of Delhi scandals. A Minister of Cabinet (name to be disclosed next week) has impregnated his daughter-in-law. There's nepotism for you! Free service to the son! 'Confessions of a Connaught Circus Girl.' Poor thing complains of misuse by the Indian staff of an African embassy. She says Africans are better endowed than Indians. They also pay more money. A college lad writes a letter complaining that his step-mother raped him while his father was out on tour. Editor appends angry footnote in italics: 'How can you put your instrument in the same place as your father's which gave you birth?..... Your step-mother is disgrace to Indian womanhood.' He promises to give advice on how to deal with such women in the next issue. I drool over drawings of 'sex cats' with bosoms like the protrusions on the fenders of American cars. The next issue also promises a full disclosure of goings-on in Tihar Jail (women's section). Bhagmati has told me quite a lot about that. She's been to Tihar many times.

I see two of our gang come in. One is a photographer, the other a journalist. Both claim to be Delhi's champion womanizers. They see me and advance with their arms wide open. 'Hullo, hullo. How's the little one?' asks the photographer, tapping my middle. 'Did it do its duty to the memsahibs?' I tap his fly: 'And how's Delhi's champion stud bull?' He shrugs his shoulders. 'Fifteen days no action. I stick to my motto: when you find a woman fornicate, when you do not be celibate. No self-abuse, no boys, no hijdas.' That's hitting me below the belt.

'And you great pen-pusher, what's your Qutub Minar been up to?' I ask the journalist. He's a big fellow with pubic-sized growth on his face. He also replies in verse. 'When I get a woman I copulate. When I don't, I masturbate. No complaints. The great Guru is in His Heaven and the mashooka in my bed!' He plucks a hair out of his beard and examines it with philosophic detachment. A third friend joins us. He is an Upper Division Clerk in the Ministry of Defence. He is utilizing his unutilized sick leave. He disapproves of this kind of talk! 'Five million Indians are dying of hunger in Bihar and all you fellows can think of is women.' He shakes his foot, then jerks his legs like the arms of a nutcracker. He puts his feet on the chair and continues to amuse himself. A fart escapes his fat arse: *poonh*. He is embarrassed. He puts his feet down and apologizes: 'Sorry, it was a slip of the tongue.'

Another of our cronies comes along. He is a politician of sorts and our political expert. He made a name during the last famine by organizing a 'miss-a-*chappati*-a-week' movement. Now he is contemplating a similar campaign for family planning based on the slogan 'If you want good luck: In one week only one...' The slogan hasn't got off the bed yet. We return to sex and corruption and inefficiency and five million starving in Bihar. We drink many cups of coffee and nibble many plates of cashewnuts. So passes the morning.

A heavy depression overtakes me. I take leave of my coffee-house friends and drive along the Ring Road which skirts the old city. I pass along the Mughal city wall and Zeenat Mahal's mosque. I slow down at the electric crematorium. No customers, no smoke. I move on through the arches of three bridges to Nigambodh Ghat cremation ground on the Jamna. I park my car and go in.

What's happened to the Delhiwallas? They are not even dying as they used to! Only one pyre burning and three heaps of smouldering ashes. No mourners. I walk up to the edge of the bank to see if there is any life there. Quite a scene!

Down the steps running into the river is a corpse draped in a red shroud. A dozen men and women are screaming and beating their breasts. A Brahmin priest pushes them aside, chants Sanskrit mumbo-jumbo and sprinkles water on the body. A middle-aged man uncovers its face. It's a young girl—very waxen and in deep slumber. The man stares at her face, moans and shakes his head in disbelief. A woman on the other side of the corpse smacks her forehead many times and clasps the dead girl in her arms. Other people gently remove the wailing couple and cover up the face of the corpse. The priest puts out his palm. Somebody gives him a rupee. He looks at the silver coin with disdain, then clip-clops up the stairs in his wooden sandals. The mourners lift the bier and follow him. They put the corpse on the ground and begin to make a platform of logs. The middle-aged couple resume their mourning. The woman throws dust in her hair and smacks her head with both her hands screaming. '*Hai*! *Hai*!

Hai!' The man again uncovers the dead girl's face, gazes intently for a minute and then groans, *'Hai Rabba!'* He cannot take his eyes off the dead child. He presses her arms and legs, massages the soles of her feet. The pyre is ready. The corpse is lifted and placed on it. More wood and pampas stalks are placed over the body and a brass *lota* full of clarified butter emptied on it. A man lights a stick with a bundle of rags soaked in kerosene and takes the torch round the pyre. It bursts into flames. Another man takes a sharp-pointed bamboo pole, prods the flaring, crackling pyre to locate the dead girl's head and then lunges into her skull.

The parents bury their faces in the dust, slap the ground and wail. The Toofan Mail from Calcutta rumbles over Jamna's iron bridge towards Delhi railway station.

I leave Nigambodh Ghat with the heat of the flames on my face and the helpless cry of the stricken parents ringing in my ears. There is real grief! It stabs through the heart like a needle. There, but for the grace of God, it could have been I pouring dust onto my head to mourn the death of my child! Here, by the grace of God, I am driving my Ambassador back to my apartment! What are my irritations, envies and frustrations compared to the sorrow of the people I have left behind! They will go home and miss their daughter. I'll get home and drink my Scotch.

Budh Singh awaits me. He presents arms with his stave. I refuse to be embarrassed. He comes closer and confides. 'Excuse me, sir, your *hijda* came to see you. I told her you have not come back from *phoren*. I hope you not angry with me. Take a woman, take a boy, but a *hijda*...'

I could slap Budhoo Singh across his bearded face. Instead I gently shut the door behind me and fix myself a drink.

That's Delhi. When life gets too much for you all you need to do is to spend an hour at Nigambodh Ghat, watch the dead being put to the flames and hear their kin wail for them. Then come home and down a couple of pegs of whisky. In Delhi, death and drink make life worth living.

2

Lady J.H.T.

I am nibbling my second sandwich with my second Scotch. The phone rings. 'Is that 420420?' It is. 'Sir, please speak to the Secretary, Ministry of Education.'

'How are you old cock?' (The Secretary and I are on Delhi's old cock network). He does not wait for an answer and proceeds. 'This is about Lady Hoity-Toity. You must have read about her in the morning papers! Famous archaeologist, cousin of the Queen, Guest of the President, V.V.I.P. etc., etc. Good contact; maybe a good lay. She wants to examine some old sites to see if she can dig up something. Everything laid on. Limousine, caviar, champagne. Everything that our poor country can afford. Can you take her around?'

'Sure!'

'Fine! The car will pick you up at five in the morning. Don't keep Her Ladyship waiting. Have a nice fuck.'

Before I can explode 'Five!' he puts down the receiver. I reason with myself. One early morning compensated by a lifetime of name-dropping. How does it go? 'Sound, sound the clarion, fill the fife, throughout the sensual world proclaim, one crowded hour of lusty loving, is worth an age without a name.' I'd have a whole day with a world celebrity, with a bit of luck seduce her and go down in the pages of history as one of her lovers.

I could take her to Moti Mahal on *Qawwali Nite*. People would ogle, whisper, envy. And to my friends: 'Jane said to me.' 'Who is this Jane *yaar*...?' 'You don't know Lady Jane Hoity-Toity...? Cousin of the Queen...renowned archaeologist! Well, we were digging for this grey earthenware pottery...we became close friends...'

I turn in early. I get little sleep. The scene at the cremation ground haunts me. I switch on the light often to see the time. The alarm clock bursts my eardrum at 4.30 a.m. Quick shit, quick shower and half-an-hour later I am standing outside my apartment.

It is March. Fragrant dawn. The morning star shines brighter than the dying moon. The block of apartments is lit by the headlights of a car. A truck thunders by. Again the silence and the morning star and the fresh morning breeze. The eastern horizon gets lighter. Big bats wing their way home. Another car. And another. My watch says 5.40. My temper begins to rise. I could have had another half-an-hour in bed. The glare of headlights blind me. A Rolls-Royce rolls up and a flunky in red and white uniform steps out and asks whether I am I. Yes. He opens the front door. I find myself wedged between the chauffeur and the flunky. I take a quick look back; a vast seat occupied by a diminutive figure wrapped in fur. She nods her colourless white face and asks, 'Are you the guide?'

'Yes Madam,' I reply gruffly. When she discovers who I am she will feel very silly. The thought soothes my temper.

'Purana Qila,' I order the chauffeur.

'No,' she squawks from the rear. 'Tilpat. He's been told where to go.' So she knows Delhi! What am I supposed to do? Act the court jester to Her Royal Bitchiness of Kennelpore!

We go along the Mathura-Agra Road, cross the ancient Barapulla bridge. The Rolls-Royce switches off its headlights. The morning light reveals scores of defecating bottoms. We go over the railway bridge, past Friends Colony and through the stench exuded by the sewage disposal farm. We bump past the Road Research Institute. We go through the village Badarpur, turn off the main highway and ride into the rising sun. The fields are littered with defecators; some face us with their penises dangling between their haunches; others display their buttocks—barely an inch above pyramids of shit. The Indian peasant is the world's champion shitter. Stacks of *chappaties* and mounds of mustard leaf-mash down the hatch twice a day; stacks of shit a.m. and p.m. We cross the western Jamna canal. Tilpat hoves into view rising on a hillock above a sea of young wheat. The chauffeur announces 'Tilpat, Madam.'

'We're there, are we!' she exclaims. Her voice is hoarse, asthmatic. 'Pull up somewhere. I'd like some breakfast.'

I tell the chauffeur to drive on to the end of the road. I switch on my Oxbridge. 'There's a palm grove beyond the village. Your Ladyship can have breakfast in peace without half of Tilpat gaping at you.'

She winces at my *haw haw*.

'Sounds lovely! I am dying for a cup of hot coffee. Bet you are too!'

I ignore her invitation. I'll punish her till she says sorry. We skirt round Tilpat. The road ends abruptly beside a temple in a grove of date-palms. The flunky hurls himself out to open the rear door. I follow him.

Lady Hoity-Toity emerges out of her ermine cocoon. I get a full view. Fifty-fivish, small (a little over five feet), bosomless, bottomless, scraggy, sexless. Muddy blonde hair, muddy blonde down all over her leathery pink skin. Cuts on the sides of the jaw indicate a surgical face-lift. She is, as the Bard put it, 'beated and chopp'd with tann'd antiquity.' Dress: grey cardigan, powder-blue denims, khaki canvas boots. Nothing feminine about her except her little size, blue eyes and a bracelet strung with gold coins.

The Presidential hamper is opened on a Presidential collapsible table. Egg sandwiches, steaming hot coffee.

'You speak uncommonly good English,' says she, offering me a cigarette. 'Bet you were schooled in England.'

I shake my head at the cigarette. 'Haileybury.' Haileybury sounds safe and very Blighty.

'Old East India school!' she says very patronizingly.

'And surely that's a King's tie!'

'It is.' I hold up the tie I have no right to wear.

'My husband is also a King's man. When were you up?'

'Seven years ago.' Her husband must be at least thirty years older than I. No danger of being caught out.

'What did you read?'

'History.'

She beams. 'So did my husband! Who was your tutor?'

I will get into trouble if I let her go on questioning me. 'I spent more time on the sports ground than in tutorials.'

She smiles. She makes up to me. 'I am awfully sorry. I took you to be a professional guide. They should have told me. Do forgive my discourtesy.'

'Don't give it a thought! Your Ladyship has Delhi's worst unpaid guide at her service.'

'You are a joker! We'll get on. My name is Jane. What's yours?' she extends her hand. Bony, strong, cold. 'Singh. A very distinguished name shared by fifty million Sikhs, Rajputs, Banias, Thakurs, Gurkhas, Biharis and many others.' She chortles happily. We are old friends. I tell her I was on the same plane. I flatter her. 'Those camera bulbs flashing! I thought you were a film star. You could be one.'

'Liar! I like compliments not flattery.' She wheezes a mixture of cough and laughter.

We sip coffee, munch egg sandwiches and engender rapport.

'What do you know about Tilpat?' she asks.

'Not much. Legend has it that it was one of the Pandava's five villages. You know about the Pandavas?'

She nods. 'Tell me again.'

'The Pandavas demanded of their kinsmen, the Kurus, their share of the inheritance consisting of five villages: Panipat, Sonipat, Indrapat, Baghpat and Tilpat. When the Kurus refused, they went to war. The battle was fought at Kurukshetra, seventy miles north-west of here. The Pandavas, helped by Krishna, won. You know the *Gita*?'

She nods again. 'Part of the *Mahabharata*, isn't it? Krishna's sermon on the righteous war...Wasn't there a woman with many husbands somewhere in the story?'

'Draupadi! She was wife to all the five Pandava brothers. Arjun, the third brother, won her at an archery contest. When he brought her home and said, "Mama, see what I've got!" his Mama without looking back replied: "Be a good boy and share it with your brothers." So like an obedient Indian son he did as he was told.

'After the Pandavas had settled the hash of the Kurus, they retired to the Himalayas: all good Indians go to the

Himalayas to die when they grow old. It is possible that the people living on that mound are descendants of the Pandavas who stayed at home.'

'Last time I was here they'd dug up grey earthenware pottery at Tilpat. I examined the specimens: Certainly 1000 BC or earlier.' She speaks in a tone of authority and emphasizes it by pouring the dregs of her coffee on the ground. The flunky runs up to take her cup. We gaze at Tilpat which is lit by the sun. It is a huddle of mud-huts around a few brick-houses and a temple.

A herd of cows and buffaloes come from Tilpat towards us. Boys run around to prevent them straying into cultivated fields. Girls follow picking up blobs of steaming dung and putting them in their baskets. Cows eye the Rolls-Royce and shy away. Buffaloes snort at its fenders and meander along. Boys let the cattle scatter in the palm grove. They put their staves between their legs and sit down on their haunches a few feet away from us. The girls line up behind them.

'What do they want?' demands Lady Hoity-Toity.

'What do you want?' I translate.

'Nothing,' replies one of the boys, 'just looking.' I repeat the reply in English. A villager alights from his bicycle and asks what it is going on. 'Nothing,' reply the boys. The cyclist joins them. More villagers come along. Within a few minutes we have quite an audience.

'Bhai! Is this a tamasha? Is it a zoo?' I ask them with kindly sarcasm.

They snigger, they shuffle. But continue to sit and stare. A lad asks me, 'Is this a mem or a sahib?'

The girls look at each other and giggle. Men grin. The lad gets cheeky. 'Arre, it wears a pantaloon like a sahib! It has nothing in front or behind. How can anyone tell!' More giggles and smirks. Hoity-Toity senses he has said something about her. She takes my arm in a firm grip and demands to be told. I tell her. She drags me towards the lad. 'Ask him to come round the bush and I'll show him.' I tell the lad. He is overcome with embarrassment. Hoity-Toity grabs the fellow by his ears and hauls him up to his feet. 'Come and see for yourself.'

The lad wrenches his ears free and runs away. The boys and girls scamper away after him. The cyclist cycles off. The other men melt away. There's the master race for you! There's a woman who, although she has no breasts to speak of, could give suck to a regiment of Grenadier Guards!

'That's that!' she says triumphantly slapping imaginary dust off her hands. 'Now I'd like to see a bit of the countryside. The river couldn't be very far from here.'

'A brisk hour's walk.'

'Let's go.'

We set our course eastwards. We go through the palm grove and out into open country. We skirt a swamp. We wade through water courses. The ground becomes sandy. Stunted *thuja* and casuarina. A herd of deer come bouncing into view and bounce away towards Tilpat. A black buck, its antlers spiralling into the air, comes to a stop a few yards ahead of us. Hoity-Toity raises her arms, takes aim and says 'Bang.' The buck turns its back on us. It has been hit; blood trickles down its rump. It ambles away slowly and sinks exhausted behind a cluster of dark casuarinas. A jeepload of Sikhs armed with rifles and shotguns comes zig-zagging through the bushes. 'Sardarji, did you see a herd of deer go by?' one asks me in Punjabi. He sees the white woman and adds in English, 'And a big black buck. I am sure I hit it.'

I point towards the river: 'Just this moment. It cannot have gone very far.'

'Thanks, thanks.' The jeep races on towards the river.

'I'd put those bloody *shikaris* against the wall...'

Hoity-Toity smiles. Her blue eyes sparkle. 'No bang, bang.' She gives me a patronizing pat on my beard.

'When I was a boy there were herds of blue bull and wild pig within a mile of the city walls. Tigers were seen on the Ridge behind Rashtrapati Bhavan where Your Ladyship is staying. There were hares, partridges, and peacocks in our parks. As for deer, I remember seeing herds fifty strong not twenty miles from here. Today you can't see anything within a hundred miles of Delhi. These foreign bastards with diplomatic privileges have shot all our game. If I had my way, I would shoot the bloody lot.'

'Those chaps in the jeep looked more like your own kind than foreign bastards,' she says.

'I'd shoot them too.'

We trudge along. Scrub gives way to cultivated fields; wheat turning from green to light yellow. A skylark pouring down song on us plummets down into the wheat. Another rises skyward, flutters at one spot and trills away. Then another. And another. The cultivated land ends. Our feet sink in sand. We come to a small pond. A flock of whistling teal rise and whistle past over our heads. I raise my arms, take aim and say, 'Bang, bang... Good shot Lady Hoity-Toity. Six birds down!' She laughs, 'You are making fun of me.'

We skirt the pond. Our feet are now ankle deep in powdery soil. Suddenly the river bursts into view.

We are on a high bank. Below us stretches the Jamna coiled like a three-mile-long grey python. She seems lifeless but for a red shroud entangled in marigolds that floats lazily downstream. Three turtles scamper down and slosh into the water. On the sandbank on the other side thousands of waterfowl bask in the sun. Terns slice the air. A white-headed fishing eagle flies over the stream scanning its surface.

Lady Hoity-Toity spreads out her arms in wonder: 'It's like a pre-historic reptile! All those bends and curves!' She takes my elbow and lowers herself on to the sand. I sit down beside her. Our feet dangle over the ledge perforated with the nest holes of bank mynahs. She lights a cigarette.

'That's because of Krishna's brother Balaram. Jamna would not yield to his lust so he got drunk and dragged her by the hair zig-zag across the plains of Hindustan.'

A fish takes a somersault on the surface of the stream.

From far away come the thuds of the *shikaris'* guns. Waterfowl on the opposite bank rise skyward. They pass overhead in a great whoosh honking and squawking as they go: geese, mallard, brahminy ducks, pintails, pochards... They fly along the river and back again to land on the stream a hundred yards from us. Peace returns to the Jamna. Once again terns slice the air and the white-headed eagle looks for fish in its heavy, purposeful way.

After a while Hoity-Toity puts her hand on my knee and asks: 'Is this one of your sacred rivers?'

'Only a fraction less holy than the Ganga! She is Sarjuga, daughter of the Sun; she is also Triyama, sister of Yama the ruler of the dead. And since she was born on Mount Kalinda, she has yet another name, Kalinda-Nandini, daughter of the black mountain. The *Vedas* were washed up by its flood; Krishna bathed in her waters. Madam, the Jamna is so holy that one dip in it washes away the sins of a lifetime. As a matter of fact if I were to push you down the bank, I would be doing Your Ladyship a great favour.' I put my hand on hers.

She extricates her hand. The gold coins on her bracelet jingle. She throws away the stub of her cigarette and digs out a packet of Caporals from her hip-pocket. She hands me the lighter and puts a cigarette in her lips.

I cup my palms to shelter the flame and take the lighter to her lips. I look up. She looks up. Our eyes meet. Her's are as blue as the Bay of Bengal under an aquamarine sky. She knows how to use them. I feel their rapier-like stab through my eyes down to my gullet. I lower my gaze. She blows a mouthful of roasted tobacco smoke into my face. 'Thanks,' she says taking back her lighter. Her hand again comes to rest on my knee.

I play with the coins on her bracelet. They bear masculine names: Jim, Freddy, Dennis, Jacques. 'Boy-friends,' she explains. She bares her yellowing teeth, cough-laughs and spits phlegm on the other side.

'Rich and of all nationalities,' I remark holding the gold coin inscribed Ali. She laughs again. 'Not all rich; I had some made at my own expense. And not of all nations. India is missing. Perhaps I'll add an Indian this time,' she says giving me a meaningful leer. She buries her half-smoked Caporal in the sand. 'I really must have a quick *dekho* at the Tilpat excavations and then this other place Suraj ... Suraj ... and some four letter obscenity.'

'Kund.'

The obscenity dawns on me. I blush.

'I am an awful tease!' she says patting me on my beard. She

stands up and brushes the sand off her little bottom. 'Come along,' she commands hauling me up by the shoulder.

She is rejuvenated. She strides on ahead. I trudge behind her. I can't make anything of her. I cannot affix any labels to this diminutive yet strong, sexless yet bawdy woman.

We see a small cloud of mobile dust over the bushes. It is the jeep with the *shikaris*. No black buck in the jeep. They see us. Lady Hoity-Toity bares her teeth and turns a victorious smile on me. They understand. One fellow clenches his fist, shakes his right arm from its elbow and yells abuse.

'What's he saying?' asks Hoity-Toity.

'He's telling me to go and bugger myself.'

'An Oriental accomplishment, no doubt! One of the yogic postures designed to make the ends meet,' she says.

The masterful female leads the way through the palm grove back to the Rolls-Royce beside the temple. A crowd of inquisitive rustics has again collected round the car. They disperse as soon as we arrive. We have coffee. And drive into Tilpat.

Word has gone around about how the memsahib dealt with the village lad. The state emblem on the car and the liveried flunkies do the rest. The village headman and his cronies welcome us with a mixture of *namaskars*, *Jai Hinds* and *salaams* to the memsahibji. Hoity-Toity nods at them. A *charpoy* is laid out. A woman with her face veiled brings a trayful of *chai* in glass tumblers. Hoity-Toity peers into the woman's veil and makes everyone laugh. She refuses to drink the *chai* but grabs the pipe of a *hookah* from the hand of a peasant and takes a couple of puffs. They clap their hands and laugh like children. Through me they inform her that the excavated sites have been covered over. 'Have any of you found any strange objects while ploughing or digging foundations for new houses?' They waggle their heads. 'No.'

We take leave of Tilpat. At Badarpur we turn left, go over a railway level crossing and turn left again along a narrow road. We descend through a defile. A peacock scuttles across and takes wing raucously crying *paon, paon*.

'A real live peacock!' exclaims Hoity-Toity.

'The place is infested with them.'

'And humans! India seems to be infested with human beings.' She waves towards the buses, scooters, cars and bicycles in the parking lot at Suraj Kund. Picnickers are scattered everywhere. Transistors, tape recorders and gramophones compete with the snake charmers' pipes.

Our arrival causes a stir. By the time we pull up alongside the verandah of the rest-house, transistors have been toned down; three snake charmers blow lustily through their gourd pipes; an old man with a king cobra twined round his neck approaches us. 'Christmas!' exclaims Lady Hoity-Toity. 'I don't like snakes and I don't like picnickers.' She surveys the scene for a moment, shudders a long *ooh* of disgust. 'How long do we have to stay here?' she asks.

'There's this amphitheatre. Then there is an old dam about two miles from here, village Anangpur another mile beyond the dam. There are the remains of the wall which protected Anangpur. It'll take us most of the afternoon and evening.'

She's a lady of quick decisions. She orders the flunky to unload the hamper. She goes in, examines the room and the bathroom, sniffs at the towels, turns up her nose at the bundle of clipped newspapers in a box beside the toilet. She dictates the order of the day to the chauffeur, 'Take the car back. Come back around 9 p.m.' She does not ask me if I am free till 9 p.m.

The flunky puts the hamper and her suitcase on the floor. The chauffeur and the flunky salute and take their leave. She flops into an armchair, glances at her wrist-watch and says, 'I am dying for a drink. Be a darling and mix me a gin and tonic. And help yourself to anything you like—Scotch, champagne, beer, gin—all on your old President.'

I act the butler. I mix Her Ladyship a gin and tonic. While I am still making up my mind what to take, I have to mix her another and light her cigarette. I make myself a dry martini and sit down on the edge of the bed. I raise my glass. She ignores the gesture. 'Tell me about this place Suraj ... Suraj ...'

'*Kund* to rhyme with the German *Bund*. Simply means pond.' I tell her about the Tomara Rajputs who ruled Delhi in the seventh and eighth centuries and their chieftain Surajpal after whom the amphitheatre is named.

She holds out her glass, 'Be a honey!'

I be a honey and give her another gin-tonic. 'And this dam and the village?' She puts her legs on either arm of her armchair just as she would do to let a man enter her. How can I talk of the Tomara Rajputs with her opening her thighs in this wanton manner? I try to keep my mind off her middle. 'The dam was built by another Tomara, Anangpal. He also built the fortified town Anangpur; we can go there in the afternoon. Then he shifted his capital westward and built a citadel of red sandstone which came to be known as Lal Kot.'

She's lost interest in my lecture. Her eyes are drooping. 'Go on,' she orders.

'No, I won't,' I reply rudely. 'You are half-asleep.'

She laughs, coughs, spits. She throws her cigarette on the floor and squashes it under her foot. 'Forgive me! I'll have a wash and get out of this,' she says holding her blue denims. 'Won't be a jiffy.' She pulls out a skirt from her case and goes into the bathroom. The bathroom has a curtain which only covers the middle part of the doorway. It also has a door; she does not shut the door. She unzips her denims and hangs them on a peg. She wears white lace panties to cover her little bottom. She bends over the basin to wash her face. I know she is doing it to rouse my curiosity. My curiosity rises. She buries her face in a towel. She turns round, bends over and slips on her skirt.

'Chalo,' she says. 'Juldi (quick). Is that right?'

We step out. It is quieter. The snake charmers are bundled under trees and the picnickers are huddled round their transistors; the women are frying *poories*. Boys in bum-tight trousers, girls in bosom-and-bum-tight long shirts stroll about the amphitheatre.

Hoity-Toity examines a bush of thorny caparis in flower. She looks across the ridge and is entranced. On one side is the vast Romanesque amphitheatre with large steps going down to the pool. A man is washing himself on a slab of stone. A safe distance from him a couple of moorhens are bobbing up and down. Swallows skim over the water in unending circles. On the other side is a densely wooded valley of flame trees and wild date-palm. She clasps her hands beneath her chin in adolescent wonder: 'So that's the flame of the forest! How perfectly beautiful! Where is the Sun temple?' she·asks.

I point to the flights of steps on the other side of the amphitheatre. I lead her down the large steps to the pool. Then up the same steps to the ruins of the Sun temple. I show her some of the surrounding countryside: massive boulders with flame and acacia sprouting from the sides.

'I have had enough for the morning. I am hot and hungry,' I plead. 'Aren't you?'

She glances at her wrist-watch. 'Okay! My watch says time for another gin-tonic and a bite.'

We return to the rest-house. I mix her more gins and tonics and lay a plateful of *tandoori* chicken and Russian salad on the table. I help myself to a bottle of chilled lager and some *kababs*. She gobbles up her lunch and brusquely orders me out of the room. ' I must have my siesta. Wake me up at 4.30. We can do your dam and fortified village in the evening.' She does not care to find out whether there is another room or even a chair for me, just puts me out on the verandah and shuts the door. 'Shake me up; I sleep heavily.'

I scrounge a chair from the kitchen, put my feet up against a column and make myself comfortable. I watch the picnickers dozing under the trees. My head is heavy with sleep. I close my eyes. I am roused by the snake charmers' pipes. The picnickers are packing up while the snakewallas make a last attempt to extract something from them. I doze. I hear charabancs, cars, scooters leave. The snake charmers' pipes fade away in the distance. Only pye-dogs snap and snarl over garbage left by the picnickers. I daydream. Hoity-Toity is trying to seduce me. I am not very difficult to seduce. I have no conscience about Bhagmati. Bhagmati is a whore; why should I feel guilty about her? I am taking Hoity-Toity when Bhagmati turns up and asks, 'Couldn't you find anyone better than this old memsahib?' It would be nicer if Hoity-Toity was younger and her mouth did not smell of gin-tonics, roasted tobacco and old age!

It is 4.30 p.m. I press open the door of Hoity-Toity's room and shut it behind me. She sleeps with the bedsheet drawn over her head like a corpse in a shroud. I shake her by what appears to be her shoulder. She flings the sheet off her face. 'What time is it?'

I tell her.

She yawns and stretches her arms. Yellow, fungoid growth in her armpits. She props herself against her pillow and holds the bedsheet under her chin. 'Be a darling and hand me a cigarette.' I give her a cigarette and light it for her. She sends jets of smoke through her nostrils, *ahs* and *oohs* with pleasure. 'Hand me my dressing-gown,' she says pointing to the garment hanging on the latch of the bathroom door.

I get her the dressing-gown. She leaps out of bed. Stark naked: small, wrinkled breasts; nipples looking downwards and dejected; wrinkled belly with a slight paunch beneath the navel; scraggy-brown pubic hair. I put the gown round her shoulders and close my hands over her breasts. She turns to stone. 'What do you think you are trying to do?' she demands.

'Well I...'

'Well, you what? Don't get silly notions in your head.' She picks up her shirt and denims lying at the foot of the bed and walks into the bathroom. She does not bother to shut the door. I do not bother to look.

She comes back, puts her hands on my shoulder. 'Don't be cross. I'm a bit of a cock-teaser.' She gives me a smelly kiss on the nose to seal her forgiveness. My feelings are hurt, I want to hurt her. Her halitosis encourages me to be rude to her. I snigger. 'What's the joke?' she asks.

'You! You remind me of my city Delhi. We have a saying: "Ruins proclaim the past splendour of an ancient monument."'

She shrivels. 'That's not a nice thing to say.'

We step out of the bungalow as strangers. We walk along-side with a wall of silence between us. It is hot. Sandstone boulders burn under the sun. In the shade of trees sit peacocks panting for breath with their beaks open. We walk a mile or more without exchanging a word or looking at each other.

We come to the end of the Ridge. In front stretch cultivated fields growing wheat and mustard. Out of the flat sea of green and pale yellow rise rocky islands covered with the flame. Beyond the islands is the village Anangpur. It is the kind of scene that cannot be appreciated by people with a wall of misunderstanding between them. I take Hoity-Toity's hand and ask, 'Isn't it beautiful?' She replies, 'Isn't it! Let's sit down somewhere.'

I lead her by the hand. We descend on Anangpal's dam. We turn our backs to the fields and sit down facing a valley of date-palms. Fifty feet beneath us is a pool of water, crystal clear. It sparkles as minnows' bellies catch the sun. From a date-palm darts a halcyon kingfisher aglitter with peacock-green and molten-gold. It hovers helicopter-like above the pool, drops like a stone into the water and is off with a wiggling minnow in its beak. The pool returns to its placid self; once more fish move in shoals of grey dots. Suddenly they leap into the air like a shower of sparks, plop back and dart to the sides of the pool. A snake wriggles upwards, raises its head above the surface and wriggles back nosing its way through the shadows of submerged rocks. Hoity-Toity smokes yet another Caporal and throws the butt into the pool. Minnows come back for the cigarette. The stub bobs up and down like an angler's float, then goes down into the water.

We spend the rest of the afternoon walking through the fields of Anangpur. We watch a camel-driven Persian wheel. We watch Gujar women patting buffalo dung on their walls. We skirt round Anangpur and see the ruins of its battlement. As the sun goes over the Ridge we retrace our steps to the dam. We return through the valley of palm trees, wading through swamps overgrown with bullrushes. As the sun sets, we are back in the rest-house.

Not a human being in sight. The *chowkidar* puts chairs and a table out for us and retires to his quarters. I bring out the President's Scotch. We sit with our legs on the table and sip our whisky. After a long walk, it is like elixir in the entrails. I stretch out my hand to her. She gives me hers to hold. We watch the sky turn a luminescent grey. Flocks of parakeets streak across squawking as they flash by. It is peacock time. They cry lustily from the valley of the date-palms. Two perched on the roof of the rest-house return their calls. Then the twilight hush. Hoity-Toity stands up and stretches her limbs. I stand up as well. She nestles her head against my chest. 'Thank you! It's been a lovely day.' She kisses me on my mouth. I enfold her in my arms, lift her off her feet and kiss her all over her leathery face. 'Would you like to make love to me?' she asks very humbly.

'Yes, let's go inside.'

We get as far as the verandah. The President's Rolls-Royce catches us with its headlights. I swear: 'Fuck!'

Very frustrating! Also somewhat of a relief. I do not have to waste my *bindu* on a battered, malodorous woman. I can preserve it for Bhagmati who despite the bashing she gets from men goes for sex with the zest of a newly-wed nymphet. And her mouth smells like a bush of cardamom in springtime.

Hoity-Toity becomes the Lady once more—cold and aloof. She sits at the other end of the seat. When we pull up outside my apartment, she says very dryly: 'Thanks for everything. Do look me up when you are in London.'

'It was a pleasure.' I do not invite her to come in. There is the omnipresent Budh Singh armed with his stave. As soon as I step out of the Rolls-Royce he springs to attention and yells: 'Parade, present arms! *Thak, thak, thak.*' As Hoity-Toity leans out to wave to me, he intones a Punjabi version of 'God Save our Gracious Queen.'

I wave to Hoity-Toity. I acknowledge Budh Singh's salute and ask: 'How's everything?'

'Parade, slope arms! *Thak, Thak.* Everything okay. Your *hijda* is waiting for you. I let it in because you were so *gussa* with me yesterday. Excuse my saying so, take a woman, take a boy, but a *hijda*...'

I complete his sentence for him. 'That's not nice.' And hurry indoors.

3

Bhagmati

She sits cross-legged in my armchair turning over the pages of a book. Her left hand is clenched into a fist with a cigarette sticking out of her fingers. She sucks noisily at the cigarette and flicks the ash on my carpet. Her hair is heavily oiled and arranged in serried waves fixed by celluloid clips shaped like butterflies. She wears a pink sari of glossy, artificial silk with a dark blue blouse of the same material. A pair of white slippers with ribbon bow-ties on their toes lie in front of the chair. Bhagmati is the worst-dressed whore in Delhi.

The light of the table-lamp reveals a layer of powder and rouge on her face. It does not lighten the colour of her black skin or hide the spots left by small-pox. The *kohl* in her eyes has run down and smudged her cheek-bones. Her lips are painted crimson. Her teeth are stained with *betel*-leaf. Bhagmati is the plainest-looking whore in Delhi.

'*Ajee*! You are back from *vilayat*!' she exclaims as I enter. And without giving me the chance to say yes, continues 'What kind of books do you keep? They have no pictures.' She waggles her head with every sentence and gesticulates with her hands in the manner of *hijdas*. 'No pictures, only black letters like dead flies.' She changes the subject. 'Did you ever think of your poor Bhagmati when you were riding those white mares in London?' Bhagmati is the coarsest whore in Delhi.

Bhagmati is not a woman like other women. She's told me something of her past life; I've discovered the rest myself.

Bhagmati was born in the Victoria Zenana Hospital near Jamia Masjid. When her father asked the doctor, 'Is it a boy or a girl?', the doctor replied, 'I am not sure.' Her parents already had three boys. So they gave their fourth child a girl's name, Bhagmati. When a troupe of *hijdas* came to their home to sing and dance and said, 'Show us your child. We want to see if it is a boy or a girl, or one of us,' her father abused them and drove them away without giving them any money. The *hijdas* gave her parents no peace. Whenever they came to the locality to sing and dance at births or weddings they would turn up at their doorstep and say, 'Show us your last born. If it is one of us, let us take it away.'

Bhagmati's mother had two more children—both girls. Both times her father had taken Bhagmati with him to the hospital and asked the doctor to examine her and say whether she was a boy or a girl. Both times the doctor had looked at her genitals and said 'I am not sure; it is a bit of both.' Bhagmati was then four years old. When the troupe of *hijdas* visited them after the birth of his last child, her father gave them twenty-one rupees and said, 'Now I have three sons and two daughters, you can take this one. It is one of you.'

The troupe of *hijdas* adopted Bhagmati. They taught her to sing, clap her hands and dance in the manner of *hijdas*. When she was thirteen her voice broke and became like a man's. She began to grow hair on her upper lip, round her chin and on her chest. Her bosom and hips which were bigger than a boy's did not grow as big as those of girls of her age. But she began to menstruate. And although her clitoris became large, the rest of her genitals developed like those of a woman. This time she went to see the doctor herself. He said 'You can do everything a woman can but you will have no children.'

There are as many kinds of *hijdas* as there are kinds of men and women. Some are almost entirely male, some almost entirely female. Others have the male and female mixed up in different proportions—it is difficult to tell which sex they have more of in their makeup. The reason why they prefer to wear women's clothes is because it being a man's world every deviation from accepted standards of masculinity are regarded as unmanly. Women are more generous.

Bhagmati is a feminine *hijda*. When she was fifteen, the leader of the troupe took her as his wife. He already had two *hijda* wives; but such things do not matter to them. Instead of shunning her as a rival, the wives stitched Bhagmati's wedding-dress and prepared her for the nuptial bed. They shaved the superfluous hair on her face and body and bathed her in rose-water. They escorted her to their husband's room. They had their eyes and ears glued to the crevices in the door. Later they often made love to her. Bhagmati had small-pox when she was seventeen. 'They gave me up for dead,' she said. 'They threw me in a hospital where people were dying like flies. *Seetla Mai* (goddess-mother of small-pox) spared me but left her fingerprints all over my face.'

When men came to expend their lust on *hijdas*—it is surprising how many prefer them to women—Bhagmati got more patrons than anyone else in her troupe. She could give herself as a woman; she could give herself as a boy. She also discovered that some men preferred to be treated as women. Though limited in her resources, she learnt how to give them pleasure too. There were no variations of sex that Bhagmati found unnatural or did not enjoy. Despite being the plainest of *hijdas*, she came to be sought by the old and young, the potent and impotent, by homosexuals, sadists and masochists.

Bhagmati regards a bed in the same way as an all-in wrestler regards the arena when engaged in a bout where no holds are barred. Bhagmati is the all-purpose man-woman sex maniac.

Although Bhagmati is a freelance, she continues to live with her husband and co-wives in Lal Kuan. She puts whatever she earns in the community kitty. In return she has a roof over her head, and a meal whenever she wants it. When she is ill, they look after her. When she is arrested for soliciting they furnish bail; when she is sentenced by the magistrate, they pay the fine.

How did I get mixed up with Bhagmati? That's a long story which I will tell you later. How did she come to mean so much to me? I am not sure. As I have said before I have two passions in my life; my city Delhi and Bhagmati. They have two things in common: they are lots of fun. And they are sterile.

'Where have you been blackening your face?' I ask her flopping down on the sofa.

'*Ajee!*' she exclaims saucily digging her finger into her chin. 'I go blackening my face but you go riding big cars and old, white women! What kind of justice is this?'

'You've been gossiping with Budh Singh.'

'That *pagal!*' she dismisses him with a wave of her hand. 'He lied to me. He said you would not be back for fifteen days. But something in my heart told me you were back.' She stubs the half-smoked cigarette on my table and sticks it behind her ear. With the thumb and finger of the hand she makes a circle. She inserts the index finger of the other hand in and out of the circle and asks: 'How was it?'

I told you she is the coarsest whore in Delhi.

'Must you be so vulgar?'

'*Uffo!*' she exclaims, 'Today you call us vulgar; God knows what you will be saying tomorrow!' She comes and sits on the floor, takes off my shoes and socks and begins to massage my feet. It is very pleasant. She massages my ankles, my calf muscles and the insides of my thigh. Every now and then her hands wander up for a spot-check. Very casually she undoes my fly-buttons, plants a soft kiss on my middle and comes over me. I don't have to do a thing except lie back and enjoy myself. I told you Bhagmati knows exactly what anyone wants at any time.

How did Bhagmati come into my life? That's in the past tense—three years ago.

*

At the time I was engaged in writing the biography of an industrialist. I was provided with a staff of research assistants to sift through his correspondence. We were allotted a few rooms in one of the newer suburbs called Patel Nagar across the Ridge which had at one time marked the western extremity of the two cities of Delhi, the Old and the New.

It took me some time to discover that the shortest way to my office was along a road which ran atop the Ridge. It was also the most picturesque; from many places you could get a view of the two cities. On either side of the road were bushes of sesbania, vasicka and camel thorn; huge boulders of red sandstone were strewn about everywhere. There were flowering trees, flame, coral and the flamboyant *gul mohar.* Ridge Road as it was known had earned a bad name.

A car or two had been held up, there had been a case of assault or robbery. The newspapers did the rest. Pedestrians and cyclists avoided it now and cars sped by without stopping. It was usually deserted. It was on this road that I first met Bhagmati.

It is curious how the first encounter remains so indelibly printed on the mind while the affair that follows is soon blurred.

I can recall every detail of our first meeting.

It was some time in April. It was very hot. I had put in a couple of hours of work in my air-cooled office which I had heavily curtained against the glare of daylight. (I read and wrote under the orb-light of an anglepoise lamp). Suddenly the electric current was cut off: those days as now this was a frequent occurrence in Delhi. For a while I waited in the stifling dark, then decided to call it a day. It was noon with a dust-laden grey sky and a scorching hot wind blowing more dust. I drove onto the Ridge Road. Through clusters of waving sesbania I could see a dense pack of houses on either side. But no signs of life, not even a kite wheeling in the sky. A hundred yards or so ahead of me I saw two cyclists struggling against the wind. And beyond them what appeared to be a body stretched halfway across the shimmering tarmac. I saw the cyclists stare at the body, hesitate a little, and then push on. I pulled up on the side. The cyclists turned back.

It was a woman lying with her arms and legs stretched out as if crucified. Her eyes were half-open; a little froth and blood trickled down her mouth. There was a damp patch beside her sari. I looked at her bosom to see if she was breathing: the flapping of the sari made it difficult to be sure. 'Is she dead?' I asked the cyclists who had joined me.

They peered into the woman's face. '*Mirgee*! (epileptic fit)' exclaimed one of them. He found a twig and thrust it between the woman's teeth. 'That will stop her from biting her tongue.' He took off one of his shoes and placed it on the woman's face. 'This is the best thing for *mirgee*....the smell of old leather.'

I noticed the woman's bosom heave. It was a very small, almost non-existent bosom, encased in a cheap, printed, artificial silk blouse. What else did I notice? Feet, very black. Toe-nails painted bright crimson. Inside of the palms, stained with henna. Very short and somewhat plump. About twenty and altogether too dark to be considered attractive by Indian standards. The little I could see of her face was pitted with pock-marks.

'What is she doing on the Ridge by herself?' I asked.

'Only the Guru knows!' exclaimed one of the cyclists.

'These are bad times,' said the other. He removed his shoe from the woman's face and slipped it on his foot. 'She'll be all right in a few minutes.' Then without giving me a chance to say anything the two rode off.

The woman began to moan and shake her head. She raised her hand and drew a circle with her finger.

'Are you all right?' I asked her.

She nodded her head. I wiped the bloody froth on her mouth with her own sari and helped her to her feet. She smelt of sweat and urine.

'*Chukkur*,' she explained, again drawing a circle with her finger. 'Be kind and take me to a bus-stand.' It was a hoarse, masculine voice.

I hesitated. Was it a trap? I had heard of people being black mailed in this way. But I had little choice. And my conscience was clear. I helped her into the rear seat of my car. She slumped down and closed her eyes. I passed the cyclists. In the rear-view mirror I saw them dismount and one of them write something in his pocket-book. It was obvious he was taking down the number of my car. What had I landed myself into?

'Where would you like to be dropped?'

No answer. I looked back. She was fast asleep—or perhaps having another fit. What was I to do? Take her to a hospital? They'd ask questions and send for the police. Take her to a police station? Oh no! Not the Delhi police! Not in a thousand years!

I drove past Lohia Hospital towards the Parliament and headed down Parliament Street towards Connaught Circus. Then it struck me that I was being very foolish! At any traffic light someone might have noticed the woman lying in a state of collapse and started a riot. I turned back towards the Parliament and took the broad road to Palam airport. At a deserted spot I pulled up to see how she was. I felt her forehead. No fever. I shook her gently by the shoulder. She opened her eyes and mumbled, 'Let me be! I am very tired.' And went back to sleep.

I drove about for an hour before I turned back to my apartment. I parked the car where I usually did alongside my window. The Guru was merciful. None of my neighbours or their servants were about. I opened the rear door and boldly dragged the woman out by her shoulders. 'Come along!'

She allowed herself to be helped out. 'You can sleep here till you feel better,' I said as soon as we were safely indoors.

'Your slave has had enough sleep,' she replied. 'If *huzoor* can show me where to wash, your maidservant will be most grateful.'

I was startled by her florid Hindustani. I showed her the bathroom and explained how the hot and cold water taps operated. I gave her a clean towel, my Princeton T-shirt and a pair of trousers. 'I have no woman's clothes, but you can wear these till your sari is dry.'

She spent a long time in the bathroom bathing and washing her soiled clothes. She waddled into the sitting-room with the Princeton T-shirt hanging loose on her shoulders and holding up the trousers with her hands. My clothes were many sizes too big for her.

I smiled. A blush spread on her pock-marked dark face. 'Too big for me,' she said looking down at the trousers. I poured her a Coke and asked her to help herself to the plateful of mangoes on the dining-table.

'I am very hungry,' she said taking a mango. 'I have not had anything to eat since yesterday.'

'What were you doing on the Ridge at noon?'

'I was on my way home from Tihar.'

'Tihar?'

'You know! The jail! They let me out last evening. I did not have a paisa with me. I spent the night outside a labourer's hovel. They would not let me in. Then I started to walk home. Tihar is a long way away from the city.'

'What took you to Tihar?' I asked her.

She fixed her eyes on me and waggled her head saucily in the manner of a dancer. 'Vagrancy, what else?' I am a prostitute.'

'What is your name?'

'What will you do with my name? Your slave is known as Bhagmati.' I had a vague suspicion that there was something besides her flat chest and masculine voice which made her different from other women. 'Where is your home?' I asked her.

'Wherever the dusk overtakes me, I spread my carpet and call it my home. My roof is studded with the stars of heaven.' She had retained all her tartish tartness. 'Your slave's abode of poverty is in Lal Kuan.' My suspicion got stronger. In Lal Kuan was the hermaphrodites' quarters. My curiosity was roused. I'd never known a *hijda*, only seen them go about in groups of fours and fives, sing in their unmelodious male voices, make ungainly movements they called dancing and clap their hands with the fingers stretched backwards. I had heard strange stories of their sex-life and the shapes of their genitals. Despite my curiosity to find out more about her, I asked her if she would like to be dropped home.

'Your honour is very anxious to get rid of me.'

'Not at all! But won't your people be worried?'

'Nobody worries about me!' she replied. 'I come and go as I please. All my husband asks me is how much have you brought?'

'You have a husband?'

'What sin have I committed that I should not have a husband? When I am old and of no use to men, he will look after me.'

She sensed I was one of the types who liked to hear about sex. 'Has *huzoor* never honoured our habitations with his blessed feet?'

'Never.'

'*Inshallah*! Your maidservant may have the honour of turning your steps in that direction.'

I was not used to being propositioned by women—much less a *hijda*. 'Your clothes must be dry,' I blurted. 'Let's go.' She came across the room, sank down on the coir mattress and put her head on my feet.

'In the name of Rama! Do not throw me out! I am too sick to go back to work. If you let me spend this one night here, I swear by Allah I will cause you no further embarrassment. For the sake of your Guru, please!' (How she mouthed the names of Gods—Hindu, Muslim, Sikh!). She looked up at me with tears in her eyes.

Women had spent nights in my apartment. But they had been Europeans or westernized Indian memsahibs aping English mannerisms; never a low-born, Hindustani-speaking, *hijda* whore, who obviously catered to perverts of the working-classes: domestic-servants, soldiers, policemen—at a couple of rupees a shot. I thought to myself that I would not know what to say to her. And she was not very appetizing. 'All right,' I said without much enthusiasm. 'But we must leave the house before my servant comes back. And while you can stay here after he has left for the night you must leave early in the morning. Go and get dressed, your clothes must be dry by now.'

She bent down and kissed my feet. She brushed her tears with the hem of my shirt. She got up and turned her back towards me. The trousers slid down baring her from her waist to her ankles. Whatever other ravages her body might have suffered at the calloused hands of the working-classes, her behind was like that of a schoolboy athlete: taut, dimpled. She looked back over her shoulder and smiled an embarrassed smile. Then bent down, pulled the trousers up to her waist and shuffled back to the bathroom.

While she was changing I made plans for the night. I put two candles on the dining-table. This was my way of communicating with my unlettered cook-bearer. One candle for 'out-for-dinner'; two candles for 'also do not come in with the bed-tea in the morning.'

We left the apartment unnoticed. 'If you would be so kind as to take me for a drive! I would like to eat some fresh air,' she said as she got into the car. 'There are not many car rides written in your slave's *kismet*.' She tapped her forehead.

'Where would you like to go?'

'Wherever *huzoor's* heart desires to take his maidservant.'

This was a different Bhagmati—relaxed and self-assured. She began to hum and tap a *tabla* drumbeat on the dashboard when we set off. As we drove past the Ashoka Hotel into the Diplomatic Enclave she began to chant the names of the embassies we passed: '*Amreekee ambassee*...and the *Roosi, Pakistani, Japanee, Germanee.*'

'How do you know all these embassies?'

'Your slave has had the privilege of serving many foreign gentlemen.' She looked sideways at me to watch my reaction.

'They must give you a lot of money.'

'They probably do. But after the pimps and the embassy chauffeurs have taken their share, a couple of rupees is all that falls into your maidservant's apron. Then there is my husband. Allah be thanked! I have enough for a cupful of lentil soup and a *chappati* to fill this belly.' She slapped her paunch.

'How do you talk to them?'

'*Ajee wah!*' she exclaimed animatedly waggling her head. 'What kind of question is that? They don't need to talk to me. They drink their whisky; they carry on their *git mit* in their own language till they need my services.' She paused, looked sideways at me and added, 'These foreigners have some very curious habits.'

'What do they do?'

'Not all in one session,' she admonished. 'A little today, a little tomorrow. But it will astonish you. They take their pleasure in strange ways. It makes me sick to think of it.' She spat out of the window.

'Will *huzoor* kill me with hunger? Take me to a nice hotel and give me some saffron *pilaf*, some oven-baked chicken and *kulfi* (ice-cream) and I may tell you more.'

'And be seen with you in public? You want me to cut off my own nose?'

She was squashed. I felt mean. But I was determined not to give in. I turned towards the old city. We went through Delhi Gate and entered Faiz Bazaar. I pulled up outside Moti Mahal. I left her in the car and went to order a packed meal for two. I brought it back to the car: 'All you desire: saffron *pilaf* and *nan*, chicken and baked fish and *rabdee* of thick clotted cream.' She turned her face away from me.

We drove out of the city along the old wall. Her silence began to irritate me. 'If you are going to sulk, I will put you out of the car right here.' I turned to look at her. She turned away and blew her nose into the hem of her shirt.

'*Accha*, if you are going to behave like this, I will drop you at Lal Kuan.'

At Kashmiri Gate I turned into the city. We drove along Chandni Chowk to where it ended at Fatehpuri Mosque. I turned left towards Lal Kuan. I could sense her nervousness. 'You gave me your word...'

'I take it back. You go home.'

'*Hai Ram*!' she exclaimed as we approached the hermaphrodites' quarters. She slid down the seat and grabbed my left foot rest on the clutch. 'I'll do anything you want, but in the name of Rama, don't throw me out here.'

'You promise to behave?'

'I'll be your slave for life.'

I slowed down. Pimps darted across from the pavement. 'Nice new goods, just unpacked...collegegirl...virgin of thirteen....you no jiggee-jig?' Bhagmati remained hidden where she was calling upon Hindu and Muslim gods. '*Hai Ramji...Ya Allah.*'

We came out of Lal Kuan to Qazi-ka-Hauz and out of the city wall. 'We are out of Ajmeri Gate,' I announced.

She peered over the rim of the window to make sure before she sat up. '*Huzoor* has a strange sense of humour!' she complained. 'If they had found your maidservant in your car, her throat would have been slit.'

'If you sulk again, I'll take you back.'

At Connaught Circus I pulled up at a drug-store. When I came back she remarked: 'May our enemies be stricken with disease! I trust your honour is in good health?'

'Just the compulsions of age!' I answered. 'A pill to whip up the appetite; another to digest what has been eaten. A third for sound sleep, a fourth to be more wide awake and a fifth to tone up the system.' From the look on her face I could tell she had not bought my story.

Budh Singh, the night-watchman, had got used to seeing me bring women to my apartment. I gave him a tip every month. Although he was crazy, he never created trouble for me. In the dark, he could not tell what I was bringing home. Although it was a common bazaar *hijda* prostitute I felt as awkward as a young groom bringing home his bride. Bhagmati walked with a self-conscious gait.

Few words passed between us while we ate.

'It would be too much to ask a Sikh gentleman for a cigarette,' she exclaimed as she belched. I brought her the cigarette-box. She took two and stuck one behind her ear and waited for me to light the other. As I lit the cigarette she looked me boldly in the eye and blew a jet of smoke in my face; then fanned it away with her hand.

I switched on the fan in the sitting-room and asked her to make herself comfortable on the sofa. 'If you need anything just knock on the door.' I retired to my bedroom.

The hum of the air-conditioner cut out the other sounds in the apartment. I wondered what she was doing? Had I insulted her? Surely living in a brothel she must have got used to being turned down in favour of other inmates! In any case I did not know what one did to a *hijda*. And she had had an epileptic fit that afternoon. What would she sleep in? I had not given her a change of clothes. Naked? She wasn't very beautiful. But what did a *hijda* look like with nothing on?

I felt a desire for sex. I tried to put it out of my mind. A sick, scruffy *hijda*—how could I? I picked up a journal. Her naked figure kept coming over the print. What kind of breasts did a *hijda* have? What shape were her genitals? Did she shave her pubis? I put away the journal and switched off the lamp.

It did not help. I could not put out the notion that I had a strange creature in my apartment; I might never again have the opportunity to add to my knowledge. I switched on the bed-lamp and once again began to turn over the pages of the journal.

The bedroom door was pushed open. The light of the table-lamp sliced Bhagmati's figure in two. She had nothing on. As I had suspected—not real breasts, just protrusions. And she had her hands between her thighs. 'Have I permission to enter?' she asked as she entered. 'This poor wretch has nothing else to offer in return for your kindness.'

I made room for her beside me. She sat down with her face turned away. For a while I stroked her navel and her underbelly. I was roused. I pulled her beside me, fished out a contraceptive from under my pillow and mounted her. She directed me inside her. It was no different from a woman's. She smelt of sweat; I avoided her mouth. She pretended to breathe heavily as if she were getting worked up. Then sensing my coming to a climax she crossed her legs behind my back and began to moan. I dismounted. I felt unclean.

I went to the bathroom and brushed my teeth a second time. I was under the shower when she came in. Without asking for permission she squeezed paste out of my tube and began to massage her gums with her forefinger. As I turned off the shower to dry myself, she turned it on to wash herself. I could not bring myself to see what she really looked like in the middle.

I left her in the bathroom and returned to my bed. I did not want any more of her. To make my intentions clear I switched off my bed-lamp. I heard the shower turned off and after a while the click of the bathroom switch. Once again she came and sat on the edge of my bed. She had daubed herself with my cologne. I felt mean and made room for her.

For a while she lay still with her head tucked beneath my armpit. She began to play with my nipples—first with her fingers, then with her tongue. She placed her head on my chest and began to stroke my paunch—first with her fingers, then with her tongue. She went on till my reluctance was overcome. I rolled over and felt under my pillow. She held my hand and murmured, 'No need of that; I am clean.' Once again she directed me inside her and held me in a vice between her legs. Her tongue darted into my ears; a shiver of a thrill ran down my spine. Then she glued her mouth on mine. This time there was no faking. With a series of violent heaves she sucked my seed into her in a frenzy of abandon.

I lay on top of her—exhausted.

We had another shower together. She was the plainest creature I'd ever made love to. Her pock-marks showed darker than before. Her teeth were stained red with *betel*-leaf and tobacco. 'What are you staring at?' she demanded looking up through the shower and coyly hiding her nakedness.

'You, who else?' And though I had not the slightest desire for sex left in me I escorted her back to my bed and let her sleep beside me.

I slept as if I had been drugged. It must have been some time in the early hours that I began to dream. It was a mixture of fact and fantasy. Bhagmati lying on the road in a puddle of urine beckoning to me. Bhagmati grabbing me by the neck and pinning me down as a wrestler puts down his adversary. I realized that it was not all a dream and that Bhagmati was in fact lying on top of me. She nibbled my earlobes and gently led me out of my dreamland into her dusky, lusty world. She was taking me as a man takes a woman: clawing my scalp, biting my neck, heaving into my middle with a violence I had not known. I submitted to her lust with supine abandon. I felt the room go in a whirl, all my life-force from the top of the crown to the soles of my feet sucked into my middle and erupt like lava out of a volcano. The three acts of sex were like the *scala menti* of a mystic's ascent to union with the Divine. The first rung in the ladder was the purgatory; the second, the seeking; the third, the final act of destruction of the individual self (*fana*) and the merging of two lights into one. In simpler terms—that of my relationship with Bhagmati—the process was masturbation, fucking and the body's rapture. But I still did not know how a *hijda* like Bhagmati was different from a breastless woman.

It was 5 a.m.

While Bhagmati was getting into her sari I opened the safe hidden behind my bookshelf and took out a wad of ten rupee notes.

'What is this?' she asked with feigned surprise when I pressed the money into her hands. She counted the money. 'One hundred! You do not have to give me money,' she said. Then she quickly changed her mind. 'I can't refuse to take what my husband gives me, can I?'

'One hundred thousand husbands!'

She put her arms about my neck. 'As Allah is my witness, hereafter you will be the only one. You have been kind to me. I will be forever indebted to you.'

'Let's go,' I said unlocking her arms.

'You don't believe me?' she demanded. She re-counted the notes and handed them back to me. 'All right, I'll take ten to give to my husband,' she said plucking out one of the notes from my hand. 'Keep the rest for me. I will come for them another day.'

I looked out to see if it was clear. Budh Singh was fast asleep on his *charpoy*. We tiptoed past him and slipped into my car. Even the starter didn't rouse the watchman from his slumber. It was a clean getaway. We went through a deserted Connaught Circus under Minto Bridge and then onto Ajmeri Gate. 'Drop me here,' said Bhagmati putting her hand on the steering wheel. I pulled up and opened the door. She pressed my hand. 'Your maidservant thanks you a hundred thousand times. Don't forget her.' Then she walked away, barefooted, in the middle of the deserted road.

Bhagmati had not bothered to ask me my name. She had not enquired about the number or even the location of the block of the apartments in which I lived. How would she find her way back to get her money? I certainly had no intention of going into the *hijda* locality in Lal Kuan to look for her.

Days went by and weeks. With the passage of time I began to think that perhaps Bhagmati was not as much of a whore as I had earlier presumed. And the memory of that one night she had spent with me came back to me with pain. I lost hope of ever seeing her again.

The way Bhagmati re-entered my life made me believe that the gods had decided to have fun at my expense.

I resumed my usual routine of life; a few hours of work in the morning, a round of golf in the afternoon, a cocktail party in the evening followed by a late dinner. In Delhi one could manage a drink and dine off other people all 365 days of the year. The Diplomatic Corps was my cornucopia. I got all the canned food and liquor I needed from diplomats. Scotch which cost a hundred-and-fifty rupees per bottle in Connaught Circus was made available to me by the crate at thirty rupees each or for free. The Corps also catered to my basic needs. Delhi had over a hundred embassies, High Commissions and Legations. Diplomats in Delhi did not have much work to do. Most of their energies were directed to wining and dining officials of the External Affairs and other ministries of the Government of India, cultivating non-official locals and celebrating their independence days. It was not difficult to find a bored wife or a spinster eager to know Indians and thus ensure a regular supply of imported victual and exotic sex.

At the time I found Bhagmati on the road I had been courting a stenographer working in the West German Embassy. I had met her at a consular reception, discovered that she was a new arrival and like many newly arrived foreigners anxious to get to know Indians. She was not particularly attractive—thirtyish, grey-eyed, thin-lipped, tall and bony. She tied her hair in a bun which made her look severe.

*

Fraulein Irma Weskermann was an easy conquest. One Sunday I took her round the monuments of Delhi and had Bavarian beer in her apartment. The following weekend I took her to the *son-et-lumiere* at the Red Fort and gave her dinner at Moti Mahal. Since restaurants were not permitted to serve alcohol I carried a hip-flask and when the waiter was not looking poured a slug of Indian whisky in her Coke. I explained that this was all an Indian citizen could afford as the cost of Scotch was prohibitive. She took the hint. (This gambit always worked with the diplomats). Thereafter whenever I invited her home or took her out she brought a bottle of Scotch or wine with her.

Fraulein Weskermann did not seem very interested in sex. Being somewhat sexless in appearance she had cultivated a kind of brashness as a defence mechanism. When I first put my arm round her waist she said 'Must you?' I answered in the affirmative and added, 'Because I like you.' Thereafter, she began to put her face forward to receive a kiss on her bony cheeks. One evening I said to her, 'Irma I am beginning to like you more than I should.' 'Zat's nice,' she replied and responded with a kiss. On another occasion I told her 'Irma, it's terrible but I think I am beginning to fall in love with you.' No woman can resist that. 'How many vomen have you said zat to before?' she asked. And let me kiss her on her lips. The relationship progressed in the conventional way with a little more intimacy each time. Soon I was fondling her breasts. How long can any woman have her breasts fondled and resist giving herself completely? My hands began to explore further. If they got too close to her middle she would open her grey eyes and firmly say 'No.' But it was only a matter of time. One evening as I was feeling her between her thighs I said 'You are ready for it.' A shudder passed through her frame. 'It must neffer, neffer happen,' she said pushing my hand out of her knickers. I apologized and pretended to be hurt. 'It's also my fault, yah?' she replied and made up with a kiss that made my ears burn. I had little doubt that the decks had been finally cleared and at the next encounter the Indo-Germanic affair would be consummated.

I had not reckoned with Bhagmati.

It must have been almost two months after the meeting with Bhagmati that Fraulein Weskermann was dining with me in my apartment. A certain strangeness, loud conversation and forced laughter indicated that she had made up her mind to say 'Yah.' Half-way through the meal we had emptied her bottle of Moselle. She agreed to try a 'tear-drop' of cognac with her coffee. As soon as my cook-bearer left we went to the sofa and proceeded to fondle each other. I whispered into her ear, 'Shall we?' She murmured, 'If you wish. Let me prepare myself.' She picked up her handbag and hurried into the bathroom. I repaired to the bedroom and switched on the air-conditioner. Irma Weskermann emerged draped in my dressing-gown. She looked coy. 'Don't look at me,' she pleaded. 'Switch off the light, please!' I laughed and put my arms round her waist—'We have a saying in Hindustani "If you are pregnant you have to show your belly to the midwife." If you are going to make love you have to bare your body,'—disrobed her and led her to my bed.

Fraulein Weskermann lay on her back and parted her thighs. I entered her without much emotion. She was not a virgin; she was damp but not very excited. All she did was to let out a moan *aah* and shut her eyes. We lay interlocked without a word or movement. Neither of us seemed to be getting very much out of it. But neither seemed to have the courage to call it off. How different it had been with Bhagmati!

Through the hum of the air-conditioner I heard the doorbell. I looked up. It rang again. 'Somebody at the door?' asked the Fraulein a little alarmed. 'Sounds like it,' I replied. To reassure her I added, 'Who cares!'

She pushed me off. 'Might be a telegram or something important like zat.'

I got up, slipped on my dressing-gown and tiptoed to the door. I peeped through the Judas hole. It was Bhagmati.

The ringing became more insistent. I tiptoed back. Fraulein Weskermann was sitting up in bed. 'Who is it?' she demanded.

'A woman,' I replied foolishly.'I owe her some money.

'What a time to visit a man!' she said very acidly.

'It is nothing like that,' I protested. 'She is a sick woman I picked up on the road one morning...'

The bell continued ringing.

'I haf been a big fool,' she said standing up. She picked up her clothes and went into the bathroom. She came out fully dressed. 'Nice to have known you, Mr Singh. Good-bye and haf a naice time.' She opened the door and looked the dazed Bhagmati up and down. 'Excuse me, Madam!' she exclaimed and marched out to her Volkswagen.

I slumped on my sofa and covered my face with my hands. I heard the door close and then Bhagmati's voice pleading, 'If your slave has been guilty of indiscretion she begs a thousand pardons.'

I refused to look at her. 'You could have chosen a better hour.'

'*Huzoor*, your maidservant had an engagement at the *Misri* embassy. I thought I would leave some money with your honour and also offer my humble services. I see I have angered your honour. I must extract a pardon before I rid myself of your sight.'

She sat down at my feet and began to press my legs. 'Your slave had only to turn her face the other side and you were unfaithful to her!' Her hands stroked the insides of my thighs. 'What was the giraffe like?' she asked saucily.

'I'll show you,' I replied and roughly hauled her up into my lap.

'*Arre!*' she exclaimed wagging her head, 'All males of the species are the same. One minute one woman, next minute another.'

*

Today is the 15th of June. Delhi had its first pre-monsoon shower. It has cleansed the atmosphere of the dust that has been hanging in the air for the past three days. A fresh breeze drives snow-white clouds across the blue sky. The earth is fragrant. The air smells of more rain. How can anyone stay indoors on a day like this?

The choice is between Mehrauli and Okhla. Mehrauli has the Qutub Minar with its gardens, monuments and acres of mango orchards. Okhla has no monuments but it has lots of water. The Jamna has a weir from which a canal branches off. At monsoon time the river is an awesome sight. She is then Triyama the sister of the ruler of Hades. Delhiwallas who have a death-wish come to Okhla during the monsoons to hurl themselves into the Jamna's muddy arms. Those who have a zest for living come with baskets full of sucking mangoes. They suck them and see how far into the river they can throw their stones. Whether it is Mehrauli or Okhla you have to have a *mashooka* to share the experience: a *mashooka* in whose ears you can whisper: 'I want to take you in the rain till your bottom is full of mud and mine full of the monsoon.'

I hear a *tonga* pull up outside. I hear argument between the *tongawalla* and the passenger. The *tongawalla* shouts, 'There is more money in buggery than in plying a *tonga*.' The passenger replies in a louder voice '*Abey ja*! Who would want to bugger you! Nobody will spit on your dirty arse.'

Who could it be except Bhagmati!

Before she can ring the bell I open the door. She comes in swaying her hips and abusing the *tongawalla*, '*Sala, bahinchod*! I give the sister-fucker one rupee from Lal Kuan to this place and he wants to bugger me for more. There is no justice in the world.' She turns on me. 'Is this a day to sit indoors like a woman in a *burqa*? I thought you'd like to take me out in your motor car to eat some fresh air and mangoes.'

I'm waiting for an excuse to get out. There is no one I'd like to be with more than Bhagmati. But not with her dressed in that red and blue sari and her head looking like a nest of butterflies. I've bought her a pair of stretch-pants and an open collared shirt which she keeps in my apartment. 'I'll change into my *vilayati* clothes,' she says as she strides on into my bedroom.

She washes off the powder, rouge and lipstick. She plucks out the butterfly-clips from her hair, combs out the waves and ties it up in a bun at the back of her head. Now it is a different Bhagmati: a sprightly little gamine in a canvas kepi, half-sleeved sports shirt and bum-tight stretch-pants. Very chic! No one can tell whether she is a *hijda* or a boy who looks like a girl.

We start with an argument. Bhagmati says, 'It's a day for Okhla. When it rains the entire world goes to suck mangoes by the weir.'

'Not Okhla,' I reply. 'I don't like crowds: least of all Punjabis. They will be a crowd there screaming, shouting, eating, making litter everywhere.'

'If you are ashamed of being seen with me, I'll stay in the motor car,' retorts Bhagmati. It's true. But I am not going to spoil her day. 'I swear by the Guru that is not true! Okhla has too many people, too many monkeys, too many snakes. Once

I killed five snuggling behind the water-gauge. Five! One after the other.'

Snakes settle the argument in favour of Mehrauli.

The road to Mehrauli has an endless procession of cycles, *tongas*, scooters, cars and people on foot. Everyone is shouting *ho, ho* or singing film songs.

A two-wheeled open cart jammed with women in veils and children comes tearing through the crowd and passes us. The driver puts the handle of his whip on the spokes of the wheel to make them rattle. He yells to everyone to get out of his way. He almost knocks down a Sikh with his wife and four children piled on one bicycle. The Sikh is very shaken. He lets out the foulest abuse he can for a family of Mussalmans. 'Progeny of pigs! You want to kill us?' Out of the huddle of *burqas* rises a six-year-old David. He loosens his red jock strap, sticks out his pelvis and flourishes his tiny circumcized penis. He hurls back abuse like pellets from a sling. '*Abey Sikhrey*! *Harami* (bastard), you want to sit on my Qutub Minar?'

Daood *Mian*'s Qutub is a mighty two-and-a-half inches long. The other Qutub only 283 feet!

Bhagmati breaks into a helpless giggle. 'What a lovely little penis he has! So much nicer than the tapering things of the Hindus. Is your fellow circumcized?'

'You should know.'

'They all look the same when they are up. Next time I will look when it is asleep.'

We get to the Qutub. The car park is full of cars, the gardens are full of people. While we are trying to make up our minds where to go there is a heavy shower and everyone scurries for shelter. 'Not here,' I say and drive on. We go past the ruins of Metcalfe's mansion, Jamali-Kamali's mosque and enter Mehrauli town. I pull up in the car park alongside Auliya Masjid. The shower turns into a downpour. The Shamsi Talab, becomes a part of the cascade pouring into it. We sit in the car playing with each other. Bhagmati slithers down the seat and parts my legs. I am nervous. Any moment someone may peep in the window and want to know what she is up to. 'Not here,' I tell her, pushing away her head. 'We'll try Jahaz Mahal.'

I take the car a few feet further up the road and park it

alongside Jahaz Mahal. We make a dash for the building. There is a crowd of rustics—obviously caught by the rain on their way home. They make way for us. I take Bhagmati down the stairs to the floor which is almost level with the water of the pool. Not a soul. I take Bhagmati in my arms and crush her till she can't breathe. 'You want to break my bones? You want to murder me?' she protests.

'If you die here you would go straight to paradise. The waters of the Shamsi Talab have been blessed by many saints.'

'*Acchaji*! Now you want to finish me! I'll go and tell them I was murdered by my lover. Allah will forgive my sins. In my next birth I will be born as Indira Gandhi and become a famous daughter of India.'

We resume our flirting. But when you have only one ear, one eye and half-a-mind to spare for sex and have to keep the other ear, eye and half-of-the-mind to confront anyone who suddenly bursts upon you, it is not much fun. Twice we try to have a quickie but both times we are interrupted by voices coming down the steps. In that light no one can tell whether Bhagmati is a boy or a girl—or both. Indians are very understanding about boys amusing each other. Only when it comes to straightforward fucking do they get censorious. We pretend we are deeply interested in archaelogy, history, architecture. I light matches, examine the tiles and try to decipher inscriptions on stones.

The downpour continues. Not a break anywhere in the leaden sky. We continue strolling in the cellars examining dark corners by matchlight. I find a stone lying on the ground with some writing on it. I pick it up and bring it to the light. It has a swastika on top, two lotus flowers on either side with 'Allah' inscribed on it in Arabic. Beneath it is a legend in Persian:

'Musaddi Lal Kayasth, son of Chagan Lal Kayasth, disciple and slave of Peer Hazrat Khwaja Nizamuddin, Beloved of God by whose blessing he received the gift of a son, Kamal Kayasth. In the reign of Sultan Ghiasuddin Balban, King of Kings, Shah-in-Shah of Hindustan.'

4

Musaddi Lal

I Musaddi Lal, son of Lala Chagan Lal, Hindu Kayastha of Mehrauli in the city of Delhi, having lost the light in one eye due to the formation of a pearl and fearing the same fate befalling the other, herewith record some events of my days upon this earth. May Ishwar who is also Allah, and Rama who is also Rahim, bear witness that what I have written is true, that nothing has been concealed or omitted.

I was born in 633 Hijri corresponding to the year 1265 of the Christian calendar. It was the beginning of the reign of Sultan Ghiasuddin Balban. My ancestors had been scribes in the service of the rulers of Delhi. They had served Raja Anangpal, the Tomara Rajput, who built Lal Kot and planted the sacred iron pillar of Vishnu Bhagwan in the middle of the city. They had also served Raja Prithvi Raj Chauhan who renamed the city Qila Rai Pithora. When Mohammed Ghori defeated and slew Raja Prithvi Raj and became ruler of Delhi my ancestors acquired knowledge of Turki, Arabic and Persian and continued in the service of the new ruler. My great-grandfather served under Sultan Qutubuddin Aibak and with his own eyes saw the destruction of Hindu and Jain temples, the building of the Jamia Masjid later called Quwwat-ul-Islam on their ruins and the beginnings of the tower of victory, the Qutub Minar. My grandfather served under Qutubuddin's son-in-law and successor Sultan Altamash. Like a common labourer he dug the earth for the Shamsi Talab at the site where the Sultan had seen the footprints of the Holy Prophet's horse, Buraq, and carried stones on his head to build the mausoleum of the Saint Qutubuddin Bakhtiyar Kaki. He saw the Qutub Minar completed in AD 1220. It was my grandfather

4

who built the stone house along the Shamsi Talab where I was born and spent most of my life. He also served under Sultan Altamash's daughter Razia Sultana who ruled over Hindustan for three-and-a-half years. My father, Lala Chagan Lal was a clerk in the *kotwali* (police station) of Mehrauli under the mighty Sultan Ghiasuddin Balban and served him for fifteen of the twenty years of his reign which lasted from AD 1265 to AD 1287. (My father died in the year AD 1280).

Like my Kayastha forefathers, I was trained to be a scribe. A *pandit* taught me Sanskrit and Hindi. Through my father's influence I was admitted to a *madrasa* to learn Arabic, Turki and Persian. At first I was treated roughly by the Turkish boys and the sons of Hindu converts to Islam. But when I learnt to speak Turki and dress like a Turk, they stopped bullying me. To save me being harassed, the *Maulvi* Sahib gave me a Muslim name, Abdul. The boys called me Abdullah.

I was the only child of my parents. I had been betrothed to a girl, one of a family of seven who lived in Mathura. We were married when I was nine and my wife, Ram Dulari, only seven. Four years later, when I was old enough to cohabit, my parents sent the barber who had arranged my marriage to fetch my wife from Mathura. For reasons I will explain later, her parents refused to comply with our wishes. Then tragedy struck our home. My father died and a few days later my mother joined him. At thirteen I was left alone in the world.

The *Kotwal* Sahib was very kind to me. When he came to offer his condolence, he also offered my father's post to me.

It was at that time that my Muslim friends suggested that if I accepted conversion to Islam my prospects would be brighter; I could even aspire to become *Kotwal* of Mehrauli. And I would have no trouble in finding a wife from amongst the new converts. If I was lucky I might even get a widow or a divorcee of pure Turkish, Persian or Afghan stock. 'If you are Muslim,' said one fellow who was full of witticisms, 'you can have any woman you like. If you are up to it, you can have four at a time.'

A Turk for toughness, for hands that never tire;
An Indian for her rounded bosom bursting with milk;

A Persian for her tight crotch and her coquetry;
An Uzbeg to thrash as a lesson for the three.

There was something, I do not know what, which held me back from being converted to Islam. I suspected that the reason why my wife's parents had refused to send her to me was the rumour that my parents had adopted the ways of the Mussalmans. If I became a Muslim, they would say, 'Didn't we tell you? How could we give our daughter to an unclean *maleecha*?'

On the last day of the obsequial ceremony for my mother, my wife's uncle came from Mathura to condole with me. His real object was to find out what I was like and whether I observed Hindu customs. With his own eyes he saw that I had my head shaved, wore the sacred thread and fed Brahmins. I asked the barber to speak to him about sending my wife to me. The uncle did not say anything and returned to Mathura.

After waiting for some days I approached the *Kotwal* Sahib. At that time people felt that fate had dealt harshly with me and were inclined to be sympathetic. The *Kotwal* Sahib made me write out a complaint against my wife's parents for interfering with my conjugal rights. He forwarded it to the *Kotwal* of Mathura with a recommendation for immediate execution. If the family raised any objection, they were to be arrested and sent to Mehrauli.

A week later my wife escorted by her younger sister and uncle arrived at my doorstep. After a few days her uncle and sister returned to Mathura.

Ram Dulari behaved in a manner becoming a Hindu wife. She touched my feet every morning and wore vermilion powder in the parting of her hair. But she cried all the time. And if I as much as put my arm on her shoulder to comfort her she shrank away from me. One night when I went to her bed she started to scream. Our neighbour woke up and shouted across the roof to ask if all was well. I felt very foolish.

Even after one month I did not know what she looked like because she kept her face veiled with the end of her *dupatta*. It was only from her neck and hands that I made out that she was fair. I also noticed that her bosom was full and her buttocks nicely rounded.

It took me several weeks to realize that my wife did not intend to cohabit with me. She cooked her food on a separate hearth and ate out of utensils she had brought with her. For her I was an unclean, Muslim *maleecha*. I tried to take her by force. I beat her. It was no use. I asked her whether she would like to return to her parents. She said that she would only go if I threw her out or when she was taken away on her bier. What was I to do? Could I go to the *Kotwal* Sahib and ask him to order my wife to spread her legs for me! Gradually, I reconciled myself to my fate. We slept under the same roof but never on the same *charpoy*.

One morning I took Ram Dulari to see the Qutub Minar. We climbed up to the first storey and I pointed out the mausoleum of the Saint Qutubuddin Bakhtiyar Kaki, the Auliya Masjid alongside the Shamsi Talab, our own little home on the other side. And right below us the tomb of Sultan Altamash. I showed her the slab on which a Hindu stone-mason had inscribed *Sri Visvakarme Prasade Rachita* and stuck it into this Muslim tower of victory. We came down and I took her towards the Quwwat-ul-Islam mosque. I explained to her how the Turks had demolished twenty-seven Hindu and Jain temples and buried the idols of Vishnu and Lakshmi beneath the entrance gate so that Muslims going in to pray could trample on them. She refused to enter the mosque. As we were retracing our steps, she noticed that the figures of Hindu gods and goddesses on the pillars of what had once been a Hindu temple had been mutilated: noses sliced off, arms broken, breasts chopped off. She put her head against a pillar and began to cry. A small crowd collected. I pretended she was not feeling well and pushed her along. If it hadn't been for the fact that I was dressed like a Mussalman and my wife wore a *burqa* (all Hindu women of rank wore *burqas*) it could have been very awkward. When we got home I reprimanded her very severely.

The Hindus hatred of the Mussalmans did not make sense to me. The Muslims had conquered Hindustan. Why hadn't our gods saved us from them? There was that Sultan

Mahmud of Ghazni who had invaded Hindustan seventeen times—not once or twice but seventeen times. He had destroyed the temple of Chakraswamy at Thanesar and nothing happened to him. Then Somnath. They said that even the sea prostrated itself twice every twenty-four hours to touch the feet of Somnath. But even the sea did not rise to save Somnathji from Mahmud. They said that Mahmud used to chop off the fingers of the Hindu rajas he defeated in battle; his treasury was full of Hindu fingers. He styled himself as Yaminuddaulah—the right hand of God and Zill-e-Ilahi the Shadow of God on earth.

The Muslims had become masters of Hindustan. They were quite willing to let us Hindus live our lives as we wanted to provided we recognized them as our rulers. But the Hindus were full of foolish pride. 'This is our country!' they said. 'We will drive out these cow-killers and destroyers of our temples.' They were especially contemptuous towards Hindus who had embraced Islam and treated them worse than untouchables.

The Hindus lived on the stale diet of past glory. At every gathering they talked of the great days of the Tomaras and the Chauhans.

'Arre bhai! Who can deny our ancients were great!' I told my Hindu friends a hundred times. 'But let us think of today. We cannot fight the Mussalmans; they are too big, too strong and too warlike for us. Let us be sensible and learn to live in peace with them.' But reason never entered the skull of the Hindu. Everyone in the world knows that if you put the four Vedas on one side of the scale and commonsense on the other commonsense will be heavier. But not so with the Hindus. They would look contemptuously at me and call me a pimp of the Mussalmans. Their great hero was Prithvi Raj Chauhan who had defeated Ghori once at Tarain in AD 1191. But the very next year, on the same battlefield, he had been defeated and slain by the same Ghori. They had an answer to that too. 'Prithvi Raj's only mistake was to spare the life of the maleecha when he had first defeated him,' they would reply. Nobody really knows the truth about this Prithvi Raj. A poet fellow named Chand Bardai had made a big song-and-dance about him. This great hero Prithvi Raj married lots of women and even abducted the daughter of a neighbouring raja. But you could not say a word against him to the Hindus. Next to Sri Ramchandraji, it was Samrat Prithvi Raj Chauhan who they worshipped.

I realized that I belonged neither to the Hindus nor to the Mussalmans. How could I explain to my wife that while the Brahmins lived on offerings made to their gods, the Rajputs and the Jats had their lands, Aheers and the Gujars their cattle, the Banias their shops, all that the poor Kayasthas had were their brains and their reed pens! And the only people who could pay for their brains and their pens were the rulers who were Muslims!

I was disowned by the Hindus and shunned by my own wife. I was exploited by the Muslims who disdained my company. Indeed I was like a *hijda* who was neither one thing nor another but could be misused by everyone.

Then I heard of Nizamuddin. 'Go to the *dervish* of Ghiaspur on the bank of the river Jamna and all your troubles will be over,' people said. They called him *auliya* (prophet) and also Khwaja Sahib. But there were many learned Mussalmans who called him an imposter who would soon meet the fate he deserved. As becomes a good Kayastha I did not express any opinion and waited to see which way the wind was blowing.

In due course this Nizamuddin was summoned by the sultan to answer charges of heresy levelled against him. On the day of the trial I took leave from my job and went to the palace.

The very name of Ghiasuddin Balban made people urinate with fear. He had a terrible temper and was known to execute anyone who as much as raised his eyes to look at him. He kept two huge Negroes beside him to hack off the heads of people he sentenced to death.

What a sight it was! The great sultan on his couch flanked by his Abyssinian bodyguards: black djinns with drawn swords! Hundreds of bearded Turkish generals! On one side of the throne-couch stood five *ulema* dressed in fine silks. Facing them on the other side was a young man not much older than I. He wore a long shirt of coarse black wool and had a green scarf tied round his head. With him were three of his followers dressed as poorly as he. This was Nizamuddin, the Sufi *dervish* of Ghiaspur.

The sultan first addressed Nizamuddin. *'Dervish*, the *ulema* have complained that you make no distinction between Mussalmans and infidels; that you pose as an intermediary between God and man; that you use words which obliterate the difference between man and his Maker; that your followers indulge in music and dancing in the precincts of the mosque and thus contravene the holy law of the *shariat*. What do you have to say in your defence?'

Nizamuddin smiled and replied: 'O mighty Sultan, it is true that I do not make any distinction between Mussalmans and Hindus as I consider both to be the children of God. The *ulema* exhort Your Majesty in the name of the Holy Messenger (upon Whom be peace) to destroy temples and slay infidels to gain merit in the eyes of Allah. I interpret the sacred law differently. I believe that the best way to serve God is through love of his creatures. As for the charge of posing as an intermediary between man and his Maker, I plead guilty. God's Messenger (on Whom be peace) said: "Whoever dies without an Imam dies the death of a pagan." We Sufis follow this precept and believe that he who has no Shaikh is without religion. The *ulema* know not that God often manifests himself in His creatures. They also do not know that Allah cannot be understood through knowledge of books or through logic. His Messenger (peace upon Him) when asked whether even he did not know God replied "No, not even I. God is an experience."'

The sultan nodded towards the *ulema*. Their leader went down on his knees and kissed the ground in front of the throne. *'Jahan Panah* (Refuge of the World),' he said addressing the sultan, 'you who are the wisest and the most just of all monarchs do not need such insects as we are to expound the holy law. Your Majesty must know that this man, Nizamuddin, talks of love only to throw dust in the eyes of innocent people.' He unwrapped a copy of the *Quran*, touched it to his forehead and read out a passage. The crowd broke into a chorus of applause *Wah! Wah! Subhan Allah!* Few of them understood Arabic. Even fewer understood what the words meant when translated into Turki.

The sultan turned to the *dervish* and asked him about his claiming unity with God. Nizamuddin replied in very poetic language, 'O Sultan! And O you *ulema* learned of the law! And all of you people assembled here! Do you know what it is to love and be loved? Perhaps all you have known and enjoyed is the love of women. We Sufis love God and no one else. When we are possessed by the divine spirit we utter words which to the common man may sound like the assumption of godhood. But these should not be taken seriously. You may have heard of the story of the dove that would not submit to her mate. In his passion the male bird said, "If you do not give in to me, I shall turn the throne of Solomon upside down." The breeze carried his words to Solomon. He summoned the dove and asked it to explain itself. The dove replied, "O Prophet of Allah! The words of lovers should not be bandied about." The answer pleased Solomon. We hope our answer will please the Sultan Balban.'

A murmur of *Wah! Wah!* went round.

The sultan asked the *ulema* for authority on the subject of music. The *ulema* opened another book (they had brought many bundles of books with them). Their leader again read out something in Arabic and then translated it into Turki. He looked back at the crowd and a section applauded *Wah! Wah!*

The sultan again turned to Nizamuddin. The *dervish* had not brought any books. From memory he quoted a tradition of the Prophet about music and dancing. 'When Allah's grace enters one's person it manifests itself by making that person sing and dance with joy. If this be a manifestation of being possessed by Allah, I say *Ameen.*'

The sultan pondered over the matter for a while. He brushed his beard and examined the hair that came off in his hand. The silence was terrible. At last he cleared his throat and spoke in a clear, loud voice! 'We dismiss the *ulema's* charges against Nizamuddin, *dervish* of Ghiaspur.'

The crowd broke into loud applause praising the sultan's sense of justice. Many rushed to the *dervish* and kissed the hem of his coarse, woollen shirt.

The next morning I asked the *Kotwal* Sahib about Nizamuddin. 'He's got up there,' he replied pointing up to the sky. 'He has shown many infidels the true path. Go to him any Thursday or on the eve of the new moon and you'll see what miracles he can perform!'

The following Thursday I hired an *ekka* to go to Ghiaspur which was more than a *kos* from Mehrauli. When I got to the hospice and asked an attendant whether I could see the man who was at the palace some days earlier, he replied. 'Khwaja Sahib is meditating in his cell. He only receives visitors in the evening. You can go and eat at the *langar* (free kitchen).'

I went to the *langar*. It was crowded with Muslims and Hindus, rich and the poor, clamouring for a leaf-cup of lentils and a morsel of coarse bread. I had to fight my way through the crowd to grab a *chappati*. I came out and sat in the courtyard where a party of *qawwals* were singing in Hindi. I was told that the song had been written and composed by one Abdul Hassan, who was very close to the holy man.

Late in the afternoon word went round that the *dervish* had emerged from his cell. People buzzed round him like bees round a crystal of sugar. I pushed my way through the throng and when I got to him I kissed the hem of his shirt. Suddenly tears came gushing into my eyes. The *dervish* put his hand on my head. I felt a tingling sensation run down my spine and the fragrance of musk enveloping my frame. He tilted my tear-stained face upwards and said, 'Just as Allah has let my tunic drink your tears, so may He make your sorrows mine!' As he spoke those words I felt as light as a piece of thistledown floating in the air.

'Abdullah, my son,' he continued, 'you live near the mausoleum of Hazrat Qutubuddin Bakhtiyar Kaki. Go there every morning and recite the ninety-nine names of Allah. Your wishes will be granted. Come whenever your heart is heavy. The doors of our hut of poverty are never bolted against anyone.'

It was on my way back to Mehrauli that I asked myself, 'How does he know that I live near the mausoleum of Bakhtiyar Kaki? How does he know that my Muslim friends call me Abdullah? And if somebody has told him who I am

and where I live, how is it that he does not know that I am a
Hindu and may not know the ninety-nine names of Allah?'

I could not contain myself. Since there was no one else I
could unburden myself to I told my wife all that had passed.
For the first time since we had been married, Ram Dulari
showed some interest in me. When I ran out of words she
asked very timidly, 'Why don't you take me along one day?'
In my enthusiasm I took her hand. It went limp in my grasp.

On the first day of the new month of the Muslim lunar
calendar I took Ram Dulari to Ghiaspur. Our *ekka* was one in
a long line on the dusty road. We passed bullock carts loaded
with women and children, the men striding along barefoot
with their shoes hung on their staves.

There was an immense crowd. A whole bazaar of bangle-
sellers, sweet-meat vendors, cloth-dealers and medicine-
sellers had gone up. I feared Ram Dulari would not get a
chance to have *darshan* of the holy man. I did not take her to
the *langar* as she would not touch anything cooked by
Muslims. We wandered round the stalls, watched jugglers
and acrobats, dancing bears and monkeys. We sat down
under a tree. I began to despair. In an hour the sun would set
and the *ekka*-driver would insist that we return to Mehrauli
before it became dark. I was lost in my thoughts when a
dervish came to me and said: 'Abdul! Isn't your name Abdul
or Abdullah? The Khwaja Sahib has been enquiring after you.'
He led us through a door at the back of the mosque into a
courtyard where the holy man was receiving visitors. The
dervish forced his way through the crowd with us following
close on his heels.

I kissed the hem of the holy man's shirt. Ram Dulari
prostrated herself on the ground before him. Khwaja Sahib
stretched his hand and blessed her. 'Child, Allah will fulfil
your heart's desire. If He wills your womb will bear fruit. Go
in peace.' That was all. The crowd pushed us away.

Her womb bear fruit? This man of God who was said to
read people's minds like a book had not read Ram Dulari's.
From the way she turned away her face I could tell she was
embarrassed. On the way back to Mehrauli she avoided
touching me. We got off opposite the Auliya Masjid. We

walked home as if we had nothing to do with each other: I in front looking at the shuttered doors of shops as if I had never seen them before; she behind me enveloped in her *burqa*.

As soon as we stepped into our courtyard she lit the hearth to warm up food she had cooked in the morning. I lit an oil-lamp in the niche and wrote down the events of the day. She gave me my meal and went back to the kitchen to eat hers. After I had finished I gave her my empty brass plate and went to the bazaar to get a *pan*-leaf.

By the time I came back Ram Dulari had rinsed the utensils and was lying on her *charpoy* with her face towards the wall. I blew out the oil-lamp and stretched myself on my *charpoy*. I could not sleep. I kept thinking about the holy man's promise that we would have children. How could Ram Dulari have them unless I gave them to her? I wondered if she was thinking the same thing. After an hour of turning from side to side I called softly to her, 'Ram Dulari!'

'Hun!'

'Are you asleep?'

'No.'

The gong of the *kotwali* struck the hour of midnight. Once again I asked Ram Dulari if she was asleep; she said 'No.' Something said she might not be averse to my touching her. I got up and went over to her *charpoy*. 'Can I lie with you?' I asked, 'I feel cold.' She made room for me and replied, 'If you wish.'

I lay beside her. The passion that I had stored up over the months welled in my body. Just as a torrent carries away everything that comes in its way my lust swept aside my fears. I fell on her like a hungry lion. I tore away her sari and tried to enter her. She spread out her thighs to receive me. But no sooner did I reach between them than my seed was spent. I felt ashamed of myself.

Ram Dulari got up to clean herself. She poured water from the pitcher into her brass *lota*. She put aside her sari and began to splash water between her thighs. Under the light of the stars I saw her pale body, the outlines of her rounded breasts and her broad hips. She dried herself with the same sari and wrapped it round her body. She hesitated, not sure which *churpoy* to go to. I stretched out my hand to her. She took it and let me pull her beside me. My passion was roused again. She let me remove her damp sari and warm her naked flesh in my embrace. This time I was able to hold myself longer. And she more eager to receive me. A cry of pain escaped her lips. I knew that I had at long last made Ram Dulari mine.

I re-lit the oil-lamp and helped her wash the stains of blood on the bedsheet. By the time we had finished our bodies were again hungry for each other. So passed the whole night.

I was woken by the sun on my face and flies buzzing in my ears.

Ram Dulari had bathed and cooked the morning meal. She was wearing the red sari she had worn when she had come to Mehrauli as a bride. She did not cover her face against me and blushed as she saw me get up from her bed. She ran indoors. I followed her and bolted the door from the inside.

Thereafter I could not have enough of Ram Dulari. I could not take my eyes off her. Every movement she made fired me with desire to take her. Every moment I was away from her was a torment and I hurried back home to be in her embrace. And she became coquetish. '*Ajee*, I am not a whore you can have anytime you like—not unless you pay me for it.' I bought her a nose-pin with a red ruby; I bought her glass bangles of all the colours I could find in the bazaar. For some months our world was narrowed to a small *charpoy* on which we sported night and day.

Ram Dulari and I became members of a community which worshipped both in Hindu temples and in Sufi hospices. We celebrated Hindu festivals as well as the Muslim. At Dassehra we went to see Ram Lila, on Diwali we lit oil-lamps on the parapet of our house, at Holi we squirted coloured water on our Hindu friends. On Id we exchanged gifts with Muslims we knew; on the death anniversaries of Muslim saints we went to the mausoleum of Qutubuddin Bakhtiyar Kaki. And at least once a month we went to Ghiaspur and watched the sky at dusk to see if the new moon had risen.

Ram Dulari continued to dress as other Hindu women did. She wore crimson in the parting of her hair, a red dot on her forehead, and a *mangalsutra* (a necklace of black and gold beads). I continued to dress like a Turk with a skull cap and turban. Like the Turks I sported a neatly trimmed beard and moustache. And I spoke the way they did. If they said *As-Salaam-Valai-kum* (peace be with you) I replied *Valai-kum-As-Salaam* (and with you too be peace). If they asked me how I was, I replied *Al-hamdu-lillah* (well, by the grace of God). But if they asked me 'Abdullah when will you become a true Muslim?' I would reply 'Soon, if that be the will of God—*Inshallah.*' If anyone asked me whether we were Hindus or Mussalmans, we would reply we were both. Nizamuddin was our umbrella against the burning sun of Muslim bigotry and the downpour of Hindu contempt.

So passed the days, weeks and months. By the end of the year Ram Dulari was pregnant and had to go to her parents in Mathura for her confinement. When news of the birth of a son was brought to me I sent plates full of sweets to the *Kotwal* Sahib and to all our Muslim and Hindu friends. After a few weeks I went to Mathura to bring back my wife and son. Ram Dulari's sisters made a lot of fuss over me. They teased me, 'Are you going to have the boy circumcized? Are you going to name him Mohammed or Ali or something like that?' I let them say what they liked. I had great fun with them.

I did not have my son circumcized. I had his head shaved and got a Brahmin to recite *mantras*. I chose the name Kamal for him—it could be either Hindu or Muslim. In Hindi it meant the lotus flower. In Arabic, pronounced with a longer accent on the second *a*, it meant excellence. We took the child to Jogmaya temple and had the priest daub sandalpaste on his forehead. Then we took him to Ghiaspur and had the Khwaja Sahib bless him. I recorded my gratitude to my *peer* by having his name inscribed on stone as my benefactor and embedding the stone in the outer wall of our home.

People who do not have a guru or a *peer* can never understand what they mean to their disciples. They are more than either father or mother to them. A disciple gives more respect and obedience to his guru than to his father. He is more devoted to his guru than to his mother; he suckles the milk of love from the guru's bosom and snuggles in his lap as would a baby in its mother's. Indeed the guru is more loved by his disciple than the bridegroom is by his bride because the disciple gives to his guru his *tan* (body), *man* (mind) and *dhan* (worldly wealth). The guru is the embodiment of God on earth. What happens when the true guru is away or you choose a wrong guru was abundantly proved to us. When Khwaja Sahib went away to the Punjab all the little towns which comprised Delhi became like a woman whose husband has gone abroad. Dust-storms of chaos began to blow. One calamity followed another.

Sultan Ghiasuddin Balban's eldest son, Prince Mohammed, was killed fighting the Mongols. The mighty sultan who had ruled Hindustan for twenty-two years with an iron hand wept like a woman. He would not eat or sleep or attend to the affairs of the state. He fell ill but would not allow the royal physician to feel his pulse. In a few days he was reduced to a skeleton—and died.

There were many claimants to the throne. They slew each other; I cannot even recall their names. Then Jalaluddin Firoze of the tribe of Khiljis, an old man with one foot in the grave, took his seat on the throne of Delhi. His sons could not wait for him to die. Many of them came under the influence of a false guru called Siddi Maula.

Siddi Maula had a hospice of his own where he ran a *langar* in which confections, the like of which were only cooked in the royal kitchen, were served to the rich and the powerful. The Siddi also had an army of followers to sing his praises. They reeled off the names of the *omarah* and princes of royal blood who paid homage to Siddi. They said Siddi Maula did not care a cowrie shell for worldly wealth or power and had even turned down the post of chief *qazi*. They said that the daughters of noble houses were eager to marry him but he would not have any of them. 'Ya Allah! What kind of *dervish* is this?' I asked myself: 'One foot in God's boat and the other in the courts of kings! Maybe he is one of those who wear the cloak of humility to cover designs of power!'

I saw Siddi Maula and at once knew he was not fit to kiss the dust of the feet of my *peer*, Nizamuddin. He was a rascally looking fellow with a glossy black beard and moustaches that curled up like scorpion tails. He assumed the airs of an aristocrat and was forever sniffing at a perfumed swab of cotton. Although he was a young man, he had developed a paunch. Even a blind man could see that this Siddi did not believe in fasting or overcoming his *nafs* (desires). He was so busy giving counsel to the rich that he had little time left for the poor. He was a proud man. Of the proud, Mustatraf has said:

> *Tell this fool whose arrogance makes his neck veins swell!*
> *Pride corrupts religion, weakens the mind, destroys*
> *reputations. So take heed!*

It is truly said that a country cannot have two kings any more than a scabbard hold two swords. In Delhi we had the Khilji, Jalaluddin Firoze. And we had Siddi Maula who was known to be conspiring with one of the sultan's sons to overthrow the sultan. It had to be one or the other.

How the old sultan outwitted the *dervish* is quite a story. He got some people to lodge a report that the *dervish* had promised to help a faction inimical to the sultan and had in turn been promised the hand of a young, beautiful princess. No sooner did this charge reach the sultan than he ordered the arrest of Siddi Maula. I was in the *kotwali* when Siddi Maula and a score of his followers were brought in handcuffs. Their feet were in irons. I knew blood would flow and Siddi Maula would curse anyone who sided with his enemies. Why risk the anger of a *dervish* even a false one! I wrote a petition to the *Kotwal* Sahib begging leave for three days as my bowels had suddenly become loose and the *hakeem* had advised rest.

I learnt of what passed with Siddi Maula from the clerks who came to enquire about my health. *Kotwal* Sahib had tried to extort a confession from Siddi Maula. He had him beaten, his testicles squeezed, red hot chillies pushed up his anus, his mouth filled with shit and urine. But Siddi Maula had refused to speak. The sultan was very angry. 'Make him and his followers walk through fire. If they come out alive, I will believe they are innocent and let them go,' he said. The next day a huge funeral pyre was prepared near village Baharpur not far from Mehrauli. I could not miss this sight as Siddi Maula was reputed to be able to perform miracles.

The sultan came to watch the spectacle. The pyre was set on fire. Just as the Siddi and his followers were being pushed towards it, the sultan lost his nerve. He sent for the *ulema* and asked them if an ordeal by fire had the sanction of the holy law. The *ulema* shook their heads. 'It is the nature of fire to burn,' they said. The sultan cancelled the order and returned to his palace. Siddi Maula and his men were flogged back to the *kotwali*. The sultan turned his wrath on the *Kotwal* Sahib. 'If you can't make him talk, send him to us. We will make him open his vile mouth.'

Despite Ram Dulari's remonstrations that I should stay at home I joined a party of clerks going to Shahr-i-Nau—the new city going up in the vicinity of the Qasr-i-hazaar Sutoon, the palace of a thousand pillars.

Siddi Maula and his gang were already present in the Hall of Public Audience when the sultan took his seat. The sultan was in a very bad mood. The way he talked showed clearly that his mind was as infirm as his body, 'Confess your crimes,' he roared, 'or we will have your tongue torn out of your mouth.' And if he confessed he was to have his head cut off.

'Bring the impostor near us,' he commanded. Siddi Maula was brought forward. The old sultan stepped down from his throne. 'Son of Satan! You call yourself a saint and meddle in the affairs of kings!' he shouted as he slapped the *dervish* across the face. Siddi did not flinch. Although his face was black with bruises and his eyes were almost closed because of the swelling around them, the ends of his moustache were still curled up and his mien was as defiant as ever. The sultan hit him again and screamed, 'Speak, you fruit of fornication!' Siddi spoke in a clear and powerful voice everyone could hear. 'Jalaluddin, listen to the words of Siddi Maula, the *dervish* of Allah!' he said as if he was speaking to a slave. 'Allah will punish you for laying hands on His servant. At the hands of your own kinsmen will you die. Your carcass will burn in the fires of hell.' Suddenly Siddi Maula spat out a blob of phlegm and blood which covered the sultan's face and snow-white beard.

The old sultan began to rave like a maniac: 'Moozi (blackguard), bastard, son of a pig!' He turned to his courtiers and abused them, 'Cowards! You allow your ruler to be insulted by this dog!' In the hall there was a party of dervishes of an order known to hate Siddi Maula. They pounced on Siddi and belaboured him till he was reduced to a bloody mess. They dragged him out into the open where he lay like a sack—alive or dead—I do not know. Then an elephant was brought to crush Siddi Maula's head under its foot. His skull burst like a coconut spilling blood and butter-like fat. My knees buckled under me; I could not stop my body from shaking. I sat down where I was and began to pray. It took me an hour to recover. My friends helped me get home.

What a terrible day it was! When Siddi Maula was taken to Shahr-i-Nau, it was a bright, sunny morning. No sooner was he dead than the sky turned as black as charcoal. A vast cloud of locusts descended on the city. Every tree and every bush became a beehive of crawling, hopping, flying insects. Within a matter of moments the trees were leafless, bushes turned to brambles.

Then followed the worst sand-storm I have ever known. It came like the charge of a phalanx of black elephants smashing walls, uprooting trees, blinding man and beast alike. It was so dark that one could not tell when the sun set and the night came on. 'It is the curse of Siddi Maula,' said Ram Dulari to me as we lay huddled together with Kamal between us.

What Siddi Maula had prophesied came to pass. Sultan Jalaluddin Firoze was murdered by his own nephew, Alauddin Khilji, who was also his son-in-law. I do not know whether the deceased sultan roasted in the fires of hell but we certainly had a foretaste of gehennum. The summer's heat turned Delhi into an oven. The sun's rays were so fierce that every day twenty or thirty people died of stroke. There was no rain. Wells dried up. Cattle began to die of thirst. Crops withered. There was no flour or rice or lentils in the bazaars. We had to get provisions at an exorbitant price from distant villages. The city was full of starving beggars dying in the streets. Hindus prayed to their gods. Muslims prayed to Allah. We prayed for the return of our Khwaja Sahib.

Our prayers were answered. One morning a *dervish* returning from the Punjab informed us that the Khwaja Sahib was only two days march from Mehrauli. That afternoon there was a meeting of the citizens at the mausoleum of Qutubuddin Bakhtiyar Kaki to arrange a suitable reception for him.

When the great day came, citizens in their hundreds poured out of the city gates to welcome the saint.

The Khwaja Sahib looked pale and tired. That was not surprising as he had walked barefoot over hundreds of *kos* of hot, dusty roads. But he had a smile and a blessing for everyone who got close enough to kiss the hem of his cloak or touch his feet. The *dervishes* had to make a cordon to protect him from the surging crowd. The bazaars were decorated with arches with banners saying *Khush Amdeed* (welcome). Women crowded on the roof-tops showered rose-petals on him. Men smothered him in garlands. A huge procession led by parties of *qawwals* wound its way through the main bazaar of Mehrauli to the mausoleum of Qutubuddin Bakhtiyar Kaki. The Khwaja Sahib begged to be left alone. He went down into one of the cells in the basement of Auliya Masjid and bolted the door from the inside.

At night we heard the rumble of clouds. Mehrauli which had not had a drop of rain during the monsoon season had a heavy shower in autumn. May the mouths of unbelievers be stuffed with dung!

The following Thursday, I took Kamal and Ram Dulari to have *darshan* of the Khwaja Sahib. Such a crowd I had never witnessed at Ghiaspur! It was very hot and my throat was parched. The Khwaja Sahib's words were like nectar cooled in mountain streams of paradise.

'There is only one God though we call Him by different names. There are innumerable ways of approaching Him. Let everyone follow the way he thinks best for him. His path may lead to the mosque or the tabernacle, to a temple full of idols or to a solitary cave in the wilderness. What path you take is not important; what is important is the manner in which you tread it. If you have no love in your heart then the best path will lead you into the maze of deception.' He told us of an incident from the life of the Prophet Musa. Musa heard a poor shepherd praying: 'Where art Thou that I may serve Thee? I will mend Thy boots, comb Thy hair, give Thee milk from my goats.' Musa reprimanded the shepherd for so speaking to God. God in His turn reprimanded Musa. 'Thou hast driven away one of my true servants.'

It was again to the Prophet Musa that Allah conveyed the essence of true religion. The Almighty said. 'I was sick, and you did not come to see me. I was hungry, and you did not give me food:' Musa asked 'My God, can you also be sick and hungry?' God replied 'My servant so-and-so was sick, and my servant so-and-so was hungry. If you had visited one and fed the other, you would have found me with them.'

The Khwaja Sahib made us memorize some Sufi catechisms:

> *Who is the wisest of wise men?*
> *One who rejects the world.*
> *Who is the saintliest of all saints?*
> *One who refuses to change with changing circumstances.*
> *Who is the richest of rich men?*
> *One who is content.*
> *Who is the neediest of the needy?*
> *One who has no contentment.*

How to be content? I asked myself. The Khwaja Sahib heard the question I had asked only in my heart. 'Reduce your wants to the barest minimum, conquer your *nafs*.'

By the time we came out, the sun had gone behind the walls of the hospice. Kamal had fallen asleep in my lap. *Ekkawallas* were clamouring to get back to Mehrauli.

These were dangerous times. We had to pass through villages inhabited by Jats and Gujars who were notorious robbers. We formed a party of ten or twelve *ekkas;* two dozen men armed with swords and spears rode on either side. We reached Mehrauli without any untoward incident.

It had been a long day. I put Kamal to bed. Ram Dulari brought me a tumbler of milk which I was in the habit of drinking before retiring. I drew her on my lap. She protested:

'All day you hear sermons on controlling your passions: but as soon as it gets dark you want to do this.'

'*Aree*! How stupid can you be! All day you hear sermons about love; but by the evening you forget everything you heard.'

'The Khwaja Sahib did not mean this kind of love,' she replied. 'Hasn't he often said, "If you want to approach God, you must first conquer your desires." Is this how you overcome your *nafs*?' she asked pressing her bottom on my middle. 'You will never achieve union with God this way,' she giggled.

'Let us first achieve union between ourselves; we can bother about union with the Almighty later,' I replied.

*

The days went by. Our *Kotwal* Sahib became too old to work. He was permitted to retire and go to Mecca. His son-in-law was appointed in his place.

The new *Kotwal* was a bigot. He spoke very disparagingly of the Hindus. He became a great favourite of Sultan Alauddin Khilji who, as I said before, was the late sultan's nephew, son-in-law and assassin.

Sultan Alauddin Khilji set about despoiling the Hindu kingdoms of the south. His General, Malik Kafur, extended his dominions right up to the seas. He brought thousands of slaves, hundreds of elephants, camels and bullocks carts loaded with gold, silver and precious stones to Delhi. Hindu women were given away to Muslims as rewards for service. Many Hindu temples were destroyed. The sultan paid no heed to the Khwaja Sahib's advice that conquests of the sword were shortlived.

The atmosphere changed so much that even Hindus like me, who had adopted Muslim ways, found life irksome. I did my job, drew my wage and kept my mouth shut. If some Mussalman needled me too much, I sought shelter at Ghiaspur. Not even the mighty sultan who assumed the title *Sikandar-i-Sani* (Alexander the Second) and proclaimed Delhi as *Dar-ul-Khilafa* (Seat of the Caliphate), who had defeated and massacred Mongol invaders by the thousands, who had raised a new city Siri and an enormous *madrasa* beside the Hauz-i-Alai and who planned to raise another Qutub Minar twice as high as the first, dared to raise his eyebrows in front of our Khwaja Sahib. Once when he expressed a wish to visit Ghiaspur, the Khwaja Sahib replied, 'We will have nothing to do with kings. If the sultan enters our hospice by one door, we will leave by another.'

One day I was at the *kotwali* singing praise of our *Khwaja* Sahib. A clerk whose tongue was coated with odious criticisms said loud enough for all to hear, '*Ajee*, what can one say about a gentleman like you! The more one says the less adequate it is! At one place you are Musaddi Lal Kayastha, at another Shaikh Abdullah, some you greet with a *Ram Ram*, others with a *salaam:* with Muslims you bow towards the Kaaba; with the Hindus you kiss the penis of Shiva; a courtier in the *kotwali*, a *dervish* in the hospice; one foot in a monastery, the other on your woman's *charpoy*. You get the best of both worlds. Yes sir, the more one praises you, the less adequate it seems.'

I did not return to the *kotwali* after my midday meal. I lay on my *charpoy* in the courtyard, gazing at the grey sky and thinking about what that clerk had said. If I'd had the power I would have had the fellow taken to the market-place, his trousers pulled down and ordered every citizen to spit on his bottom.

Ram Dulari sat down beside me and asked, 'What's the matter?'

'Nothing.'

'Can't be nothing. It's written on your face. Why don't you tell me?'

I told her. She listened quietly. When I had finished, she gaped at the wall; I gaped at the sky. 'There are many like us,' I told her, 'There is that poet Abdul Hassan who also calls himself Sultani and Ameer Khusrau. His father was Muslim, his mother Hindu. For Hindus he writes in Hindi, for Muslims in Persian. For Indians he praises everything about India; for Muslims he praises everything in the lands of the Muslims. He flatters the sultan and he flatters the Khwaja

Sahib. And he is the favourite of both. He writes poems praising the *omarah* and extracts many *tankas* from them; at the same time he pretends to be a *dervish*. No one dares to say anything to him because he is Muslim. It is only poor Hindus like us who wish to befriend Hindus as well as Muslims who get spat on by both; we are neither one nor the other. They treat us as if we were *hijdas*.'

'Let our enemies be *hijdas*!' exclaimed Ram Dulari angrily. 'You talk to this man Abdul Hassan or Khusrau or whatever his name is. Ask him for advice.'

'I don't like him. He never says anything without a sting in it. He is too clever for the likes of me.'

'If you speak nicely to him, he may become your friend.'

'*Aree*! You are very innocent; you don't know the ways of the world. The rich only make friends with the rich. The clever only like admirers and flatterers. Khusrau is both rich and clever. I am not important enough to matter to him. And I will not waste my time pandering to his vanity.'

However, the next day when I went to Ghiaspur I ran straight into this chap Abdul Hassan Ameer Khusrau. As usual he was surrounded by a ring of admirers. Also as usual the only voice you could hear was his. As soon as he saw me he aimed a barbed shaft at me: 'Lala Musaddi Lal *alias* Abdullah brings his august presence amongst us.' I exchanged greetings with the others without looking at the fellow. His friend, another poet named Amir Hassan Dehlvi, was more amiable. 'Say brother Abdullah, how goes it with you?' he asked. '*Al hamdu-Lillah*,' I replied as I sat down.

Khusrau realized I had taken offence and tried to make up. 'Brother Abdullah I have composed a new riddle for you in Hindi. Let us see if you can get it':

> *Twenty I sliced, I cut off their heads*
> *No life was lost, no blood was shed.*

He had obviously put it to the others before I came. They said in a chorus, 'This is really a clever one!' I could make nothing of it. Khusrau reverted to his ill-mannered self. 'Fool!'

he cried, 'The answer is in the riddle itself. It is *nakhoon*. Don't you see *nakhoon* means both nails and no blood? You have to have brains to work out Khusrau's riddles.'

'Allah gave you wisdom, Ishwar gave me the gift of good manners,' I replied in as sharp a tone as I could manage. It hit the mark. Khusrau changed his tone. He was like that, blowing hot one minute blowing cold the next. 'Don't take it ill, brother,' he said. 'We are *dharam bhais* (brothers in faith). Try this one':

> *All night he stayed with me.*
> *Came the dawn and out he went;*
> *At his going my heart bursts*
> *O friend, was it my lover?*
> *No friend, it was the ....*

'It was the...? It was the...?' demanded Khusrau clicking his thumb and finger in my face. Fortunately someone gave an answer. 'No friend, it was the lamp.' Khusrau went on from riddle to riddle. '*Bhai*, the prophecy that you will be greater than Khaqani of Persia has certainly been fulfilled,' remarked one of his cronies. Khusrau did not deny it. 'I am but the dust under the feet of the Khwaja Sahib! If the great Nizamuddin honours me with the title of *Toot-i-Hind* (The Nightingale of India) and calls me Shaikh Saadi of Hindustan, what power on earth can prevent me from becoming the greatest poet and singer of all time? It's not I, it is divine spark that the Khwaja Sahib has lit in my bosom that shines in my wretched frame.

What could anyone say to such mock humility and such bare-faced bragging? It is true that as soon as someone achieves success, people vie with each other to discover newer facets of his genius. So it was about Khusrau. If one man said Khusrau was a great poet, another said he was a greater musician. If a third one said Khusrau was a great statesman, a fourth one would insist he was an even greater swordsman. Khusrau knew the art of spreading stories about himself. Since it was fashionable among Muslims to trace their ancestry to some foreign land, Khusrau who was darker than I and had more Indian blood than Turkish in his veins talked of Turkey as his 'home'. The poetic pseudonyms he had chosen for himself were designed to convey nobility of birth, power and wealth. At first he was Sultani (drop the *i* at the end and it becomes Sultan). When he became Khusrau he added Ameer (rich) to it. God had given him brains and talent but had forgotten to temper His gifts with modesty. This braggart who compared himself to Shaikh Saadi had not read what had been written about people who chant their own praises:

> It does not behove a man of wisdom
> By his own tongue to praise himself;
> What pleasure does a woman beget
> If with her own hand she rubs her breast?

What a change came over Khusrau when the Khwaja Sahib made his appearance! He was like an actor who takes off a mask which has moustaches painted insolently upwards and puts on another which has them hanging down in humility. The arrogant boaster suddenly turned into an ardent hem-kisser and tear-shedder. And he alone of all the thousands present was always honoured by a pat on the head and a solicitous enquiry, 'Is all well with you, Abdul Hassan?'

On my way back to Mehrauli, I was full of angry thoughts about Khusrau. How was it that other people could not see what a double-faced man he was? He had served innumerable masters. If anyone knew when to turn his back to the setting sun and worship the new one rising, it was Khusrau! He had first been with Sultan Balban's nephew, Malik Chajjoo. How he had extolled Chajjoo! Then he had joined the sultan's younger son and denounced Chajjoo. Next he'd served the heir-apparent; thereafter the ruler of Avadh. When the ruling dynasty was half-Hindu he boasted of the Hindu blood in his veins and extolled the greatness of Hindustan. He praised its *betel* leaves and its bananas, its chess players and musicians. When the ruler was a Muslim bigot, the same Khusrau proclaimed: 'Do not count Hindus among men for they venerate the cow, regard the crow superior to the parrot and read omens in the braying of an ass!' According to Khusrau what made India the greatest nation of the world was the fact that he, Khusrau, was Indian! I said to myself: this Khusrau is a cunning sycophant. Why should I waste so much of my time and temper on him! By the time the *ekka* pulled up at the stand outside the Auliya Masjid I had made my peace with Khusrau; for me he was just a successful joker, a *khusra* (a castrated male).

Ram Dulari heard my footsteps and undid the latch to let me in. Kamal was already asleep. She warmed milk for me and sat down beside me. I told her of what happened at Ghiaspur. I asked her the riddle about paring nails. She had heard of it and gave me the answer. I asked her about the other one of the 'spending all night and going out at dawn.' She nudged me in the belly: 'Do you have anything else on your mind except this?' I took her hand and put it on my member. 'It's not this, you silly woman! It is the lamp.'

She rose and blew out the lamp.

*

The years drifted by. Despite the thousands of conjugations in which our hips met to pump ecstasy into each other and the Jamna flood of semen which I poured into her—none of these efforts bore more fruit in Ram Dulari's womb. The hair on my head thinned till there was none left. My right eye began to turn grey; antimonies prescribed by *hakeems* did not arrest the cataract which soon deprived me of the sight in my left eye. Ram Dulari's hair also turned grey. No sooner did she stop menstruating than she started getting fleshy about her middle. Every time she had to get up from her *charpoy*, she had to rest her hands on her knees and invoke the assistance of Ramji. At times we lay on the same *charpoy*. But more often it was with our bottoms that we kissed each other than with our lips. We decided that Ishwar had given us enough and we should devote the days that remained to us in prayer.

Kamal had become a man. He had acquired knowledge of Turki and Persian at the *madrasa* at Hauz-i-Alai near Siri. I pleaded with the *Kotwal* Sahib, gave him a handsome *nazrana* of eleven gold *tankas* and got Kamal appointed in my place as a clerk in the *kotwali*. Ram Dulari found him a wife from among the daughters of one of the Kayastha families who frequented both the temple of Jogmaya and the hospice at Ghiaspur. From the way Kamal and his wife behaved, we were assured that our branch of the Kayasthas would not end with us.

We began to spend more time at the Khwaja Sahib's hospice in Ghiaspur than in our home in Mehrauli. Then we rented rooms in Ghiaspur and began to live there. We went to Mehrauli to visit our son and daughter-in-law once every month. Kamal brought his wife to see us every Thursday.

We saw the Khwaja Sahib every day. Khusrau was also there more often than he used to be. The years had deprived him of his teeth and cleansed his tongue of its coating of sarcasm. He became quite friendly and began to address Ram Dulari as *bhabi* (sister-in-law). I responded to his friendship and we were often in each other's homes.

What more could one ask for in old age? Peace, prayer, security, friends—all under the shade of a massive banyan tree—and our Khwaja Sahib, Beloved of God (*Mahboob-i-Ilahi*) and Beloved of Man! We lived in the world without being a part of it. We were like people who stroll through a bazaar without wanting to buy anything.

Rarely did the world intrude into our sanctum. One occasion that I recall was on the death of Sultan Alauddin Khilji. At first we heard that he had died in his sleep and that Malik Kafur, the slave he had raised to the rank of Commander, had taken over the administration till such time as a successor could be named by the *omarah*. Then we heard that Kafur had taken his master's senior widow to his couch, put out the eyes of two princes and murdered many others. The Khwaja Sahib, who seldom bothered about the comings and goings of sultans, put his hands on his ears and exclaimed 'Tauba!' Even Ameer Khusrau who had, as he said himself, 'woven a false story in every reign' wrote a satire on Malik Kafur which he recited to a gathering in Ghiaspur. We knew that if our Khwaja Sahib said something against someone, he was sure to be punished. So it came to pass. The servants of the palace rose against Malik Kafur and slaked the thirst of their daggers in his vile blood.

Qutubuddin Mubarak Shah, who became the next sultan, did not like our Khwaja Sahib. It did not take flatterers much time to fan the ashes of hate that smouldered in the sultan's breast into a vindictive flame. They said, 'Nizamuddin tells people that he does not give a cowrie shell for anyone; he defies royal commands to lower Your Majesty in the eyes of Your Majesty's subjects. (This was in reference to the Khwaja Sahib not attending Friday prayers in the Quwwat-ul-Islam mosque). He spreads all manner of gossip about Your Majesty and Khusro Khan.'

Who was this Khusro Khan? He was a Hindu Pawar boy captured during an expedition to Gujarat. The men of Gujarat are handsome but effeminate. And, of the Gujaratis, Pawars are known to be the most handsome and at the same time the most womanlike. I never saw this fellow, but he was said to be fair, gazelle-eyed with eyebrows curving like scimitars and buttocks as large as a woman's. By some quirk of fate the sultan who was known for his prodigious appetite for women turned his back upon his well-stocked harem of the beauties of Hindustan, Iran and Turkistan and fell in love with this boy from Gujarat. He had the fellow colour his lips and put kohl in his already dark eyes. They drank out of the same goblet. The royal hakeem was asked to prepare perfumed oil to smear on the boy's bottom. Then yet another change came over the sultan. He started colouring his own lips, smearing his own bottom with scented oil and making the Pawar do to him what he had been doing to the Pawar. As details of the affair travelled from lip to ear more pepper and spice were added to it.

The Muslims were more upset by these goings-on than the Hindus. They said it was a disgrace that a manly Turk should allow an infidel to mount him as a horse mounts a mare. The sultan thought the Muslims were unhappy because his beloved was a Hindu. He ordered the boy to be converted to Islam and re-named Khusro Khan. The two celebrated the occasion by getting drunk and carousing with each other in the open. Bawdy jokes about the Gujarati stallion and the Turkish mare could be heard in the bazaars. They reached the sultan's ears. The ulema who had reason to hate our Khwaja

77

Sahib told the sultan that the source of all the filthy stories about him and Khusro Khan was the hospice at Ghiaspur.

The sultan believed this calumny. He forbade the supply of provisions to the hospice; a police post was established at Ghiaspur to check the coming and going of people.

Strange are the ways of God! Our Khwaja Sahib who was the Sultan of all Sultans, simply wrote the name of Allah on a piece of paper and stuck it on the entrance of the hospice. He announced that the quantity of food cooked in the *langar* kitchen would be doubled. Allah saw to it that we were never short of flour, lentils, salt or *ghee*. Although the *omarah* discreetly stayed away, the number of poor pilgrims to the hospice increased.

This was like a cup full of chillies in the already hot curry of the sultan's temper. He ordered that the hospice be closed down. But the ways of God are mysterious! He heard of the plight of His Beloved Friend and decided to teach the sultan a lesson. The sinful cohabitation of the sultan and his lover-boy bore its monstrous fruit. Boils erupted on the royal penis and blocked the passage of urine. Physicians applied all kinds of unguents but the boils would not heal nor a drop of urine trickle out. What can medicines do against affliction visited by God! And how long can man live without urinating? Within a few hours the sultan was tossing in agony and crying to Allah for mercy. His mother came to Ghiaspur tearing her hair and pouring dust on her head. She clung to the Khwaja Sahib's feet and would not let him go till he forgave her son. 'Let your son abdicate and give his kingdom to us,' said the Khwaja Sahib. We knew the Beloved of God had some other miracle in mind.

The Queen Mother rushed back to the palace. The sultan was in terrible pain and agreed that as soon as he was able to urinate he would give up his kingdom. 'No,' said our Khwaja Sahib to the emissary, 'first abdicate, then urinate. Write the deed of renunciation in your own hand and put the royal seal on it.'

The sultan was almost on the verge of death when he signed the deed of abdication. As he pressed his seal on the wax, his bladder, which was on the point of exploding, emptied itself of its poisonous contents. The Queen Mother carried the jar containing her son's urine on her head and walked barefoot all the way from the palace to Ghiaspur. Women of the royal harem, eunuchs and guards followed her. She prostrated herself before the Khwaja Sahib and placed the scroll of parchment at his feet. The Khwaja Sahib broke open the seal and read aloud the deed of transfer of the kingdom of Hindustan made by Sultan Qutubuddin Mubarak Shah in favour of Hazrat Khwaja Nizamuddin, *dervish* of Ghiaspur. He then crumpled up the parchment and dropped it in the jar of urine. 'This is all we *dervishes* care for earthly kingdoms,' he said and retired to his cell to pray.

When a man's instincts are evil, repentance has a short lease and brief is his gratitude towards those who have done him good. No sooner had the sultan's penis healed than he began to misuse it as he had done before. And since the story of what our Khwaja Sahib had done with the deed transferring sovereignty of Hindustan to him had become common knowledge, the sultan's chagrin got the better of his gratitude. He issued an order reminding Mussalmans they were expected to be at the Quwwat-ul-Islam mosque on the eve of the new moon to pay him homage. He knew that our Khwaja Sahib dedicated this day of the month to the sacred memory of his departed mother. The Khwaja Sahib heard of the order and went to his mother's tomb to pray for guidance. After prayer he laid down where he was and fell asleep. When he woke he told us that he had dreamt of an enormous bull charging towards him. He had caught hold of the beast by its horns and pulled it down into the dust. We did not have to consult a soothsayer to know what the dream foretold.

Came the fateful day and there was the usual congregation to join the Khwaja Sahib at the afternoon prayer. As the shadow of the western wall spread across the courtyard of the mosque, the Khwaja Sahib took some of us with him to the roof to see the new moon. Just as the lower rim of the sun sank below the battlements of Shahr-i-Nau, we saw the pale, silver crescent of the moon. The Khwaja Sahib said a short prayer, ran the palms of his hands over his eyes and beard and recited a Persian verse which went somewhat as follows:

Oh fox! Why did you not stay in your lair?
Why did you join issue with a lion and bring about your
doom?

We continued to stroll on the roof enjoying the fresh evening breeze. Both the sun and the moon disappeared. The short dusk turned into a dark night. Suddenly the western horizon was aflame. We heard the sounds of horses' hoofs. It seemed as if an army bearing torches was galloping towards us. Was it the Royal Constabulary sent to arrest the Khwaja Sahib? The *Kotwal* came in person. He had come not to arrest the Beloved of God but to break the news that the sultan had been murdered and that the city was in turmoil.

The next morning we learnt the details of what had transpired. It appeared that the sultan and his Pawar friend had come to a settled arrangement whereby each played the male and female role on alternate days. To heighten their enjoyment they would go through the elaborate charade of a marriage ceremony. One evening the sultan would arrive as a Turkish groom, sign a contract of marriage with the Pawar and then escort him to the royal couch. This was followed by the feast of deflowering (*dawat-i-valima*) for their cronies. The next evening the roles would be reversed. Apparently on the fateful evening it was the sultan's turn to play the woman and the Pawar's to bestride him. The sultan decked himself out like a Turkish bride, wearing a spider-net veil over loose-fitting garments of silk. The Pawar rode to the palace as a Rajput bridegroom would, accompanied by a band of musicians. They were married by Hindu rites, going round a sacrificial fire to the chanting of *mantras*. The Pawar then led his Turkish 'bride' to his couch and with much banter proceeded to disrobe 'her'. When the Pawar mounted the Turk, the latter made modest protestations as would a virgin on her first initiation. When the Pawar was fully ensconced he began to play with the sultan's now perfectly healed penis. People who know about such matters say that this is customary in the unnatural cohabitation of male with male. As the Pawar approached the climax of his passion he withdrew his member and rammed it back into the sultan's bottom with great violence. The sultan screamed. The Pawar was overcome with an insane frenzy and crushed the sultan's testicles in his hands. As he was drained of his mad lust, the vapours that had clouded his vision lifted. He acted boldly. He cut off the sultan's head and had his body thrown down from the ramparts. He proclaimed that he had executed the sultan because the people did not want to be ruled by a degenerate transvestite. Thus ended the rule of the sodomite-catamite Sultan Qutubuddin Mubarak Shah. The year was AD 1320.

Delhi had a new king! One sodomite-catamite succeeded another. The Hindu Pawar Rajput from Gujarat re-named Khusro Khan had himself proclaimed emperor of Hindustan under the title Sultan Nasiruddin Mohammed.

We wondered whether the Divine Maker of Destinies would permit the new sultan to go unpunished after He had reduced his partner-in-sin to dust.

Nasiruddin squandered largesse on the *omarah* hoping thereby to buy their loyalty. He sent robes of honour to the governors of the distant provinces. Most accepted them and sent gifts in return. But one, Ghiasuddin Tughlak, who guarded the western frontiers against the Mongols, kicked the trays bearing the robes. No Turk he said would recognize a double-faced *hijda* as his monarch.

The Mussalmans of India rose against Nasiruddin. He had to turn to the Rajputs and the Jats for help. He invited them to take over the defence of Shahr-i-Nau. The battle was fought on the outskirts of the city. It appeared that just as the Turks were giving ground, the Muslims of the city rose against the Jats and the Rajputs and turned the tide of battle in favour of their co-religionists. Ghiasuddin Tughlak had Nasiruddin torn limb from limb and his torso thrown over the ramparts. Thousands of citizens were put to the sword. Ram Dulari and I spent the rest of the night praying for the safety of our son and his *bahoo*. (But as becomes wise Kayasthas they had locked themselves inside a room, painted the numeral 786 on the door to indicate that it was the house of a Muslim and so escaped the blood-thirsty Turks).

A wise man has said that a subject should not look at the warts on the face of his ruler but only at the nobility of his features. The new sultan, Ghiasuddin Tughlak, was of noble birth. He had taken a Hindu princess as wife and also had his son, Prince Juna, marry into a noble Hindu family. With a Hindu as his chief consort and a Hindu daughter-in-law we expected the sultan to be lenient towards his non-Muslim subjects. Our hopes were belied. Ghiasuddin Tughlak turned out to be headstrong tyrant. Flatterers created mischief between him and the Khwaja Sahib. 'Is it right that this old *dervish* (Khwaja Sahib was over four score years and ten) should receive the homage due only to Your Majesty as God's viceregent on earth?' they asked.

Half-way between Mehrauli and Ghiaspur, Ghiasuddin Tughlak built a new city of gold-coloured bricks with high battlements around it. It came to be known after his tribe as Tughlakabad. He expected everyone to come to pay him homage and praise his handiwork. Everyone did, except our Khwaja Sahib. When Ghiasuddin demanded an explanation our Khwaja Sahib prophesied that the new city would soon be a wilderness inhabited by Gujar robbers.

When this was reported to the sultan, he swore he would teach the Khwaja Sahib a lesson. The foolish man did not know that God spoke through His Beloved Saint, Nizamuddin. God in the role of the Divine Mahout struck the sultan with a goad and made him act like a rogue elephant. He granted him a victorious campaign in his eastern domains and filled him with delusions of invincibility. His courtiers did the rest. 'O mighty Sultan! You who slice off the heads of thousands of your enemies like a reaper gathering wheat, can you not destroy this insignificant *dervish*?' they asked. Ghiasuddin Tughlak who was only a few marches from Delhi sent orders that before he entered the capital the hospice at Ghiaspur should be razed to the ground.

The *Kotwal* came with tears in his eyes and placed the royal command at the Khwaja Sahib's feet. The Khwaja Sahib comforted him: 'Son, I have seen the coming and going of many sultans. When I first came to Delhi, it was Ghiasuddin Balban. Thereafter there was Kaikobad and Jalaluddin Firoze;

then there were Alauddin and Qutubuddin of the Khilji tribe followed by Nasiruddin. And now Ghiasuddin Tughlak. That makes seven. Kings come and kings go. The will of Allah is eternal.'

The *Kotwal* did not understand the meaning hidden in the Khwaja Sahib's words. 'Beloved of God! You are more to me than my father and mother. The sultan is only three marches from Delhi. What am I to do?' he wailed.

'Go home in peace. *Hunooz Dilli Door Ast!* (It is a long way to Delhi),' remarked the Khwaja Sahib.

As soon as the *Kotwal* returned to Shahr-i-Nau he received the news that the sultan had met with an accident. The next day runners brought the news of his death which had occurred when an archway he was passing under fell on him. This was in AD 1325. Allah is indeed the greatest of plotters and the strength of the feeble! And as the Khwaja Sahib had prophesied, the great citadel that Ghiasuddin had raised was soon deserted; the river Jamna receded from its walls and all its wells dried up. It became the abode of jackals, owls, bats and Gujars. Its once golden walls began to crumble—all that remained intact was the tomb in which Ghiasuddin Tughlak was buried—it was as if Allah wanted him to see what had happened to his dreams of glory.

God is the author of the Book of Destiny in which are written the past, the present and the future. God allowed our Khwaja Sahib to read the chapter on events to come. One day in his sermon the Khwaja Sahib said no one should ever fear death because it was a lover's tryst with his Beloved. 'For ninety years I have been separated from Allah,' he said, 'but every hour of every day of those ninety years I have longed to be reunited with Him.'

His words cast a gloom over Ghiaspur. I sought audience with the Khwaja Sahib. When I came before him I broke down and wept. 'If it is for me you cry,' he said, 'be assured you will follow us soon. And your wife will not linger in this caravanserai very long after you.'

I cried! 'O Beloved of God! Take us with you so that we may continue to serve you in paradise.'

I became very low in spirits. Much as I told myself that life

was no longer worth living because I could hardly see or walk
unaided and that death would be a release from the sufferings
of old age, I was afraid of dying. I would prefer being ill and
in pain than going into the dreaded kingdom of Yama. I did
not desire union with the Beloved; my toothless Ram Dulari
was good enough for me.

One day in the month of *Rabi-us-Sani* of the year 725 of the
Hijri of the Prophet (peace be upon Him) corresponding to AD
1324 of the Roman calendar, the Khwaja Sahib told us that he
could hear the angels singing songs of welcome. But before he
left the world he would purge his body of earthly dross by
fasting for forty days. We pleaded with him. 'O Beloved of
God! *Hakeems* say that your body needs nourishment and
even a week's fast may be too much for it.' He rebuked us. 'Is
this all you have learnt from me? Know you not that fasting
and prayer are food for a better life than we lead on earth?'

A pall of melancholy spread over Ghiaspur. The Khwaja
Sahib sensed our concern. 'I will be with you till Thursday; on
Friday I will depart,' he told us. 'Bury my remains in this
courtyard. Do not let Khusrau (he was then in Lakhnauti)
come near my grave lest I am tempted to defy the laws of
nature and rise to embrace him. The message of Allah and His
Holy Prophet (may peace be upon Him) will continue to be
delivered to you by my chief disciple Makhdoom Nasiruddin.
He will be your guide in this dark world, for he is *Roshan
Chiragh Dilli*, light of the Divine Lamp in Delhi.'

It happened exactly as the Khwaja Sahib had foretold. It
was on the morning of Friday, the 18th of *Rabi-us-Sani* 725
A.H. (3 April 1324) that the Khwaja Sahib's soul winged its
way to paradise. What cries of lamentation rent the skies!
Hundreds of thousands of people from the neighbouring
towns came to Ghiaspur. Women beat their breasts chanting
Ya Allah!Ya Allah! Hazrat Roshan Chiragh, whom the Khwaja
Sahib had named his successor, came out and pleaded in a
tearful voice that such demonstrations of grief were forbidden
by the holy law; he divided the mourners into different
groups and gave them passages from the *Quran* to chant in
unison.

The Khwaja Sahib's body was bathed. The bier was placed

in the courtyard of the mosque for the last prayer. Then it was taken out in procession round Ghiaspur. *Qawwals* sang as they went along. The party closest to the bier sang one which began with the following words:

> *People crave to see thy face*
> *Why hast thou turned thy back on the world?*
> *Whither art thou bound, O Fair One?*
> *Beloved of God! Who hast thou gone to meet?*

Someone shouted that the Khwaja Sahib had put his hand out of the shroud. The bier was placed on the ground and the mob surged towards it. It took a while to restore order. The pall-bearers insisted that they had heard the Khwaja Sahib's voice replying to the questions in the song. Hazrat Roshan Chiragh cupped his mouth and spoke loudly into the ears of the Khwaja Sahib. 'Beloved of God! Does thy *dervish* have to remind thee that speaking after death is against the ordinance of Allah? Go in peace to thy tryst.' He put the Khwaja Sahib's hand back into the shroud and the procession proceeded on its way.

The Khwaja Sahib's sainted dust was interred in the centre of the mosque courtyard. Some people placed oil-lamps on the grave; others lit joss-sticks in the fresh earth. People put their ears to the grave to catch sounds that might come out of it.

*

Khusrau has returned from Lakhnauti. A huge mob has collected to see how he will conduct himself and whether the Khwaja Sahib will rise from his grave to embrace him. Khusrau has come to the hospice wailing and beating his breast like a woman who has lost her husband. Hazrat Roshan Chiragh holds him in a tight embrace. After he has wept his heart out the *dervish* tells him that the Khwaja Sahib had forbidden him from going to the graveside. Khusrau stops by a *kewra* bush a few yards away from the grave and fixes his eyes on the spot where his departed friend sleeps. Tears run down his eyes into his beard; he sobs like a child crying for its mother. In a wailing voice he recites:

> On her couch sleeps my fair one
> Her black hair is scattered over her face.
> O Khusrau! 'tis time thou too the homeward path did tread,
> The shades of twilight over the earth are spread.

Khusrau shaved his head just as Hindus do on the death of their parents. He gave away his property. He began to wear a coarse cloak of black wool prescribed for the Sufis. As he had prophesied for himself, a few weeks later he took the homeward path. We buried him beside the *kewra* bush.

*

I come to last chapter of the book of my life. I hasten to write these lines before my right eye, which has also developed cataract, loses its light and I am no longer able to put pen to paper.

After many weeks of absence Kamal has brought his wife and two children to be left in our care. He says Sultan Mohammed Tughlak has gone mad. For many years we had been hearing of his eccentric habits. In fits of generosity he gives away lakhs of *tankas*, in fits of madness he cuts off lakhs of heads. He issues copper coins to represent silver rupees and gold *tankas*. Cunning people forge copper coins and take their value in silver and gold till there is nothing left in the treasury. Kamal says that the sultan has been talking of conquering China and then the rest of Asia. And now he has issued a proclamation transferring his capital from Delhi to Daulatabad 700 miles down towards *gehennum*. He has ordered every man, woman and child to evacuate Tughlakabad and travel southwards with him. This is indeed madness! Delhi by whatever name it is known—Lal Kot, Mehrauli, Shahr-i-Nau or Tughlakabad—has always been the seat of the emperors of Hindustan. Delhiwallas would rather die than live in any other city in the world. Poor Kamal as a

86

government servant must comply with the order; but no sultan's writ has ever extended to the sacred precincts of the mausoleum of Hazrat Khwaja Nizamuddin.

5

Bhagmati

May. The lid is off the fires of *gehennum*. Searing heat, spiralling dust devils, eye-scorching glare, tarmac on the road shimmering like quicksilver. Not a breath of life. No mad dogs, no nothing. Only the noonday sun.

The car seat burns. '*Hai Ram!*' groans Bhagmati and raises her bottom to let the seat get cooler. 'Ouch!' I cry in my wog style. 'Just touch the steering wheel.' I grab her hand and put it on the steering wheel. She withdraws it with a jerk. 'Has some doctor ordered us to go out and get sunstroke?'

We take the Qutub road. Past the mausoleum of Safdar Jang, through the rash of bungalows that have smothered Yusuf Sarai and all the Khilji, Tughlak and Mughal monuments that once dominated the landscape. At Qutub Minar we turn sharp left and go through village Lado Sarai. There is a lot of activity at the well. Jat women vigorously hauling up buckets of water and pouring them into pitchers lined on the parapet. Two young ones bathing. Not a stitch on them. They see our car. They put their hands between their thighs and turn their large buttocks towards us. I slow down to have a good look. A woman picks up a clod of mud and hurls it at us. I laugh. They laugh. These Jat women are tall, full-bosomed, slender-waisted, well-stacked. They carry their pitchers on their heads and stride along flouncing their skirts like the queens of Amazonia. I ask Bhagmati 'Don't you think these Jat females are the most beddable women in Hindustan?'

'Other men's wives and sisters are always more fuckable than one's own. A home-bred chicken tastes no better than lentils.' Bhagmati believes in the wisdom of cliches.

We are out of Lado Sarai. And again the hot, shimmering tarmac and an expanse of dun-coloured plains. The shadow of the car speeds ahead of us. A tumulus on our left gradually becomes a stone wall, the stone wall becomes a massive battlement of grey and red rock towering sixty feet or more above the ground. We go along an avenue of ancient banyans. I pull up under the shade. On my left is an arched gateway leading into the citadel of Tughlakabad; on my right a viaduct leads to the tomb of the builder Ghiasuddin Tughlak. Its sloping red walls and white marble dome rise above its fortress-like enclosure.

What's happened to all the urchins who hang around to look after visitors' cars? Midweek, midsummer. No visitors no urchins. Calls for a celebration. We celebrate.

'What's that?' shouts Bhagmati pointing to a furry hand with black, tapering fingers clutching the rim of the windscreen. Up comes the face of a rhesus monkey with a request for food *kho-kho-kho-kho*. Bhagmati screams and clings to me. The monkey takes fright, scampers away across the road displaying its bright red posterior.

Bhagmati nestles in my arms, I push her away. There is another somebody at the door. 'Sahib, I'll look after your car.'

Before I can say 'Okay,' another boy turns up. 'Sahib, it is my turn. He looked after the last car; didn't you?'

They begin to quarrel, 'Sahib, didn't I ask you first? Sahib, it's not his turn—you decide.' More urchins come along and clamour for the right to guard my car. I step out, take one by the scruff of his neck. 'This fellow will look after my car. He's the only one I will give money to.'

That settles it. Or does it? Four boys follow us up the path leading to the gate of Tughlakabad fort.

'Sahib, we will show you round the ruins of Tughlakabad.'

'I know them quite well,' I reply. 'We don't need a guide.'

'Sahib this is the main gate of the fort.'

'I know. You don't have to tell me, *jao*.'

'This hollow on the left was a tank; it used to supply drinking water to Tughlakabad.'

'I've told you once, I do not need a guide. Go away.'

'Sahib, these are the remains of the Meena Bazaar, the women's market.'

I turn on them. 'Bugger off!'

They run away a little distance and shout back at me: 'Bugger off.' Bhagmati and I proceed up the paved pathway through the ruins: gun emplacements, mosques, markets and up to the highest point. We survey the landscape: the Qutub Minar to the west, Ghiasuddin Tughlak's tomb to the south, the ruins of the Qasr-i-hazaar-Sutoon palace and Shahr-i-Nau to the east. We retrace our steps and turn off on a path, thread our way through the debris and goats nibbling at *vasicka* bushes. We are at the edge of the battlement. A hundred feet below us is a pool full of water buffaloes. This is all that remains of what was once a moat encircling the citadel of Tughlakabad. And what goes by the name of Tughlakabad today is a huddle of flat-roofed brick-houses and mud-huts. The rest of the landscape is a rocky, treeless plain dotted with ruins among which new buildings are erupting like red fungus.

Bhagmati takes my hand.

'*Arre*! She's taken the Sardar's hand.' The bastards are still there. Bhagmati takes over. 'Will you get away from here or do you want a rod up your arses?' she asks striding towards them. They run away as fast as they can with the goats scampering after them. Bhagmati comes back triumphantly. We sit down on the rampart. She nestles her head on my chest. 'Tell me why are some monkeys' balls and behinds red?'

'I don't know. I am told they become red when they are randy.'

'Do your balls become red when *chotey mian* (the little gentleman) becomes *badey mian* (big gentleman)?'

It takes me a while to catch on. 'I have never looked; besides I am not a monkey.'

'Our fathers' fathers were,' she pronounces very scholar-like. 'I must look next time. I'll bring a flashlight with me.'

We sit and talk and look at the world below us. Bhagmati nibbles my ear and feels my middle to make sure that *chotey mian* is still there.

90

The sun's rays lose their sting. The sun becomes a large, orange balloon. Lines of crows flap their wings towards the city. Flocks of parakeets streak across the grey sky. From Tughlakabad village a million sparrows rise, wheel over the tops of *keekar* trees and then settle down on them in a bedlam of twitters.

The orange sun goes down in a haze of dust. Village lads urge their buffaloes to get out of the pond. Their shouts mingle with chirruping of the sparrows and the forlorn barking of dogs. Then an eerie silence descends on the ancient ruins. Even Bhagmati has run out of words. I tell her of the varieties of silence in a language she does not understand.

> There is silence where hath been no sound,
> There is silence where no sound may be,
> In the cold wave—under the deep, deep sea,
> Or in wide desert where no life is found,
> Which hath been mute, and still must sleep profound;
> No voice is hushed—no life treads silently,
> But clouds and cloudy shadows wander free,
> That never spoke, over the idle ground:
> But in green ruins, in the desolate walls,
> Of antique palaces, where Man hath been,
> Though the dun fox or wild hyaena calls,
> And owls, that flit continually between,
> Shriek to the echo, and the low winds moan-
> These true silence is, self-conscious and alone.

The evening stars shine in the grey sky. A soft breeze begins to blow. After the hot wind it feels cool, soporific. My eyes are heavy with sleep. I ruffle Bhagmati's hair. She has fallen asleep. I shut my eyes and am lost to the world.

I waken with a feeling of someone looking at me. It is the full moon shining in my face. A *papeeha* comes out of the grey sky and settles on a crag a few feet away. It raises its head to the moon and fills the haunted landscape with its plaintive cries *pee ooh, pee ooh*.

'Listen Eugenia!' Her name is not Eugenia but Bhagmati. The bird is not the nightingale but a Hawk Cuckoo.

Nevertheless its full-throated bursts come crowding through the moonlight.

Eternal passion!
Eternal pain!

*

Sometime after this I have my encounter with the bees.

Delhi has a rich variety of bees of which one species, the *apis historicus Delhiana*, is noted for its attachment to the past. Habitat: high vaulted arches with special preference for the pre-Mughal, Mughal, post-Mughal, Lutyens and Baker. Size of hive: the most massive known in the beeworld. Natural enemies: the urchins of Delhi who torment it with stone, brick, dung smoke and flaming rags. Natural victims: unsuspecting, absent-minded, old men who visit historical monuments to daydream.

One afternoon I find myself at Hauz Khas. Although it is late April and very hot, this old *madrasa* is so designed that hot winds passing through the maze of its ancient walls turn cool. I am seated on the floor of a colonnaded verandah reclining against a grey, sandstone column. On my left is a freshly mown lawn with a sprinkler spreading rainbows; the bullock and the lawn-mower both rest in the shade of a *neem* tree. Facing me is the tomb of Sultan Firoze Shah Tughlak with its lofty plaster-dome black with age. And about fifty feet below me on my right is a muddy pond black with buffaloes. This is all that remains of the huge tank, the Hauz-i-Alai, dug by Sultan Alauddin Khilji to provide water for his new city, Siri. Of the city the only surviving evidence is a litter of disjointed walls and a gate.

The warm breeze-turned-cool drones in my ears. Above my head martins chitter in their mud-feathered nests. From the floor below come the strains of a Hindi film song and the voices of men playing cards. In the lengthening shadow cast by the ancient school of learning, village boys play tipcat. Bhagmati is not with me and the calm and peace of the surroundings are conducive to daydream.

What did they teach at this *madrasa*? Astronomy, astrology, mathematics, chemistry and the *Quran*? Boys sitting in rows chanting their tables? Whatever happened to Siri and the great tank which supplied its drinking water? Was it still there when Taimur, the club-footed Mongol, sacked Delhi and slew 50,000 of my citizen-ancestors? How long did it take to repopulate the city?

I see the scenes of horror which must have taken place around Hauz-i-Alai during the massacre. Men sitting on their haunches with their hands tied behind them and necks bent low; the flash of scimitars and heads rolling away from bodies; spurts of blood, the tops of spines sticking out. Shrieking, wailing mothers, wives and sisters. Children benumbed with terror. The Mongolian shadow of God on earth enjoying the scene from somewhere near where I am sitting. If only I had been there, armed with a modern sharpshooters's rifle fitted with a telescopic sight, I would have climbed a tree beyond bowshot and shot the lame bastard dead. I would have picked out his generals and one after another sent them to hell. I would have created panic in the ranks of the Mongols, Turks, Tartars and all the other Central Asian savages. The Delhiwallas would then have risen against them, slaughtered thousands like goats and sent the rest screaming back to Samarkand.

A stone narrowly misses my head and crashes down on the floor. I see a pack of urchins scuttling away into Firoze Shah's tomb. 'Oi, oi, oi,' I yell. 'You *harami* ...' Before I can tell them what I will do to their mothers and sisters, a swarm of *apis historicus Delhiana* descends on me. I flail my arms. I run like one pursued by the devil. They follow me attacking my face, neck, arms. I unwrap my turban, wrap my face and arms in its folds, and crouch on the ground. I can hear the card-players shouting for help as they run to safety and the grass-mower's bullock bellowing on its way to the village. The assault continues for five hellishly long minutes before it is called off. I pluck dead bees off my body. I pick two caught in the meshes of my beard and get stung on the tips of my fingers. My flesh begins to swell, my fingers become too fat to be useful, my body tingles all over. I run back to my car and drive as fast as I can to Ram Manohar Lohia Hospital.

By the time I enter the emergency ward my eyes are almost closed and parts of my body are numb. I muscle my way through the crowd into the clinic. It looks like the third-class passengers' waiting-room of Delhi railway station. Men, women and children are sprawled all over the floor. A bearded patriarch lies on a stretcher tracing patterns on the wall with his legs. There is a cluster round the doctor's table. I push my way through: I am more 'emergency' than most of them. Bee-stings on the neck and the ears can be fatal unless attended to at once. The doctor is talking on the phone. In his left hand he holds the instrument; in his right, a syringe. He talks away as he presses air bubbles out of the needle. Facing him is a fourteen-year-old girl with her chemise raised over her shoulders. My half-shut eyes focus on her young bosom-buds. Her mother glowers at me and turns angrily to the doctor: 'You want to expose my child to the world?' The doctor says 'One minute,' puts the receiver on the table, stabs the needle into the girl's belly and tells her to come again tomorrow. He picks up the phone. 'Doctor, I've been stung by bees, please...' He says 'Excuse me,' into the phone in English and snaps at me in Punjabi. 'You are not dying! Take your turn.' He apologizes to the phone and lists his favourite restaurants: Moti Mahal, Gaylord, Laguna. He warns the fellow or lady at the other end of the line about crows being served instead of chicken and blobs of blotting-paper mixed in *kulfi*. *Ha, ha*. I slap my numbed hands on the table and scream. The fellow says 'Sorry, too many patients. I'll ring later. Ta-ta.' Then he turns to me in a raging temper. 'You bee-stingwalla, don't you see I am busy?' he says in Punjabi. I reply in my *haw haw* Oxbridge: 'Busy, my fucking foot! Discussing restaurants and food with some broad while people here are in agony. I'll report you to the Health Minister; I'll write letters to every paper. Who the bloody hell do you think you are?' English works like magic in independent India. The bugger examines my stings, gives me a massive shot of something and tells me that I am lucky to be alive. Then adds humbly, 'Please forgive me for the delay. I am only an intern.'

The shot does not improve my vision. I go out of the door closest to me. I find myself in a room with a corpse lying on a marble slab and a policeman counting the number of bruises on 'the aforesaid deceased so-and-so'. He asks, 'Are you a relative or something?'

'No, I am the corpse. Count the stings on my dead body.'

Before he can retort, I retrace my steps and hurry back to the car.

Budh Singh is alarmed at my appearance. He asks me how and where it all happened. I tell him as best as I can. He raises an admonishing finger and ticks me off. 'I have warned you many times not to go near graveyards. They are full of ghosts. Places where hundreds of thousands have been murdered have hundreds of thousands of ghosts. You were not attacked by bees but by evil spirits of those slaughtered by that Taimur *lang* (the lame one).' He spits into his own hand.

I cannot argue with Budh Singh. I tell him to keep his *charpoy* near the door so he can hear me if I shout for help. I take my temperature: 103 degrees—high enough to make a man of my age delirious.

I sleep a little, groan a lot. I feel sorry for myself. How close had I come to dying? Scenes from the past come vividly before my eyes. I wonder what kind of savage was this Taimur who revelled in the massacre of innocents! I have his *Memoirs*. To his own words, I add some gloss.

6

The Timurid

One night in the spring of the Year of the Ox when we were sixty-two years old we had a strange dream. We saw ourselves in an orchard with trees loaded with fruit. The trees also had many nests and birds were pecking away at the fruit. The gardeners were making a lot of noise to frighten away the birds. We arrived in the orchard armed with a sling and a bag full of pebbles. With our slingshot we drove away the birds and destroyed their nests. The gardeners then prostrated themselves before us and gave thanks to Allah for being thus delivered of the pests.

Whenever the tablet of our mind was heavily over-writ with our designs, we were wont to dream about them. We asked the saintly Shaikh Zainuddin Abu Bakr Tatyabady to tell us what this dream signified. The Shaikh, who was the pole star of religion, confirmed that we were about to undertake an expedition to a distant land which was being despoiled because it had too many rulers; that we would drive away these rulers, as we had driven away the birds in our dream, take possession of their kingdoms and their subjects would kiss our feet. At the time we were in two minds. We were not sure whether we should conquer China—or proceed towards Hindustan. We consulted Syed Mohammed Gesudaraz, the saint with long hair, who we had also adopted as our guide in matters of religion. The Syed was more specific. He interpreted the dream as follows: 'The Holy Prophet (on Whom and on Whose progeny be peace) has taken you under His care and protection in order that you propagate Islam in the extensive regions of India.'

By then we had already subjugated most of the kingdoms

of Asia. Now Hindustan through its disorders had opened its gates to us.

Nothing happens in this world save as Allah wills it. When we were born in the spring of the Year of the Mouse sparks had flown out of our royal mother's womb and our hands were found to be full of blood. Men of wisdom foretold that the flash of our scimitars would be like sparks of an ironsmith's anvil and we would wade through rivers of blood. We were taken by our parents to be blessed by Shaikh Shamsuddin. He was reading the sixty-seventh chapter of the Holy Book and intoned 'Are you sure that He who dwelleth in heaven, will not cause the earth to swallow you up... and behold it shake (*Taimura*)?' And so we came to be given the name Taimur. Our horoscope had promised that we would be superior to all monarchs of the age, we would protect religion, destroy idols and be the father of our people. At twenty-seven an injury caused a deformity in our foot compelling us thereafter to be more in the saddle than on foot. We knew that behind our backs, common people called us *Taimurlang* (Taimur the lame) but in our presence they addressed us as the Uncompared Lord of Seven Climes and the Lord of Fortunate Conjunction.

We summoned the *kuriltay* of the nobles who had attached their destinies to our apron. We told them of our dream and the interpretations made by wise and saintly men. We told them that our object in undertaking the invasion of Hindustan was to bring infidels to the path of true religion and to purify the country from the filth of polytheism and idolatry. We exhorted them to place helmets of courage on their heads, don the armour of determination, gird on the swords of resolution and like alligators dive into the river of blood: if victorious they would gain renown as warriors who had carried the flag of Islam to the farthest horizons of the earth; if subdued they would gain admittance to paradise as martyrs. We told them of the enormous wealth of Hindustan; of the city the Tughlaks had built of gilded bricks that glistened in the sun and of the cistern in this citadel which was said to be filled with molten gold. We warned them of the rising power of infidels and said that if we did not destroy them by stuffing their mouths with lead they would swallow up everything that the line of sultans starting with Mahmud of Ghazna followed by the Ghors—Mohammed, Qutubuddin Aibak, Altamash and his daughter Sultana Razia—followed by the mighty Ghiasuddin Balban and the house of Khiljis—Jalaluddin, Alauddin—down to the dynasty of the Tughlaks—Ghiasuddin, Mohammed, Firoze and Nasiruddin—had amassed over two centuries.

The minds of Turks are as narrow as their eyes. In order to gain their support and to tie up their tongues, it is necessary not only to excite their zeal for Islam but also their greed for gold. We reminded them that as in the past whatever had fallen into our lap after a victorious campaign we had divided amongst them without keeping anything for ourselves, so would we divide the gold, silver, cattle and slaves that fell into our hands during the expedition to Delhi.

The *kuriltay* was moved by our words. Every man present drew his sword to follow us to victory or paradise.

We decided to send a probing force ahead of us under the command of our grandson, Prince Peer Mohammed Jahangir. The Prince was a youth of only twenty-three summers but he had accompanied us on many campaigns and we had gauged that the star of his destiny was in the ascendant. We summoned him to our tent to apprise him of his duties. 'He who wishes to embrace the bride of royalty must kiss her across the edge of the sword,' we told him. 'We give you the throne of Ghazna. From there you will proceed to Hindustan and capture the city of Multan.' We then told him of the state of affairs in Delhi. Sultan Firoze Tughlak had spent more of his time raising mosques, caravanserais, *madrasas* and laying canals than in keeping his subjects in fear. Rightly had the Holy Prophet (on Whom be peace) said that a just king is the shadow of God on earth and from the dread of that shadow people render him obedience. But Sultan Firoze had allowed infidels to raise their heads. He had also given sanctuary to many traitors who had fled our wrath and thus behaved in an unbrotherly manner towards us. Firoze had been dead ten years but the seeds of disrespect towards the supreme ruler that he had sown had grown into a thicket of nettles and this displeased us.

His sons and grandsons followed each other in quick succession and now Mahmud sat on the throne of the Tughlaks. However, it was not Mahmud Tughlak who ruled Hindustan but two upstarts: Sarang Khan who had Multan under him and his brother, Mallu Khan Iqbal, who crowed over the ramparts of Tughlakabad and the Qasr-i-hazaar Sutoon. The smoke of vanity had clouded their brains.

Soon Prince Mohammed Jahangir marched from Ghazna, crossed the river Indus and besieged Sarang Khan in Multan.

Now it was the Year of the Tiger. We sent messengers throughout our kingdom to announce that we were ready to march on Delhi. The men who flocked to our standard were as numerous as drops of rain—of these the largest number were our own kin, Chughtai Turks of the Barlas clan, who had shared the perils and profits of many campaigns with us. By the time the almond trees ushered in the spring we had upwards of 90,000 cavaliers and cross-bowmen under our command. We led a small task force into the mountains of Kafiristan and carried out great slaughter amongst the tribes of infidels who had defied even the mighty Alexander of Macedon.

By rapid marches we overtook birds in flight and reached the river Indus. We crossed the mighty river and entered the domains of the Tughlaks. Meanwhile our grandson had occupied Multan. We overcame attempts to impede our progress and crossed the rivers of the Punjab. We stopped at Pak Pattan to pray at the tomb of Fariduddin *Ganj-i-shakar* and promised to convey the blessings of the saint to his successor Shaikh Nizamuddin buried in Delhi.

Our expedition had been carefully timed in consultation with astrologers and men of learning who knew the movements of the sun. When we traversed the Punjab, its plains were still muddy from the recent heavy rains of the summer. By the time we arrived on the banks of the river Jamna it was cool; the skies were as blue as the tiles of our palace roof and the breezes as balmy as those during spring in Samarkand.

We rode along the Jamna then in flood and drew rein in full view of the city which Sultan Firoze Tughlak had built and which was known after him as Firozabad or Kotla Firoze Shah. On the top of his palace Firoze had planted a slender pillar fabricated at the time of the infidel Ashoka who had ruled this country over 1500 years ago. It was said to bear inscriptions of Ashoka's prophet named Gautama the Wise. The citizens of Firozabad did not put up any resistance; indeed many Mussalmans came to offer us their services.

Our nobles warned us that the thousands of infidels we had taken as slaves in the Punjab might use the opportunity to rise against us when we were engaged in battle against the Tughlaks. Some advised us to slaughter them before we engaged the enemy. We refused to spill so much blood as there was upwards of 1,00,000 slaves in our custody. Instead we picked a few who had tried to escape and had them brought before us. We ordered them to be beheaded in front of the others as a warning of the fate that awaited those who dreamt of breaking the bondage we had imposed on them. Thus we crushed the thorn of rebellion under our foot before it could prick us.

On the 19th of December 1398 Mahmud Tughlak, misguided by his minister Mallu Khan Iqbal, came out of the city with a great clamour of drums and fifes and a vast army to meet us. His generals confronted us with a line of elephants covered with armour and loaded with archers. They were like slow-moving fortresses. We were prepared for them. We had sharp stakes dug in the ground behind the front line of our cavalry. Like the Cossacks we relied on suddenness of assault and retreat. Our horsemen galloped up to their elephants, discharged their arrows and galloped back. This repeated many times took a fearful toll of the Tughlak's army and drove its commanders to desperation. As their elephants advanced, we retreated. Beasts in the front row got their feet entangled in the stakes; those behind them refused to move forward. We ordered camels (animals which elephants are known to dread) to advance from the sides. We had loads of hay put on their backs and set alight. The remaining elephants turned back in terror exposing the Tughlak's cavalry and footmen to us. We gave the *Tekbir*. Our Turkish warriors replied with full-throated cry, *Allah-o-Akbar* and sprang like lions on their quarry. The Tughlak army broke ranks and fled. Allah, who presides over battlefields, blessed our swords with victory.

Two days later, on Thursday the 21st of December, we encamped in the ancient *madrasa* along the spacious tank called Hauz-i-Alai. We recited the *fateha* at the tomb of Sultan Firoze Tughlak and after the *zohar* prayer commanded the citizens of Siri, Jahanpanah and Mehrauli to make their submission. They came in their thousands, presented *nazranas*, laid their turbans and caps at our feet and craved our forgiveness. A party of *ulema* presented us with copies of the Holy *Quran* and appealed to us as a fellow Mussalman not to shed more Muslim blood. They brought us the keys of their townships and pleaded with us to let them arrange a befitting welcome for us. We acceded to their request and asked them to discuss with our generals details of the indemnity to be paid to us.

The next day being Friday the *khutba* was read in our presence at the Quwwat-ul-Islam mosque. We recited *fatehas* at the tombs of Sultan Altamash and Sultan Alauddin Khilji before inspecting the Qutub Minar and the entrance to the Royal Mosque. We marvelled at their craftsmanship: how these Hindvis began their work as giants and finished them like goldsmiths! We decided to take their master craftsmen with us to work on the mosque at Samarkand. We then proceeded to Mehrauli to pay our homage to Saint Qutubuddin Bakhtiyar Kaki and visited the Auliya Masjid where he had performed many austerities. The citizens made a great display of welcome and arranged swimming contests at the Shamsi Talab beside the mosque. We saw signs of prosperity everywhere.

The ladies of our harem were anxious to see Qasr-i-hazaar Sutoon. We allowed them to be escorted thither while we proceeded to Ghiaspur to fulfil our vow to pray beside the tomb of Hazrat Nizamuddin Auliya.

It does not take long for the men of Hindustan to switch their minds from fawning flattery to deadly hate. They began to make excuses for their failure to pay the indemnity we had imposed on them. Under the cover of darkness many stole out of Siri, Mehrauli and Jahanpanah with their possessions. Guards we had posted at the city gates were slain. We ordered our troops to enter these towns and extend the hand of rapine, to slay every able-bodied man and take his women and children as slaves. For the next ten days our men drenched their swords in blood. There was no count of the numbers killed: some said 50,000 others 5,00,000. Nor was there any measure of the quantities of precious stones, gold and silver taken by our valiant soldiers. Even the humblest of our footmen took over two dozen slaves. The wealth they acquired in Delhi would last our men many generations. We recalled that once the Holy Prophet (on Whom be peace) had appeared in a dream and told us that the Almighty had declared that seventy-two of our line would sit on the throne of sovereignty. That prophecy seemed to be fulfilling itself. We decided to tarry no more.

We loaded innumerable elephants and camels with the wealth of Delhi and with thousands upon thousands of slaves in our train began our slow march homewards. We crossed the river Jamna, ransacked Meerut and proceeded along the foothills. We destroyed, as we had undertaken to do, many temples of idolatry. At one place the Brahmins warned us not to touch the image of their god, Krishna, who was said to be so powerful that he could in one night impregnate 1600 women. His image which was made of gold stood as high as ourselves. Under the eyes of the pleading, wailing priests we smashed the idol with our own hands and ordered the priests to be beheaded

A month later we and our victorious armies were back in Samarkand.

We received sad tidings from Delhi. We were informed that after our departure there was no one to bury the dead. The rotting corpses had spread pestilence and the few who had survived had succumbed to disease. For many months the towns of Delhi were deserted save for crows, kites and vultures by day and owls, jackals and hyaenas by night...

But we had fulfilled our life's mission. We had realized early in our youth that just as there is one God in heaven, so the earth can support only one king. In the years granted to us by Allah we strove to bring the nations of the world under our rule. In order to preserve our sovereignty, we took justice in one hand and equity in the other and by the light of these two lamps kept our royal palace illuminated. Many people blamed us for the blood we had spilt. At one time the ill-informed Khwaja Obeyd forbade Muslims to recite the *khutba* in our name because we had also shed the blood of Mussalmans. That night the Holy Prophet (peace be upon Him) had visited Khwaja Obeyd in his dream, refused to acknowledge his salutations and reprimanded him in the following words: 'Although Taimur has shed much blood of my followers, as he has been a friend, the supporter and respecter of my posterity and descendants, why dost him forbid the people to pray and bless him?'

May Allah forgive us for any sins we may have committed.

7

Bhagmati

It has rained in the night and the damp fragrance of the earth steals into my bedroom as I wake. It is cold. The hot-water-bottle at my feet has lost its warmth and I shiver under my quilt. Sounds of muffled voices pass along my apartment like the babble of a stream. I switch on the table-lamp. It is 4.30 a.m. I switch off the light, tuck my hands between my thighs and try to go back to sleep. The stream of voices continue. What on earth are these people up to on this cold, winter morning?

I am woken with finality by my cook-bearer with a steaming mug of tea. He switches on the electric radiator; the bedroom has a glow of pink warmth. 'It's very cold,' I tell him.

'Yes,' he agrees. 'It rained during the night. Can I serve your *chota hazri* soon? I'd like to get away early.'

'What for?'

'To see the parade; it is Republic Day. People have been leaving their homes since the early hours to find a place in front to get a good view. Budh Singh also wants leave for the day.'

What could be better than having both out of the way. If only that stupid Bhagmati would know it is a holiday and get to this side of the city before the police put up barricades on the roads (to mark off the route of the parade) we could celebrate *gantantra divas* on the carpet by the fireside. But she never reads newspapers nor listens to anything on the transistor I gave her except film music on Vividh Bharati. However, there is hoping. I haven't had sex for many weeks and it's accumulated to explosion point. I ask the cook-bearer to put the breakfast on the table and light a fire in the sitting-room before he and Budh Singh take off.

By the time I come into the sitting-room there is a blazing log fire in the grate. The sky is clear and the sun is streaming through the windows. A regular procession of men, women and children wrapped in shawls, and mufflers goes by on its way to Rajpath and Connaught Circus. I feel very superior in my singular isolation. I can read about it in the papers, hear the commentary on my radio, and, if that Bhagmati has any sense, sing the national anthem and hoist the tri-colour flag atop her quivering torso. There is reason to hope because she seldom misses a holiday.

The stream of humanity ceases to flow. The block of apartments becomes strangely deserted. Everyone has gone to see the caparisoned elephants, camels of the desert patrol, tanks and troupes of folk-dancers. The President, Prime Minister and everyone else who is anybody in Delhi will be there. My window-panes rattle. I switch on the radio and hear the deafening roar of cannon. Twenty-one salvos in honour of the Rashtrapati! He will take the salute of the units of the Army, Navy, Air Force and then proceed to tell the world of Gandhi, his message of non-violence and peace. And there will be Nehru kissing children, being *chacha* (uncle) to all the snivelling little bastards.

The twenty-first cannon explodes. My doorbell rings. Bhagmati has not let me down. 'How wonderful! I thought you'd forgotten. How did you manage to cross over the traffic barriers?' I ask her with unconcealed pleasure.

'The mortal who can stop your faithful servant going where she wants is yet to be born,' she replies, spreading her hands in front of the fire. 'The ice has got into my bones. What kind of *chootias* are these Dilliwallas. Year after year they go out in the cold to see the same parade!'

I make her a cup of coffee and put a slug of rum in it. She is so involved in talking she doesn't notice the smell or the difference in the taste. By the time she has drained the mug she is as warm inside as she is toasted on the outside. And I am possessed by the urge to celebrate *gantantra divas*. I get to the job with an adolescent eagerness. A minute later I lunge into an exultant cry of *'Jai Hind'*. A million Delhiwallas echo *'Jai Hind'* over my radio. It's all over in sixty seconds.

I would like Bhagmati to return to Lal Kuan. But Bhagmati has no intention of obliging me. She is disappointed with me and she is not the sort of person to spare my feelings. 'So many lessons I have taught you but you have forgotten even the first one: patience. How can I get to the second lesson; consideration for the *mashooka*? Lesson three in also very important: when you light a fire, you must see that you put it out before going *phut*. While your *mashooka* is like Sri Lanka burning on Dassehra you are like a fire brigade hose with no water in it, *hain*?'

Horrible bitch! She will give me no peace till I dowse the fire I've lit in her body. She must cool off and I must re-warm myself. I mumble an apology and suggest that we go out before the millions start moving back to their homes. She is in a sulk. She throws up her hands and sighs.

The breeze is cold but the sun is warm. The world looks washed, clean and green. Delhi is at its best and saying it with flowers: roses, poinsettias and bougainvilleas. I drive to the zoo to show her the family of white tigers. Other people have had the same idea and the entrance is crowded. So we opt for the Purana Qila towering over the northern end of the zoo. It is deserted. I take her down the steps of the *baoli* (well) and touch the icy cold water. Then back into the sunlight to Sher Shah's mosque. She covers her head with a scarf. Even after the years I have known her I am not sure whether she is a Muslim or Hindu. She says she is both—and more, because now she is also Sikh. We stroll about in the sunshine. I tell her about this being the site of Indraprastha, the first city of Delhi built by the Pandavas. That invites trouble because she knows all about Draupadi and her five husbands. She remarks acidly, 'Seeing what the men of today are like, every woman should have five husbands.'

Indian Air Force jets scream across the blue sky leaving streaks of white ribbons behind them. Then follow a clutch of helicopters showering rose and marigold-petals. The Republic Day parade is over. We go up the Sher Mandal tower to get a better view. I tell her that it was a library built by Sher Shah Suri. 'But it has no books,' she remarks waving to the empty octagonal-shaped room on the top. I tell her that the library existed more than 450 years ago. She understands.

We watch the lines of buses, cars and scooters honking, hooting and spluttering down Mathura Road. It is cold and breezy at the western end so we go to the sunny eastern side. 'I know that one,' she says pointing to the marble dome, half-a-mile away from us, 'that is the mausoleum of Humayun Badshah. His begum built it over his tomb. Will you build a tomb like that for me when I die?'

Her irritation is over. She takes my hand in her's. We descend the narrow dark steps together. I miss a step and fall heavily on my bottom. '*Ya Allah!* Be more careful of these murderous steps. If you had fallen on your face, you would have broken your head.'

'That's right,' I tell her cheerfully. 'That's exactly what Emperor Humayun did on these very steps exactly 430 years ago to this day—on 26 January 1530.'

Bhagmati is now impressed with my learning. But she cannot resist a back-hander. 'He must have been running down to meet his begum. I tell you an impatient lover always comes to grief.'

'No he wasn't impatient to bed his begum. He heard the call to prayer and was impatient to meet Allah, so Allah sent for him.'

Bhagmati raises both her hands in front of her face and mumbles something for the soul of the departed emperor. We return home to fan the dead embers of lust and make them glow.

It is a bad day. It had an inauspicious start and much as Bhagmati ministers to me, I cannot rise to the occasion. I tell her I am getting old and nothing will rouse me any more. She tells me, again very acidly, that I am not getting old but indifferent and need a memsahib to re-activate me.

Bhagmati has a sixth sense about other women in my life. I try to ward off her pointed enquiries and avoid meeting her eyes. We pass the afternoon bickering over little things. I pretend to make up by offering to drive her around in the evening to see the Republic Day lighting. Once again she shrugs her shoulders and sighs. She takes very little interest in the grand display of the Secretariats and Rashtrapati Bhavan. The crowds make the going very slow. By the time I get through Parliament Street and Connaught Circus to Ajmeri Gate, it is after 9 p.m. I press two ten rupee notes in her hand as I open the door for her. She looks at them disdainfully, throws them on the seat and disappears into the crowd.

Something has happened to Bhagmati. She is becoming jealous and possessive. 'I know you will ask who I am to object to anything or anyone?' she says on one occasion. She brushes the back of her hand to wipe tears that are not there and continues, ' I am like the Purana Qila you have conquered; now you want the Red Fort and its white marble palaces.'

Sarcasm does not suit Bhagmati's style of speech. She has begun to irritate me. But the more I dodge her, the more she pursues me. Every night after she is through with her chores, she comes to my apartment to see if I am in. If I am not, she questions Budh Singh. And Budh Singh has become something of a mischiefmaker. 'He's gone out with that *Amreekan* Missy Baba,' he tells her.

The American Missy Baba is sixteen-year-old Georgine. Why Bhagmati should worry over a gawky, snub-nosed, freckled, red-headed teenager is beyond me. She never bothered about any of the other women. In any case, what right has a common whore to object to what one of her many patrons does when she is not with him? However Georgine has become an obsession with Bhagmati. I admit that Georgine has also become an obsession with me. I am always talking about her. It was I who first told Bhagmati about her.

*

It had been a bad year for me. I didn't have many writing assignments and the articles I sold to Indian papers did not get me enough to keep me in the style I was accustomed to. So I registered myself as a guide with the Tourist Department of the Government of India and left my card at foreign embassies and international organizations. During the tourist season between October and March I made quite a bit in tips in foreign currency which I exchanged for rupees at rates higher than the official. I earned commissions from hotels, curio dealers and astrologers for the custom I brought them. Men left me the remains of their bottle of Scotch. Sometimes middle-aged women invited me to their rooms and gave me presents for the services I rendered them.

It was not very hard work. After I had memorized the names of a few dynasties and emperors and the years when they ruled, all I had to do was to pick up a few anecdotes to spice my stories. At the Qutub Minar I told them of the number of suicides that had taken place and how no one could jump clear of the tower and come down in one piece. I told them of Humayun's father, Babar, going round his son's sickbed four times praying to Allah to transfer his son's illness to him and how Humayun had been restored to health and Babar died a few days later. About the Red Fort and its palaces I had picked up a lot of interesting details from the time Shah Jahan had built it—the kings who had sat on the peacock throne and were later blinded or murdered; the British who had taken it after the Mutiny of 1857; the trials of INA officers, down to 15 August 1947 when Lord Mountbatten had lowered the Union Jack and Nehru hoisted the Indian tri-colour on the ramparts. Having once done my homework, there was little more to do than impress the tourists with my learning.

After a while I began to enjoy my work. Although I did not find anyone who would give me a free round-the-world ticket, I could boast that the world came to me. Once a cousin who had found a job as a worker in England told me of the number of white girls he had 'killed'. They were English girls working in the same factory. I told him that I had 'killed' many more Europeans, Americans, Japanese, Arabs and Africans, sitting where I was in Delhi, without having to pay a counterfeit four-anna coin to anyone. The fellow began to drool at the mouth and scratch his testicles with envy.

The only thing that troubled me was that I never got a chance to make friends with anyone. All the Marys, Janes, Francoises and Mikis darlinged and honeyed me for a day or two then vanished for ever. After a few weeks I could not recall their names or faces. All I could recollect was the way they had behaved when I bestrode them. Some had been as lifeless as the bed on which we lay; some had squirmed and screamed as they climaxed. A few had mouthed obscenities, slapped me on the face and told me to fuck off.

It was different with the American Missy Baba, Georgine. My contact with the US Embassy was a man named Carlyle. I do not know what he did in the embassy except that he looked after what he called 'visiting firemen'. He had tried out other guides. Once he was assured that 'I did no hanky panky' with visitors, he put a lot of custom my way. Americans were my best customers. Despite their brash manners they were more friendly and generous than other foreigners. I was particularly careful with Carlyle's 'visiting firemen'. I was respectful, polite and kept my distance. I opened car doors for them, did not angle for tips or look eagerly at their tape recorders, cameras and ball-point pens. (I knew they would leave some memento for me). I did not take them to emporia to earn commissions but helped them with their shopping at the best and cheapest stores. I never made passes at Carlyle's introductions and only obliged those who insisted on my obliging them.

My Oxbridge accent impressed Americans more than it did the other nationalities; to them I was a gentleman guide, a well-to-do fellow fallen on evil days, which was true.

Carlyle introduced me to Georgine. Georgine was Mrs Carlyle's niece and had come to Delhi to spend her Christmas vacations. 'This is Georgine,' Carlyle said without mentioning her second name. 'And this is your guide,' without mentioning mine. I bowed. She said 'Hi.'

As I said before, she was very young, gawky, freckled, pimpled, snub-nosed—but also large-bosomed and even larger-assed. She wore a tight-fitting sweater with 'Arizona' printed across her boobs and bum-tight jeans frayed at their ends. I asked her what interested her more, people or monuments. She shrugged her shoulders, stuck out her tongue and replied in a voice full of complaint: 'How should I know? A bit of both, I guess.' She proceeded to take snapshots of the Carlyles, the house, the car—then handed me her mini-camera so she could be in the pictures as well. She spoke very fast and dropped the g's at the end of most words: goin', comin', gettin', seein'. She was very animated and spoke with her grey eyes and hands; she interspersed her speech with noises like *unh, shucks, crikey* — and was constantly sticking out her red tongue.

'What are we waitin' for?' she demanded turning to me the first day after she had finished the photo session.

I opened the rear door of the car for her. She ignored me and bounced into the front seat beside the chauffeur. I took my place in the rear seat. 'Miss....'

'The name is Georgine.'

'Miss Georgine, have you...'

'Not Miss Georgine; just plain and simple Georgine, if you don't mind.'

'I was going to ask you, if you had read any Indian history. We are going to see...'

'That's a stoopid question to ask an American high school girl. Why in the name of Christ should I have read Indian history?' I decided to keep cool. We passed through Delhi Gate into Faiz Bazaar. 'What are all these jillions doin'?' she demanded.

'They are not jillions, they are vegetable-sellers. They...'

She turned round as if to make sure I were human. 'You don't know a jillion? It is the highest number—more than millions of millions. Even the dumbest American kid knows that.'

'Oh, I see,' I replied tamely. 'The population of Delhi has more than trebled in these last twenty years. It is over four million now.'

'I don't want to know that!' she snapped.

We went out of Faiz Bazaar—on our left the Royal Mosque, Jamia Masjid, on our right massive red walls of the Fort. She ordered the chauffeur to stop and took more snapshots. We drove up to the entrance of the Red Fort. While I queued up to buy a ticket for her, she took photographs: Chandni Chowk, the *tongas*, hawkers, beggars, everything. She stopped outside the entrance to take pictures of the guards, looked up at the towering walls and exclaimed 'Yee!'

No sooner had we entered the arcade with its rows of shops aglitter with brass, gold-and-silver thread embroidery, miniature Taj Mahals and other bric-à-brac, than she stretched her arms wide and exclaimed, 'I want everythin' in this crummy bazaar. How much?' She went from shop to shop picking up things and putting them down with a grunt. But she was canny. She parried every attempt to sell her anything. A marble-seller would say, 'Yes memsahib, some *marbil-varbil*?' and she would shake her head and reply firmly 'No thanks.'

We came to the Naqqar Khana gate. I cleared my throat. She pulled out her *Murray's Guide* and said: 'Don't tell me. This is where drums were beaten, right? And that red buildin' in front is the Dear one somethin'-or-the-other where the kingee received common folk, right?'

'Right on the mark. It is the Diwan-i-Am, the Hall of General Audience. You don't need a guide, you know everything.'

'No. I don't,' she snapped. Armed with *Murray's Guide* she instructed me about Emperor Shah Jahan, when he had lived, when he had built the palaces, pointed out the figure of Orpheus behind the throne, the Rang Mahal, the 'Dreamin' Chamber', the octagonal Jasmine tower and the 'Dearonee...'

'Diwan-i-Khas.'

'Where kingee sat on the peacock throne to receive noblemen. Right?'

'Right.'

'Goodee! That pearly mosque built by the kingee's son who locked up Dad and became King Orangeade.'

'Aurangzeb.'

'Aren't I clever?'

'Very! You could make a handsome living as a professional guide.'

'I could at that! I am thirsty. Can I get a carton of milk or a Coke some place?'

'Coke, yes. Milk, no.'

We returned to the arcade. She drank two bottles of Coke, pressed her belly and belched. 'Sorree! I feel good.'

It usually took me over an hour-and-a-half to take visitors round the Red Fort. Georgine did it in twenty minutes. I picked up a marble Taj Mahal encased in glass and nodded to the shopkeeper. He wagged his head to indicate I could have it for free. 'Miss... I mean Georgine, this is for you. With my compliments.'

'Me? What for?' she demanded blushing. She grabbed it from my hands and clasped it to her big bosom. 'It's lovely. Thank you.' She gave me a peck on my nose, 'And that's for you bein' so nice to a horrid girl.'

This time she took the rear seat beside me. When I asked the chauffeur to take us to the Royal Mosque, she protested: 'Nope. One mornin' one buildin'. Okay?'

'That would take us a whole month to do Delhi.'

'Goodie! You can spend every mornin' with me. Won't you like that?'

We drove through Chandni Chowk, Khari Bawli and Sadar Bazaar. Georgine kept taking snapshots and making unintelligible sounds. She suddenly turned round, stared at me and giggled, 'Gawd! You are a funny lookin' man!' she exclaimed. 'If somebody had told me last week that I'd be ridin' around with a darkie with a bandage round his head and a beard round his chin, I would have died.' I made no comment. She sensed my resentment. 'Don't mind me,' she added, 'I am always sayin' such dumb, stoopid things. Anyway what have you got under that bandage?' I made no reply. She grunted *unh* and said no more till we were back in Carlyle's home. As she got out of the car she asked, 'Can I pull your beard?' Before I could raise my hand to protect myself she grabbed it in her hand and gave it a violent tug. She threw three ten rupee notes on the seat, jumped out with the miniature Taj in her arms, and with a jerk of her big bottom ran to the door. 'Bye! See you tomorrow.'

The bloody bitch! I muttered to myself. What she needs is to be put across the knee, her jeans ripped off and a few hard smacks on her large, melon-sized bottom. Followed by buggery.

At the Coffee House I found myself telling my cronies about Georgine. I didn't like my Sikh journalist friend referring to her 'as another quail I had trapped.' Nor the politician warning me against carnal knowledge of a girl of sixteen. When I came out of the Coffee House, it was late in the afternoon. The *jamun* trees were alive with the screeching of parakeets. I wanted to fill my chest and yell her name so loudly that it would be heard all over Connaught Circus, 'Georgeeen,' and the traffic would come to a halt, 'Georgeen' and the parakeets would stop screaming. And the only sound to be heard would be 'Georgine, Georgine, Georgine,' echoing round and round the Circus.

That evening I told Bhagmati about Georgine. As usual she did not like my being so enthusiastic about anyone except her. I tried to laugh it off by reminding her that Georgine was forty years younger than me. That did not reassure her. And when I took her with greater gusto than usual, she asked, 'What is the matter with you today?' Meaning *you are not taking me but that fat-bottomed sixteen-year-old white girl*. She was right.

I was less exuberant in the morning. However, I spent twenty minutes in my cold, damp bathroom dyeing my beard. By the time I turned up at Carlyle's house I was apprehensive of the kind of reception I would get.

Georgine was outside soaking in the sun. She looked more grown up. 'How do you like my new hair-do?' she asked turning her head sideways. The hair was bunched on top of her head and tied in a chignon. It made her neck look longer and bared her small pink ears.

'Very nice! Makes you look like a lady.'

'I am that. *Shucks!*'

In the car she asked me if I slept with my turban on my head.

I replied: 'If you were a little older, I would have said "Come and find out for yourself!"'

Her face flushed. 'You are an ole lech! You makin' a pass at me or somethin?'

It was my turn to be embarrassed. 'I said if you were older and I meant a lot older. I must be older than your father.'

' I don't buy that kind of crap!'

I laid on some flattery. White people are not used to flattery and succumb very easily. She gave me an opening by taking my hand and apologizing: 'Don't be mad with me. I don't mean to be nasty.'

'You are not nasty,' I replied taking a grip on her hand, 'you are the nicest Missy Baba I've met.'

'Messy what?' she asked, raising her voice.

'Not messy, Missy. No flattery, it is not often I have anyone as pretty to take around.'

'*Unh*' she growled. 'I am not pretty or good lookin' or anythin' like that.'

But it was clear my compliment had hit the mark. Her face had gone pink with happiness and after a pause she said 'You're a nice ole man. Can I call you pop? I don't know your name anyhow.'

Girls are more easy to seduce when they are sixteen than when they are a year or two older. At sixteen they are unsure of themselves and grateful for any reassurance you can give them about their looks or brains—either will do. Georgine, despite her brashness, proved very vulnerable. I took her to the Coffee House, as I said, 'to show her off to my friends.' She blushed again and repeated, 'You are an ole lech you know? But I like you.'

At the Coffee House we sat in the section marked 'Families Only.' I ordered a Coke for her and went to greet my friends. They were not very complimentary about Georgine. Said my Sikh journalist friend: 'From the way you described her, I thought you had picked up a Marilyn Monroe. Nice fat boobs and bum though!'

'She's no Noor Jahan,' opined the political expert. 'Like any American schoolgirl. Must have a nice pussy. But you must be madder than I thought; you try any tricks with that one, you will be in for seven years rigorous imprisonment.'

Ugly, vulgar words. I rejoined Georgine. 'What did they have to say about your girl-friend?' she asked.

'Girl-friend? Oh you mean you?' I replied pretending to have been taken by surprise. 'They said you were very beautiful.'

'Liar! I bet you a hundred dollars, they said, "What are you doin' with a lil girl like that? Foolin' around with anyone under seventeen can land you in a jail." How 'bout that for a guess?'

'Wrong, wrong, wrong,' I protested vehemently. I could see she was happy.

This time she put my fee in an envelope and gave it to me with 'Thanks a whole lot.'

That evening I was by turns exhilarated and conscience-stricken. In my confusion I rang her up without having anything to say to her. Her uncle picked up the phone. 'You must not let Georgine make a nuisance of herself,' he said, 'and let me have your bill for the time she's been with you.' He put down the receiver without asking me why I had rung. But I was excited to know that Georgine had paid me without telling her uncle.

I decided to use the information at an appropriate moment. Meanwhile I became bolder in my compliments. Since she changed her hair-style every day I got many opportunities to say something that would please her. One day she dressed herself in a bright red sari. It did not suit her, nor did she know how a woman in a sari should walk—like most Caucasians she had a masculine stride. I said 'How charming'—and she replied: 'Oh thank you, I thought you'd sort of like to see me in your native costume.' I explained that the sari was not native to the Punjab and that a *salwar-kameez* would look even nicer on her. 'O great!' she exclaimed. 'I must have these thingees at once.' I took her to a tailor and while she was choosing the material I told him in Punjabi to send the finished products with the bill to me. Georgine could not make up her mind. What she liked best she said was too expensive for her. So she settled for the second best. I spoke to the tailor (again in Punjabi) to use the material of her first choice.

'You think it will look nice on me?' she asked me when we were in the car.

'I am sure it will. We have a word in our language *jamazebi* which means the ability to fit into any clothes. I think you will look nice in anything you wear.' (Far from being *jamazeb*, because of her large bosom and broad hips she had difficulty in fitting into readymade clothes). 'You are nuts,' she said dismissing the compliment. 'I know none of the nice things you say are true, but I like you sayin' them. So don't stop, O—Kay?'

Getting her into my apartment was easy. Two days after she had been measured, I offered to drive her around in my own car. When I went to pick her up, I said, as casually as I could, 'Your things have been delivered to my apartment. Would you like to pick them up before we go sightseeing?'

'O—Kay.'

She looked around admiringly at my books and pictures. 'Nice, comfy pad,' she remarked.

'Thank you. Do sit down.'

She took off her shoes, bounced onto the settee and crossed her legs. '*Nunc!* What you starin' at?'

I quoted Ghalib, first in Urdu and then translated it for her: 'She has come to my house. Sometimes I look at her, sometimes I look at my house.'

'That means you're pleased to have me here. Where are my thingees?'

I brought the bundle and untied it. 'I didn't order that one; it was too expensive, you remember? That old tailor is tryin' to rob me. All you Indians try to touch us Americans. You think we're a bunch of suckers, don't you?'

'He's not charging you any more for this material. He knew you liked it better, so he's just made it for you.'

She was nonplussed. 'I am sorry. That's very nice of him. And this?' she asked, opening out a sequined *dupatta*, 'It is very pretty, but I didn't ask for this.'

'That goes with the other things. Nothing extra.'

She draped it over her head and looked around for a mirror. 'Where can I try them on?' she asked, taking the bundle under her arm. I showed her to my bedroom. I was left alone for some time. I poured out a whisky and gulped it down neat. I moved from the chair to the sofa.

Georgine came out in Punjabi clothes. The *dupatta* was like a small white cloud studded with stars haloing her red hair, face and shoulders. The clothes fitted her: it seemed as if she were formed to wear Punjabi clothes. 'How's that?' she asked pirouetting on her toes.

'Very becoming! Much nicer than anything you've worn.'

'Thank you, I sort of like it too.'

She came and sat beside me on the sofa. She opened her handbag, 'How much does he want for this?'

My voice stuck in my throat, I forced it out. 'Nothing. Allow me the privilege of making this a present. Please!'

'Thank you and all that. But I know you can't afford it?'

'Yes I can; and it'll make me very happy.'

' Okay, if it'll make you happy.' She turned round and gave me a quick kiss on my beard, 'Thank you, pop.'

The kiss paralyzed my tongue. After a while I was able to say: 'And I owe you money. You paid me for the outings out of your own money, didn't you?'

'How do you know?'

'I rang up your uncle.'

She turned scarlet. 'That was a dumb thing to do! What did he say?'

I took her hand in mine. 'Don't worry. I did not tell him you had paid me. Now I can earn a double fee.'

'You cunning ole Oriental!' she laughed. 'I'm relieved to know my ole uncle doesn't know.'

'Why didn't you tell him?'

'I dunno.'

The initiative was now mine. 'Maybe you wanted to be with me without his knowing.'

'Maybe,' she replied tossing back her hair.

Any experienced lecher knows that one should not waste words with a teenager because when it comes to real business she gets tongue-tied or can only say 'No.' It is best to talk to her body with your hands. That excites her to a state of speechless acceptance. I ran my fingers up and down her lower arm. She watched them till goose pimples came up. Thereafter all I had to do was to put my arm around her waist, draw her towards me and smother her lips, eyes, nose, ears and neck with kisses. She moaned helplessly. I slipped my hand under her *kamiz* and played with her taut nipples. Then I undid her pyjama cord and slipped my fingers between her damp thighs. A little gentle ministration with the hand made her convulse and she climaxed groaning 'O God! O God!' She lay still like a human-sized rubber doll. I put my hand on her bosom. She slapped it and pushed it away. She picked up her clothes and went to the bedroom. She came back in her jeans, tossed the bundle of *salwar-kameez* and sequined *dupatta* on the settee and strode out of the apartment.

That was the last I saw of Georgine.

She was the last customer Carlyle put my way. I do not know whether what I had done amounted to having carnal knowledge of a girl below the age of consent. But for many long days and nights I pondered over the words in the *Mahabharata:* 'As two pieces of wood floating on the ocean come together at one time and are again separated, even such is the union of living creatures in this world.'

*

After many years I have come to Delhi by train. The railway station has changed. But not beyond recognition. The platforms bear the same numbers they did fifty years ago. The same line of coolies in dark-red shirts and dirty white *dhoties,* bearing metal brassards with identification numbers on their arms, line up on their haunches along the platform. There are the mynahs chittering and quarrelling with cows. The same hawkers; the same melodious cries: *lemon-soda-barraf* (ice); *chai, garam chai.* And the same all pervading stench of shit, urine and phenyl.

It is an early morning in October. Pleasantly cool and somewhat misty presaging the advent of winter. I skirt past people sleeping on the platform, go up the stairs, across the footbridge over rail tracks with mounds of shit on the sides, and down the stairs alongside the retiring-rooms. No one asks me for my ticket. I come out of the station and face the Company Gardens with its Hardinge library. Clean, fresh air. Motor scooters and taxis are lined up on the road as far as the eye can see. The drivers are sprawled on the seats, snoring lustily. I hail a passing *tonga.* The *tongawalla* is wrapped up in a dirty shawl. He eyes me suspiciously. He is Muslim. I am Sikh. 'Where to?' he demands. 'Raisina! How much for Raisina?' He hasn't heard anyone use Raisina for New Delhi for many years and rightly concludes I am an old Delhiwalla. Raisina is also a good four miles away and will therefore have more money to it. 'Give me whatever you wish; a taxi would cost you over ten rupees. You are my first customer so this will be my *boni*.' I clamber up on the rear seat and place my valise beside him in the front.

He decides to go through the city; it is shorter, not crowded at this hour and safer than the deserted Ring Road. So we set off through the Company Bagh to the Fountain which has not spouted water in half-a-century. On the balcony of Roshan-ud-Daulah's mosque men are lined up for prayer. Alongside is Sees Ganj Gurdwara festooned with coloured bulbs. There is much coming and going of worshippers. Swarthy, long-bearded men in blue and yellow armed with spears guard the entrance.

The *tonga* turns left. I see the ramparts of the Red Fort. The *tonga* turns right into Dariba. Herds of Hindu women in white carrying brass plates full of flowers and coconuts are shuffling along towards the Jamna. We emerge from Dariba with the Jamia Masjid towering above us. The sun has just caught the eastern minaret in its noose. Hundreds of figures wrapped in sheets sleep on the broad steps. A weary oil-lamp flickers on the headstone of Sarmad's grave. It has been given a fresh coat of green; withered jasmine and marigold are strewn over it. We go through a very smelly Urdu Bazaar, past the lane leading to Razia Sultana's grave, the high-plinthed Kali Masjid and out of the old walled city through Turkman Gate. The air is fresher. Hundreds of RSS boys drill with staves under the podium in the wide acres of the Ram Leela ground. Middle-aged Punjabis take their walking-sticks for brisk walks. We pass the massive equestrian statue of Shivaji brandishing his sword towards New Delhi. 'When did they put this up?' I ask the *tongawalla*. 'Two years ago,' he mumbles as he gives the statue a baleful look. We go down below the Minto rail bridge and up again into Connaught Circus. 'Drop me at the Coffee House on the other side,' I tell him. We drive round the colonnaded shopping centres and pull up outside the Coffee House. 'How much?' I ask him as he hands me my valise. 'Whatever pleases you, you are doing the *boni*; and I have yet to feed my son,' he says patting the flanks of his horse. The horse has apparently had plenty to drink; it sends a powerful jet of wine-coloured fluid splashing on to the asphalt road. I hand him a tenner. He fumbles for change in his pocket. 'Keep it; give your son a good feed.' He invokes Allah's blessings on me, my kith and kin and drives off.

I buy the six English daily papers published in the city. It is a waste of fifty paise six times over. But old habits die hard. I flip through pages to read the announcements of citizens who have 'left for their heavenly abode'. Quite a few have. I don't know any of them. Nor any whose loss is mourned in verse and syrupy prose in the Memoriam columns. *Delhi Diary* states it is a sectional holiday for the Sikhs on account of the anniversary of the martyrdom of Guru Tegh Bahadur. And the column alongside mentions the promulgation of Section 144 of the CPC forbidding the assembly of more than five persons in certain areas. The Inspector General of Police states that—'*goondas,* miscreants and anti-social elements have been rounded up.' You don't have to read between lines to know that trouble is anticipated.

By the time I have disposed of my *idli-sambar* and the papers, the regulars who have little to do beside being regular at the Coffee House are at their respective tables holding forth on political developments. My regulars have dwindled. The bald, beady-eyed photographer left for his heavenly abode last year; the farting clerk in the Ministry of Defence who resented our calling him a farter has dropped us. That leaves the Sikh journalist and the political expert. They are not getting along too well. The Sikh journalist arrives first, plucks a hair from his sparse beard and says 'You are back! When?' and orders coffee. The politician follows: 'I thought all *goondas* have been rounded up,' he says in lieu of greeting. The journalist, usually quick-witted, is stuck for a proper retort. I ask, 'What's all this fuss about today? We've had hundreds of the Guru's martyrdom anniversaries without Section 144 and the police *bandobast.*' The politician—he is Hindu—fires another barbed shaft at us, 'You can never trust the Sikhs. They couldn't do much when their Guru was executed, so better 300 years later than never. Isn't that so?' The Sikh journalist explodes: 'We settled our scores with the Muslims long ago. It is you Hindus, whose mothers and sisters they raped, who provoked us against them. You can't bear to see Sikhs and Muslims becoming friendly.' I try to defuse the tension. 'How different would have been the story of India if instead of Aurangzeb, Dara Shikoh had become Emperor of India!'

The politician proffers his version: 'He would not have executed your Guru and the Guru's son would not have had any excuse to make you grow all this fungus around your chins. Also India would have become a real Hindustan—the land of the Hindus; and...'

'And,' interrupts the Sikh journalist, 'if there had been no bearded Khalsa the only thing your Hindu ancestors could have offered in the way of defence against invaders like Nadir Shah and Abdali was their bare buttocks to be buggered.'

'Don't buk buk,' snaps the politician warming up.

'You are doing all the bakwas not I.'

So does the past cast its baleful shadow on the present. But nowhere do the shadow of history assume such bizarre patterns as they do in Delhi's Coffee House. I pick up my valise and leave the two to dispute the past.

*

Bhagmati bursts in like a hurricane, flailing her arms and spouting torrents of words. 'The Sikhs are up in arms. They are all over the city carrying long swords and are marching towards their gurdwara in Chandni Chowk. Do you know what they are saying? Three hundred years ago someone murdered their Guru in Dilli so they are going to murder every Dilliwalla today. Does that make any sense?'

'Why don't you ask your friend Budh Singh?'

'Hai Ram! You should have seen the way he looked at me! He asked me "On whose side are you, Badshah Aurangzeb's or our Guru's."'

'On whose side are you ?'

'He is mad. I told him as politely as I could, "I am on no side—neither Emperor Aurangzeb's nor your Guru's." You know what he says to me? "So you are neutral, *hain*? If you were a man or a woman you would have been on one side or the other. "But I shut him up for all time to come; he will never bandy words with me again. I said *"Arre*, son of Budhoo Singh! The great Bhagwan who lives up in the heavens can perform many miracles. He can make a Bhangi (sweeper) into a Brahmin. He can turn a timid Bania (shopkeeper) into a Kshatriya (warrior). He can make a poor *hijda* into a man or a woman. But even Bhagwan cannot put sense into the skull of a *budhoo* like you.'"

Bhagmati flops into the sofa with a triumphant *hoon*. She takes out a cigarette and flings the matchbox across the room to me. I go over and light her cigarette. 'You think there will be trouble in the city? There are policemen everywhere. Truckloads of them in Chandni Chowk and Nai Sarak and Qazi-ka-Hauz and Ajmeri Gate and Connaught Place— everywhere!'

'Maybe!' I reply. I have been a little off colour for some days and have not much appetite for Bhagmati. She has shown me a way out of my difficulties. 'That's the route the Sikh's procession is to take this afternoon. And they will be in all the gurdwaras including the one right behind this apartment. You will be safest with your husband in Lal Kuan. I can drop you there.'

Bhagmati looks at me very suspiciously. I don a sanctimonious look. I tell her that I had forgotten about the anniversary of the martyrdom of the ninth Guru, Tegh Bahadur. I tell her that it is a day for prayer not fornication. Bhagmati is very superstitious about having sex on sacred days. She often says, 'We have 364 days to do this; one day of abstinence won't kill us.'

She finishes her cigarette. I give her twenty rupees. 'What's this for?' she asks as she tucks the notes in her bra. I drive her back to Lal Kuan.

8

The Untouchables

It was a few days before Diwali that news of the Badshah Jahangir's death was heard in Dilli. No one was allowed to light a lamp or kindle a fire in their hearth for some days. Our elders said that anyone seen smiling or heard laughing during the next forty days would have his head cut off. My mother would not let me go out to play with the other boys lest I forgot not to shout or laugh. That is why although I was only a small boy I can never forget that badshah's death.

When I asked my *Bapu* the name of the badshah who had died, he said 'What will you do with the badshah's name?' None of the sweepers or cobblers in Rikabganj knew his name. Only the Mussalmans who lived in the *sarai* alongside the mosque and the contractor, Lakhi Rai, who lived in a big stone house with his wives, eight sons and their wives knew the badshah's name. These Mussalmans and Lakhi Rai's family went about with long faces as if their own mother's mother had died. Some people feel very big if they can cry over the deaths of big people.

'What have we poor untouchables to do with kings!' I remember my *Bapu* saying. 'They are all the same to us. One goes, another comes, *zulum* goes on.'

I did not know who *zulum* was. When I was a little older my *Bapu* told me that *zulum* was not a man but what the rich did to the poor. We untouchables were the poorest of the poor. No one did anything to us except run away if we came near them. That, said my *Bapu*, was also a kind of *zulum*. It was in our *karma*. We had done bad things in our previous births. That is why we were born black and had to do all the dirty work.

My *Bapu* called every badshah a *zalim*. This one who had just died, said my *Bapu*, was a very bad man because he drank more wine than Uncle Reloo who was drunk most of the time. Uncle Reloo told me that the badshah could drink twenty cups of *arrack* and eat *tolas* of opium every day and yet poke his queen and the other women of his harem every night. He told me that his queen had been married before. But when she saw the badshah who was only a prince at the time she knew at once that he would become a badshah. So she put some magic powder in his cup of wine and made him fall madly in love with her. The prince had the husband murdered and when he became badshah he made her his queen. Uncle Reloo said that it was not the badshah but this queen who had ruled over Hindustan.

It was not so much the badshah's drinking or womanizing that had made my father angry with him as what he had done to our Guru. 'What is it to us how much he drinks and whose mother he fucks,' he used to say, 'but perish the man who raises his hand against our Guru.' Most of us untouchables of Rikabganj had attached ourselves to the lotus feet of the Guru and begun to call ourselves the Sikhs of Nanak. No one had seen Nanak or the Gurus who came after him to save us. The badshah who had just died had killed our fifth Guru Arjun and put his son Hargobind in jail. So there was no reason for us to beat our breasts on this badshah's death.

If there was a death in our family we did not light lamps at Diwali or squirt coloured water at Holi for at least one year. But the Mussalmans have strange customs. Three full moons after the death of the Badshah a fellow came from the city *kotwal̤i* and began to beat his drum in front of the mosque. When everyone had collected he shouted: 'All you people listen to the order of the new badshah.' Then he gave his name which was as long as the road from Rikabganj to Paharganj—His Majesty Abul Muzaffar Shahabuddin Mohammed Sahib-i-Qiran Sani, Shadow of God on Earth, King of Kings, Monarch of the Universe, Emperor of Hindustan. He told us that we were to light our homes and pray for his long life.

We untouchables had no oil to light our homes and we had no temples to go to say our prayers. So we decided to see how others lit their homes and prayed for the new badshah's long life.

My mother gave me a clean shirt to wear. Everyone wore their best clothes. The sweepers and cobblers of Rikabganj formed a party. The men in front danced to the beat of the drum; women followed singing as they went along. I took hold of Uncle Reloo's hand. He was more fun to be with than *Bapu*. Aunt Bimbo was happy. 'You stick to your *chacha* and don't let him drink or get into mischief,' she said.

We drank lots of *sherbet* which was served free outside *nawabs'* mansions and we ate lots of sweetmeats which were also given free by rich tradesmen. My *Bapu* did not give me any money but I got a handful of coins in the scramble when a *nawab* showered them from his elephant.

The new badshah who called himself Shah Jahan or King of the World was not as *zalim* as his father had been. Although he had killed his brothers' families when he came on the throne, he did not hurt any one else. But Uncle Reloo who knew everything told me that like his father, grandfather and great-grandfather and others before them, this badshah also liked women. His favourite was a queen whom he kept pregnant from the day he married her. In the fourteen years they were married she had fourteen sons and daughters. She couldn't take any more and died giving birth to her fourteenth child. The badshah was so sad that he decided to make the biggest and most beautiful grave over her body. This was very good news for the stonemasons of Paharganj. They moved to Agra. It took over twenty years to make. People who came from Agra said it was higher than our Qutub Minar and much more beautiful than the tomb of Badshah Humayun at Arab-ki-Sarai. One day Aunt Bimbo asked Uncle Reloo: 'When I die, will you make a Taj Mahal for me?' He replied: 'You die first, we'll talk about a Taj Mahal for you afterwards.'

Some years after he became king, this badshah, Shah Jahan, came to Dilli. He liked our city very much and said: 'I am going to live here.' He sent for his chief builder, Mukarram Khan, and told him: 'Make a big fort along the river Jamna, and inside that fort make palaces for myself and my queens.

I also want the biggest mosque in the world.' Mukarram Khan bowed three times before the badshah and replied: 'Badshah, peace be upon you! If Allah wills I will build you as big a fort as at Agra with as many canals and gardens and fountains. You will also have the world's biggest and most beautiful mosque. I will build it on Bhojla Hill so it can be seen from Palam and Qutub.' Then Mukarram Khan asked Ustad Ahmed and Ustad Hira to make maps. When that was done he asked the badshah to come to Dilli. 'Badshah, peace be upon you! Now put down the foundation stone, so we can get on with work.'

What years they were! Everyone got work. We gave up skinning dead cows and buffaloes and carrying other people's shit. Lakhi Rai got a contract to supply labour. As I was now old enough, he gave me a job to carry mud and stones.

Dilli began to change. Every day a new building! Every day the city wall rising higher! Every day new minarets and domes rising into the sky! And so it went for many years. When the work was finished we had nine days of *tamasha*. Princes showered silver coins on the crowds. The badshah rode through the city on his biggest elephant and scattered gold coins by the palmful. His courtiers said, 'We won't call "Dilli" "Dilli" any more. We will rename it Shahjahanabad.' But Dilli is Dilli and no king or nobleman can give it another name.

When a person is busy making money he forgets his God. As soon as he has made ninety-nine rupees he wants to make a hundred. For the years I was working in the city I hardly ever thought of my Guru. When my *Bapu* died and I became the head of the family, the Guru's agent sent for me. I went along with the messenger to the agent's camp. He reclined against a big pillow set on a big *charpoy*. I thought he was the Guru himself and so I went down on my knees and rubbed my forehead on the ground in front of him.

'Who are you?' he asked me.

'I am Jaita Rangreta of Rikabganj,' I replied.

'Are you a Sikh of Guru Nanak?' he asked.

I told him I was what my *Bapu* had been.

'You paid nothing for your father's soul nor on the accession of the new Guru,' he said.

I replied that I had no money left as I had to feast all the Rangretas in Rikabganj on my *Bapu's* death. His servant smacked me on the back of my neck and exclaimed angrily. 'You argue with the Guru's agent!' I had to borrow money from Lakhi Rai to pay him. I said to myself, 'At least I am something—a Sikh of Guru Nanak. I do not know what it means but it is better than being nothing but a Rangreta untouchable.' Thereafter every year I had to give this agent of the Guru something when he came to Dilli. Although he never allowed me to go near him or even touched my money with his own hands (his servants did that) I felt different. I was told that the new Guru did not like people to cut their hair or their beards. So I let the hair on my head grow long and wrapped a turban over it. I had quite a growth of beard on my face. The Mussalmans did not allow Hindus to wear beards but they did not bother us untouchables. We bearded Rangretas began to look different from other untouchables. And although after the building of Dilli was over I had to become a sweeper again, if anyone asked me who I was I would reply: 'I am a Sikh of Guru Nanak.'

For some years after the building of Shahjahanabad, the badshah liked Dilli more than Agra. Then he began to like Agra more than Dilli. His visits to our city became less and less frequent. Tradesmen and artisans began to move back to Agra. People began to say that very soon Shahjahanabad would become like the other old cities of Dilli: Mehrauli, Siri, Chiragh, Tughlakabad, Kotla Firozeshah and Kilokheri, the abode of Gujars, jackals, hyaenas and the owls.

I did not earn very much sweeping drains and cleaning latrines and had to borrow money from the Bania and Lakhi Rai. I had to pay interest on their money and when I was unable to do that, they refused to lend me any more. Because of this I was forced to take employment in the executioner's yard attached to the *kotwali* in Chandni Chowk. This was really dirty work: first I had to get used to seeing a man's head being hacked off; then see his arms and legs cut off. After this had happened it was my job to put the pieces together and lay them out for the people to see. As I worked I could hear the onlookers avoiding me as if I were a murderer. Every evening there were at least three to four unclaimed corpses to be carted off and dumped in the river or on the garbage mound. What will man not do to fill his belly!

As I said before, I did not like this work. I did not like to shout *dom, dom* whenever I went out with the cartload of corpses. I did not like people covering their children's eyes against me and blocking their nostrils against the smelly load I carried. Even the sentries at the city gates would draw aside to let me pass. I used to console myself by recalling my *Bapu's* words: 'Son, only two people can pass through the gates of Shahjahanabad without being questioned: the King and the untouchable!'

It was on one of his visits to Dilli that Badshah Shah Jahan was taken ill. They tried to keep it secret but within a few hours everyone knew about the sultan's ailment mainly through the badshah's doctor who was a gossip. This is how it happened. The badshah had got up at night and complained of pain in his belly. The queen had sent for the *hakeem* who lived in Ballimaran. The *hakeem* told many people of having had no sleep because he had to stay up all night with a patient whose name he could not disclose—which is how news of the badshah's ailment spread.

When I came to work one of the *doms* shouted '*Chhuttee!*' (holiday). 'Orders from the palace, no executions today.' Executions were only stopped on religious holidays or if the king or one of his queens or their princes was ill and desired to earn merit and good health. By the time the sun had risen over the walls of Red Fort people were gathering in groups and speaking in whispers. Butchers were forbidden to slaughter animals; *mullahs* were ordered to pray to Allah to restore the king to good health; priests were ordered to clang their temple bells. Shops closed. People hurried to their homes and barricaded their doors. At night they dug holes under their hearths to bury their gold and silver.

The king it turned out was constipated. The *hakeem* gave him a purgative made of laburnum pods. For two days and nights the king emptied his bowels till there was nothing left in them and he started shitting blood. But big people's illnesses are always made to sound big. The simple shutting and opening of the royal arse-hole was made to sound as if the world was coming to an end. At first he was said to be dying of constipation; then he was said to be dying of dysentery.

My *Bapu* used to say that when a father hiccups his sons go for his purse. That was certainly true about the badshah's four sons. No sooner had they heard of their old man's illness than their hands were on the hilts of their swords. But they wanted to make sure he was really dying before they drew them. So they sent messengers to Dilli with gifts for their father. The old fellow knew these tricks as he had tried them in his own time. He seated himself at the window of his palace so that the crowd could see him. He had prayers of thanksgiving said in the mosques. However, his sons were not fooled and started raising armies to march to Agra and Dilli. The badshah decided to get to Agra and sit on his throne before one of his boys got to it. Despite this, one after another his sons proclaimed themselves kings of Hindustan. First, Shuja who was in Bangladesh from where the sun rises put a crown on his head and said: ' I am King of Hindustan.' A few days later Murad, who was somewhere in the south, sat himself on a throne and said: 'I am King of Hindustan.' Aurangzeb was more clever. He went to Murad and told him: 'Let me help you to defeat our brothers. Then we will lock up our old man who is now too feeble to rule and you can become King of Hindustan. I will then go off to Mecca and pray for you.' Dara who was the badshah's eldest and the favourite son was incensed at the behaviour of his brothers. He said, 'My father is King of Hindustan. After him, I will be King of Hindustan because I am his eldest son. Shuja, Murad and Aurangzeb are bastards. I will kill them.'

We were not sure which of the sons would make the best king. The contractor Lakhi Rai was in favour of Dara. 'He is the eldest and the eldest son always succeeds his father. Besides he is god-fearing and treats Hindus and Muslims alike,' he said. The Muslims did not like Dara. They said he was a *kafir* because he made the stone gods of the Hindus equal to Allah and His Prophet. Their favourite was the third son Aurangzeb.

At this time there was a Yahoodi *fakeer*, Sarmad, who went about naked like a Naga *sadhu*. Sarmad told everyone in the bazaars that Dara would win. The people of Dilli were frightened of Sarmad because he was a friend of God and could ask Him for any favour he wanted. One day I casually told one of the Muslims at the *sarai* what *fakeer* Sarmad was saying. The Mussalman spat on the ground and exclaimed: '*La haul valla quwwat!* That shameless fellow who dangles his penis before women! If I ever catch him alone I will cut it off and throw it to the dogs.'

Fakeer Sarmad was wrong. The king's sons fought each other as hungry dogs fight over a bone. Dara's son, Sulaiman Shikoh, defeated Shuja. Meanwhile Murad and Aurangzeb defeated Dara, captured Agra and made their old father prisoner. Then this fellow Aurangzeb tricked his brother Murad: he got him drunk, tied him up and threw him into a dungeon. He then finished off Shuja, Dara and Dara's sons. This was how we had a new badshah—Aurangzeb—while the old badshah Shah Jahan was still alive. The Mussalmans in the *sarai* were happy. They said that the new badshah was a good man. He did not drink wine; he did not have concubines or courtesans; he did not allow dancing and singing in the palace; he ate little, slept little and prayed a lot. He spent on himself only what he earned by making copies of their holy book and selling them. They said if all kings had been like him, Hindustan would have long ago been rid of *kafirs*. Alamgir was the name they used for him—'Alamgir, *Zinda Peer*, is a living saint,' they said.

Lakhi Rai was not happy. The new badshah did not give him any contracts. One day many years later when I was eating his leftovers in his courtyard I told him that the Mussalmans said Aurangzeb was a man of God because he did not drink wine or womanize. He lost his temper and said 'What about that slut Hira Bai?' Then he got frightened and made me swear that I would never tell anyone of what he had said. But I could not get Hira Bai's name out of my mind. I asked the Bania, who also sometimes gave me his leftovers, about her. He made a ring with the thumb and index finger of his left hand and pierced it with a finger of his right hand. 'But that Hira Bai is dead,' he said. The Bania did not like Aurangzeb because he had imposed *jazia* tax on the Hindus. 'Don't tell anyone I told you,' he said in a low voice, 'but a tribe called the Marathas are going to finish him. Their leader Shivaji has stuck a big bamboo pole up the bottoms of these Mughals. Haven't you heard how this Shivaji tore out the bowels of one of the badshah's generals with his hands? In the name of Rama, don't breathe a word about this to anyone or they will slit my throat.'

I couldn't keep secrets. One day I asked the Mussalman cook at the *sarai* if he had ever heard of Shivaji. He almost spat in my face. 'Where did you pick up the name of that dirty *kafir*?' he asked angrily. 'He murdered the brave General Afzal Khan who was embracing him as a friend. That is the kind of *moozi* he is. The badshah has sent an army against him. If Allah wills, the rat will be flushed out of his hole and destroyed. *Inshallah!*'

Some months later the Mussalman cook gave me an extra large portion of leftovers. He looked very happy. 'Have you heard of that Shivaji of yours? He has been captured and brought in chains to Agra. He will be sent to hell ' When I told this to the Bania, he said it was a lie and that Shivaji had come of his own free will to talk to the king. For many days everyone in Dilli was talking of this man Shivaji. The Mussalmans said he was a great villain and that the king would cut off his head. The Hindus said he was a great hero. Then we heard that he had escaped and returned to his mountain kingdom in the Deccan. 'Didn't I tell you so?' said the Bania to me. 'They can never catch him. Ramji is his protector.'

The king was very angry. He ordered Hindu temples at Varanasi and Mathura to be destroyed. The Bania who was so frightened of the Mussalmans called the badshah a *zalim*. 'Whenever there is too much *zulum*,' he said 'God sends an *avatar* to destroy *zalims*. It is written in the *Gita*.' Even Lakhi Rai who kept up with the Mussalmans wagged his head and said, 'This is *Kaliyuga* (the dark age), God will send an *avatar* to save us.'

The *zulum* went on but no *avatar* came to stop it. When the Jats and Brahmins of village Tilpat, which is a few *kos* in the direction of the rising sun, claimed land which belonged to their temple, the badshah sent his army against them and blew up their village. Their leader, Gokula Jat and all his supporters were brought to Dilli and executed. No *avatar* came to save them.

Three years later there was a worse *zulum* at Narnaul. A sect of *sadhus* called Satnamis were slain by the thousand. No *avatar* came to save them or punish the *zalim* badshah.

I asked Lakhi Rai about the coming of the *avatar*. He just shook his head. I asked him whether our Guru could be the *avatar*. 'Which Guru?' he asked. 'There are so many. And all they do is to send their agents to collect money.' That was strange talk from Lakhi Rai!

I began to lose faith in the Guru. The Mussalmans in the *sarai* made fun of him. 'Who is this robber you worship?' one fellow asked me. The *mullah* of the mosque (may his mouth be filled with dung!) said: 'The badshah will soon bring this Guru of yours to the path of obedience and teach him that the only way of approaching Allah is through His only Messenger, Mohammed—upon Whom be peace.' Although I knew nothing about this Guru I did not like Mussalmans talking like that about him. When the Guru was captured at Agra and brought to Dilli in chains, the Mussalmans mocked: 'We told you this Guru of yours is a robber! The entire gang will be hanged.'

I saw the Guru and three Sikhs who had been arrested with him. I said to myself: 'If he was an avatar *he will save himself and destroy the* zalims.' I prayed that he would fly out of his cell or perform some other miracle so that I could show my face to the Mussalmans of Rikabganj.

But who cares for the prayers of poor untouchables? There was this judge Qazi Abdul Wahab. His Allah had made him so deaf that everyone called him *behra qazi*. He sentenced the Guru and his three followers to death. He ordered their bodies to be displayed in front of the *kotwali* for everyone to see. For the first time even the timid Lakhi Rai became brave. 'This must not happen,' he said to me. 'The Guru has refused to save his life, but we must not allow them to dishonour his body.' The rich contractor addressed me as Jaitaji. Before this he had always called me 'Jaitoo' or worse 'O, *choorha* (sweeper).' How was I to know Lakhi Rai was not a spy? I kept quiet. Silence is the best friend of the poor.

Strange things happened in Dilli that autumn. Dassehra passed without any Ram Lila or the burning of the effigies of Ravana and his brothers. The Hindus said the badshah had forbidden the celebration of Hindu festivals. The Muslims said that this was a lie and said they knew why Hindus were not celebrating their most important festival. A few days later came Diwali. Not a light in anyone's house! Not a sound of a cracker! No fireworks! No one sending sweets to anyone! The whole world was like a dark, moonless night. You know how much darker the night looks when you expect millions of oil-lamps twinkling and there are none! So no Diwali for the Hindus. And the Mussalmans feeling as if ants were crawling up their bottoms! The *mullahji* of the *sarai* mosque asked Lakhi Rai very discreetly why he had not lit any lamps on Diwali night. 'The death of a very near and dear one,' he replied. 'All the Hindus seem to have lost someone near and dear to them,' exclaimed the *mullahji* very sarcastically. ' I hope it is not because someone very near and very dear is going to die, yes?'

Lakhi Rai did not answer. The *mullahji* turned his temper on me. 'And you, Jaitoo! Have you lost your mother's mother that you did not light lamps at Diwali?' I replied: '*Mullahji* in poor men's houses there is a death every day. We never have enough oil to light a lamp. If you gave me money, I would have lit up every home in Rikabganj.' He mumbled in his beard, 'You have learnt to talk big, haven't you?'

Everyone in Dilli was talking about the miracle the Guru would perform. They said anyone who raised his hand against him or his companions would go blind. The *Kotwal* could not find anyone in Dilli to carry out the sentence of death and had to send for one Jalaluddin all the way from

Samana in the Punjab. This Jalaluddin hated the Sikhs and their Gurus.

A few days after the Diwali-without-lights, Jalaluddin cut off the heads of the Sikhs captured with the Guru. Jalaluddin did not go blind; nothing happened to him. Now it was the turn of the Guru. The *behra qazi* said, 'Jalaluddin we'll cut off the Guru's head on Thursday. His body will be exposed to public gaze after prayer on Friday. Everyone in Dilli will see which is mightier, the sword of Islam or the neck of an infidel!' Everyone in the world knows that whenever the blood of a good man is spilled in Dilli, the Great God who lives in the sky makes His anger known. On Thursday the sun came up like a ball of fire. Everyone said: 'Something terrible is going to happen today.' Even the Mussalmans were anxious and hoped the badshah who was away beyond the Punjab would get to know and would cancel the order of the *behra qazi*. The *Kotwal* told me that he had prayed all night. 'It will be very bad for the Mussalmans if this Guru is martyred,' he said shaking his head.

The Guru performed no miracle. With the name of God on his lips he permitted the monster Jalaluddin of Samana to sever his head from his body. The town-crier went round beating his drum and yelling that 'justice' had been done and that the Guru's body would be exposed in front of the *kotwali* for two days and nights for all to see and learn a lesson.

I brought the news to Rikabganj. In the afternoon all the Sikhs and Hindus of Rikabganj gathered under a tree. No one said anything. The men sighed and the women wept. The Mussalmans of the *sarai* watched us from a distance. Even they seemed to be touched by our grief.

As I sat in that crowd listening to the sighing and whimpering a strange feeling came over me. We had done nothing to save the life of our Guru—and now they were going to expose his naked body to the gaze of crowds and for animals to tear and birds to peck! What kind of devotees were we? My blood boiled within me; I felt very hot and angry with myself. Most of the Guru's disciples were high-born Kshatriyas and Jat peasants who boasted loudly of their bravery. They had done nothing to save their Guru. I, an untouchable, could teach these high-caste fellows how a Guru's Sikh should act. It might cost me my life, but I would win the respect of the world for my untouchable brethren.

I slipped away. Lakhi Rai saw me get up and followed me. 'I have some work for you Jaitaji,' he said, putting his hand on my shoulder, adding meaningfully, 'if you are man enough to do it.' This was the first time he had touched me. I was not sure of this rich contractor—one can never be sure of rich people. I replied, 'I have to be on duty at the *kotwali*.' Lakhi Rai said: 'I will come with you. I also have business at the *kotwali*.' What was his game? I really did not care to find out. However, I felt not Lakhi Rai's but my Guru's hand on my shoulder. I was not afraid of anyone in the world—not of the badshah or the *behra qazi* or that Jalaluddin; not even of the Mughal soldiers or the *Kotwal* and his constabulary.

Lakhi Rai had several bullock carts lined up on the road. They were loaded with bales of cotton. His eight sons were with him. As he was a government contractor, he and his family were allowed to carry weapons. All the men were armed with swords and spears. Lakhi Rai always guarded his caravans in this way and everyone knew him. We left Rikabganj in the afternoon.

When we reached Paharganj, the sun suddenly disappeared. The wind dropped. Hundreds of kites began circling above us. We could see a dark brown wall come sweeping in from the west. As we came to the city wall, the circle of kites moved overhead towards the Royal Mosque. Then the storm overtook us with a fury I would not have thought possible.

The guards at Ajmeri Gate had muffled their faces with the ends of their turbans and waved us on. The storm swept us through Qazi-ka-Hauz, through Lal Kuan and past Begum Fatehpuri's mosque into Chandni Chowk. We arrived at the *kotwali*.

Who knows the inscrutable designs of the Guru? The dust-storm had turned the day into night. Every door and window had been shut against the dust. The guards had bolted themselves in their barracks. And the only sound was the howling of the wind.

I had no difficulty in finding the Guru's body. I touched his feet and then slung his body over my shoulders. I took his head in my hands and walked through the blinding dust-storm. Lakhi Rai and his sons also touched the Guru's feet. We laid his body and head on one of the bullock carts, piled bales of cotton over it and turned our carts around. The same storm that had driven us into Chandni Chowk drove us backwards through the same bazaar, out of Ajmeri Gate to Paharganj. When we arrived at Rikabganj, the wind suddenly dropped and the dust disappeared. The night had come on.

Lakhi Rai's wife and daughters-in-law had made a pyre of sandalwood in the centre of their courtyard. We placed the Guru's body on it. All the family touched his feet. Lakhi Rai said a short prayer and lit the pyre. His wife brought out a shawl and wrapped the Guru's head in it. 'Take this to the Guru's son in Anandpur,' she said, handing me the bundle. 'The Guru will take you there in safety.'

*

As I went up the ridge, I looked back to make sure no one was following me. In the distance the flames of the funeral pyre in the courtyard of Lakhi Rai's house flickered. The storm had gone as suddenly as it had come and the sky was clear and full of stars. It was a few days after the full moon. I quickened my steps. By the time the moon came up, I was many *kos* from Dilli on the way to Anandpur.

At last the Guru had performed the great miracle. He had given a carrier of shit and stinking carcasses the privilege of carrying his sacred head in his arms. Hereafter anyone who called me unclean would have his mouth stuffed with dung. I was now Jaita Rangreta the true son of the Guru.

9

Bhagmati

I haven't seen Bhagmati in weeks and, worse, haven't even thought of her—so engrossed have I been in a series I've been doing for Doordarshan TV entitled: 'The Delhi you do not know.' I began with monuments in the suburbs of Mehrauli—the tombs of Altamash, Sultan Ghari, Balban and Jamali-Kamali. I threw in a few dilapidated mosques and some *baolis*. The appearance on Doordarshan has brought me an unexpected bonus—letter from a lady saying she had watched the programme and would like to meet me. She has signed herself by her first name, Kamala. Neither Miss nor Mrs nor anything else about who she is—what age or what she does for a living. The address is the room number of an army mess. Usually women who write letters to men they do not know turn out to be serious-minded bores. However, something impels me to write back to say that I would be happy to meet her. And this is when I think with some guilt of Bhagmati.

I spend an hour or two in the library of the India International Centre where I have asked Kamala to meet me. Since she knows what I look like she should find it easy to locate me.

Though I usually love flipping through the magazines and papers at the Centre, this morning I find I cannot keep my mind on what I'm reading but keep looking up at every woman who comes in. Will she be fifteen or fifty? Fat or slim? Fair or dark? And what the hell does she want to get to know me for? To bore me or to get laid?

At last she comes in and walks straight towards me, holds out her hand and says with a smile, 'I am Kamala.'

I get up, take her hand and reply, 'Pleased to meet you. Let's have some coffee in the garden.'

She is small, dark and looks in her thirties. We find a table, I order coffee for two. I open the dialogue: 'What is your full name, Kamala what?'

'You are very curious. Okay, I am Kamala Gupta, wife of Brigadier Gupta. We have three school-going children — one girl, two boys.'

I express surprise. 'Mother of three! You look young enough to be in college.'

She beams with pleasure. 'Not as young as you think. I am over forty. Been married more than twenty years. People mistake my daughter to be my younger sister.'

'Are you a Delhi girl?'

'No. I am Tamil. My husband is from Delhi itself.'

The 'itself' is her first Indianism. It could as well have been 'Delhi only.'

'Convent of Jesus & Mary, Miranda House and arranged marriage,' I guess.

'Wrong on all three. Modern School and St Stephen's College where I met my husband and eloped with him. Later forgiven by parents on either side for intercaste, interstate marriage. He is a Bania, I am a Mudaliar. He speaks Hindi; I speak Tamil. We speak English. Our children speak all three.'

'Sounds wonderful! Where is the rest of the family?'

'My husband is posted at a non-family station. The children are in boarding schools in Mussoorie. I've been allowed to stay on in the army mess. We get together during vacations.'

There is a lull in the dialogue. I try to size her up. She is lost in the depths of her coffee-cup. 'A paisa for your thoughts,' she says breaking the silence. 'I can tell you what you are thinking, why did this woman want to meet me?'

'You tell me.'

'Well, I have nothing much to do. Can't stand army wives. So I thought I'd write a book or something. Your programme on TV gave me an idea. Why not something on Delhi and its monuments? What do you think?'

'There are hundreds of them on the market.'

'Maybe. But they are all the same. None of them have those

things you were showing on your programme. I know many old *havelis* lost in tiny lanes nobody knows about. My husband was born and brought up in Parathe Vali Gali. Ever heard of it?

'Heard yes, seen never.'

'There you see, even you don't know! Ever heard of Gali Namak Haraman? I bet you haven't. You show me what I have not seen. I'll show you what you have not seen. And we do a book together. What do you say?' She puts out her hand as her part of the deal. I take it as my part of the deal. 'Done.' And give it a gentle squeeze. It is firm but leathery.

We chat for an hour. It seems as if we have known each other for years. I have little doubt that I can extract more out of the deal.

I drop her outside the army mess, an old building raised during the war to house American G.I.s. She agrees to meet me at the Centre the following Sunday to be driven round the sites I had shown on TV. 'Better the Centre than the mess. Too many prying eyes and bitchy wives,' she says as she waves good-bye.

*

She is there waiting for me at the gate with a small basket containing two thermos flasks and a box of sandwiches. 'Much better to carry your own stuff than go to those crowded cafeterias or *dhabas*,' she explains.

I give her a miniature jade Ganapati that I had lying with me. 'It is my good luck totem. I always carry one in my wallet. This one is to see nothing goes wrong with our friendship.'

She cradles the figurine in both her palms and kisses it. 'Thank you. I am sure it will bring me luck.'

As we pass the Qutub Minar, she remarks: 'I believe that the latest research has proved that this is a Hindu monument.'

'So is the Taj Mahal and the Red Fort,' I add sarcastically. 'Where did you pick up this bullshit. All these buildings have the names of the builders and the dates of completion inscribed on them in Arabic. You've been reading Hindu fascist propaganda?'

We spend the morning in Mehrauli. I park the car alongside Auliya Masjid. We walk along the Shamsi Talab, past Jahaz Mahal into the crowded streets. I take her to the mausoleum of Qutubuddin Bakhtiyar Kaki and show her the tombs of Mughal kings in the neighbouring graveyard. At Emperor Bahadur Shah's tomb I tell her about the execution of Banda Bairagi and 700 of his Sikh followers. 'He was ordered to kill his own child before they hacked him to pieces, limb by limb.'

'When?'

'Sunday, 19 June 1716.'

'You must hate Muslims,' she mutters. 'You remember the day and date as if it was your birthday.'

'No, I don't hate Muslims.' I protest. 'Banda had slaughtered them by the thousands before they caught him and his band. Those were savage times.'

I take her to Jamali-Kamali's mosque. She pours out the coffee, gives me a sandwich. She takes out a notebook and a ball-point pen. 'Tell me of the places we've seen this morning. If I don't write it down I'll forget everything.'

I go over the itinerary while she makes notes and sips her coffee. When I come to Banda, she repeats, 'I don't believe you like Muslims.'

Once again I lodge a protest: 'Most of my friends are Muslims, not Hindus or Sikhs.'

'You couldn't possibly like someone like Aurangzeb—a man who killed his brothers and nephews and put his father in prison. He destroyed Hindu temples and had one of your Gurus executed. How can you like a character like that? If you ask me, all our Hindu-Muslim troubles of today can be traced back to Aurangzeb.'

'My dear young lady, you've been properly brainwashed! You've never been told that this Aurangzeb also gave grants to build Hindu and Sikh temples.'

'That's news to me. You've just made that up.'

She asks to be dropped at the corner of the road near the army mess.

Our next tour is to be in the city where she will act as my guide and mentor. This time I give her another miniature

Ganapati made of crystal! 'This is to double your luck.' This time she gives me a kiss on my beard. We drive up to the Red Fort where I park the car. She takes me into Chandni Chowk. 'I can't take you through Dariba or the Parathe Vali Gali; I have many in-laws living there who may want to know what I am doing with a Sardarji.'

'And I don't want to be shown round Lal Kuan. I have friends living there.' I reply.

'Friends in Lal Kuan? What kind of friends?' she asks suspiciously.

'Very respectable, very likeable. I'll tell you about them in course of time.'

We branch off onto Nai Sarak, into a narrow lane. She points out several old *havelis* and shrines beneath *peepal* trees. At places the stench from open sewers is overpowering. Stray cows, hawkers, and scooters and passers-by make the going difficult. It gives me the excuse to occasionally hold her hand. She presses mine whenever I do so. There is no want of response.

After an hour-and-a-half of wandering through winding lanes we find ourselves behind the Jamia Masjid. We cross the *maidan* to get to the parking lot outside the Red Fort.

'Drop me at Connaught Circus,' she says. 'I have some shopping to do.'

I know it is an excuse to avoid being seen with me by the other residents of the mess. I am somewhat puzzled by her attitude. When I suggest she comes to my apartment, she says no firmly, though in our conversations she makes no secret of her being unhappy with the life she is leading. 'What kind of life does an army wife lead? The husband is away for weeks and months. When he gets back for a few days he can think of nothing besides sex. He gets as much of it as he wants whether his wife likes it or not. And then he is off again, while the wife is left twiddling her thumbs.'

If it isn't going to be my apartment and she is not going to let me come to her room, where in Delhi can we find a place where we can do what we are heading for? The initiative has passed out of my hands to hers. But I am determined to bring matters to a head. If she says no, I will drop her.

Our third rendezvous at the Centre is on a warm October afternoon. I give her yet another Ganapati—this one made of ivory. 'How many Ganapatis are you going to give me?' she asks as she kisses me on the lips. We drive away towards Purana Qila.

'You know what I'd really like to give you?' I ask her in the car.

'No, tell me.'

'What I'd really like to give you is a baby.'

She does not bat an eyelid but keeps looking straight ahead of her. After a while she replies, 'That may take some doing as I had my tubes sewn up when I had the third child. But there is no harm in trying, is there?'

How does one cope with a woman like this one? I flush with embarrassment. I grab her hand and kiss it. We do not bring up the subject all afternoon as we trudge round the monuments. On the way back she asks me to take her to the INA market to buy fruit and provisions. 'You stay in the car,' she orders. 'I won't take very long.'

I know she doesn't want to be seen with me in the market which is frequented by government officials and armed forces personnel. She comes back after a few minutes followed by a coolie carrying apples, tins, biscuits and cheese in a basket. He dumps the basket on the rear seat. This time she asks me to drive to the mess. 'I can't carry all that stuff up to my room,' she explains. 'You can have a quick drink with me.'

I carry the basket and follow her up the stairs and down a verandah. She has the last room. She unlocks the door and switches on the light. I can see she is relieved that no one has seen us come in. 'I don't mix with my neighbours,' she says. 'They are a nosey lot.'

I dump the basket in her kitchenette. She puts some of her purchases in a tiny fridge and others on the shelf. 'I am afraid all I can offer you is army rum. Can't afford anything else. With soda or water?'

'I've never had it. Give it to me on the rocks.'

It is a sparsely furnished bed-sitter. She sits on her bed; I on the sofa. I take a sip of the sweet, smelly rum. It is raw, rough and heady. I cannot think of what to say. I break the silence with the first thing that comes to mind. 'The other day you said something about Aurangzeb being a bigot. That's not how Muslim historians see him. Even the ordinary Muslims of today think he has been unfairly maligned.'

She laughs. 'Can't you think of anything more interesting to talk about with a woman than a dead emperor?'

'I could say how lucky I am being in the company of an attractive woman. But where will that get me?'

'You know very little about me. Not even how attractive I can be. You've not even tried to find out,' she says. She removes her sari *pallau*, undoes the clasp of her blouse and exposes her breasts. 'Have you seen anything like these before? And on a woman who has suckled three children?'

I certainly had not. Ebony black, perfectly shaped and taut as that of a virgin of sixteen. Blacker nipples pointing directly at me. 'You have the most perfectly shaped bosom I've ever seen the pictures of nudes included,' I say. I have a strong urge to get up and sit beside her. She notices my hesitation. 'Feel them. Nothing flabby about me.'

I go and sit beside her. I run my palms over her bosom; they are firmer than any I have ever encountered. I lay her head on her pillow and run my tongue round her nipples. 'This is coming in your way,' she says removing my turban from my head. My long hair spreads over her face. She pulls me down by it and presses my head closer to her bosom... I stop for a breather and take a look at her face. She has closed her eyes and is breathing heavily. As I press my lips on hers she opens her mouth to entangle her tongue in mine. My hand goes reconnoitring over her buttocks and then between her thighs. 'Come inside and give me the baby you promised,' she murmurs.

I do her bidding. She is a quick comer. It is all over in a matter of seconds. I go back to my rum on the rocks. She gets up, plucks a cigarette from her bedside table and lights it. 'Now that we've got this off our minds, you can tell me about Aurangzeb,' she says.

10

Aurangzeb Alamgir: Emperor of Hindustan

In the name of Allah, the Beneficent, the Merciful and in the name of His Messenger, the Refuge of the World, I, Abdul Muzaffar Mohiuddin Mohammed, on whom Allah in His Divine wisdom bestowed the sovereignty of the Empire of Hindustan, pen this brief account of the ninety years of his life and forty-eight years of his reign. I do this so that Allah who is just will punish those who have transgressed against truth in writing about me. And may He forgive His humble servitor for presenting his side of the story in his own words.

This sinner, full of iniquities, was born in Dohad, a small town in the province of Gujarat. A poet composed for us the title *Aftab-e-Alamtab* meaning the Sun-whose-Radiance-would-take-the-World-in-its Embrace. Another bard composed the chronogram: *Gauhar-e-Taj-Muluk-Aurangzeb* meaning Aurangzeb-a-Pearl-in-the-Emperor's-crown. The letters of both these titles when added up gave the year of our birth 1027 Hijri corresponding to 1618 of the Christian calendar. We were born on the 15th day Zi'qad (3 November) under the dual signs of Libra and Scorpio. Astrologers predicted that our character would partake of the qualities of both: justice and mercy from the scales; and from the scorpion which carries venom in its tail, tenacity of purpose and the power to destroy those who dared to trample on our rights.

At the time of our birth our Sire, then known as Prince Khurram, was Viceroy of the Deccan and his Sire, Jahangir, Emperor of Hindustan. Our royal mother who reposes in the peace of the marble mausoleum in Agra named after her as the Taj Mahal, bore fourteen children in fourteen years of happy conjugation. Seven of these children were summoned to paradise by Allah. Of the seven who were permitted to sojourn in the world, the eldest, Jahanara, was followed by Dara Shikoh, Shuja and Roshanara Begum. This creature of dust was the fifth surviving child and the third son of our parents. After us came Murad. Gauhar Ara made her entrance into the world the same day as our revered mother took leave of it on 7 June 1631.

Since the memory of mortals begins to accumulate only after the sixth or the seventh year, we remember little of our childhood. We were told later that our grandfather, Emperor Jahangir, being for some reason displeased with our father, had our elder brother Dara Shikoh and ourselves taken as hostages to reside with him at Lahore. We were then eight years old.

The Emperor appointed men of wisdom and piety to be our teachers. Mir Mohammed Hashim Gilani and Aitmad Khan taught us the sacred word of Allah, the traditions of our holy Prophet (on Whom be peace). We were also taught Persian, Turki, Hindi and the art of calligraphy. We were content to learn whatever was considered worthy of learning. Indeed what more is there to learn than the word of God and the precedents of His chosen Messenger! However, Dara Shikoh preferred reading the books of infidels and holding discourses with heretics. He gave up saying his prayers and fasting during Ramadan. On one of his fingers he wore a ring with the word *prabhu* inscribed in Devnagri characters. He also bestowed patronage on men who created the likenesses of living things on paper and stone, singers, lute-players, dancers and such others. The gift of intellect that God had given him he magnified into something of his own making. He became haughty in his manner, pompous in his speech and arrogant towards the *omarah*. Of such it has been truly said: 'If the blanket of man's fate has been woven black, even the waters of Zam Zam and Kausar cannot wash it white.'

As often happens in families, some members were closer to each other than to others. Our father's favourite children were the two eldest, Jahanara Begum and Dara Shikoh, and the two were perforce drawn closer to each other than to any of their other brothers or sisters. Although we maintained equal affection towards all our kin, Roshanara sought our company more than that of her other brothers. Likewise the youngest, Gauhar Ara, attached herself to Murad.

Our father, Shah Jahan, when he became Emperor of Hindustan in October 1627 once spoke of his four sons in the following words: 'Dara Shikoh has made himself an enemy of good men; Murad has set his heart on drinking; Shuja has no good trait except contentment. The resolution and intelligence of Aurangzeb prove that he alone can shoulder the burden of ruling India. But he is physically weak.'

We had seen only fifteen summers when we proved to the world that just as our heart did not lack resolution our arms did not lack strength. In the early hours of one morning, when the sun had only made its presence known to the minarets of the Royal Mosque, a vast concourse assembled along the sandbanks of the river to watch a fight between two elephants—Sudhakar armed with spearlike tusks and Surat Sundar which, despite its tusks being removed, was as big as its adversary. The beasts had been fed on hashish. After entangling with each other for some time, Sudhakar, goaded by its mahout and angered by the yelling of the people, suddenly wrenched itself free, turned upon the crowd and crushed many people under its mighty feet. Everyone except us fled in panic and terror. Seeing us alone, Sudhakar charged towards us. We held our horse in check. As the maddened elephant bore down upon us we struck its forehead with our spear with such force that it was stunned to a halt. However, with a swipe of its trunk it knocked down our horse beneath us. We rose to our feet, drew our sword and slashed its trunk. By then others, including Shuja and Raja Jai Singh, galloped up and attacked the beast. The other elephant, Surat Sundar, came back into the fray as well and chased Sudhakar off the ground. His Majesty chided us for our rashness. We replied: 'Death drops the curtain even on emperors; that is no dishonour. The shame lay in what our brother did.' Since Shuja had done whatever he could, it was apparent to everyone that our words were aimed at Dara Shikoh for he had behaved like a coward. His Majesty pretended as if he had not heard us. He had us weighed against gold coins which he presented to us and bestowed on us the title of *Bahadur* (the brave). A few months later he appointed us governor of the Deccan. Dara Shikoh's heart became heavy with envy.

At the age of seventeen we were married to Dilras Bano Begum, daughter of Shah Nawaz Safawi. The following year Murad, then only fourteen, married Dilras Bano's younger sister and so, besides being our brother, he also became our brother-in-law. Though we were in the prime of youth, and youth has its compulsions, we wasted little time on the nuptial couch. Living in camp amongst our comrades-in-arms became us more than dallying with the ladies of the harem. Gilani Sahib, our teacher, had impressed upon us that a ruler should always be on the move; being in one place gives the impression of repose and repose brings a thousand calamities. We realized early that it is bad for kings as it is for water to remain in the same place; stagnant water goes putrid and a stagnant king's power slips out of his hands. Unlike other monarchs of Hindustan and the nobility of the times, no more than five women enjoyed our intimacy; they produced ten children from our seed. Only one of these women we really and truly loved but her sojourn was brief and bore no fruit.

*

We were thirty-five years old. The searing heat of summer had given way to the season of dark clouds, cool breezes and rain. We had gone to call on our aunt at Burhanpur and were strolling in her deer park along the banks of the river Tapti. We heard the laughter of young girls at a swing and stopped where we were in order to save them embarrassment as they were unveiled. The girls began to sing in chorus. We caught some words of their song which was about a young bride pining for her groom. They were singing in *Raga Megh Malhar* which was appropriate for the time and the season. One voice rose above the others; dulcet, clear it seemed to spread over the verdant greenery like drops of dew glittering under a morning sun. Our feet were drawn towards the voice. The girls fled from our presence but the voice stayed. Till then only our ears had been bewitched. What we saw bewitched our eyes as well: a young girl clad in diaphanous white, her jet black hair hanging down to her waist, her hands clasping the bough of a tree loaded with mangoes—exposing her chemise bursting outward. She continued to sing as she swayed and regarded us with her large gazelle-like eyes. We stood rooted to the earth a few footsteps from this apparition of matchless beauty. The girl leapt up, plucked a mango from the branch and tossed it towards us. It hit us on our heart and we felt we had been struck by lightning. Then the girl turned and ran away into the palace. 'Allah be praised!' we exclaimed. 'Is that a mortal or a houri from paradise!' One of our companions who had joined us replied. 'Sire! Allah forgive me if I am wrong but that could be no other than your aunt's slave, Hira Bai. Her fame as the comeliest of women and a nightingale amongst singers is the talk of the Deccan.' We tarried for a while to recover our composure. But when we paid our respects to our *mausi* (mother's sister) Saliha Bano, she could read our misfortune in our countenance and in the confusion of words in which we addressed her. We implored her assistance to give us our heart's desire. 'Take all the women of my harem and in return give me Hira Bai,' we beseeched her. Saliha Bano said she would do anything, even sacrifice her life for us but was afraid of what her husband Saif Khan, governor of Burhanpur (who was notorious for his ungovernable temper), might say. Our friend and companion, Murshid Quli Khan, undertook to murder Saif Khan. But we restrained him from acting against the *shariat* law. Instead Murshid simply went to Saif Khan and put our proposal as bluntly as he could. Saif Khan pondered the matter and then informed our aunt that he would exchange Hira Bai for one of our slaves, Chattar Bai.

It was thus that Hira Bai was brought in a palanquin to our harem. For many months we thought of nothing but her and sought no company save hers. From her hand we even took a cup of wine which had hitherto been an abomination to us— and would have as gladly sipped it even if it had been deadly poison. She herself forbade us to do so. Stories of our infatuation were carried by tale-bearers to Dara who further poisoned our father's ears against us. He was reported to have told the Emperor:' See the piety and abstinence of that hypocritical knave! He has gone to the dogs for the sake of a wench of his aunt's household.'

Allah in His infinite wisdom decided that we were straying from the path of duty and took Hira Bai from us. We buried her in Aurangabad beside a tank full of our tears.

Our father was given to lending his ear to gossip and the prattle of soothsayers. It was narrated to us that once an imposter who passed for a holy man gave His Majesty two apples and said that as long as the smell of the fruits remained on his hands no illness that afflicted him would take a fatal course. When asked which of his sons would destroy his dynasty the knave is said to have replied, 'Aurangzeb.' We who had kissed our father's hands many times never detected the smell of apples on them. And far from destroying the kingdom, we extended its domains beyond the furthest limits known to our forefathers. Nevertheless our father's mind was poisoned against us; it was reported to us that to mock our fair complexion and our character he had described us as 'a white snake'.

An incident confirmed our suspicions. One evening Jahanara Begum, while carrying a candle to her bedchamber, stumbled and let the flame touch her muslin garments. She suffered grievous burns; two maidservants who took her in their embrace to smother the fire were burned to death. Dara Shikoh delayed sending the news to us. Consequently, it was only after a month that we were able to reach Agra. His Majesty was out of countenance with us and relieved us of the governorship. All our explanations were ignored. Ultimately we wrote in anguish: *If His Majesty wishes that of all his servants I alone should pass my life in dishonour and at last perish in an unbecoming manner, I have no recourse but to obey ... Ten years ago I realized this fact; I knew my life was a target.*

Later the same year Dara Shikoh invited us to his palace by the river Jamna. Having been slighted by him many times we preferred to keep our distance from him by staying near the entrance, whereupon he incited the emperor to rebuke us about the necessity of keeping our rank. We were forbidden from attending court for seven months.

This was only one among many such incidents. The emperor put us away as if we were not of his seed. To our brothers and their sons he sent presents of gold and jewellery on their birthdays; never to us or our children. Recommendations we made for promoting loyal servants were turned down. We were accused of misappropriating the wealth of Golconda which had fallen into our hands and even of eating Deccani mangoes meant for the emperor's table. It was reported to us that, while on a visit to Delhi, the emperor had recognized Dara as the future King of Hindustan. He appeared in the *darbar* wearing a robe of honour conferred by the emperor and sat on a gold chair placed beside the peacock throne. If Dara is speaking the truth, which is seldom, His Majesty apparently said to him: 'My child, I have made up my mind not to do any important business or decide on any great undertaking henceforth without your knowledge and without consulting you first... I cannot sufficiently thank Allah for blessing me with a son like you.'

As we have said before, and will say a hundred times, we had no desire for power or kingship. But, as our teachers had often reminded us, since Allah in His wisdom had given us birth in a dynasty of kings, it was our duty to serve humanity and to spread Islam by making mankind bear witness to the true faith. Gilani Sahib used to say that Hindustan was like a piece of bread given by the Bestower of Gifts to our ancestors Taimur, Babar, Humayun, Akbar, Jahangir and Shah Jahan. He used to impress upon us that though Allah was bountiful, it was the duty of those who received His bounty to extend the domain of Islam. 'Make the best of life,' he said, 'but remember it is transitory: only the name of Allah is immortal.'

> When in the garden enjoy every moment,
> Every moment of every day.
> Spring passes into summer, summer into autumn,
> And the flowers of henna
> Shall wither away.

While Dara Shikoh clung to his father's apron at Delhi and Agra, we administered the Deccan, restored order in Balkh, Badakshan, Kandahar and Multan. We measured swords against the misguided Persians. We were continuously on the move from one field of battle to another. The only part of our life which never changed was the routine of our devotions. It mattered not to us where we were or how critical the battle, as soon as it was time for prayer we put aside our weapons and turned our face towards Mecca to pay homage to our Maker.

Misguided historians have written many falsehoods about the way we came to acquire sovereignty over Hindustan while our father Emperor Shah Jahan was still alive. They have maligned our name as a scheming self-seeker and a plotter. They forget that the holy book says; 'God is the best of plotters.' We were but the instrument of His design.

The stars and saints had foretold the shape of things to come. Our agent in the court of our father had informed us that once the emperor had asked a saint, who could read the book of future events, which of his four sons would sit on the peacock throne. The saint asked him the names of his sons.

'Dara Shikoh is the eldest,' replied the emperor.

'His fate will be the same as of his namesake Darius who fell to Alexander.'

'Shuja is the second.'

'Though his name means 'fearless' he is not without fear.'

'Murad is our youngest.' (His Majesty, as was his wont, often overlooked our existence).

'Though his name means ambition, he will not achieve it.'

'Then there is Aurangzeb.'

'He has been justly named for he alone is fit for the throne. Wisdom and fortune are closely connected to each other. He who lacks wisdom will have no fortune either.'

We were in Burhanpur when we received the news that His Majesty had been taken ill on 6 September 1657. Our agent in Shahjahanabad sent us a message in code saying that His Majesty had been unable to pass motions or urine for several days and the physicians attending on him despaired of his ruling Hindustan for much longer.

We instructed our agent to keep us posted on His Majesty's state of health and at the same time ordered our agents in the courts of our brothers to keep us informed of every move they made. In our letter praying for his speedy recovery, we sought His Majesty's permission to attend on him at Delhi.

His Majesty sent us a very curt note to say that rumour-mongers had exaggerated a minor stomach upset; that he was in perfect health and proceeding to Agra. At the same time our agent in Delhi informed us that the royal *hakeem*, on being given a handful of gold *mohurs*, had expressed the opinion that unless Allah performed a miracle His Majesty's sojourn in this troublesome world might soon be over. Our dear sister Roshanara Begum, who was in attendance on His Majesty, also sent us a cryptic message hinting at the machinations of our brothers and wishing us success.

We advised our brothers Shuja and Murad to behave in a manner becoming of the descendants of Taimur and Babar. They did not heed our counsel. First Shuja, who was in Bengal, proclaimed himself Emperor with the title Abul Fauz Nasiruddin Mohammed Taimur III, Alexander II, Shah Shuja Bahadur Ghazi. A few weeks later Murad, who was in Gujarat, proclaimed himself monarch of Hindustan with the title Maruwwajuddin and asked us to join him in the march to Agra. Being unable to govern his hot temper he soiled his hands by murdering his minister, Ali Naqvi, on suspicion of conspiring with Dara Shikoh. Our agent in Agra sent us news that Dara Shikoh had already made himself master of the Red Fort where His Majesty was convalescing and had opened negotiations with the infidel Rajputs to help him become the Emperor of Hindustan.

We pondered the matter for many days. We could not believe our brothers would behave in this unseemly manner. Dara Shikoh's pretensions disturbed us most. If he became king, the empire of Hindustan would cease to be Dar-ul-Islam and the work of our Mughal forefathers, and the Afghan and Turki monarchs before them, would come to nought.

There was another matter which caused much disturbance in our mind: the viciousness of sibling rivalry. We knew that kingship knows no kinship. No bridge of affection spans the abyss that separates a monarch from his sons; no bonds of affection exist between the sons of kings. Sired though they may have been by the same loins, lain in succession in the same womb and suckled the same breasts, no sooner were they old enough to know the world than they understood that they must destroy their siblings or be destroyed themselves.

Since the Mughals had ruled over a domain larger than that ruled by any other dynasty in the world, it was the Mughals who had spilt more royal blood than any other succession of monarchs. Our great ancestor Zahiruddin Babar had laid the foundation stone of the empire in Hindustan in 1526. His two sons, Humayun and Kamran, had then drawn their swords against each other. Allah had granted the throne to Humayun and so he took the light out of the eyes of his brother and sent him off to Mecca to die. When Akbar succeeded Humayun he disposed of Kamran's only son. Likewise Emperor Akbar's reign was disturbed by the revolt of his beloved son Salim Jahangir—who in his turn had to keep his own impatient son Khusrau in confinement. The same fate had befallen our father who had also to suffer his sc as Dara Shikoh and ourselves being taken hostage. When Allah bestowed the empire of Hindustan on our father, he was compelled to remove his own brothers Dawar Baksh and Shahryar along-with their male progeny. Truly does the prophet Jeremiah say: 'Fathers have eaten sour grapes and the children's teeth are on edge.'

Only one of us four brothers could sit on the peacock throne; for the other three it had to be the scaffold. The Hindvis summed it up in an aphorism; *taj ya takhta* (the crown or the gibbet). A kingdom is like a scabbard which can' hold only one sword at a time.

The ambition to be Emperor of Hindustan possessed Dara Shikoh like a fever; his ambition had been fed by assurances given to him by a mad charlatan, Sarmad, who went about the streets of Delhi without as much as a 'loin-cloth to clothe his nakedness. This Sarmad had proclaimed that Dara would be King of India.

Allah who knows the innermost secrets of our hearts knew that we had no thought of royalty when we responded to

Murad's request to join him on the march to Agra. Our only aim was to save the empire from falling into the hands of an enemy of Islam like Dara Shikoh.

Soon our worst fears were confirmed. The infidel Rajputs aligned themselves on the side of Dara Shikoh. His son Sulaiman Shikoh and the Rajput Jai Singh defeated Shuja near Benares. He sent another Rajput, Jaswant Singh of Jodhpur, against us and Murad. We routed his army and proceeded apace towards our goal. Dara Shikoh met us at Samugarh, ten miles from Agra. Once more our swords were crowned with success. While we gave our thanks to the Granter of Victories, Murad, as was his wont, took the daughter of the grape to bed and remained drunk for many days.

Even in the flush of victory we penned respectful words to our father, the Emperor: 'Obedience was my passion as long as power was vested in your venerable hands, and I never went beyond my limit, for which the all-knowing Allah is my witness. But owing to your Majesty's illness Prince Dara Shikoh, usurping all authority and bent upon propagating the religion of the Hindus and idolaters and suppressing the faith of the Prophet, had brought chaos and anarchy throughout the empire. Consequently I started from Burhanpur lest I should be held responsible in the next world for not providing a remedy for disorders.'

Our victorious armies arrived at Agra. Dara fled. Then Jahanara Begum sent us a note of remonstrance saying: 'Your armed advance is an act of war against your father. Even if it is directed against Dara it is no less sinful, since the eldest brother both by common law and common usage stands in the position of the father.' We felt it was time to kill the serpent of falsehood with the staff of truth. 'Dara is doing everything to ruin his younger brothers. Witness how he has crushed Shuja already,' we wrote in reply. 'He has poisoned the Emperor's ears against us.'

His Majesty, though old and sick, continued to weave the net of intrigue against us. He sent us gifts including the famous sword *Alamgir* and invited us to visit him in the fort. He flattered us for our piety and addressed us as 'His Holiness'. Our spies warned us that preparations were afoot to have the women of the harem assassinate us as soon as we set foot in the palace. We refused to walk into the trap laid for us and cut off the water channel that ran from the river into the fort. In his next communication, His Majesty pleaded for our sympathy: 'Why should I complain of the unkindness of fortune, seeing that not a leaf is shed by a tree without the will of Allah? Only yesterday I was master of 9,00,000 troops, and today I am in need of a pitcher of water! Praise be to the Hindus who offer water to their dead, while my devout Muslim son refuses water to the living!'

We ordered water to be sent to His Majesty but declined to call upon him till we were assured of our safety. When on 8 June 1658 the gates of the Red Fort were thrown open to us, we beseeched the emperor and Jahanara Begum to move into the palace with their retinue and ordered our trusted eunuch Etabar Khan (aptly named by its parents) to allow no one save our beloved sister Roshanara Begum to come and go whenever it pleased her.

Then we decided to go in pursuit of Dara Shikoh who had fled to Delhi. But we first had to deal with Murad. After the victories that Allah had granted us, he had lost his balance of mind. In his camp there was nothing but music, dancing, wine-bibbing and revelry. It became clear as daylight that if the reins of the empire were left in Murad's hands, the empire's chariot would soon be wrecked. We decided to let Murad retire to a place where he could drink and carouse to his heart's desire without any harm to the empire of the Mughals.

We also heard reports that while in his cups Murad not only foolishly boasted of having won the victories that Allah had bestowed upon us but had also confided to his drinking companions that after finishing with Dara and Shuja he would turn his attention to us. We did not allow such impious thoughts which poisoned our ears to poison our heart but resolved thereafter not to be misled by Murad's professions of affection and kept a watch on his actions.

We awaited Murad at Mathura, a city regarded as holy by the Hindus. When he arrived we invited him to our tent, and with our own hands offered him a cup of wine which we, as a pious Muslim, heartily abominated. Murad drank many cups. Slave girls in our employ massaged his besotted limbs and divested him of his weapons. On a sign made by us, the girls put gold handcuffs on his hands and feet. We ordered that he be given generous libations of opium and wine for as long as he lived. Then we proceeded on our march. We arrived in Delhi and took the management of the city's affairs in our hands.

Dara fled before our victorious army leaving the entire country at our feet. With our father too old and too ill to bear the burden of the empire and our brothers having proved inept we were compelled to overrule our heart's desire to retire to a hermitage and instead forced to take upon us the crown of thorns which adorns the heads of kings. This we did (after consulting astrologers) on 21 July 1658. We received felicitations from monarchs of distant lands: Iran, Bokhara, Mecca and Ethiopia.

It took us another year to remove the thorn of Dara from our side. Our troops pursued him through the Punjab, Rajasthan, Gujarat and in a skirmish at Seorai scattered his following as the breeze of autumn scatters dead leaves. Dara was finally captured trying to flee to Afghanistan. A few weeks after the celebrations of our first anniversary as King of Hindustan had ended, our loyal servant Malik Jeewan brought him, his sons and entourage in chains to Delhi.

We consulted the *ulema*. With one voice they replied that by the holy law the punishment for heresy was death. Our dear sister, Roshanara, equally related to Dara as she was to us, expressed the same opinion. Dara Shikoh begged us to pardon him.

'My brother and my king,' he wrote to us, 'my execution is an unnecessary preoccupation for your lofty mind. Grant me a house to live in, and a maid from my former retinue to attend to my needs, and I will devote my life in retreat to praying for your good.'

We did not wish to enter into controversy with Dara Shikoh. At the bottom of his petition for pardon we appended one line in Arabic: 'You usurped authority and you were seditious.'

The fate of Dara Shikoh excited the passions of the misguided citizens of Delhi. They wept in sympathy with him and pelted the loyal Malik Jeewan who had brought him to justice with pots full of urine and excreta. Though our heart was heavy with sorrow we again reminded ourselves that kingship knows no kinship and signed the warrant of death. He was separated from his son Siphir Shikoh and executed on the evening of 30 August 1659. His severed head was brought to us in the Red Fort for inspection. The next morning his headless body was paraded through the streets of Delhi before being interred in a vault of the tomb of our great, great-grandsire, Emperor Humayun.

Dara's son, Sulaiman Shikoh, who had fled into the mountains was likewise apprehended and brought in irons to Delhi. On the morning of 5 January 1661, he was led to our presence in the Diwan-i-Khas. We had not seen him for many years and were struck by his handsome and manly bearing. We had to remind ourselves that though the skin of the serpent may be beautiful, within it there is deadly poison. We explained to him the enormity of the crimes committed by his father and himself and ordered him to be sent to prison in Gwalior fort where he was executed.

We had yet to deal with the charlatan Sarmad who had falsely prophesied the crown to Dara Shikoh. Apart from going about naked in front of men and women alike his attachment to a Hindu boy had become scandalous. Although professing Islam, he was reported to have used expressions lowering the dignity of the Prophet. We summoned him to our presence and questioned him about his prophecy. The villain had the audacity to reply; 'God hath given him (Dara) eternal sovereignty!' We further asked him if it was true that he only recited half the *kalima*—'There is no God but Allah'—leaving out 'and Mohammed is His Prophet'. He replied:

The Mullahs say, Mohammed rose to the skies
But I say, 'God came to him'—the rest is lies!

Sarmad juggled with words: 'I am absorbed in the negative and hence have not yet arrived at the positive.' Questioned about his nakedness, he replied that the Prophet Isaiah also went about naked. We ordered him to be executed in front of the steps of the Royal Mosque in full view of the populace. It was later reported to us that his severed head acknowledged the truth by reciting the entire *kalima*.

While our father lived we decided to stay away from Agra. We had a small mosque built besides the Diwan-i-Khas so that we did not have to disturb the prayers of other Mussalmans by the screen that was provided for kings. It took us five years to complete it and we gave it the name Moti Masjid—because it did indeed look like a pearl without blemish. We spent many hours in this mosque praying and telling the beads of our rosary.

It was not written in the tablet of our fate to see our father. For many months he kept sending us letters accusing us of conduct unbecoming of a son and wickedness towards our brothers. We thought it was time to state the bitter truth. Our father, despite his predicament and his grey beard, was reported to be indulging himself in wine and carousal. 'Kingship means protection of the realm and guardianship of the people, not the enjoyment of bodily repose or lusts of the flesh,' we wrote. We also reminded him that after the way he had disposed of his collaterals when he ascended the throne, it did not befit him to point an accusing finger at us or threaten us with the wrath of Allah. To put an end to this pointless dialogue we wrote: 'If God had not approved of my enterprise, how could I have gained victories which are only the gift of God?'

In January 1666, our father was taken ill and at his desire his bed was placed in the octagonal Jasmine Tower from which he could gaze on the Taj Mahal. On the evening of the 22 January 1666, with the name of Allah on his lips, he passed out of this world into paradise.

Urgent affairs of state kept us in Delhi for two weeks. Then, as soon as we were able, we repaired to Agra and with our tears washed the sacred earth in which our parents were laid.

It was not till two years after our father had been summoned to paradise that we first took our seat on the peacock throne. We then felt we should fulfil the mission that we had been charged with by Allah. We ordered our commanders Mir Jumla, Shaista Khan and others to extend the domains of Islam to the furthermost corners of Hindustan. Our victorious armies marched eastwards to Chatgaon, northwards over the mountains to Tibet, westwards beyond Kabul and southwards beyond Karnatak. In turn we crushed the Jats, the Rajputs, mischievous sects of the Satnamis and Nanak Prasthas who had raised their heads against us. We ravaged the lands of the wily Marathas and forced their leader, Shiva, to pay homage to us. We levelled temples of idolatry to dust and raised mosques on their ruins. We imposed the *jazia* tax on non-believers to induce them to tread the righteous path. In everything we did, our only guide was the holy law of the *shariat*. We forbade the distillation of liquor and severely punished those we suspected to be under its influence. It was a common saying that when we ascended the throne there were only two men in all Hindustan, ourselves and the chief *qazi*, who did not drink. Within a few years we made drink a rarity. Since drinking was often indulged in to the accompaniment of dancing and singing, we forbade them too. We forced prostitutes and dancing girls to marry or leave our empire. Once when musicians and singers carried fake biers of corpses of music and dance, and accosted us as we were going for our Friday prayers, we told them to bury the corpses so deep that they would never rise again. Our Mussalman subjects were happy with our ordinances and acclaimed us as *Zinda Peer* (a Living Saint.)

We waged a ceaseless war against the infidel. Wherever he raised his serpentine hood we crushed it under foot. Most of our later years were spent in the Deccan contending with the mountain rats that Shiva had bred. We caught his son Sambha and sent him to eternal damnation. However, we realized that the land would not be purged of idolatry in our lifetime and exorted our sons to keep up the crusade.

Other kings would have treated the state treasury as their personal property and wasted it in extravagant living, women, wine, jewels and monuments. We looked upon ourselves as God's chosen custodian to use it for the good of the people. On ourselves we spent no more than the poorest of our subjects. We sewed prayer caps and made copies of the holy *Quran*: whatever we got for them in the market we spent on our food and personal raiment. How many monarchs who ruled empires as large as ours could claim to have lived like *dervishes* as we had done?

We had only three sisters left in our world. Roshanara, who had been closest to us, had of late shown indifference to our wishes and had been indiscreet in her behaviour towards strangers. Before we could fully remonstrate with her, Allah summoned her to His court. She had in her lifetime designed her own resting place. She used to spend many evenings in this garden and had a variety of exotic, fragrance-emitting shrubs planted alongside water channels and tanks. She had desired that her tomb should have the sky as its vault so that the dew and the rain that Allah sent down could refresh her remains. Her wishes were carried out.

We turned to Jahanara Begum and pleaded that now the people who had come between us had gone, she should show us the affection due from an elder sister to her brother. On the anniversary of our coronation we presented her with 1,00,000 gold pieces, fixed a pension of 1,700,000 rupees and invested her with the title of *Padshah* Begum. She agreed to share our loneliness and guide us with her counsel. When she was summoned by Allah we commanded that in all historical documents she should be referred to as *Sahibat-uz-Zamani*, because she was indeed the mistress of the age. In accordance with her wishes, she was buried near the tomb of Hazrat Nizamuddin Auliya. On the tombstone we had inscribed a Persian couplet she had composed:

Let green grass only conceal my grave:
Grass is the best covering for the tomb of the meek.

In the spring of the year AD 1706 when the last of our brothers and sisters, Gauhar Ara Begum, was summoned by Allah to His presence we knew it was our turn to fold up our prayer mat. We were in Ahmednagar when our health began to deteriorate. We realized that Ahmednagar was to be the end of our travels. Our beloved daughter Zeenat-un-Nissa, to whom Allah had given the gift of prayer (which she had translated into a large mosque in Delhi) and our ageing wife Udaipuri Begum ministered into needs. A hundred *hakeems* felt our pulse every day; but what can mortals and medicaments do against Allah's decrees? We divided our time between re-reading the tablet of our deeds in our mortal's existence of ninety lunar years, and what rewards and penalties awaited us on the day of judgement.

What now sorrowed us most was the treacherous path taken by the progeny of our own loins. Mohammad Sultan had earlier blackened his face by joining his uncle Shuja against us, and now Akbar went over to the infidels. Azam, to whom we had given Dara's daughter as wife, turned out to be a worthless braggart. We had to put him in prison for a year to keep him away from wine and to teach him to govern his temper. Our youngest, Kam Baksh, had neither ambition nor competence, but of all the slights that our children had aimed at us, none hurt us more than the conduct of our gifted daughter Zebu-un-Nissa to whom Allah had given the gift of poetry (she composed verse under the pseudonym 'Makfhi'). She encouraged her brother Akbar to carry on treasonable conduct against us and with a heavy heart we were constrained to order her to be detained in Salimgarh fort. She aimed her last barbed shaft at us:

> *I have experienced such cruelty and harshness in this land of Hind,*
> *I shall go and make myself a home in some other country.*

Saying which she went to the land of the dead.

We had reposed faith in our eldest-born, Muazzam. Even he betrayed our trust during our victorious campaigns against Bijapur and Golconda by treating with the enemy. We did not let our affection stand in the way of justice and had him put in prison and forbade him to either cut his hair or pare his nails or drink anything except water. We kept him in confinement for seven full years.

Came the summer of 1705. As we camped in village Devpur, on the banks of the river Krishna, a severe fever seized us. In our delirium we recited a quatrain of Shaikh Ganja:

> When you have counted eighty years and more,
> Time and Fate will batter at your door;
> But if you should survive to be a hundred,
> Your life will be death to the very core.

A nobleman attending our sickbed added the last lines:

> In such a state lift up your heart:
> remember
> The thought of God lights up a dying ember.

We had little will to tarry longer in the world and the succession of fevers that ravaged us confirmed our hope that before long Allah would summon us. In one of these feverish bouts we composed another couplet:

> A moment, a minute, a breath can deform,
> And the shape of the world assumes a new form.

We thought it proper to address words of counsel to our errant sons. To Azam we wrote: 'I came alone and I go as a stranger. I do not know who I am, nor what I have been doing. The instant which has passed in power has left only sorrow behind it. I have not been the guardian and protector of the empire. Life, so valuable, has been squandered in vain. God was in my heart, but I could not see Him. Life is transient, the past is gone and there is no hope for the future...I fear for my salvation, I fear my punishment. I believe in God's bounty and mercy, but I am afraid because of what I have done...'

And to Kam Baksh: 'Soul of my soul...I am going alone. I grieve for your helplessness; but what is the use? Every torment I have inflicted, every sin I have committed, every wrong I have done, I carry its consequences with me. Strange that I came into the world with nothing, and now I am going away with this stupendous caravan of sin! Wherever I look, I see only God... I have sinned terribly and I do not know what punishment awaits me...'

These were not words written by an old man who feared death when he knew his end to be near but who feared that he was taking leave of life without fulfilling his mission. We saw the infidel Marathas, Rajputs, Jats and Sikhs rising in arms all over Hindustan. And we saw how feeble of mind and purpose were the progeny we were leaving behind us. We knew that after we were gone the empire of the Mughals founded by Babar would begin to totter to its fall and only tumult remain: *Azma hama fasad baki.*

We had already chosen our place of rest, a simple, unadorned grave in the courtyard of the tomb of the saintly Shaikh Zainuddin at the foot of Daulatabad fort.

We knew our end was near. Our companions also understood that the time for farewell was nigh. They asked us if we would give away our elephants and diamonds in charity to ward off the final hour. Our tongue had lost its speech but we scribbled on a piece of paper that such practices were not becoming to Muslims. 'Give all you want out of the treasury to the poor. And build no mausoleums over my body,' we wrote. 'And carry this creature of dust quickly to the first burial place and consign him to the earth without any useless coffin.'

11

Bhagmati

All my life I have been tormented by ghosts. Since Delhi has
more ghosts than any other city in the world, life in Delhi can
be one long nightmare. I have never seen a ghost nor do I
believe they exist. Nevertheless for me they are real. I have
tried to overcome this 'ghostophobia' by exposing myself to
the dying and the dead, visiting cremation grounds and
graveyards. It has not helped very much. I come back feeling
àt peace with myself and imagine that I have exorcised the
fear. But no sooner does the day begin to die, than spirits of
the dead come alive. Doors open by themselves, curtains
rustle without any breeze and I feel the invisible presence of
dead people around me. The only one to whom I have
confessed these fears is Bhagmati because she believes in
ghosts. She is not sympathetic. She laughs and calls me *baccha*
(child) and adds, 'When I die, I will come to lie with you. Then
you will be free of this childish fear. But if I catch you making
love to someone else, I will never let you have one night of
sleep.' (She has not yet forgiven me for fucking Kamala, the
Brigadier's wife. But Kamala is gone now with her husband to
a family posting so Bhagmati is no longer as angry with me!).
Of the many encounters I have had with ghosts, there is one
I can never forget. This was some years ago. I was rung up
and told that my uncle was very sick and I should see him
before he died. This uncle had been dying for many years.
Asthma had reduced him to a bearded skeleton with large,
fiery eyes. He had been a kind of living ghost for a long time
and something told me I should keep away from his bedside.
But my morbid fascination with death, and wailing over the
dead, made me ignore my inner promptings and so presently

I found myself in a room full of solicitous relatives seated round the sick man's bed. Some were praying, others whispering to each other. He was reclining against a bolster with his head tucked between his knees. His wife sat beside him holding a spittoon full of phlegm. He began to cough— a long never-ending gurgle—then raised his head. His wife held the spittoon under his chin and yellow, pus-like phlegm drooled down his black beard into the receptacle. The wife wiped his beard with a towel and told him I had come to see him. He fixed his large eyes on me without a trace of recognition. Then he lowered his head between his knees. A minute later he fell sideways with his eyes and mouth wide open. He was dead.

My aunt slapped her forehead with both her hands and screamed. '*Hai*! I am dead! People, I have become a widow!' She smashed her glass bangles against the bedpost. Others came crowding round to comfort her. Someone closed the dead man's eyes and mouth, tied a band round his chin and stuffed wads of cotton in his nostrils. The wailing continued for some time followed by the loud chanting of prayer: 'There is One God. He is the Supreme truth,' etc. etc.

It was monsoon time and the sky was clouded. But I dared not sleep alone in my apartment. I had no means of locating Bhagmati and persuading her to spend the night with me. I asked Budh Singh to put my bed out on the lawn behind my apartment as the air-conditioner was out of order. The lawn was overlooked by other apartments and the comforting sound of human voices and lights from the servants' quarters drifted down to it. I fixed a mosquito net and lay down in the gauzy security it provided.

Despite all these measures I could not shut my eyes. Whichever way I tried I could see the dead uncle's eyes staring at me. The lights went out one by one. The human voices faded into an eerie silence. A grey moonlight spread over the sky. Owls screeched in the mulberry tree. I saw one flit across, dart down on to the road and carry off a mouse... Of their own volition my eyes had closed and I was re-living the scene of the death in the morning. The dead man came alive. With measured steps he walked across the lawn towards me, parted the flaps of my mosquito net and brought his face close to mine. I was petrified with terror. I lost my voice. Then a gurgle rose in my throat and burst out into a loud moan. The dead man shook me by the shoulder and exclaimed; 'Wah Guru! Wah Guru! It's only I, Budh Singh. It has begun to rain. Let me take your bed inside.'

I was bathed in a cold sweat. I saw the lights go up in the neighbouring apartment. A voice asked: 'What's the matter?'Budh Singh answered for me 'Nothing! He was having a nightmare.'

I went indoors, switched on the lights in all the rooms and told Budh Singh to go. I sank down in my armchair and began a silent argument with myself. I felt very foolish. I had made an ass of myself. Now Budh Singh would tell everyone how his sixty-year-old master had behaved like a frightened child.

I resolved to get the better of this stupid, irrational phobia. It was 3.30 a.m. I got into my trousers and walked out into the drizzle, determined to take the dead in my stride. I strolled down the deserted road to Lodhi Park. It had many tombs. I would sit on them I decided and say 'hullo' to the chaps lying buried underneath.

First I called on Mohammad Shah, the third ruler of the Sayyid dynasty who died in 1444. Big, octagonal-shaped mausoleum on a high plinth. I told him he had no business to be there because the park belonged to the Lodhis. He didn't say anything but the bats in the dome replied: 'He came here first; the Lodhis came later. And that fellow Sikandar Lodhi has even less right to be here because he spent more time in Agra than in Delhi.'

I went out into the drizzle again towards the Bara Gumbad, mosque built by Sikandar Lodhi. Beautiful dome! Exactly like the bosom of Kamala, the woman from the south, the land of coconuts: firmly rounded, with its taut nipple poking the sky. I walked round the mosque, sat on a dilapidated grave and examined the Sheesh Gumbad which was a few metres away. Its dome was a little less wanton. The surrounding frills of coloured tiles which looked like lace brassieres in the daytime were not visible in the grey moonlight. From the mosque to Sikandar Lodhi's tomb. My nerve began to fail me. The fellow was buried inside a square garden with high walls. I could not trust myself in the enclosure at night. What if some ghost blocked my exit?

I went up the steps and down again. I tried twice but both times I failed to go further than the entrance. 'Taken as visited,' I assured myself. In any case the fellow didn't like Delhi and I didn't have to bother with him. Besides it was his son Ibrahim Lodhi who let himself be defeated and killed by the Mughal, Babar, at Panipat. So no more honour was due to the Lodhis.

By now the eastern horizon had turned bright and the drongos were announcing the dawn. Early morning walkers were striding over the Athpula bridge. An open-air yoga class had assembled on the grass opposite Bara Gumbad. The living world was awake; the world of the dead had retired for the day.

12

Nadir Shah

Many years ago, when we shepherded our father's flocks of goats, ate the bread of humility and slept on a couch of sand we had a dream. We dreamt that from a shepherd we had turned into a fisherman and in our net we had trapped a fish with four horns. A fish, we knew, was the emblem of royalty. We also knew that it was in the nature of an empty stomach to produce illusions of grandeur. Nature provides that a man who slaves all day should spend the hours of the night in a palace full of houris whereas a king who wields the sceptre by day should have his sleep disturbed by nightmares of rebellion and assassination. Thus does Allah dispense justice; to one man He gives pleasure by day, misery by night; to another He gives travail from sunrise to sunset, the joys of paradise from sunset to sunrise.

However, the dream remained embedded in our memory. When we became ruler of Isphahan we consulted a seer who had mastered the science of interpreting dreams. A fish, he confirmed, was indeed the emblem of royalty, and its four horns symbolized four kingdoms. In short, Allah had destined us to rule over four domains. We were ruler of Isphahan and had become *Padishah* (Emperor) of Iran. Afghanistan would soon yield to us. What could the fourth kingdom be save Hindustan?

We were besieging the city of Kandahar when we had a second dream. We dreamt that Hazrat Ali Murtaza came to us and with his own blessed hands girdled our waist with the all-conquering sword, *Zulfiqar*. We pondered this dream. We recalled that when someone had asked him: 'How far is it from the east to the west?' The Blessed One had replied: 'A day's journey by the sun.'

'Tahmas Quli Khan,' we said to ourselves, 'the road to Delhi beckons you!' And so it came to pass. A few days later we received an invitation to come to Delhi. It was not from Nasiruddin Mohammed Shah, who was then seated on the throne of the Mughals, but from two noblemen of his court— Asaf Jah Nizam-ul-Mulk, who was governor of the Deccan, and Saadath Khan, who was governor of an equally important province eastward of Delhi known as Avadh. The secret manner in which the invitation was delivered to us, and the way it was worded, convinced us that its authors knew the art of impregnating sentences with more than one meaning. We said to ourselves: 'Nadir Shah, you have ruled over men long enough to know the art of striking the heads of serpents with the hand of your foe!'

We use the word 'foe' for the Mughal because he had shown grave discourtesy towards us. He neglected to maintain commerce between his court and ours, was negligent in answering our letters and had even detained our envoys in Delhi. And what could better describe men like Nizam-ul-Mulk and Saadath Khan who, while eating their master's salt, were plotting for his downfall than the vile serpent which crawls on the ground but is ever ready to bite the man who stands above it?

On important matters we deemed it wise not to dilute our judgment by watering it with the advice of lesser men. We dipped the pen of diplomacy in the ink-well of our own interests and had the reply written on the parchment of stratagem. We neither accepted nor rejected the invitation; we only enumerated the difficulties we would encounter on the way to Delhi. The deep defiles of the Sulaiman and Hindu Kush mountains through which we would have to traverse, the warlike tribes of the Afghans and Pathans that we would have to contend with, the ill-will that the *subedars* of Kabul and Lahore had against us. We ended our epistle with a reference to the powerful army that the Mughal Emperor was said to have under his command. The reply to our letter would tell us whether those who had invited us were conspiring to wield us as a sword in their hands or whether their fount of loyalty had been so poisoned by their sovereign's ill-use that they would become pliable weapons in ours.

We did not have to wait very long for their reply. They not only pledged assistance to us but also sent us copies of letters they had addressed to other *omarah* advising them to look upon us as their redeemer. They informed us that their monarch, 'His Imperial Majesty Nasiruddin Mohammed Shah employs his time in wine and women... The great heritage of the Mughals is being squandered and may soon pass into the hands of the infidel Marathas.'

Reports of Mohammed Shah's profligacy had come to our ears from other quarters. It had been reported to us that he was seldom without a mistress in one arm and a glass of wine in the hand of the other. He was known as 'Rangeela', the colourful monarch. Although he was said to be well-versed in Persian he had not heeded the admonition of Shaikh Saadi: 'Account as an enemy the passion which is between thy two loins.'

> *He whose wishes you fulfil will obey your orders*
> *But passion when obeyed will forever command.*

We took Kandahar and Ghazni and then the city of Kabul. The whole of Afghanistan, which was nominally a part of the Mughal's domains, yielded to us. We thought it best of address Mohammed Shah in the following words: 'Be it clear to the enlightened mind of Your High Majesty that our coming to Kabul, and possessing it ourselves thereof, was purely out of zeal for Islam and friendship for you. We never could have imagined that the wretches of Deccan (the infidel Marathas) should impose a tribute on the dominions of the King of Mussalmans. Our stay on this side of Attock is with a view, that, when these pagans move towards Delhi, we may send an army of our victorious Qazilbash to drive them to the abyss of hell... History is full of the friendship that has subsisted between the Kings of Iran and Your Majesty's predecessors. By Hazrat Ali Murtaza we swear that excepting friendship and concern for religion we neither had, nor have, any other interest. If you suspect the contrary you may. We always were, and will be, a friend of your illustrious house.'

Mohammed Shah did not reply to our letter. '*Ameen*,' we said to ourselves, 'but we will not allow an Islamic kingdom to be despoiled by heathens just because it has the misfortune to be ruled over by a man who thinks that paradise is a garden where fountains spout grape-juice and common harlots are as bewitching as houris.'

We sent another letter to Mohammed Shah. In this letter we stated our terms clearly enough to pierce his besotted skull. We told him that we would soon be taking the road to Delhi to put the House of the Mughals in order and to restore the Kingdom of Hindustan to Islam. Our price for so doing would be four crore rupees in silver and the ceding of four northern provinces of the Mughal empire to Iran. Our experience of Mohammed Shah's earlier conduct persuaded us to append a warning. 'We expect a reply within forty days,' we wrote.

Forty days went by. Then the whole year. Not only did we get no answer, but our envoy was not allowed to leave Delhi.

We ordered a general muster. Men were drawn to our ever-victorious standard as moths are drawn to a lamp and they were as willing to sacrifice their lives for us as winged insects are for the love of the flame. There were Qazilbashes and Turks and Georgians, Uzbegs, Afghans, Pathans and Biloches. We enlisted engineers and gunners from Inglistan, France and Italia. Very soon we had 1,25,000 men under our command.

On 6 November 1738, kettle drums were beaten and we started our long march to Delhi. It had already turned cold. In the valleys through which we passed the nights were bitter with frost. The tribes which inhabited the region between Kabul and plains of the Punjab, being robbers by nature, often looted our baggage. We would have liked to have taught them a lesson but the affairs of Hindustan demanded that we quicken our steps.

We arrived at the western mouth of the Khyber. We had been told that this pass was like a trap and that large bands of robbers had assembled on the mountaintops to prey on us.

We made a brief halt and joined our men for the *maghreb* prayer. As the sun was about to set we gave orders to strike camp and proceed forward. While the robbers slept in the warmth of their quilts we rode through the fifty miles of the treacherous defile with no light to guide us save that of the stars that twinkled in the clear, cold sky. By the time the robbers were rubbing their eyes to the rising sun we were on the outskirts of the city of Peshawar. We captured Peshawar without any difficulty.

We pressed on. We crossed the broad stream of the Indus after which this country is named and entered the vast champaign of the Punjab so named after the five (*punj*) rivers (*ab*) that flow through it. The land was flatter than any we had visited, but at that time of the year, not unpleasing to the eye. For many marches the snowcapped hills were visible towards the north and the west. How much more beautiful snows appear at a distance than when one has to wade through them!

The skies were as blue as lapis lazuli; the sun as warm as amethyst. The khaki plains were dotted with oases of green wheat, mustard and sugarcane. There was an abundance of game: partridges, peacocks and herds of deer. Many varieties of waterfowl swarmed over the ponds and rivers. We were told that tigers, panthers and leopards were also to be found in plenty. In the middle of these islands of prosperity were villages walled like fortresses. Most of the inhabitants—being Muslim—knew that we had come to save the country from the infidel Marathas and were friendly towards us. For provisions that we took from them we paid in silver and gold. If our men were found taking anything by force we had their heads chopped off; if they molested Indian women we had them castrated and gave their month's wage and their testicles to their victims.

Zakarya Khan, governor of Lahore, made a show of resistance before he came to us with the shawl of submission over his head. He pleaded that he had misunderstood our motives for coming to Hindustan. We knew he was lying. We recalled the saying of Hazrat Ali Murtaza: 'Accept his excuse who seeks your forgiveness,' and allowed him to kiss our feet and offer twenty lakh rupees towards the expenses of our troops.

We spent sixteen days in the pleasant surroundings of Shalimar Gardens, a few miles south of the city. The days began to get longer, the sun began to get warmer. At Shalimar the silk cotton trees burst into large red blossoms. Gardeners said that from the colour of the *simbal* (that was what the natives called it) one could foretell the heat of the summer to come; the brighter its fiery red the fiercer the sun's rays would be.

Our agents in Delhi informed us that Mohammed Shah had raised a huge army to impede our progress towards Delhi. We ordered our troops to resume march as we realized that if we tarried much longer in Lahore the spring would turn to summer and the heat become too oppressive for our warriors.

We followed our advance guard till we arrived at the village Tilauri where our tents had been pitched. A few musket shots away the Mughal army was entrenched between the town of Karnal and the canal named after one Ali Mardan Khan.

The next morning we rode out to see the disposition of the enemy's forces. He had indeed come in great strength— upwards of 3,00,000 men. Yet it was apparent that the Mughal was still a baby in the art of war. Despite being twice as numerous as us, and possessed of over 2000 war elephants, thousands of camels mounted with swivels, parks of artillery and innumerable cavalry, he had thrown high breastworks about his forces, and thus deprived himself of the power to strike at us. Allah had verily deprived him of sense and delivered him into our hands!

We ordered our mobile columns to cut off the Mughal's food supplies. Verily has the learned Saadi said: 'When a warrior is full, he will be brave in fight; but if his belly is empty, he will be brave in flight.' We let our enemy go hungry for a few days. When his stomach was empty we struck him at various points to create confusion in his mind. He fired his artillery in all directions without ever hitting us.

On the afternoon of 14 February 1739, driven by hunger,

the vast army that the Mughal had collected emerged from its earthworks to give us battle. First a wall of elephants was sent against us. We sent camels loaded with burning naphtha on their backs to meet them. The elephants took fright, turned tail and trampled over their own host. Before the Mughal could restore order in his ranks we sent our cavalry to charge him. Our lion-hunting warriors broke the lines of the enemy. In a two-hour engagement, 20,000 of the enemy were killed and many more taken captive. Among those mortally wounded was Samsamudaulah regarded as one of the pillars of the Mughal court. This nobleman was also reputed to be a patron of poets. We were truly sorry to hear of his death.

We allowed the dust of defeat to settle on Mohammed Shah's face before agreeing to receive him. And who did he send to plead for him but Asaf Jah Nizam-ul-Mulk, who had invited us to Hindustan! This man had been untrue to his master's salt; but as he had also become the instrument of our designs we bestowed on him a robe of honour and agreed to let Mohammed Shah lay the sword of submission at our victorious feet.

The following day Nasiruddin Mohammed Shah, Emperor of Hindustan, came to our presence. He feared that we might take his life and stopping outside our tent sent a eunuch in with a copy of the *Quran* as a pledge of our forgiveness. We kissed the Holy Book and asked our dear son, Prince Nasrulla Khan, to bring in the Mughal. Mohammed Shah entered our tent, bowed and placed his sword at our feet. We rose and embraced him. We told him to banish fear from his mind. 'Our policy towards our enemies is open war, not treacherous assassination,' we said.

He did not believe us. When food was laid before him, we saw the veil of suspicion drop over his frightened visage. We took his plate and placed ours before him. We did the same with the goblets of wine. To reassure him further, with our own hands we poured a cup of *kahwa* and handed it to him. Since kindness failed to kindle the flame of friendship in his breast we thought it best to give him some plain words of advice.

'It is strange that you should be so unconcerned and

regardless of your affairs that notwithstanding the fact that we wrote you several letters, sent you an ambassador to testify to our friendship, you should not think it proper to send us a satisfactory answer!' We paused for a reply but Mohammed Shah maintained a mute silence. We continued: 'You show no concern for your affairs; when we entered your empire you did not send an envoy to ask who we were, or what our design was! None of your people came with a message or salutation, nay, not even with an answer to our salutation to you!'

We pointed to him the errors he had committed in the conduct of the battle. 'You foolishly cooped yourselves up in your trenches, not considering that you could not remain within barricades without either water or grain. You have seen what has happened!'

The Mughal's head remained lowered in shame. We did not want to leave him with any misgivings of our motives for coming to Hindustan. 'Only your indolence and pride has obliged us to march so far,' we told him. 'We shall not take the empire from you. But we have been put to extraordinary expense; our men, on account of the long marches, are much fatigued, and in want of necessities. We must proceed to Delhi, and remain there for some days until our army is refreshed and the compensation that Asaf Jah Nizam-ul-Mulk has agreed to is made to us. After that we shall leave you to look after your own affairs.'

Mohammed Shah listened to us without as much as raising his eyes from our feet. We gave him permission to leave. We had it conveyed to him that his Empress, Malika-ul-Zamani, and his son Sultan Ahmed be sent as hostages to our camp.

We proceeded onwards to Delhi with the Mughal King following in our train. When we arrived outside the capital of the Mughals, we detached a posse of Qazilbash cavalry to escort the Mughal king to his palace and prepare the city to receive us.

Our camp was pitched in a suburb called Shalimar where the omarah had their pleasure houses amidst the greenery of massive banyan trees whose branches hung down to the earth. Here also were orchards of a fruit called the mango, much relished by the natives. At the time, they were in flower— barely visible clusters of pale green which attracted a pestilence of flies, bees and spiders. The mango tree was also the favourite abode of a black bird of the size of a crow called the *koel* which screamed incessantly all through the day. Besides mangoes, the orchards had a large number of guavas which were again not in season. How different spring was in our gardens in Khorasan and Meshed! There, when the new leaf burst through the brown of grapevine, the days and nights were filled with the melodious songs of nightingales. We said to ourselves, 'Allah! One day in Iran is worth a hundred in Hindustan.'

The next day we entered the city of the Mughals through the northern gate which opened into Lahori Bazaar. We left most of our army outside the city walls so that no untoward incident between our men and citizens would spoil our sojourn.

We rode through a succession of floral arches with words of welcome in Persian, *Khush Amdeed*, cunningly woven of roses, jasmines and marigolds. From the balconies women in veils showered rose-petals on us. These Hindvis certainly knew the art of flattery! The fragrance of flowers mingled strongly with the sharp smell of asafoetida and garlic which pervaded Lahori Bazaar. We passed a large mosque built, we were told, by one of the begums of Emperor Shah Jahan and named after her: Masjid Fatehpuri.

We turned into a broad street called Chandni Chowk. It had a water channel running in the centre and was lined with trees on either side. When we passed by the jewellers' quarters, known as Jauhari Bazaar, we were presented with a trayload of precious stones. Next we passed a newly built mosque. This, we were told, had been erected by Nawab Roshan-ud-Daulah the keeper of Mohammed Shah's treasury. Although it was small, its marble and gold spoke eloquently of the wealth of the treasury keeper. (We later learnt that Roshan-ud-Daulah was a notorious bribe-taker. As in Iran, so in Hindustan money-makers were also the builders of mosques).

Immediately following the mosque was the city *kotwali*,

with its jail and execution yard. And next to the *kotwali* was the flower-sellers' market, Phool-ki-Mandi. Here there were many patterns of floral decorations; the balconies on the opposite sides of the bazaar were linked with strings of garlands, making the bazaar appear like a tunnel of flowers. At the gate of the next bazaar, Dariba, silversmiths presented us with salvers inlaid with precious stones. Some of them were allowed to touch our stirrups before they flung palmful of coins in our name to beggars who abounded in the city. Near the entrance to the fort was Urdu Bazaar, the soldiers' encampment. This had been vacated by the Mughal for our Qazilbash bodyguards.

As we entered the fort, Mughal guns fired a salute in our honour. We were pleased with the reception given to us. By beat of the drum we had it proclaimed that Delhi was under our protection and that as long as the citizens conducted themselves with propriety they could go about their business without fear. We presented robes of honour to Lutfullah Khan, Governor of Delhi, and to the *Kotwal*, Haji Faulad Khan. We complimented them on the excellent arrangements made by them.

Several places around the Diwan-i-Khas had been prepared for our stay. Here we received princes of the Mughal household and accepted tributes from them. We presented them with robes of honour.

In the evening we watched a display of fireworks on the bank of the river Jamna. It was followed by dancing and singing. Although we felt that our recent victory called for celebration, we did not deem it wise to indulge ourselves in the company of strangers. However, to please our host, Mohammed Shah, we took a goblet of wine from his hands and accepted a girl, said to be the most beautiful of her sex in Delhi. Without as much as looking at her we told her to await our pleasure in our dreamchamber.

Mohammed Shah drank so much wine that he forgot himself and the guest he was entertaining. He tied bells to his ankles and joined the nautch girls. He could dance as well as they— with the same sauciness in his eyes, the same delicacy of movement in his hands and the same nimbleness of feet.

When one of the *omarah* applauded his performance and said
that His Majesty had more to him than any dancing girl in
Hindustan, Mohammed Shah grinned like an ape and
suddenly took out his member from the folds of its privacy.
'No dancing girl has this!' he boasted as he waved it about. 'A
hundred gold coins for anyone who can produce a bigger
one.' We smiled at this foolish exhibition. Encouraged by our
smile he doubled his wager: 'And two hundred for anyone,
Turk or Iranian, who can put it to better use!'

No one deigned to take up his challenge. The foolish man
was emboldened to direct a barbed shaft at us. He quoted
Saadi:

> *...O little mother of ancient days:*
> *Thou hast cunningly dyed thy hair but consider*
> *That thy bent back will never be straight!*

He turned to his cronies with a meaningful smile. The
besotted sycophants applauded: 'Wah! Wah!' We knew the
allusion was to us for we had not had the time to dye our
beard and its roots showed the same grey as the hair on our
head. The double-faced Saadath Khan, who only a few hours
earlier had been kissing the ground before our feet, took up
the refrain with another quotation:

> *I have heard that in these days a decrepit aged man*
> *Took fancy in his grey head to get a spouse*
> *A beautiful lass, Jewel, by name.*
> *And when he had concealed the jewel casket from other men*
> *He tried to perform the feat customary at weddings*
> *But in the first onslaught, the man's organ fell asleep.*
> *He spanned the bow but failed to hit the target.*

We wanted to slap Saadath Khan there and then but
decided to postpone his punishment to another day.
However, we did not want these besotted men to get away
with the notion that we were not aware of the direction in
which they had aimed their poisoned darts. As soon as their
laughter subsided, we replied:

> *A nice face and a gown of gold brocade*
> *A haw of rose, aloes, paint and scent*
> *All these a woman's beauty aid,*
> *But man, his testicles are his real ornament.*

They applauded us at the top of their voices: 'Marhaba! Subhan Allah!'

We dismissed the *mehfil* and retired to the bed prepared for us. No sooner had we reclined on our couch than the slave girl made her bow, took off our shoes and began to massage our feet. After the tiresome journey of many days the sensation was most pleasurable. We placed our legs in her lap and let her press our legs as well. We noticed that she was young and beautiful. 'Girl, what is your name?' we asked.

'Your slave is known as Noor Bai. Can your slave have the honour of presenting a goblet of wine to Your Majesty?'

She looked up at us. What eyes Allah had given her! Larger, darker and more limpid than those of a Persian gazelle; and how she could speak with them! She poured wine from a silver decanter into a gold goblet and offered it to us with both her hands. We took it but, as was our wont, put it aside on a table. We never took wine, water or a morsel of food from a stranger's hands. Noor Bai did not press us to drink. 'Do I please Your Majesty?' she asked, digging her forefinger into her cheek and wagging her head.

'Your face is very pleasing to us. Of the rest we have as yet no knowledge,' we replied.

She sensed what we meant. She placed our feet on a footstool and stood up. She unbuckled her trousers and let them drop at her feet. Then she took off her chemise and flung it on the carpet. Overcome by bashfulness she covered her face with both her hands, thus exposing herself completely to our gaze. We had never seen a girl fashioned as she: dark as cinnamon; bosom bursting with wanton impudence, waist so slender that we could enclose it within the palms of our hands. She was small but her buttocks were as large as the melons of Herat.

'Noor Bai, how old are you? Have you known a man before?' we asked her.

She pretended to be shocked. 'How could anyone dare to offer Your Majesty something soiled by another? I was raised for your pleasure. No other man has touched, or ever will touch my body after it has been honoured by Your Majesty.'

She was a child in years but adept in the art of seductive speech. We asked her to draw close to us. We ran our hands over her face and body; firm and smooth as polished walnut without a trace of hair on her limbs, armpits or privates. She had rubbed her body with aromatic oil and exuded the fragrance of jasmine. It occured to us that our hosts had some design in sending so young and wanton a girl to our bedchamber.

Fifty summers spent in hardship and strife reduces a man's appetite for women. But we were determined to prove to our hosts that the men of Persia are as potent in the harem as they are powerful on the field of battle. We had a snow-white sheet spread over our couch. We ordered Noor Bai to minister to us till our passions were fully roused. She had been well-groomed.

The look of childish curiosity on her face changed to alarm when she saw what we were to present to her. We were gentle with her. She cried in pain and the bedsheet received ample testimony of her virginity and our manliness.

When we had finished, we loaded her naked body with gold ornaments studded with precious stones. We told her she was the most comely woman we had taken to couch. She wiped away her tears and smiled. But when we expressed our wish to take her into our harem, she began to cry again: 'If Your Majesty stays in Delhi, your slave will serve you till her last breath, but if Your Majesty takes me away from Delhi, she will take poison and kill herself,' she said very stubbornly.

We had heard that the people of Delhi loved their city as bees love flowers. But we could not believe that the child of a courtesan would prefer to live in a Delhi brothel rather than in our palace in Iran!

However, we did not wish to converse with the girl nor make her unhappy. We told her to be in attendance on us during our sojourn in her city. Perhaps she would change her mind. Or we, ours.

The next day being Friday we ordered the *khutba* to be read in our name in all the mosques of the city. This would make it as clear as the sun that we had come to Delhi only to restore order in the country of Islam.

In the afternoon we sent for Saadath Khan. He came accompanied by his sons and a cavalcade of retainers. Because he, along with Asaf Jah Nizam-ul-Mulk, had addressed the letters of invitation to us to come to Hindustan and told us of the enormous wealth collected in the vaults of the Red Fort, he presumed a degree of familiarity with us. He also wanted to impress his entourage with his own importance. We felt that we should strip him of his delusions. We said nothing about his behaviour on the night before but reminded him that we had come to Delhi on the assurance that if we saved the empire from the Maratha infidels, they would meet the expenses of the expedition. We told him that his behaviour since our arrival in Delhi gave us the impression that he did not mean to honour his undertaking.

Hazrat Ali Murtaza has rightly said that: 'Often a word pierces like a sword and the tongue can have a sharper point than the lance.' So it was with the tongue of anger that we spoke words of admonition. 'Saadath Khan, the army of the defenders of Islam has not been compensated for its sacrifice,' we said bluntly. 'Not one cowrie shell of the four crores promised has so far been given. If an earnest of this sum is not paid by tomorrow sundown, we will make our displeasure known.'

This remonstrance failed to impress its seal on the wax of Saadath's brain. 'What is money to the conquerer of the world!' he said jauntily as he turned to his entourage for approval. 'What is money!' he repeated. 'We will lay down our lives for the Great Nadir!'

His followers applauded his audacity. Our temper rose. 'Come here, Saadath Khan!' we commanded. The silly grin disappeared from his face: his knees shook as he approached us. As he bowed to us we grabbed him by his left ear and pulled him up. 'We do not like this kind of clever talk! We do not like men who break their word!'

Saadath's face first turned red, then yellow. He began to

stutter. We boxed his ear and slapped him on his face. As he reeled back we gave him a kick in his belly. 'Get out of our presence!' we roared. 'If we do not get what is due to our army by tomorrow we will have you flogged in front of the *kotwali* in Chandni Chowk.'

Saadath Khan had to be carried away from our presence. The chastisement proved too much for him. That very night he plunged a dagger in his heart and ended his miserable existence.

The people of Delhi are both ungrateful and cowardly. Instead of thanking us for the trouble we had taken by coming hundreds of miles over mountains through ravines and desert waste to save them from the infidels, they had the audacity to insinuate that it was not the love of Islam but the love of gold that had brought us to their country.

We were informed that the natives had created a tumult at the Royal Mosque when the Imam was declaiming the *khutba* in our name. Our officers brought reports that our Qazilbash bodyguards had been spat upon in the streets; women had thrown refuse on their heads as they passed below their houses. Grocers and butchers were demanding higher prices from our Iranian soldiers than from their own people. The citizens of Delhi did not appreciate that it was for their safety that we had kept the bulk of our army outside the city. Seeing that there were only a few hundred Iranians in the walled enclosure of Shahjahanabad, the citizens had the effrontery to raise their cowardly eyebrows at us. Thus did they invite the angel of death to visit their city.

On Saturday, 10 March 1739, the sun entered Aries. It was also the holy day of Id-uz-Zuha, commemorating Hazrat Ibrahim's offering of his son, Yusuf, to Allah. Our bodyguards took a few stray bulls and heifers loitering in the streets to offer as sacrifice. The Hindus, who regard all bovine species of animals sacred, were incensed. They refused to sell rice to our men. We ordered our soldiers to buy instead of rice, flour from Muslim dealers. It was then that the perfidy of the Muslims of Delhi was brought to our notice; they trebled the price of wheat flour. Once more we controlled our temper.

Had not Hazart Ali Murtaza said: 'Anger is a species of madness!' We fixed the price of wheat at ten seers to the silver rupee and ordered grain depots to be thrown open.

In the afternoon we received reports that our men who had gone to buy provisions at a grain market called Paharganj, a musket shot to the west of Ajmeri Gate, had been assaulted. It was not our habit to lend ear to rumour. We sent a party of seven of our bodyguards to verify the facts. Only three of the seven were able to return; these three bore evidence of violence on their persons. They told us that the leaders of the rabble were two Pathans, Niaz Khan and Sheh Sawar Khan.

These thugs had surrounded a party of our musketeers and burnt them alive. We were told that a large number of our soldiers had been killed and an armed mob led by the villain Niaz Khan was heading towards the Red Fort to try and lay their impious hands upon our person. We went up on the ramparts above Lahori Gate which commanded a view of Urdu Bazaar and Chandni Chowk. We heard sounds of gunfire. We saw a sea of spears, swords and matchlocks flooding Chandni Chowk and the bazaars right up to the Jamia Masjid surging towards the fort.

Our bodyguards posted in the Urdu Bazaar were valiantly holding their own against this ocean of madness. We sent instructions that they should evacuate Urdu Bazaar and retreat to the sandbank between the river and the eastern wall of the fort. We had a cannon mounted on the Lahori and Delhi Gates which faced west and south and ordered grape to be fired into the rabble. We sent word to the commanders of our troops at Shalimar to send reinforcements immediately and be prepared to march into the city the next morning.

The night was made hideous with the howling of the mob and the roar of cannons. Our peace of mind was further disturbed by the fact that Mohammed Shah made no attempt to apologize for the conduct of his subjects. We received a report that it was being openly said in the bazaars that we had been poisoned by Noor Bai and were on our deathbed. When the Mughal's Chamberlain came to call on us we could read in his visage that he had come to see for himself whether mischief had been done to our person. Our mind was made up. We did not allow memories of the earlier evening to sweeten the bitterness that now flooded our soul. We hastened to our bedchamber. We sent for the decanter of wine which had been sent to us earlier and ordered Noor Bai to be brought to our presence.

Noor Bai came swaying her hips and smiling as saucily as the night before. Her eyes did not betray treachery. But as soon as she saw the anger on our face she took fright. She clasped our feet and asked: 'Has your slave been guilty of some misdemeanour?'

If she was a liar she must have been the world's best liar under sixteen years of age. 'Who gave you this decanter of wine?' we demanded. She looked innocently puzzled. 'No one, Your Majesty. It was lying here. I thought it was Your Majesty's favourite wine from Shiraz. Has it upset Your Majesty?' We picked up the decanter, filled a goblet and held it out for her. 'Drink!' we commanded.

A look of fear came in her eyes. She took the goblet from our hands. 'I have never touched wine to my lips.'

'Drink! Or we'll force it down your throat.'

Noor Bai dipped a finger in the goblet and put it on her tongue. She puckered her face in distaste. Then she shut her nostrils with the fingers of one hand and with the other tilted the goblet into her mouth. She brought up some of it and was convulsed by a fit of coughing. Her face became a deep red, she held her throat as if she was choking. 'Your Majesty drinks this poison for pleasure?' she asked us through her tears.

We were not sure whether this wine was the same as the one that had been left in our bedchamber the night before. But since neither we nor Noor Bai had suffered any ill-effect from taking it, we were assured that it had not been tinctured. We asked Noor Bai to draw closer to us. We cupped her face in our hands and looked into her tear-stained eyes.

'Noor Bai, if anyone says anything about us to you or asks you to do something to us, you must tell us. You will have our protection and we will load you with as much gold as you weigh.' She slipped down on the ground and kissed our feet. We placed a necklace of rubies around her neck and dismissed her. We deputed a spy to watch her movements for some days.

On Sunday, we rose earlier than was our practice. We said our *fajar* prayer in Aurangzeb's Pearl Mosque and had a light repast. The commanders of our garrisons had come into the city and awaited our orders. We told them to take positions in front of Lahori Gate.

As the sun rose, Delhi's rabble reassembled in the streets. We saw that the breezes of mischief had roused the populace like a stormy wind rouses the seas to turbulence. We thought that our presence would becalm their senses.

When the sun had risen above the walls of the Red Fort we rode with our escorts into Chandni Chowk. What we saw there brought tears to our eyes. Many of our faithful comrades lay dead about the streets. Their bodies had been horribly mutilated. The double-faced wretches, who only two days earlier had welcomed us with flowers and tributes of precious metal and stones, now yelled abuse at us. The flower-sellers of Phool-ki-Mandi, who had showered rose-petals over us, now pelted us with clods of mud and stones. We dismounted at Roshan-ud-Daulah's mosque and took our seat on the balcony.

Filth and stones were hurled on us from the balconies of neighbouring houses. Then somebody fired a gun. The bullet whizzed past us and hit our fly-whisk-bearer. The poor man fell on us; his blood poured over our tunic; he expired in our arms with a cry of anguish: '*Ya Allah!*'

We laid our faithful servant on the floor. Our cup of patience was full to the brim. We drew our sword. 'As long as this sword is out of the scabbard the life of every citizen of this wretched city is forfeit. Spare no one,' we ordered.

We saw yet another aspect of the character of the people of Hindustan. They were cunning in the way they had invited us to come to their help. They were double-faced in the way they continued to protest their loyalty to their monarch and to us till they were sure who was going to be victorious. We had seen how timid they were in the field of battle and how abject in the hour of defeat. We had suffered their florid speeches in which they concealed insinuations under a sugar-coating of

flattery. We saw how violent they could be when they came
in large numbers upon a few unsuspecting soldiers. And now
that the angel of death hovered over them they were as supine
as a flock of sheep. Our soldiers slew them by the score till
their hands were tired.

We left Roshan-ud-Daulah's mosque to return to the Red
Fort. While passing the gateway of Dariba we ordered our
men to level every home in that accursed street inhabited by
the infidels. Our soldiers slew every man, woman and child in
Dariba and then set fire to the bazaar. The only parts of
Shahjahanabad we spared were the bazaars around Jamia
Masjid and Delhi Gate, because Nawab Sarbuland Khan came
and pleaded with us that no one from these localities had
joined the rioters.

In the afternoon Mohammed Shah craved permission to
present himself. The fire of our anger had by then been
dowsed in the river of blood. We allowed him to kiss our feet.
He knew the art of stringing words.

'Not a soul has been spared by your avenging sword,' he
whined. 'If it be Your Majesty's wish to carry on the work of
destruction further, infuse life into the dead and renew the
slaughter.

We had no idea how many had been slaughtered except
that for six hours thousands of our brave soldiers had done
nothing else but kill. We put our sword back into the scabbard
and ordered that our pleasure be announced by beat of the
drum.

We did not wish to expose our eyes to the results of the
carnage and ordered that the streets be cleansed of blood and
corpses. It was a strange coincidence that this day happened
to be Holi when infidels celebrate the advent of spring by
dowsing each other with red water, the colour of blood! The
infidels burnt their dead as was their custom and thus sent
them to hell as was their desert. The Muslims buried their
slain along the sandbanks of the river. Those that had no one
to burn or bury were disposed of by kites, crows, cats, dogs
and jackals that abound in this city.

Although we allowed the sweet breeze of forgiveness to
blow over the accursed city, we did not want its citizens to

believe that their crimes had been atoned for. We sent our men to enter the homes of the *omarah* and rich merchants and take everything they could find.

Those who remonstrated were brought before us. We had them flogged in front of their kinsmen. The floors of their homes were dug up and their women stripped naked. Many, unable to face themselves after the chastisement they had received, ended their miserable existence with their own hands. Gold and silver and precious stones flowed into our treasury as the waters of the Oxus flow into the sea. We sent the good news to Iran with the proclamation that no taxes would be levied on our Iranian subjects for the next three years. For rightly has Hazrat Ali Murtaza said: 'The better part of generosity is speedy giving!'

After all this we found we were out of countenance with ourselves. We dismissed our attendants and told them we wanted to be alone. We sat for many hours taking counsel with ourselves. We had conquered the four kingdoms prophesied for us in our dreams. With the spear of Islam we had pierced the heart of the land of infidels and sent thousands of idolaters to hell; we had served Allah and His Prophet (peace upon Him).

We had amassed wealth and lit the lamp of prosperity in millions of Iranian homes; our sons and their sons up to seven generations could eat their fill and not finish the harvest we had reaped with our sword. The people of Asia stood in awe of our name. All men were eager to follow our banner to wherever we chose to take it. We had the fairest of women in our harem: Caucasians, Turks, Iranis, Arabs, Afghans and Hindvis. Our loins had yielded a host of sturdy sons and comely daughters. We had everything a man could ask for. And yet a strange melancholy pervaded our being.

Noor Bai was ever in our mind. We went over the night she had spent with us. We could not believe she could have wanted to harm us or even let herself be used as an instrument of another's mischievous design. We were not even sure whether any mischief had in fact been contemplated. But our ears had been filled with venomous rumour with Noor Bai's name mixed in it. We clapped our hands and asked the attendant to bring the girl to our presence.

Noor Bai washed our feet with her tears. She lay on the carpet and between sobs asked us many times to tell her why we had ever suspected her. We had no reason; so we did not deign to reply. We only gazed at her prostrate form— a waist that curved like a bow and buttocks that would delight those who desired to take their pleasure in them. Our appreciation of her did not kindle any desire in our loins. Besides, by now we knew that although we could command her body, we could not rule her heart.

Once again, to atone for the suspicion we had harboured against her, we slipped a pair of gold bangles on her wrist and told her to leave. She refused to go. She sat with her head between our knees, peering into our face. 'Your Majesty is angry with the world, she remarked, truthfully reading our disposition. 'It is all the people you have had killed. That was not a good thing to do.

We were amazed by her boldness. We stroked her head and were suddenly overcome with revulsion against ourselves. We covered our face with our hands to hide the tears that welled up in our eyes: but we could not hold back a sob that convulsed our chest. Noor Bai became bolder and without seeking our permission made herself comfortable on our lap. The unmanly spasm of weakness passed. We gently removed Noor Bai from our middle and asked her to leave us alone. Before she left she made us promise that we would send for Hakeem Alavi Khan of Ballimaran. 'He will apply leeches and remove the angry blood that courses through Your Majesty's frame, she said.

The next day we sent for Hakeem Alavi Khan who, we were told, had the healing powers of Jesus (upon Whom be peace). He was bent under the weight of years and his long white beard; he walked with the aid of a stick. He had the audacity that old men gain when they know they have not very long to live. He began reprimanding us. 'If you do not learn to control your temper, your temper will control you, he said.

We agreed we were quick to temper. 'Not only quick to

anger, Your Majesty,' retorted the *hakeem* 'but dangerously ill-tempered; anger is a species of madness. If not checked, it becomes incurable. ' His words were more bitter than his medicines. But after the braying of sycophants and flatterers, this man's blunt speech sounded like the music of the lute. It was from his tongue that we heard of the havoc that had been caused in the city. We tried to explain to him that it was the people of Delhi who had first laid hands on our soldiers and we had but given them freedom to retaliate.

'La haul valla quwwat!' exclaimed the old *hakeem.* 'Retaliate against women and children! Kill innocent people! Is that the kind of justice that prevails in your country?'

We did not take offence but let him speak on. Thereafter we sent for Hakeem Alavi Khan, more to hear what he had to say than for his prescriptions. While he had the temerity to bring our shortcomings to our notice, he also gave us aphrodisiacs compounded of crushed pearls and Yemen honey. For although we were in robust health, we felt that the thirty-three ladies in our harem and now the young and ardent Noor Bai might strain our constitution.

We cannot recall whether it was the advice of Hakeem Alavi Khan or the ministrations of Noor Bai that changed our mind. We passed no sentences of death for fifteen days. We began to laugh and joke with our companions. We asked Qazmaruddin Khan, who was Chancellor of the Mughal Exchequer, if it was true that he had 850 women in his harem. When he admitted that it was so, we remarked, 'You should take another hundred-and-fifty and become a *mim-bashi* (commander of one thousand).' People laughed and laughed till tears came into their eyes. The joke was repeated to us many times by many flatterers.

We left the Mughal to his own counsel in the hope that he would have the good sense to make *peshkash* of his own accord. But Mohammed Shah's skull was stuffed with cunning instead of commonsense. He tried to match our patience with guile. He had it conveyed to us that our two households should be linked by a marriage alliance. We gave our consent in the belief that he wanted an excuse to pay his dues in the form of dowry. Consequently our well-beloved son, Prince Nasrulla Mirza, the second fruit of our loins, was betrothed to the daughter of Yezdan Baksh, son of Kam Baksh, son of Emperor Aurangzeb.

On such occasions it is customary among the people of Hindustan to indulge in jest. Women of the Mughal seraglio who were very proud of their lineage asked our son to name his ancestors up to seven forefathers. Prince Nasrulla Mirza became speechless with embarrassment; he knew of the days when all our worldly wealth consisted of a camel and a flock of sheep. His tongue remained locked between his teeth. We intervened on his behalf: 'Son, tell them that you are the son of Nadir Shah, the son of the sword, the grandson of the sword; and so on to seventy instead of seven generations.' The women responded with *'Ash! Ash! Marhaba!'*

All this was happening only fifteen days after the terrible punishment we had meted out to the citizens of Delhi but they seemed eager to forget it and join the marriage celebrations. The walls of the Red Fort were lit with oil-lamps and there was a grand display of fireworks. There was much drinking and nautch. The *nikah* took place on 26 March 1739 followed by *dawat-i-valima* (a grand feast of consummation). The Mughal made presents to us and our officers. Perhaps he hoped that having given one of his kinswomen to our son he could settle his account with a few trinkets. We decided to teach him a lesson that an Iranian could as easily outwit an Indian in wile as he could outmatch him on the field of battle.

We were informed that there were two very precious things in the possession of the Mughal royal family. One was the *takht-i-taoos* (the Peacock Throne) made of solid gold, inset with diamonds, rubies and emeralds. It was valued at nine crore rupees. The other was the diamond *Koh-i-Noor* (the Mountain of Light), said to be larger than a pigeon's egg and worth all the world's income for seven days. We ordered a search of the palace vaults but neither the throne nor the diamond could be found.

We questioned Mohammed Shah. He told us that the throne had been broken up nineteen years earlier and that he had never seen the *Koh-i-Noor*. Saadath Khan had however told us that the *Koh-i-Noor* was in the possession of

Mohammed Shah. Instead of wearing it on his arm, as was the custom of his predecessors, he hid it in the folds of his turban. We planned a stratagem by which we would acquire this diamond without betraying our desire to have it.

We assembled a *darbar* where all the Indian *omarah* and our Iranian generals were present. First we explained to Mohammed Shah the duties of a king. Then we escorted him to the marble seat of his ancestors and beckoned to one of our servants to bring a crown we had ordered to be prepared for the occasion. We removed Mohammed Shah's turban and placed the crown on his head.

'May Allah grant you prosperity and long life!' we said. The courtiers applauded. We noticed that Mohammed Shah's eyes hovered round the turban which now lay between us. The speech he made in response seemed as much addressed to us as to his headgear. He said he looked upon us as his elder brother. That made our task easier. As he sat down we rose to our feet and said that we were given to understand that in Hindustan it was customary for men who pledged fraternal friendship towards each other to exchange turbans. We removed the crown from his head and placed our turban in its stead. We bowed our head for him to do likewise. The poor fellow did as he was told. He gave us the *Koh-i-Noor* with his own hands. We embraced him and dismissed the court.

The diamond was indeed in the folds of his turban. It was the size of a hawk's egg and so brilliant that it seemed to have captured the soul of the sun in its breast. We made no secret of having acquired it and wore it on our right arm.

By the end of April the sun's rays had become like tongues of flame from the fires of *gehennum*. Our body was covered with prickly heat and despite Hakeem Alavi Khan's *sherbets* we lost appetite for food and female company. 'Delhi is not the place for you,' said the old *hakeem* to us. 'Ameen,' we replied. 'A day in Isphahan is worth a lifetime in your country.'

We spoke truly for though we had heard so much in praise of Delhi there was little that pleased us about it. We did not like the people or their manners; we did not like their food or their wines. Their watermelons were without flavour and produced wind in our stomach. The mango which had been lauded so much we found too sweet for our taste; besides it soiled our hands and beard. And Delhi's climate produced only laziness, prickly heat and bad temper.

We ordered that all that had been taken from the city should be loaded on elephants, camels and asses and preparations made for our return to Iran. We made arrangements for the administration of the country. We attached the four *subahs* beyond the Indus to our empire but the rest we left to Mohammed Shah and Nizam-ul-Mulk. The king was simple and pleasure-loving; the minister cunning and ambitious. If the arrangement did not work, we would have the right to annex the country.

On Saturday, 5 May 1739, we left the capital city of the Mughals. There were only two people with whom we left some of our heart. One was the sharp-tongued Hakeem Alavi Khan and the other the saucy Noor Bai. An Emperor may command anything within his empire except an honest man and a woman's heart. We could have forced both to accompany us but we knew that the old man would not be able to make the journey and Noor Bai would have cried all the time. We realized that we could take her body with us, but her heart would remain behind in Delhi. And what is a woman's body worth if her heart not be in it!

We loaded the *hakeem* with presents and gave Noor Bai her weight in gold and bade them and the city of Delhi farewell.

13

Bhagmati

Bhagmati has just left. I suspect she was not happy with the previous night's love-making but what am I to do. I am old now. I feel morose. The phone rings. The Tughlak Road police station on the line. 'Am I Budh Singh's employer?'

'Well, sort of, he is *chowkidar* of the entire block, I pay him a little extra to keep an eye on my flat. What's the matter? Has he been run over; accident-shaksidant?'

'No, he has been molesting women.'

I can believe anything about Budh Singh, but not molesting women. There must be some mistake. If the poor fellow has named me as his employer, I must not let him down. I drive to the police station.

Budh Singh is sitting on the floor of the verandah chained to a policeman who is seated on a chair chewing a *betel*-leaf. Neither of them take the slightest notice of me. I bend down and ask Budh Singh to tell me what happened. He glowers at me without saying anything. I plead with him to tell me what transpired so I can get him out on bail. 'He's mad,' says the policeman spitting *betel* phlegm on the floor. Budh Singh slowly turns his head, fixes the constable with a baleful look and mutters: 'You mad! Your mother mad; your sister mad. Who are you to call me mad? *Bahinchod*!'

'I told you he is mad,' says the constable calmly chewing the cud. 'No use talking to him. Go inside and speak to the inspector sahib.'

I go in to the reporting room, tell them what I have come for. The sub-inspector offers me a seat and tells me that Budh Singh has been arrested for 'eve-teasing'. I protest. I tell him that Budh Singh is a man of impeccable character, has never shown

194

any interest in women and so on. But at times something happens to him. I point to my head.

The sub-inspector nods and tells me of Budh's eve-teasing. He was apparently walking along the corridors of Connaught Circus mumbling to himself ('Prayer,' I interject, 'he prays all the time') when he suddenly grabbed a young woman's bosom pressed it and said *bhaw, bhaw*. Before she could recover from the shock, he grabbed the other bosom and likewise pressed it with a *bhaw, bhaw*. 'Ah yes, poor man! You know he was once a truck-driver in the army; he must have thought they were bulb horns,' I explain. The sub-inspector is more understanding than the women in Connaught Circus. Apparently Budh Singh pressed many other female bulb horns. There was a hue and cry and some students beat him up. That wasn't the end. There was a woman banana-seller with her basket full of bananas sitting on the pavement. Budh Singh examined them and asked the price. He thought they were overpriced and offered to sell his own at a much cheaper rate. And showed it to the banana-seller. The lady did not appreciate the gesture and told Budh Singh to offer it to his mother. What could Budh Singh do? He grabbed the banana-seller's bosoms with both his hands and said *bhaw, bhaw*. Then the police got him. 'He must have been thinking of his trucking days,' I explain again. 'It comes over him once in a while.' The sub-inspector is most kind. They've already beaten Budh Singh. 'That's enough punishment for pressing four bosoms and showing his penis. He did not fuck anyone's mother, did he?' he says. 'But don't let him do it again.'

14

Meer Taqi Meer

I do not know which I was more, a lover or a poet. Both love and poetry consumed me. An affair of the heart brought me into disrepute; my poetry earned me a name which resounded all over Hindustan. Love brought me anguish; poetry a feeling of ecstasy. What neither love nor poetry brought me was money. Whatever I earned was by stringing garlands of words. Living amongst people who could not tell the difference between a finely cut diamond and a bead of glass, it was more the whims of my patrons than the excellence of my craftsmanship that determined what I had to eat. My father, the saintly Meer Mohammed Ali, once said to me; 'Son, I worry over your future. A fire has been lit in your heart. I fear for what it will do to you.' I was only nine years old and laughed at his words. He had the wisdom of age; he wept because he knew that the fire of love would both make me and destroy me.

One evening after he had said his afternoon prayer, he said to me; '*Beta*, the world changes very fast and there is very little time to catch up with it. The road of life is also very uneven; you must watch your steps. Whatever time you have, devote it to knowing your self.' I was only ten years old and had plenty of time to do whatever I liked. Also I did not think there was very much about myself that I did not know.

We lived in a hermitage on the outskirts of Akbarabad (Agra). Besides my father's children from his two wives, there was *Chacha* Amanullah who lived with us and like my father spent most of his waking hours in prayer and meditation. When they were not praying or meditating they argued about love. My father said if you love God you love everything created by God. *Chacha* put it the other way round : If you love

God's creatures you love God. I could not understand how two old men could go on talking for hours on end about the same thing day after day. It was only later that I understood the kind of love which was on *Chacha* Amanullah's mind. I used to wonder sometimes why when he talked so much about loving God's creatures, he never raised his eyes from the ground when women were around. Then one evening he was taking the air in an Agra bazaar when he happened to exchange glances with a beautiful boy and fell madly in love with him. After this incident he lost his appetite for food and his peace of mind. A few days later he died pining away for the love of that lad.

Love meant something quite different to my father. Once he told me: 'Son, make love your only companion. It is love that maintains the universe. All that you see in the world is a different manifestation of love. Fire is the heat of love, earth its foundation, air its restlessness, night its dream-state, day its wakefulness.' At the time his words made no sense to me. However, all unknowing, the quest of love was enjoined upon me from my infancy and became the guiding star of my life. Unfortunately it was neither the kind of love that consumed *Chacha* Amanullah nor the sort my father spoke of that became my abiding passion but the type that envelopes a man when he loses his head and his heart to one woman.

My father married twice. From his first wife, the sister of the well-known poet, Aarzoo of Delhi, he had a son, Hafiz Mohammed. My mother, who was his second wife, bore him three children of whom I was the eldest. My step-brother had no love for his father, his step-mother or her children. Most of all he hated me. My father was well aware of this and thought it best to divide whatever he owned between us in his lifetime. One summer afternoon, when the sun was at its zenith and hot winds blew, he went to Agra to see some ailing disciple. When he returned, he had a heat stroke. He smelled the breeze of paradise in his nostrils and sent for Hafiz Mohammed and me. He spoke to us, 'Sons, I am a *fakeer*. I have no money, land or property. All I have are some three hundred books. I also owe about three hundred rupees to creditors. Before I shut my eyes to the world I would like to divide my books and debts equally between you.' At this my step-brother replied, '*Abba Jan*, you know perfectly well that I am the scholar of the family and the only one who can profit from the study of books. What will Taqi do with them except make kites of their pages and fly them?' My father was very upset with him but being close to death only admonished him weakly, 'Hafiz Mohammed, mark my words! The flame of learning will never illumine your home but that of Taqi.' He turned to me and said; '*Beta* , do not bury my body till you have paid off my creditors. Do not worry. Money will come to you.'

With the name of Allah on his lips my father took leave of the world. As news of his death reached Agra, people began to collect at our hospice to pay their last homage to him. Among them were some Hindu shopkeepers who offered me money. I declined to take it from them but when one of my father's Muslim disciples put a bag with five hundred rupees in my lap, I accepted it. I paid off my father's creditors and buried his body next to the grave of *Chacha* Amanullah. At the age of eleven I was left alone in the world to look after my widowed mother, younger brother and sister. Besides the hundred rupees that remained with me after I had paid for the burial expenses and creditors my only wealth consisted of the words of wisdom bequeathed to me by my father.

Chacha Amanullah had taught me Farsee and Urdu as well as the technique of composing poetry. I used this little knowledge to coach the children of rich families. Some evenings I would go to *mushairas* and hear the famous poets of Delhi and Agra recite their compositions. I found most of them were commonplace rhymesters without a single new thought in their poems. Such poets, particularly a songster named Masood who was a great favourite at *mushairas*, roused my contempt. Masood was a handsome, roguish looking fellow who could make up for the execrable quality of his verses by singing them in a dulcet voice. No sooner would a *mushaira* start than the audience would clamour for 'Parwana' (moth) the pseudonym which he used. (I always referred to him as *patanga* which is the pejorative for a moth). Women loved him. At every gathering I saw maidservants bring slips of paper from their mistresses seated behind the *purdah* (screen) with requests for songs composed by him. These songs were usually about the moth's love for the flame in which it burnt itself. It amazed me how a theme as old as Moses and Abraham could rouse people's emotions. What irritated me about Parwana was that even on this hackneyed theme he could not produce a single new variation. I confess that it was envy of this worthless moth that first impelled me to try my hand at composing poetry.

While the others in my household slept I would sit beside an oil-lamp and compose verses. They poured out of me like the waters of the Tasneem. Although I was too shy to recite them in public I showed them to some poets whose work I thought was above mediocre. They expressed surprise that one so young could have such facility with words; some suspected I had stolen someone else's writing. 'If these verses are really yours, the days of Parwana will soon come to an end,' said one. 'He will have to leap into a flame,' said another. 'You call that *patanga* a poet?' I asked somewhat rashly. 'He is a mere *tuk-baaz* (rhymester) with the voice of a castrated male.' The story went round that a twelve-year-old *chokra* had the audacity to use insulting words about the reigning monarch of Agra's *mehfils*. In due course Parwana got to hear of what I had said. 'Who is this son of Meer Taqi?' he roared. 'I will teach him a lesson he will never forget.' Some families known to him dispensed with my services. Not satisfied with this, he decided to humiliate me in public.

At a *mushaira* in the *haveli* of Agra's richest Nawab, Rais Mian, whose begum was said to be enamoured of Parwana, somebody whispered in his ears that I was present in the crowd. I could see his eyes scanning the audience while his informant directed his gaze towards me. He nodded his head and said in a voice loud enough for everyone to hear: 'Now watch the *tamasha*.' After a poet had finished his recitation, his cronies began to shout, 'Parwana Sahib, Parwana Sahib!' He raised both his hands asking for people to be quiet. 'Gentlemen, I am grateful to you for your appreciation of my poor talents. I am your slave ever ready to comply with your commands. But this evening, before your humble servant opens his mouth, I pray silence for the rising star of Hindustan. Parwana is a mere *patanga* before him. It is no fault of yours that you have not heard of his name because the world has yet to hear his *kalaam*.

He is still wet behind his ears but regards himself as the *ustad* of *ustads*.' His voice was loaded with sarcasm. His cronies sniggered with pleasure. He turned to one of them and asked loudly, 'What did you say is this *launda's* (urchin's) name? Ah yes, Meer. Full name, Meer Taqi Meer. Let the candle be placed before his august visage.'

I was taken aback. I had never opened my mouth in a *mehfil* nor had I brought any of my compositions with me. The candle was placed in front of me and hundreds of eyes were fixed on me. Sweat broke out on my forehead and my hands began to tremble. I shut my eyes and thought of my father. I prayed, '*Ya Allah!* Thou art my help and my refuge.' I could not think of what to say except a couplet I had composed on the *shama-parwana* (flame-moth) theme only to prove that it could be handled in ways other than by this hack trying to humiliate me. 'Parwana Sahib,' I said with all the humility I could command, 'before I recite my composition, I crave permission to present you a humble gift which I beg of you to accept.' Then in a clear voice I recited:

> *The flame it saw,*
> *But thereafter nothing besides the curving, leaping*
> *lungues of fire.*
> *By the time its eyes were on the flame,*
> *The moth was in the fire.*

None of them had seen this aspect of love—love that thinks of nothing except to be consumed by its beloved. As the words sank in the minds of the audience it exploded '*Marhaba! Subhan Allah!* How beautifully put!' Emboldened by the appreciation, I sought permission to recite a poem on love that I had composed the night before and which was still fresh in my mind:

> *It is love and only love whichever way you look;*
> *Love is stacked from the earth below to the sky above;*
> *Love is the beloved, love is the lover too,*
> *In short, love itself is in love with love.*
> *Without love none can their goal attain,*

Love is desire, love its ultimate aim.
Love is anguish, love the antidote of love's pain.
O wise man, what know you what love is?
Without love the order of the Universe would be broken
God is love, truly have the poets spoken.

The audience was moved by my recitation. Every line was applauded with *Wah! Wah! Wah! Mukarrar!* I had to repeat them over and over again. Many people came and showered silver coins on me. A maidservant handed me a gold *ashrafi* with a note asking me to make a copy of the poem in my own hand and deliver it personally at the *haveli* the next morning. The note was from the mistress of the house. This was the beginning of my career as a poet and a lover.

I got no sleep that night. The applause I had received rang in my ears. I had humbled that charlatan Parwana and he would never again be able to show his face in a *mehfil* where I was present. But who was this lady who had asked for my poem? My head was in a whirl. Despite the sleepless night, in the morning I felt fresh and triumphant. I told my mother what had happened and handed over the gold *ashrafi* and silver coins showered on me. 'All this is due to your *Abba*,' she said. 'He is watching over you. He will see that you become the most famous poet of Hindustan.'

I made a fair copy of my poem, hurried back to the Nawab Rais Mian's *haveli* and had myself announced. Nawab Rais was out exercising his horses. After a while a maidservant came to escort me into the women's apartments. 'You are only a little boy; you don't even have hair on your upper lip,' she said to me saucily. 'No one will object to your presence in the *zenana*.' I found myself in a heavily curtained, dark room with a few bolsters laid on a Persian carpet along the wall. Some moments later Begum Sahiba entered the room. I bowed and made my salutation and with both hands presented the parchment on which I had written my poem. 'I am greatly honoured by your appreciation of my humble talent,' I said. She protested. 'It is I who should feel honoured by your presence. When you become the most famous poet of Hindustan you may remember this creature who was the first to appraise your greatness.'

Her words were celestial music in my ears. I dared to raise my eyes to see her. She was seated on the carpet reclining on a bolster. Since her eyes were fixed on me, I could not look at her for too long. She was a short, stocky woman about thirty years of age. She was fair, round-faced with raven-black hair long enough for her to sit on. The only other things I noticed about her were her taut bosom and big rounded buttocks which almost burst out of her tight fitting pyjamas. Her steady gaze unnerved me; it felt as if she was eating me up with her eyes. It was quite sometime before she asked me to be seated and ordered her maidservants to serve me refreshments. Even while I was partaking of the repast placed before me, I felt her eyes hovering over me. She invited me to the *bismillah* ceremony of her younger son. She asked me if I would condescend to see some of her verses and advise her how to improve them. She offered me the post of tutor to her children. I felt like a bird on whom a silken net was about to fall. I was happy but also somewhat apprehensive. My days of penury were over but my days of freedom seemed to be coming to an end.

When I told my mother about the meeting she shared both my joy and my apprehension. 'I have heard a lot of things about this Begum Sahiba. She comes from a poor family and was given away to Nawab Rais when she was barely sixteen and he over fifty and the father of many children through his first begum. They say that her second son is not her husband's but is of that poet fellow Parwana she had taken on as an *ustad* for some time. Nawab Rais is getting old and is often away in Delhi.' After a pause she added; '*Beta*, you are old enough now to get married. I will look for a nice girl for you.' Although I was only fifteen years old, I understood what disturbed her mind. She thought it would be a good idea if she called on Begum Sahiba to thank her and at the same time seek her advice about a suitable wife for me.

Begum Sahiba was very gracious to my mother. She gave her a silk dress and flattered her for having a son who would soon become the brightest star in the firmament. When my mother broached the subject of finding a wife for me, she replied without a pause; 'Leave it to me. I have just the right girl for him. Would you like to see her?' My mother protested; 'Begum Sahiba, if you approve of her what is there for us to see or say? May your choice be blessed!'

The next day Begum Sahiba teasingly told me that she had found a wife for me. 'She is not a houri; only a simple-minded girl, chaste as white marble. With a wife like her not a breath of scandal will ever pass your home. Her parents are not rich but we will look after the marriage expenses and provide her with a suitable dowry. You will not regret my choice.'

The father of the girl the Begum Sahiba had chosen for me was a distant relation of the begum and was employed as a caretaker in one of the Nawab's orchards. It was only after I had married this girl, Saleema, that the Begum Sahiba's designs became clear to me. My wife was indeed no houri: she was as thin as a bamboo rod, I could grasp her waist between my hands. Her breasts were hardly perceptible. Her front teeth stuck out even when her mouth was shut; when she spoke you could see her gums as well. She had no choice except to be chaste as white marble; but her being my wife tempted me to take the path of infidelity.

Begum Sahiba was a designing, masterful woman who had her way in everything. In old Nawab Rais she had the husband she wanted; with the singing rhymester who passed for a poet, she had a part-time lover she wanted. Her taste for poetry was determined by the applause a poet received and not its real worth. Since Meer Taqi's star was in the ascendant, she was determined to be his patron and his mistress. She found Taqi a wife he could ignore.

I will not divulge the name of the Begum Sahiba. Of all the crimes listed in the Holy *shariat*, the worst is to betray a woman who has willingly given herself to you. I will only reveal the name I gave her because of her fair, round face, Qamarunnissa— like the full moon. She was flattered by the comparison. She had a thousand years of womanhood in her: she knew how to seduce; having seduced, how to give the man of her choice the illusion that no one else in the world mattered to her. She as willingly surrendered her soul as she surrendered her body to her lovers. For the time she was my mistress she made me feel as if I was the only God she knew and every sentence I wrote was like a *sura* of the *Quran*. She became at once my mother, mistress, nurse and companion. She could not bear to be parted from me for a moment, unable to tolerate my having any other friends save those she approved of. She swore eternal fidelity to me in this life and for lives to come. I often felt handcuffed and shackled by her and wanted to break loose; at the same time I felt the long silken tresses with which she bound me were plaited by God to fulfil man's eternal quest for his beloved. When she discarded me like a pair of worn-out slippers, and turned her attention to yet another rhymester whose only qualification was that after I left for Delhi he became the favourite butterfly in the *mehfils* of Agra, I was shattered. This woman made me and destroyed me. That in brief is the life story of Meer Taqi Meer, the poet and the lover.

*

I have already narrated how I came to be invited to Nawab Rais's *haveli* and was appointed tutor to his sons. Begum Sahiba was always present during the lessons. While I taught the boys, her eyes rested on me. After the lessons were over, she insisted on my reciting whatever I had written the previous night. She praised every line and when I recited the *qita* she would exclaim *Subhan Allah*! then take the paper on which I had written the verse out of my hands and press it against her bosom. She would give me her own compositions. They were poor poetry but quite clearly addressed to me. I praised them, made suggestions on how to improve the rhyme and metre and at times took the paper from her hand and pressed it against my forehead. She gave me my midday meal. When I returned home in the evening, I would find she had sent *biryani* and other delicacies for the family. Thus she made me feel the most important man in the Mughal empire. Later in the night when I took my skin-and-bone wife to bed I would fantasize about the Begum's broad hips heaving upwards to receive me.

Once Begum Sahiba made up her mind to get something she spun a web of intrigue that ensnared everyone concerned. She was the master puppeteer with all the strings in her fingers;

they the puppets to act out her commands. From our exchange of verses she had assured herself that I was a willing victim. She then turned her wiles on her husband. She persuaded him that for his own future he should visit Delhi and find out what truth there was in the rumours that the Persian Nadir Shah was planning to invade India. At the same time she asked him to persuade Nawab Samsamuddaulah, the royal paymaster, who was the most powerful man in Delhi, to present me to the emperor. Who would suspect this strategy: if she desired me why would she want to send me away from Agra? Her husband not only agreed to both her proposals but also pressed me to stay in his *haveli* while he was away so that there was a reliable man to look after his household and his sons' education was not interrupted.

Soon after Nawab Rais left for Delhi with his retinue of horsemen the living arrangements in the *haveli* were reorganized. The boys were shifted to their father's bedchamber and their room was given to me. Between the two rooms was Begum Sahiba's own retiring-room.

She did not believe in wasting precious moments which she knew would not last long. Her duplicity was as astounding as her audacity. In the morning she bade a tearful farewell to her old husband; in the afternoon she busied herself with having the hair shaved off her legs, armpits and privates and her body massaged with perfumed oil. I discovered all this an hour after the evening repast when the children were asleep and the servants had retired to their quarters. She came to me as if she was coming to the bed of her husband awaiting her. Like people long married we did not waste time exchanging words of love. (In any case words that lovers exchange before they engage in love-making had been exchanged in the poems that we had passed to each other and in the dialogue our eyes had carried on since the first day they had met). Without bothering to blow out the lamp, she shed her clothes, stripped mine off my body and put her arms around me. We drank honey out of each other's mouths till we could drink no more. She pushed me quietly on the bed and spread herself over me. Her thighs were moist as dew on a rose-bud on a summer morning. She pressed her face into mine till my teeth hurt. After a while she began to moan, and with a shudder that shook her entire frame, collapsed drenched in sweat. Such ecstasy I had never known; nor can I put it into words.

When she tried to get up I held her down by her buttocks and did not let her move. She was of riper years and richer experience; I was younger and had more lust. She gave me a smile of approval and as a gesture of subservience turned over to let me play the master. I bit her all over her face and neck and bosom and with my tongue ravished her ears. This time she climaxed many times before I spent myself. We rested for half-an-hour and resumed the game of love. So it went on throughout the night. I do not know when it ended or when she slipped out of my room to retire to her chamber. When I woke my eyelids seemed as if they had been stuck together with glue. Instead of feeling tired I felt more refreshed. Instead of feeling guilty of having betrayed her husband's trust or having been unfaithful to my wife, I felt that Allah had blessed this union of minds and bodies; it was not profane but divine love.

I went down to the courtyard and found Begum Sahiba seated on a *moorha* with two maidservants massaging her feet. The floor was littered with the Nawab's pouter pigeons billing and cooing. As I made my *adaab* she smiled and said: 'I trust our poet-friend had a restful night,' and ordered one of her maids to serve me breakfast. She read out a letter her husband had sent her from Sikandra where he had camped for the night and informed me that she had sent a tray of dry fruit to my wife.

She planned our lives as it suited her. The money she gave me to teach her sons was more than my wife and mother had ever seen. 'Aren't my sons also your sons?' she asked my wife. 'You will be putting us in an eternal debt of gratitude if you allow your husband to teach them. What am I offering in return except a pittance barely enough to chew *betel*-leaf!' Through money and gifts she kept my wife and mother happy. To her husband she wrote that she had prevailed upon me not to take on any other work except teaching the children.

With me she was very truthful. She lied to the rest of the world but never to me. She told me of her marriage to Rais Mian who had already had children of his own. All he needed was someone to look after him and his affairs. This she did and left him with plenty of time to exercise his horses and train his pigeons. Once every few months, when roused by drink, he had sex with her. To restore his self-esteem she pretended to be worn out by his passionate love-making. She even confessed her liaison with Parwana and what trouble she had had to abort the foetus she had conceived from him. There was nothing left unsaid between us. Such was the intimacy she created that I felt guilty when I approached my wife. The Begum Sahiba persuaded me that while it was necessary for our relationship for her to keep up a pretence of loving her husband there was no need for me to consort with my wife. And because the poor thing was too modest to make demands on me she did not protest. She believed that all my energies were consumed in writing poetry and teaching.

I spent many blissful days in the Begum's company. It was in her tightly-clad, firm body that I learnt the true meaning of life. We spent long hours fulfilling the yearnings of our hearts and bodies hoping thereby that our hunger for each other would be forever satiated. But that was not to be: each time we were left to ourselves it seemed like the first time. We would pass our nights lying naked in each other's arms, but no sooner came the dawn, than, like a newly-wedded bride, she would coyly cover her face. I was overcome with the desire to find out the mystery that lay behind her veil. The more I saw of her the more my passion for her body grew. Her beauty shone like a pearl in limpid water. Whenever the moonlight of her radiance spread, real moonlight appeared no better than a spider's web:

> *A simmering fire burns our hearts away;*
> *We sink and my heart in depth of agony lies;*
> *As with the dawn the taper of the lamp*
> *Laps up the last drops of oil and dies.*

I became indifferent to the world, my mother, my wife and child. My relatives set their faces against me for neglecting my family; but what greater joy than to be tormented for the sake of love!

Nawab Rais returned from Delhi after a month. By then I had come to assume that he meant nothing to her and she would contrive to send him away on some other mission. I was taken aback by the show of affection she put up to welcome him and the formality with which she addressed me in his presence. She dressed herself in her best silks, darkened her eyes with *kohl*, reddened her lips with *missi* and showed great eagerness to be left alone with him. No sooner had we partaken of the midday meal than she announced, 'After his arduous journey Nawab Sahib needs to rest.' She followed her old man into their private apartment. I was left alone, holding my pen.

I could not sort out the confusion in my mind. After the intimacies we had enjoyed it seemed scarcely possible that either of us could bear anyone else's touch. I could not understand the shameless wantonness she displayed in wanting to be with her husband. Even more upsetting to me was her appearance after she came out of her room late in the afternoon: her hair was dishevelled and *kohl* was spattered on her cheeks. It was as if she wanted everyone to know what she had been up to. While I sulked she made solicitous enquiries about my comfort. In the presence of her husband she told me that she had sent a note to my wife that I had been detained in the *haveli* on important business. 'My husband will tell you of what transpired between him and Nawab Samsamuddaulah,' she said. Her husband said: 'Yes, I have to return to Delhi as soon as I can as there are rumours afloat of a Persian invasion. If they are true we have to gird our swords to our loins; if they are not true I will be back home within the month. Meanwhile you will stay here and look after the ladies.' The Begum Sahiba pleaded: 'Please! Please! I swear by the hair on your head if you do not accede to our entreaties, we will never speak to you again.' Though I was very angry I was left with little choice and agreed to stay. That evening a large number of Agra citizens came to call on Nawab Rais to enquire about his health and get news of Delhi. He was very discreet in his replies and quickly changed the subject: 'Don't bother about what they say in Delhi; you must stay to share our dry bread and *dal* and listen to Taqi Sahib. If you have not heard Meer Sahib's *kalaam* you have heard nothing.'

After a lavish feast, a *mushaira* got going. I listened to the rhymed *tuk-baazi* rubbish without comment. A slip of paper was handed to me by a servant. I recognized Begum Sahiba's handwriting—'Let your *kalaam* be worthy of your humble maidservant.' The candle was placed in front of me. From behind the screen I felt her eyes fixed on me and her ears awaiting what I had to say:

> How downhearted was Meer at night!
> Whatever came to his lips became a cry for help.
> When he started on the path of love, he was like fire;
> Now it's ended he is a heap of ashes on a pyre.

The *mushaira* went on late into the night with repeated requests for my *kalaam*. While it lasted I felt flushed with the wine of applause; when it ended, and I was alone on my *charpoy* on the roof with a myriad stars looking down on my wretchedness, my liver churned up angry vapours. Below the roof on which I lay, the woman who had made herself a part of my person was welcoming another man between her parted thighs. She had made me a stranger to my wife without any intention of changing her relationship with her own husband. I felt deserted and betrayed.

Nawab Rais decided to return to the capital. I accompanied him as far as Delhi Gate. That day, instead of returning to the *haveli* I went back to my family.

In the afternoon I took my wife to bed and savagely ravished her as I had not done since the first time I had deflowered her. The poor woman suffered my mauling with gratitude. She saw it as proof that I liked her. (That afternoon she conceived my second child, another son). In the evening the Begum Sahiba's servants arrived with a trayful of food and fruit. The maidservant, Naseema, in whom the Begum Sahiba confided her secrets slipped a note in my hand. It began with a couplet I had composed: 'For a long time no letter or message has been sent. A rite of faithfulness has been ended.' It continued that without me her world was desolate and if I did not return by the next morning, she would take poison and her death would be on my head. My anger vanished. I was full of remorse. I told Naseema I would present myself the next morning.

I went to the *haveli* like a criminal to a court of justice appealing for forgiveness. Without looking at me the Begum Sahiba remarked sarcastically: 'Meer Sahib treats us like beggars. When it pleases him he throws a few crumbs of his favour in our begging bowl.' I made no reply. I spent some hours taking the boys through their lessons. She sat gazing dolefully at me without saying a word. I had my afternoon meal and retired to my room. There I found a note on my pillow, again a couplet I had recited to her:

> Life is somewhat like a line drawing,
> Appearances a kind of trust,
> This period of grace we call age;
> Examine it carefully!
> It is a kind of waiting.

I awaited her all afternoon. She did not come. In the evening when I found her alone in the courtyard I asked her in dry tone, if I had her permission to return home. She replied: 'Don't bother to come to my funeral,' covered her face with her *dupatta* and ran inside.

I was not used to playing the role of villain in a melodrama. I wished Nawab Rais had taken me with him to Delhi and I would be free of this woman who made me feel like a fly stuck in a pot of honey. More was yet to come. No sooner did I retire after the evening meal regardless of the servants who were rinsing the utensils, than she came into my room, bolted the door from the inside and came towards me. Before I could stop her she fell at my feet and began to cry. The wife of Agra's richest Nawab crying at the feet of a poor teacher and poet! 'You are angry with me,' she said through her tears. 'Punish me any way you like. Beat me, treat me like a prostitute, do whatever you like but don't be angry with me!' I forced her up on my *charpoy* and brushed away her tears with my hands. She drew her breasts out of her chemise and pressed my head towards them. 'Bite them as hard as you can till you draw blood.' I kissed them tenderly. Then I kissed her eyes and lips. When I entered her she entreated: 'Let us run away to some place and get married; I hate that husband of mine. I don't want him to touch me ever again.' I smiled and asked, 'What about your children.

And the scandal?' She looked intently into my eyes: 'I will give up everyone and everything to be with you and serve you. Promise you will marry me.' I promised. Soon I was about to climax and tried to withdraw; she held me tightly between her legs and cried hoarsely: 'Don't! Come what may this night I am yours.'

When the first bout was over, I asked her timidly whether she had extended her favours to her husband. 'What kind of woman do you take me to be?' she demanded angrily. 'When I am in love with you can I offer my body to another? I knew it upset you to see me so solicitous about the old man. But one has to keep up appearances with the world, doesn't one? Were you unfaithful to me with your wife?' I lied by putting the question back to her, 'You think that is possible?'

We slipped back into the game of love. Everything ever written in books on sex and much that is written nowhere we practiced on each other. We had our own private language: she was Qamar to me; I Jaan (life) to her. We gave our genitals pet names: mine was *Raja babu,* hers *Bahoo rani.* When she was unclean she described it as a visitation of a gossiping crone she did not like. We made it a point that every coupling was a complete success. If I was hasty she patiently rekindled my lust. If she felt exhausted by what was permitted she would generously offer other avenues for my pleasure. Could any man have known a woman better? Or a woman a man? I composed the following lines:

> *Passions have made mortals of us men*
> *If men were not slaves of passion*
> *They would have been Gods, each one.*

Thus the days went by. And the nights. Whenever we were left by ourselves we told each other of our past. I had very little to say about myself but she kept nothing back from me. How she had fallen for that useless fellow *patanga* because of the way he sang only to discover that he was a philanderer and betrayed her trust by boasting about his conquest. There was nothing that we did not know about each other. A man can get away with his affairs with women, but a woman known to be promiscuous can be ruined for ever. That this woman should lay herself bare before me, convinced me that there would never be another man in her life. How little I knew of womankind!

It was not long before tongues began to wag. However, it seemed that the Begum Sahiba was not concerned about anything so long as the scandal did not get to the ears of her husband. Her servants knew that the slightest slip of the tongue about their mistress would bring ruin on their families. So they made it a point to tell Nawab Rais how, when he was away, the Begum Sahiba hardly ate anything and spent hours praying for his return. The old man would become most solicitous. Such is man's vanity! However, the *haveli* was not Agra. Whenever I went out in the bazaar, people who knew me would talk in words which had two meanings: 'Meer *Bhai*, what power you have in your pen! It can tear hearts as well as pyjamas.' Or slap me on the back and say, 'Meer Taqi, how fortune smiles on you!' One evening, when I was visiting my family, my mother took me aside and spoke in a voice full of alarm. '*Beta* Taqi, there are as many stories as there are tongues. No one can lock up people's mouths. Everyone in Agra is talking about you and the Begum Sahiba. I don't believe any of it; but if such tales are carried to her husband, do you know what he can do! He has a terrible temper and will think nothing of having all of us murdered. I beg of you to stop going to the *haveli*. Make any excuse you can. Say your old mother is dying. Say anything you like.'

I told the Begum Sahiba what my mother had said. For once she became pensive. Then she said: 'People have such dirty minds!' Thereafter there was less ardour in her passion. And she began to tell me how important it was for me to gain recognition in the Mughal court. A month later she read out a letter from her husband saying that he had arranged for my presentation at the exalted Fort Palace as well as a patron and I should proceed post-haste to Delhi. She said: 'My life will become desolate; but when I see your star shine brightly over Hindustan, I will say this man was my lover, I his beloved.'

When the day of my departure came she wrapped several

gold *ashrafis* in a green silken scarf and put her lips close to my
ear to whisper; *'Fallahu Khairun Haafiza wa huwa
arhumurrahimeen*—Allah is the best protector, He is
compassionate and merciful.' She tied the scarf round my arm
and added in plain Hindustani: 'Allah be with you wherever
you go; may He preserve you from harm, and bring you name
and fame.' However her prayer did not include this sentiment—
'May Allah bring you back to me.'

Before leaving I composed a few lines which I left with her
as a keepsake of our love:

> *You came here of your own accord and are lost in yourself;*
> *I know not what you search for, or who.*
> *If I want anyone it is you, if I want to see anyone it is you.*
> *You are the desire of my heart and my eyes' prayer.*

*

I wasn't sure whether Begum Sahiba was more grieved or more
relieved to see me leave Agra. I was not even sure of my own
feelings. At first I felt like a bird let out of a cage and wanted to
sing with the joy that freedom brought me. Then I missed the
golden cage in which she had imprisoned me for more than two
years, sang love songs to me, fed me and taken care of me. Was
I in love with her? I did not know. Perhaps it was her love for
me that made me feel worthwhile and fall in love with myself.
Whatever it was, before I had passed Mathura which was our
third halt, I found myself thinking more of my Qamarunnisa
than of my aged mother, my younger brother to whom I had
entrusted the care of the family, my wife or even my two-year-
old son, Kalloo.

These were disturbed times. Gangs of Jats, Gujars, Marathas
and Rohillas roamed over the country to prey upon hapless
travellers. Even the royal road from Agra to Delhi was not safe
from their depredations. I said to myself; 'O Meer why complain
of thorns at the start of the journey, it is still a long way to Delhi.'
I had attached myself to a caravan which had armed horsemen
and matchlockmen to guard our front and rear. We travelled
only during the day and halted at night in fortified *sarais*. At

Ghiaspur I took leave of my travelling companions to pay homage to the tombs of Hazrat Nizamuddin Auliya and Khwaja Ameer Khusrau whose works had inspired me. I stayed two days and nights in an Arab *sarai* close to the mausoleum of Emperor Humayun. It was from its marble tower that I had my first look at the city of the Mughals which was to be my home for many years to come.

I approached the city by the Delhi Gate. Nawab Rais had sent word to the *havaldar* guarding the gate to let me in. The *havaldar* detached one of his sentries to escort me to the house where Nawab Rais was staying. The Nawab Sahib was exceedingly kind to me—a man who after having eaten his salt had betrayed his trust by becoming his wife's lover. I told him how much the Begum Sahiba, the children and the household missed him. If nothing else she had taught me how to lie with a straight face.

Through Nawab Rais's influence I was able to rent a couple of rooms in a bazaar close to Fatehpuri Masjid. It was a mean-looking hovel but it was the best I could afford with the money in my purse. I called it the 'boaster's grave' and wrote a description of it in my diary: 'There are fissures and cracks in the walls, dust dropping from everywhere; in one corner a mole, a mouse peering out of another hole; bandicoots share my home, ever present is the mosquitoes' drone; spiders' webs hang from the walls; at night the crickets' grating call; edges crumbling, shutters tumbling, stones edging out of their places. Beams and rafters with soot-black faces. This was poor Meer's bower; there he spent hour after hour.'

A few days later Nawab Rais presented me to Mohammed Wasit, the nephew of the great Nawab Samsamuddaulah who was the power behind the Mughal throne. He promised to help after I had proved my worth at a *mushaira* which was due to take place soon and where his uncle was expected to be the guest of honour.

The *mushaira* was arranged on the roof-top of a mansion in Faiz Bazaar called Daryaganj. It was the night of the full moon which always reminded me of my Qamar. On the floor were carpets covered with snow-white sheets with jasmine and rose-petals scattered on them and bolsters placed along the sides; *surahis* (pitchers) of *sherbet* were lined on the parapets; a soft breeze blowing across the Jamna mingled with the fragrance of *khas*, rose and jasmine. Only the nobility of the town had been invited. Over a dozen poets of repute were present including the most famous—Sirajuddin Ali Khan 'Aarzoo', the brother of my step-mother. Most people had heard my name but none had seen my face or heard my voice. I was very nervous and kept rubbing my palms against my shirt to keep them dry. I did not know which of my compositions I should recite before such an august assemblage.

The *nawabs* of the court began to arrive. As their names were announced we rose from our seats to *salaam* them. The last to arrive was Nawab Samsamuddaulah. Everyone made a low bow to greet him. He acknowledged our greetings and asked us to be seated. After a while, the host announced that it was Nawab Samsamuddaulah's pleasure that the poets and guests should be allowed to wet their moustaches before the proceedings began. The announcement was greeted with applause. It was the first time in my life that besides *sherbet*, wine was served at a *mushaira*. Goblets went round and soon everyone was in high spirits. I had tasted wine before but never of such excellence—made from Kandahar grapes and chilled in snow brought down from the Himalayas. I had a poor liver for liquor. I realized that if I made a fool of myself at my first public appearance I would become the laughing stock of the city and decided to refill my goblet only after I had recited my piece.

The *mushaira* began with the recitations of the Delhi poets. Their compositions were on worn-out themes of moth and flame, *bulbul* and the rose, Leila and Majnun. Not one new idea, not one new turn of phrase. Nevertheless they were dutifully applauded. At long last the candle was placed in front of me. The host announced my name. He said that although I was young in years, I had become a household name in Agra and was appearing for the first time in Delhi. I acknowledged the compliments he paid and said that I had planned to recite an old poem on love which had been acclaimed in Agra but seeing the mood of the audience sought permission to recite one which I had composed in my mind while the wine-flask was going round. (To be truthful, I had composed it one night in

Agra when Qamar had passed wine from her mouth into mine as she lay above me). 'Irshad! Irshad!' they cried. I recited my poem on drunkeness:

> Friends forgive me! you can see I am somewhat drunk,
> If you must, an empty cup let it be,
> For I am somewhat drunk.
> As the flask goes round, give me just a sip—
> Not full to the top, just enough to wet my lip;
> For I am somewhat drunk.
> If I use rude words, it is all due to drink,
> You too may call me names and whatever else you think,
> For I am somewhat drunk.
> Either hold me in turn as you hold a cup of wine
> Or a little way come with me, let your company be mine,
> For I am somewhat drunk.
> What can I do, if I try to walk I stumble,
> Be not cross with me, please do not grumble;
> For I am somewhat drunk.
> The Friday prayer is always there, it will not run away,
> I will come along with you if for a while you'll stay
> For I am somewhat drunk.
> Meer can be as touchy as hell when it is his whim
> He is made of fragile glass, take no liberty with him;
> For he is somewhat drunk.

The audience was enthralled. One nobleman after another embraced me, pressed money into my hands. I was taken to be presented to Nawab Samsamuddaulah. He allowed me to kiss his hand and spoke very graciously to me. 'Beta, I was one of your father's disciples. Seeing you here in Delhi I presume he has departed from the world. I owe a lot to him and will repay his debt to you. Present yourself at our residence in the morning and we will see what we can do for you.'

I kissed his hand again and took my seat. I had my goblet refilled several times and drank the chilled wine as if it was water. My head was full of noises. I did not hear what the other poets had to say. Before the repast was served, I slipped out of the house. The world forgives a drunkard. I stepped out into a moonlit Delhi. Drunk with Kandahari wine everything looked beautiful: the streets bathed in silver, a deep blue sky with a few stars twinkling. I was a little unsteady on feet but had no difficulty in finding my way from Faiz Bazaar to Jamia Masjid and through the prostitutes' street, Chawri Bazaar, to the eunuchs'quarters Hauz Qazi. I kept thinking about my Qamar and how happy the two of us would have been and how we could have celebrated my victory over the other poets. I stopped by a *pan*-shop. I pushed my way through a ring of clients and ordered; 'Roll me the best *pan* you have.' The *panwalla* regarded me for a while before replying : 'Meer Sahib I'll make you one the like of which you have never tasted before. Perhaps you will compose a *qaseedah* on my *pan* and include my name in it.' I was pleased to know he recognized me. 'How did you know me ?' I asked. He smiled. 'Who in Delhi has not heard of Meer's *kalaam*. It is on everyone's lips.'

From his brass copper bowl he pulled out a bundle of *maghaee* leaves, selected the smoothest, smeared lime and catechu paste on them, added scented *betel*-nut and tobacco and then a powder of crushed pearls and powdered gold. He folded the leaf, stuck a clove needle in it and wrapped it in gold leaf. 'In Delhi we call this *palang tor* (bed crusher). You try it out and if what I am saying is not true, my name is not Hari Ram Chaurasia, the best *pan*-maker of Shahjahanabad.'

I did not like his talking like this to me in front of other people. I gave him a silver rupee and proceeded on my way towards Lal Kuan. I put the *pan* in my mouth. It was strong stuff and brought out the sweat all over my body. I then noticed that one of the fellows I had seen at the *panwalla's* was following me. I turned round and accosted him: 'Sir, have you any business with me?'

He addressed me very courteously: 'Meer Sahib, a night like this is made for love, not for walking through deserted streets. I can take you to the most beautiful girl in Delhi, no less than a princess of royal blood and barely sixteen years old. If she does not give you the time of your life, my name is not Chappan Mian.'

I do not know if it was the wine, the *pan* or the thoughts of my moon-faced Qamar that made me throw away the cloak of caution and follow the pimp through a dark, narrow lane branching off Lal Kuan. He slapped on a mean-looking door. A woman's voice demanded: 'Who is it at this hour ?'

'Open, I have a customer.'

An old woman unlatched the door and let us in. She *salaamed* me and said: 'Sir it is very late but I will wake up my daughter and get her ready to welcome you. *Huzoor* may give this poor hag something to buy *pan*.' I gave her one of the gold *ashrafis* presented to me earlier in the evening. She was obviously pleased with my bounty but being an experienced woman, turned the coin in her fingers and said 'I had bigger expectations from a gentleman of your rank.' I gave her another gold coin. She paid off the pimp and took me indoors.

Lamps were lit. She placed a tray of dry fruit before me which I waved away. Some minutes later a girl she called *beti* (daughter) entered the room rubbing the sleep out of her eyes. She was certainly young and beautiful—just as my Qamar had probably been at that age: fair and round-faced but somewhat shy. 'Be gentle with her, she is only a child,' said the old woman as she left the room.

I gave the girl a gold *ashrafi*. 'This is for you. Don't tell your old woman or the pimp.' She took it, put her head in my lap and began to sob. I stroked her long hair, then bare back. I slipped my hand in her *garara* and stroked her rounded buttocks. My sex was roused. She undid the cord of my pyjamas. I laid her on the bed and entered her. Was I being unfaithful to Qamar ? No. In this little girl I recreated her and relived the times we had lain together. Drink and the *pan* loaded with aphrodisiac made me stay in for an hour. She climaxed over and over again and was drenched in sweat by the time I spent myself in her.

She washed herself and then with a wet rag wiped my middle. Then he sat down beside me: 'That Chappan fellow says you are a famous poet,' she said. 'Give this maidservant a couplet as a gift.' I was not in a mood to compose poetry but did not want to hurt the girl's feelings. 'Give me a piece of paper, pen and ink and I'll scribble something for you.' She tore out a page from a notebook and gave me a reed pen and held an earthen inkpot in her hand. After thinking for a while I wrote:

218

> *The season of clouds, a flask of wine too.*
> *Roses in the rose garden, aş well as you.*

When I got to my home in Fatehpuri, the dawn was about to break. My head throbbed with pain, my mouth was parched. It was when I was changing my clothes that I noticed that all the gold and silver coins I had received were gone. Who could it have been except the sixteen-year-old girl passing for a Mughal princess! Meer, better look after your terrain, this is no ordinary habitation ! This is Delhi !

I was in ill-humour when I presented myself before Nawab Samsamuddaulah. So it seemed was the Nawab Sahib. His nephew Mohammed Wasit pleaded with him to fix an allowance for me. The Nawab Sahib regarded me with his bloodshot eyes and said: 'Yes, we heard him last night. He is a deserving case. Besides we are beholden to his late father. Let him be paid one rupee a day. Next !'

Before the next supplicant could open his mouth, I presented a parchment before him and said: 'Nawab Sahib may be pleased to put his order in writing.' Though young in years, I knew the ways of civil servants who never did anything without demanding proof in writing.

My simple request put the Nawab Sahib out of composure. He snapped in Farsee *'Waqt-e-Qalaam Daan ne'st*—this is not the time of the pen-inkholder.' I stood my ground. 'Sir, I do not understand the way you have framed your sentence,' I said. 'If your honour had said, "This is not the time for signing," or that "the pen-and-ink-bearer is not on duty," I would have understood. But to say that "pen-and-inkholder have no time" sounds extremely odd. It is not an animate object and therefore does not have proper or improper times; it can be brought at your honour's command.'

The Nawab Sahib's face lightened up with a smile. 'Meer Taqi, you are a saucy lad. We will gladly put our promise on paper.' With his own blessed hands he wrote out my allowance, signed and stamped it with his signet ring.

'Go and prosper. Let your *kalaam* be worthy of your father and bring you name and fame.'

How wonderful life was in the Delhi of those days! People thronged to my home to solicit my opinion on their compositions. Wherever I went people recognized me and praised me; there was not a *mushaira* in the city where I was not the star performer. Friday prayers at the Jamia Masjid were a treat by themselves. Although I could hardly call myself a Mussalman and saw no great difference between Believers and Idolaters, I made it a point to join the Friday prayer because of the adulation I received from the congregation after the prayer was over. The people of Delhi loved me; I loved them and their city.

Alas ! The days of happiness were not to last for ever. It was reported that the Persian, Nadir Shah, had occupied Afghanistan and was on the banks of the Indus. While preparations were being made to meet the invader, panic started growing in Delhi. Rich merchants began to leave the city. I received several letters from my wife, begging me to return to Agra. She also wrote that the Begum Sahiba had stopped sending food or gifts and had employed another tutor for her sons. People coming from Agra told me that the Begum Sahiba to whom I had sold my soul was enamoured by her son's new *ustad* and was showering gifts on his family. I did not believe these tales and decided to call on Nawab Rais, who happened to be in Delhi on a short visit before returning to Agra to raise troops to fight the Iranians. He was full of praise for the man appointed as my successor; he was not much of a poet, he said, but a good teacher and his sons were devoted to him. He had become like a member of their household and during Nawab Sahib's absence from Agra stayed in his *haveli*.

My mind was more disturbed by what was happening in Agra than by the Persian invasion. However, I stayed on in Delhi for as long as it was safe because Delhi provided me sustenance. I said to myself if a woman can be so perfidious it is best to consider her dead and forget about her rather than lose sleep over her. But the more I tried to wipe her from my mind, the more painfully she kept coming back to me. A heart on fire needs a stream of tears to put it out; a drop or two only makes it burn more fiercely. And the betrayal by a woman who my words had made divine and with whom I had exchanged my body and my soul soured me against humanity. I became short-tempered, quarrelsome and morose.

By the autumn of 1737 Nadir Shah had advanced into the Punjab plains. The Mughal army went out of Delhi to check his progress. Amongst the commanders were Nawab Samsamuddaulah. I prayed for a Mughal victory and the safe return of my patron.

One day in the spring of AD 1738 the two hosts clashed at Karnal. Allah granted victory to the Persians; the Mughals were routed. Amongst the thousands who attained martyrdom was Nawab Samsamuddaulah, royal paymaster, patron and protector of Meer Taqi Meer. No panegyric I write in his praise could do justice to his greatness and magnanimity. He was like a rain-cloud of generosity above my head. May Allah rest his noble soul in peace! I was left with no one to shield me from the darts of envious pen-pushers. Neither was there anyone before whom I could spread the apron of my poverty. I was left poor, weak, helpless and alone. It is in the nature of lightning to strike; it has struck your nest O Meer!

No sooner did I hear of the disaster at Karnal, than I hired a horse and took the road to Agra. There was no need to join any caravan as the entire route was one long caravan of people fleeing from Delhi to neighbouring towns and villages. On the way more than the Iranians we feared our own countrymen—Marathas, Jats and Gujars who robbed and killed any man they could lay their hands on and raped any woman who fell into their clutches. It took me five days to reach Agra. By then Nadir's horde was busy pillaging and looting Delhi. I said to myself : ' No matter a city can be rebuilt and repopulated but no power on earth can put together a heart that has been shattered.'

Agra was the city of my heart's ruination. I returned to see with my own eyes the debris that remained. Friend, it is my business to cry, how long will you keep wiping tears from my eyes! I recalled how our liaison had progressed and how we were carried away by our infatuation like paper-boats cast on a powerful stream. Love is an affliction which spares no one, neither the old nor the young, neither married nor single. How in my infatuation I had strewn flowers of homage at her feet;

how a woman, who I had at first not thought particularly beautiful, had become the most beautiful in the world to me after she became my beloved. In a *mehfil* of fair women, she had shone like the full moon amidst a galaxy of stars; her smile was like a rose-bud burgeoning into full bloom; her tresses lent their fragrance to the morning breeze; all this she became to me because she was cast in the mould of my desire. That this woman should have proved false to me and taken on another lover was beyond my comprehension.

But I still desired her. And now that I was back in Agra the raging fire of passion which I believed to have been reduced to ashes was once again fanned into a flame.

I returned home empty handed but was warmly welcomed by my family and saw my second-born for the first time. With some anguish I learnt that barely a month after I had left Agra, the Begum Sahiba had turned cool towards my family (so the rumours had been true!) and on their last visit to the *haveli* refused to see them on the pretext of being unwell. My step-brother who enjoyed hurting me told me with some relish how her affair with the new teacher she had hired for her children was commonly talked about. His words pierced my heart like arrows.

Next morning I went to pay my respects to Nawab Rais. Far from raising troops to fight the Iranians, he denounced the Mughals for not having made terms with Nadir, who he was reliably told, was an upright and just man, a devout Mussalman who would uproot idolatry from Hindustan. He took me inside to the *zenana* where the scene was exactly as I had left it except that instead of me there was this other teacher teaching the boys with the Begum Sahiba sitting on her *moorha* watching them. The boys greeted me very warmly, as did the teacher. But I could discern the look of triumph on his ugly face.

The Begum Sahiba had put on weight. The sparkle that had lit her eyes whenever she saw me was gone. She was as deferential towards me as she would have been to a stranger; her heart as cold as an extinguished oil-lamp. 'Meer Sahib, we hear Delhi resounds with your name. It is a matter of great pride for the people of Agra,' she said. How composed this woman was in the presence of three men, all of whom she had bedded! My face was flushed with anger and recrimination. I wanted to run out screaming and tell everyone in Agra that this woman had not only been unfaithful to her husband but also to her lover. They would have stoned her to death, not once but thrice. However, I did not open my mouth but made some excuse and took my leave. And the people of Agra. Far from being proud of me, they turned their faces against me. Men who had used the dust of my saintly father's feet as collyrium for their eyes averted their gaze from me. My voice was like the echo of a caravan bell in the wilderness. After six months of this humiliation I decided to quit Agra.

I arrived back in Delhi in the middle of summer. Strangely though I had left Agra a bitter at the betrayal by a woman who had sworn to be my companion in lives to come and was plotting ways to avenge myself, I could not get her out of my mind. I sought her everywhere among the ruins of Delhi. Like the cup of the narcissus I carried the begging bowl of my eyes asking for alms of her sight. At every dawning of the day like the morning breeze I went knocking at every door of every street. I became like the flame of a candle flickering in a gusty morning wind. I burnt inside, melted, diminished and came close to death. A strange madness came over me. Physicians told me that insanity ran in my family and that it had now erupted in my blood and could only be cured by being bled out. They cauterized me, stuck leeches on my body and locked me up in a dark, dingy cell as if I was a raving lunatic. The Hakeem Sahib who came to see me was astonished at my condition. 'What can I prescribe for a man who is stricken with the pangs of love !' he said. The only one who showed any sympathy for me was a distant relative, an old woman who brought me changes of clothes and food and words of comfort. Allah bless her !

I despaired and said to myself, 'Better be enchained, locked up, even die in a dungeon than be enmeshed in the net of love and longing.' I wrote a couplet of despair :

> 'The eye hath ruined me,' the heart complained.
> 'The heart has lost me,' the eye replied.

I know not which told the truth, which lied
Between the two, it was Meer who died.

I wanted to write my last will and testament with words of
warning to myself : 'Friend Meer, do everything your heart
desires but never let it fall in love; love spares neither lover nor
beloved.'

At long last they let me out of the cell in which they had
confined me for many weeks. I loitered about the streets and
bylanes. Whichever way I turned my eyes I saw signs of
devastation caused by Nadir's vandals. Not a house had been
spared. The Qila-i-Mualla had been stripped of its precious
stones and furnishings. Princes of royal blood had been reduced
to beggary; some had to go without food for days. Who was I
to complain! In despair I went looking for the dingy hovel
where I had spent a night in the arms of the girl passing for a
princess. Not one house in the lane had been spared. No one I
asked knew what had become of the old woman and the girl.
Perhaps the old woman was dead and the girl taken as a slave
by some Irani soldier.

What misfortunes had visited my beloved city! Sikhs,
Marathas, thieves, pickpockets, mendicants, rulers—all preyed
on us. Happy was he who had no wealth; poverty was the only
wealth. Seeing things in that light, I was the wealthiest of the
wealthy and at the same time the poorest of the poor.

One day sauntering through the city I came to buildings
recently destroyed. I had known the locality well but I
could not recognize the houses because little was left of them.
Nothing was known of their inmates. If I asked for someone by
name, they replied: 'He is not here any more.' If I asked for their
whereabouts, the reply was the same or 'I know nothing about
where they have gone.' Entire rows of houses had been razed
to the ground—as far as the eye could see it was one vast scene
of desolation. The bazaars had gone and with them the swains
who had frequented them. Where would I look for beauty
now? Where had fled all my pleasure-loving companions of
yesterday? Comely youths and aged men of wisdom—all had
vanished. I recalled a verse composed by someone :

Once through this ruined city did I pass
I espied a lonely bird on a bough and asked
'What knowest thou of this wilderness?'
It replied : 'I can sum it up in two words:
'Alas! Alas !'

*

In the wilderness that the Delhi despoiled by Nadir Shah became, I was left with hardly anyone I could turn to for help. In despair I sought the company of Sirajuddin Ali Khan 'Aarzoo', who before my coming, was Delhi's most celebrated poet. At first he seemed well-disposed towards me and even helped me to find patrons. It was on his advice that I gave up writing in Farsee and instead concentrated on composing poetry in the language spoken by the common people, the kind who thronged the broad steps of Jamia Masjid. This brought me popular acclaim. Then suddenly and for no reason known to me Aarzoo turned against me. I thought perhaps my step-brother had written to him about my affair with the wife of my benefactor. Or maybe he thought that because my mother was Shia, I had leanings towards the Shiites (Aarzoo was a bigoted Sunni). But I was neither Shia nor Sunni, neither Muslim nor Hindu. About my faith I wrote:

I have gone beyond the temple and the mosque,
I have made my heart my sanctuary;
On this thorn-strewn path end
All my wandering and my journey.

Like other Muslims I went to the mosque every Friday. Like Hindus I had drawn castemarks on my forehead, worshipped in temples of idolatry and ages ago abandoned Islam. However, the most likely cause of Aarzoo's anger was my growing popularity. He saw the crown worn by the *Sultan-ul-Shoara* (King of Poets) slipping off his head and being placed on mine. Envy slays friendship quicker than the sword. Aarzoo's hostility cost me many patrons and made life more difficult for me. As I had no regular income, I owed money to Banias, vegetable-sellers, milkmen and the like.

But as I've written earlier why should Meer mourn his own fate when loud cries of lamentation rise from every quarter of the city extending from the marble palaces of the exalted Red Fort to the humblest hovel in Paharganj ! The accursed Nadir Shah had left behind him in Delhi thousands of widows to beat their breasts over their dead husbands and forced thousands of orphans to go begging in the streets. Of the *bandobast* the less said the better. We had one king, Mohammed Shah, and three rulers: Chief Minister Nawab Safdar Jang on the one side, the Paymaster—General Nawab Imadul Mulk, and Nawab Intizammuddaulah on the other. The Emperor's writ did not run even in his own harem; it was his Hindu wife who had once been a dancing girl and her adviser, Nawab Javed Khan, who issued orders on his behalf. Javed Khan was a *khwaja sara* (eunuch) in charge of the royal harem, and despite his shortcoming was reputed to be the paramour of the Hindu empress. Why should Meer complain ? Javed may have been deprived of his manhood in one way but he proved his manliness by ignoring my detractors and spreading the umbrella of his bounty over my head. I was assured of at least one meal a day and a change of clothes when those I had on were tattered.

For a while fortune favoured Nawab Safdar Jang. When Mohammed Shah died he put the emperor's twenty-one-year-old son, Ahmed Shah, on the Mughal throne. Ahmed Shah preferred the company of nubile damsels and his wine-cup more than the business of State which he left to his mother and her confidant, Javed Khan.

Javed did not like Safdar Jang and joined Nawabs Imadul Mulk and Intizammuddaulah to plan his overthrow. A few months after Safdar Jang had become Chief Minister an attempt was made on his life. At Nigambodh Ghat in the vicinity of which he had his mansion a fusillade of gunfire was opened on him. Safdar Jang escaped by falling off his horse but many of his retainers were killed. Safdar Jang suspected Javed Khan of being the brain behind the conspiracy and plotted his destruction. He feigned friendship towards Javed and invited him for a morning repast along with Raja Suraj Mal Jat of Bharatpur. After the repast he took Javed aside and one of his retainers stabbed him in the back. His head was struck off his body and thrown on the sands of the Jamna. The empress went into mourning. I was deprived of yet another patron.

A regular war started between the soldiers of Safdar Jang and the empress's retainers. Every day they clashed, bullets flew, swords flashed and blood flowed in the gutters. They hired Rohillas, Jats, Marathas and Sikhs to fight for them. These hirelings fought for their paymasters by day and robbed the poor by night. The people of the city did not feel safe even in their own homes and pleaded with the empress to give them sanctuary. She acquiesced in their request and thousands of families moved into the open space of Sahibabad gardens alongside Chandni Chowk. Mercifully the monsoons were gentle and not many people died of exposure.

Ultimately Nawab Safdar Jang gave in. He was a Shia but there were few Shias even amongst his Muslim troops. After trying to win over the Jats and Marathas (who proved to be most untrustworthy), he quit in disgust. He spent his time erecting his final resting place on the road between Raisina and the Qutub and looking after his estates in Avadh.

The rule of Ahmed Shah came to an end while he was still living in the Fort Palace. The Marathas under Holkar after plundering Delhi's suburbs installed Mohammad Azizuddin, the great-grandson of Emperor Aurangzeb, as the new emperor. He was crowned on 5 June 1754 and assumed the title of Emperor Alamgir II. This self-styled conqueror of the Universe ruled an empire no larger than the enclosed space between the walls of the Red Fort.

Why labour the tragic tale of the King of Cities? Delhi was never the same after the Iranians had slain its soul. Kings, noblemen and their hirelings came like flocks of vultures to peck at its corpse. I stayed on in Delhi because there was nowhere else I could go except Agra. But one woman's perfidy had made me turn my face against that city forever. Through all these killings and massacres she did not send me even one letter enquiring about my health or safety. It is best to forget that such people exist. My wife and children—by now I had two sons and a daughter—joined me in Delhi. We lived in extreme poverty. I earned very little besides name and fame. I taught my children and found that all three were more inclined towards writing poetry than doing anything that might bring us money.

In the winter of 1758, Nadir's successor, the Afghan, Ahmad Shah Abdali, staked his claim to the empire of the Mughals. The Afghans marched through the Punjab without anyone daring to stop them and occupied Delhi. Abdali promised us security of life and property. But night had scarcely fallen when the outrages began. Fires were started in the city, houses were looted and burnt down. Afghan ruffians broke down doors, tied up those found inside, burnt them alive or cut off their heads. There was bloodshed and destruction everywhere. People were stripped of their clothes to wander naked in the streets. For many days no one had anything to eat. The cry of the oppressed rose to the heavens. Abdali who styled himself *Dur-i-Dauraan* (a Pearl among Pearls) and a pillar of the faith, was as rapacious as a hungry lion and remained unmoved by the plight of his fellow Muslims. People in their thousands fled from Delhi into the open country where many died of hunger or exposure to the elements. I, who was poor, became poorer. My house, which stood on the main road, was levelled to the ground.

In my constant search for patrons, I turned from the Muslim *nawabs* who no longer helped me to the Hindu nobility. Raja Jugal Kishore and Raja Nagar Mal were fond of poetry and sent their compositions to me for correction.

In the winter of AD 1759 events took a turn for the worse : Nawab Imadul Mulk once again soiled his dirty hands by spilling the blood of Alamgir II. Mirza Abdullah Ali Gauhar, the late emperor's eldest son, fled to Avadh and proclaimed himself Shah Alam II (he was the seventeenth in the line of Babar). As for me my hardships in Delhi were too much for me to bear. I put my trust in Allah and decided it was safer to be among the Hindu Jats in the countryside than live in a capital that was little better than a wilderness laid waste every six months.

I moved to Bharatpur ruled by Suraj Mal Jat. When I was there the Maratha armies marched northwestwards to meet Abdali and his Afghans who had once again descended on

Hindustan. On 17 January 1761 we received the news that two days earlier the Marathas had been decimated on the field of Panipat. Those who had managed to escape the Afghans' swords were set upon by gangs of Gujars and Jats and robbed of everything including their lives. I decided to stay on in Bharatpur until the Afghans departed and peace was restored in Delhi.

Six months later I ventured to return home. I quote from my diary written in the summer of 1761 :

'I am back in my beloved city. The scene of desolation fills my eyes with tears. At every step my distress and agitation increases. I cannot recognize houses or landmarks I once knew well. Of the former inhabitants, there is no trace. Everywhere there is a terrible emptiness. All at once I find myself in the quarter where I once resided. I recall the life I used to live : meeting friends in the evenings, reciting poetry, making love, spending sleepless nights pining for beautiful women and writing verses on their long tresses which held me captive. That was life! What is there left of it? Nothing. Not a soul with whom I can pass a few pleasant moments in conversation ! I come away from the lane and stand on the deserted road, gaping in stunned silence at the scene of devastation. I make a vow that as long as I live, I will never come this way again. Delhi is a city where dust drifts in deserted lanes; in days gone by in this very city a man could fill his lap with gold.

'Raja Nagar Mal has withdrawn his bounty. So what ! I will no longer have to correct verses which are beyond correction. I have been left with nothing. I go out begging, knocking at the doors of noblemen. Because of my fame as a poet I manage to live—as a dog or a cat might live.

'I pray that Delhi will never again see the accursed Afghans. Abdali's troopers have more loot than they can carry on the camels and elephants they have captured. They have told their king that if he wishes to stay in Hindustan he will have to do so by himself. Wisely, Abdali has given in. He has made arrangements for the administration of the territories he ravaged and is on his way back to Afghanistan. Allah be thanked for small mercies !

'The Afghans had become so arrogant and proud that Allah decided to teach them a lesson by having them humiliated at the hands of the Sikhs who were the lowest and the worst elements of society. A force of some forty to fifty thousand Sikhs blocked the passage of the retreating Afghans and fought them with a courage rarely seen in battle.

'Everyone knows that though severely wounded a Sikh will not turn his back on the enemy. Their bands move rapidly, surround straggling groups of Afghans and put them to the sword. No sooner the sun sets, than they descend on the Afghans from all directions and disappear in the morning. They make life hell for the Afghans. These Sikhs grow their hair and beards long and have a fierce aspect. Sometimes they let their long hair down before they fall on the Afghans and make them fly in terror. They fill the nights with their weird cries. Their footmen fight Afghan horsemen and their swords hack through Afghan saddles. In short, these Sikhs humiliated the Afghans in a manner never seen or heard of before. The Afghans lost the will to fight and the best they could do was to flee for their lives and to leave the governance of the State in the hands of a Hindu.

'The Sikh armies pressed on toppling crowns and thrones on their way, and chased the Afghans right upto the Attock river. Then they returned to the Punjab, slew the Hindu governor of Lahore appointed by Abdali, and became rulers of the Punjab. Now they have turned their bloodshot eyes on Delhi. What worse fate could befall a beautiful city than it become the abode of savages !'

*

Heavy as a rain-bearing cloud I wandered from one place to another. Delhi no longer could provide the food to keep me and my family alive. Once again I sought refuge in Bharatpur. My fame preceded me and people came from the south, east and west in the hope of getting a glimpse of me.

However, fame and words of praise do not fill an empty stomach. I know I have only one life to live, a hundred aspirations and a thousand desires to fulfil. I feel the weight of years on me and have become more and more like the flame of a candle flickering in a strong wind.

After the Persians, Afghans and the Marathas, came the Jats. I was still in Bharatpur when the Jat Raja Suraj Mal plundered Agra and Delhi. There was nothing left in Delhi for anyone to plunder but letters from my friends said that *Jaatgardi* (Jat lawlessness) was worse than the *Nadir Shahi* of the Iranians. The only hope left for Delhi was Nawab Najibuddaulah who kept both the Jats and the Sikhs at bay. That hope died with Najibuddaulah's death. The Marathas whom Abdali had routed at Panipat only four years earlier again became powerful. It seemed that either they or the Sikhs, both accursed races, would become the rulers of Delhi. Allah preserve us from such a calamity !

For ten long years I went from one city to another like a homeless wanderer. When Shah Alam II returned to Delhi I also decided to return and resume my quest for fame and fortune. I pinned my hopes on Mirza Najaf Khan, the Chief *Wazir*, who being Iranian was Shiite, a faith with which, because of my mother, I had a close affinity. Mirza was a veritable *Zulfiqaruddaulah*—master of the sword. He had freed Agra from the Jats and had beaten back Sikh brigands and Rohilla freebooters. Even the Marathas were afraid of measuring swords with him. Would Allah keep his sabre ever victorious ?

That, as it turned out, was not Allah's will. In April 1782 Mirza Najaf Khan died and was buried in a garden facing the mausoleum of Nawab Safdar Jang. The bloodstained dagger of destruction was once again pulled out of its scabbard. Najaf Khan's nephew, Mirza Shafi, wrested power from the hands of Mirza Afrasiab—the dead ruler's adopted son. In September 1783 Mirza Shafi was murdered by an assassin hired by Afrasiab. And a few months later Afrasiab was slain by the brother of Mirza Shafi. Not a day passed without someone murdering someone else. No one was safe.

Hunger and insecurity drove me from my beloved city to Lucknow. Here Nawab Asafuddaulah received me kindly and fixed a stipend for the upkeep of my family. However, the Lucknowis, who prided themselves on their etiquette and polished speech, displayed neither towards me. At the first *mehfil* which I attended, they looked disdainfully at my large turban, my loose-fitting clothes and asked me where on earth I had come from. When the candle was placed before me I gave them a befitting reply :

> *You men of these eastern regions*
> *Knowing my beggarly state you mock me;*
> *You snigger amongst yourselves and ask me*
> *Where on earth can you have come from ?*
> *Let me tell you !*
> *There once was fair city,*
> *Among cities of the world the first in fame;*
> *It hath been ruined and laid desolate,*
> *To that city I belong, Delhi is its name.*

*

The Lucknowis do not understand me and I do not understand them. How can I tell my tale in their strange land ? I speak a language they cannot comprehend. They do not know that every word of Meer has a meaning beyond meaning. The language I speak is best understood by the common folk of Delhi. O Meer why bother to speak to this assembly of the dead? Tears flow like rivers from my weeping eyes; my heart like Delhi lies in ruins. The fresh bloom of the rose gives me no joy; its piercing thorn no pain. Within my heart I know that I must return to Delhi where I passed my life intoxicated with love which I drank with the rose-red wine of my heart's blood. With a sigh I recall a couplet I had composed : 'Already you bewail your blistered feet; it is a long way to Delhi, my friend !'

The news from Delhi brings tears to everyone's eyes. Neither Nadir Shah nor Abdali, neither the Marathas, nor the Jats, nor the Sikhs caused so much havoc as is reported to have been caused by the ill-begotten Ghulam Qadir, the grandson of Najibuddaulah, and his ruffianly gangs of Rohillas. This villain insulted and deposed Shah Alam II before putting out his eyes. May Allah burn his carcass in the fires of *gehennum*! Only Allah

232

knows how long murder and looting will go on in Delhi ! They will have to revive the dead to find victims and bring back some loot to be able to loot again. Delhi is said to have become like a living skeleton.

> Burnt in flames till every building was reduced to ashes
> How fair a city was the heart that love put to the fire !

*

There is some good news. The Marathas have inflicted a severe defeat on the Rohillas. Ghulam Qadir has been captured alive, tortured and beheaded. Not a tear is shed for him. I am at peace with myself because at long last one villain who desecrated my beloved city has been punished. Will Delhi ever return to its days of glory? Only Allah knows.

I have now seen eighty-eight summers and winters on this wretched earth. The light in my eyes has dimmed; in three years I have lost four members of my family—my sons, daughter and my wife. I can neither read nor write and have no one left to look after me. Fain would I have mingled my dust in the scented dust of Delhi, but even that last wish is denied to me. Fate brought me to Lucknow into a *mehfil* where the *saqi* serves wine to everyone else but puts poison in my goblet. Here Meer will find no resting place; he must go like running water flowing through the gardens of the world.

Why do people tell frightening tales of the road to death when there are so many going along the same way to keep one company? I have no fear of dying. I had two loves in my life, Begum Qamarunnissa and Delhi. One destroyed me, the other was destroyed for me. I have nothing more to live for. For my two loves I compose the following lines :

> As I opened my eyes after my death
> My only wish was to once again see your face;
> It was in my heart you had your habitation
> Where will I find eyes to see this plundered place?

15

Bhagmati

Bhagmati is to spend the evening with me. She will expect me to take her. If I do not show enthusiasm she will say I am growing indifferent or worse, impotent. I must have a good excuse for abstaining: high fever, a broken arm or a fractured penis. But all I have is wind in my stomach. Anyone who suffers from wind knows that until expelled, it will not allow the flame of lust to be kindled.

A long time ago when this trouble first started I made a list of wind-producing items. It included many of my favourite foods: raw onions, mangoes, *cheekoos*, ice-creams, cakes ... I got over the problem that faced me by making a slight change in my love schedule. I ate them after and not before. With the years I had to add other items to the 'after-not-before' list: rice, lentils, potatoes, fried foods. The list continued to grow till it included just about everything edible. Nevertheless by the evening my belly would be full of air. I gave up lunch and moved the trysting hour from the evening to the afternoon. It worked well for some time. But it takes two to make a tryst and Bhagmati is not a nooner. So whenever I was sure Bhagmati would visit me I restricted my breakfast to black coffee and Vitamin B tablets— the closest thing I've discovered to an aphrodisiac.

Today all I have had since the morning are two mugs of black coffee and a capsule of Vitamin B Complex. Still there is a balloon full of wind in my stomach and no lust in my loins. I do not desire sex; instead I pray for a long, satisfying fart. I have tried hopping round the room on one leg, lying on my back with my knees pressed against my paunch, massaging my belly. All to no avail. Verily hath Shaikh Saadi said:

> *O Sage ! the stomach is the prison house of wind,*
> *The sagacious contain it not in captivity,*
> *If wind torment thy belly, release it, fart;*
> *For the wind in the stomach is like a stone on the heart.*

O Sage of Shiraz! The wind doth truly torment me like a stone on my heart! How shall I release it?

Farting is one of the three great joys of life. First, sex; second, oil rubbed in a scalp full of dandruff; third, a long, satisfying fart. With the onset of middle age I have reversed the order of merit: farting now tops my list of life's pleasures.

The king of farts is the Trumpet—known to our ancestors as *Uttam Paadam*—its noise rendered as *phadakaam*. It is an act of will, it is proclamatory, it is masculine. It has much sound, little smell. The louder, the less odorous. My friend, the bald, beady-eyed photographer who has done considerable research on the subject is an exponent of the Trumpet. He is of the considered opinion that the Trumpet can only be produced by people who restrict their diet to fresh fruits and non-fibrous vegetables grown above the ground. Such food is *sattvik* (pure). (Poultry, fish and meat, though nourishing, are of the secondary *rajas* category. Spices, stale foods like pickles, preserves and chutneys; vegetables which grow underground like potatoes, radishes, carrots and garlic, or are attached to the earth like onions, cabbages, turnips and cauliflowers are definitely *tamas*). My photographer friend demonstrated the Trumpet by consuming a succulent watermelon on an empty stomach. An hour later he was airborne like a jet plane.

Second in the order of farts is the *Shehnai*—our ancestors also give it a secondary status *madhyamaa*—and its sound is rendered as *thain, thain*. I prefer to compare it to the *shehnai*, a wind instrument made famous by the maestro Ustad Bismillah Khan of Varanasi. Like the Trumpet, the *Shehnai* is also an act of will and may be produced by a simple shift in position or gentle pressure on the paunch. It differs from the Trumpet in its softer tone and longer duration. The opening notes of a Scottish bagpipe sounds very much like it—*pheenh*.

The third variety is the Scraper which makes a sound like the squelch of uncured leather or the rustling of old parchment. It is in fact not one but a succession of little farts—*pirt, pirt, pirt, pirt*. The Scraper is a by-product of eating too much of *tamasik* food. It is also a phenomenon of rectal muscles softened by age.

The fourth is the *Tabla*. It proclaims itself with a single *phut* like a tap on a bongo drum. The *Tabla* is its own master as it escapes without the host's consent causing him or her deep embarrassment if they happen to be in company.

The fifth is the noiseless stink bomb, the *Phuskin*. Since it is unspoken it is best-suited to be planted on a neighbour as a secret gift—*gupta daan*. The donor can assume a 'not-I' look on his face or hold his nostrils and turn towards someone else with an accusing look. But he must heed the Japanese saying: 'He who talks is the one who farted'. If you have let off a stinking *gupta daan*, let others guess the identity of the benefactor.

Nations have different attitudes towards farting. The Europeans and Americans are quite shameless about it. It is a part of their Greek inheritance. Niarchos (1st century AD) extolled the virtues of farting any time wind built up in the belly:

> *If blocked, a fart can kill a man;*
> *If let escape, a fart can sing*
> *Health-giving songs; farts kill and save.*
> *A fart is a powerful king.*

Niarchos knew the difference between a noiseless stink bomb and the audible varieties of wind-breaking. To wit:

> *Does Henry sigh, or does he fart?*
> *His breath is strong from either part.*

Exhortations to the fart are also found in contemporary English literature:

> *Men of letters' ere we part*
> *Tell me why you never fart?*
> *Never fart? Dear Miss Bright,*
> *I do not need to fart, I write.*

Although white races eat bland *rajas* food which does not

236

produce much wind, when they have it, they release it in company with total unconcern for propriety. This is particularly revolting in the case of the wine-drinkers making a *gupta daan*: wind produced by wine is singularly stenchful. The ultimate in white people's vulgarity was a Frenchman who displayed his fart-power on stage. He had a slit made in the back of his trousers and for a small wager would blow out a candle placed three feet away from his posterior.

If the Whites are disgusting, the Indians are not much better. Indians have a very poor sense of humour and treat farting as a topic of jest. Since they eat highly spiced *tamasik* foods, they are the world's champion farters and have much occasion to laugh at each other. Once a Minister of Cabinet recording a talk for the External Services of All India Radio let out a Trumpet. The talk had to be re-recorded. However, when the time came, by mistake the original recording was put on the air. It gave an Indian the unique distinction of having his fart heard around the world. The *Guinness Book of Records*, please note.

For an unrelenting attitude towards farting the palm must be given to the Persians and the Arabs. There is a tale told of a young Iranian who broke wind in a *mehfil*. He was so overcome with remorse that he left the town. After many years in self-imposed exile he returned home hoping that his small misdemeanour would have been forgotten. Naming himself, he asked some boys to direct him to his old home. 'You mean the home of so-and-so the farter?' demanded the urchins. The poor man went back into exile.

The first prize for courtesy extended to farters goes to Sufi Abdul Rahman Hatam Ibn Unwan al-assam of Balkh, known for reasons of his noble attitude to farting as Hatam the Deaf. It is said that while he was explaining a matter of some theological import to an old woman, the lady farted. The saintly Sufi raised his voice and said, 'Speak louder, I am hard of hearing.' And for the fifteen long years that the woman continued to live, Hatam pretended to be hard of hearing and suffered people shouting in his ears. Hatam the Deaf is the patron saint of embarrassed farters.

I wonder if Bhagmati will accept this learned thesis on wind-breaking in lieu of the real thing.

16

1857

Alice Aldwell

I can never forgive myself for persuading my hubby to move to
Delhi. 'What's wrong with Calcutta? We are quite happy here,'
he used to say.

There wasn't anything wrong with Cal but there were many
reasons why I did not want to go on living there. For one the
place was full of Eurasians and if you didn't cut yourself off
completely from them, English gentry began to suspect you
were one of them. Mind you I have nothing personal against
Eurasians! I know some fine gentlemen who have a bit of the
tar-brush in them. Being half-caste is not their fault, is it? But I
simply had to get away from them. Mum had lived in Cal so
long that she had forgotten where she had come from back
Home. She had also picked up that awful *chichi* of the half-
castes. For another I had married a pucca English gentleman:
Alexander Aldwell Esquire of Her Majesty's Post and Telegraph
Services. Although yours sincerely was only a sweet eighteen
and he going into his fifties when she went up the altar with
him, he was, as I said before, of pucca English stock—sixteen
annas to the sicca rupee! I didn't want him to mix with the riff-
raff of Cal.

Alec gave me two girls in the first two years of our marriage.
Then he went *phut* just like that, *phut*. At fifty-five he was retired
from service. I hoped he would take us back to Ole Blighty. But
he refused to leave Cal. 'Livin' is cheaper here,' he said. 'Back
home we won't have an *ayah* or *chokra*.' In any case he hadn't
saved up anything so we did not have money to pay the ole P.
& O. our passage money. We had to move into cheaper digs in

the Eurasian quarters between Chowringhee and the native bazaar. I tried to have as little to do with our neighbours as possible. But Alec took to them like a duck takes to water. He started drinking toddy with Eurasians and going to their homes. I pleaded with him: 'Alec, I don't want my girls to grow up in India, I want to send them to a good school at Home. If you can't afford it on your pension, let's go up country where they are short of sahibs. I am sure you could get some kind of job. With your salary plus the pension we could give the girls what they deserve. We can save up and then join them in England. Meanwhile we could mix with the right kind of people.' If I said this once, I said it a hundred times. You think that Mister Alexander Aldwell would listen! In through one ear, out of the other! 'Who'll give me a job at my age?' he would say and go out of the house as fast as he could.

I got fed up. Without telling Alec I went to see Mr George Atkins who had been his boss. Mr Atkins was real nice. Only forty and a bachelor. He listened to me and said he'd like time to think it over. He asked me to dine with him at the Calcutta Club. Real swanky it was! Gentlemen in tails, ladies in long dresses! Bearers, *khidmatgars, abdars* and what have you! And Mr Atkins so gallant! He said he was mighty proud to be seen with anyone as pretty as yours sincerely. I gave him a friendly peck on his nose. After dining and dancing he drove me back in his *buggy*. I gave him a real mouthful of a goodnight kiss.

A few days later, Mr Atkins invited me to dine with him at his bungalow. So romantic it was! Candle-light and champagne and all that kind of thing. English ham, Cheddar cheese and everything of the best from Calcutta's poshest store—the Hall of All Nations. I knew what he wanted. And I knew what I wanted. After supper we got down to business: I gave him a real nice time. As I said, my hubby had gone *phut*. I was only twenty-six and hadn't known a man for more than a year.

George Atkins did not know the first thing about making love—I mean full twenty shillings to the pound worth of love. No sooner he put his thing in, he was finished. He worked himself up for a second bout. This time he was very rough; he bit my breasts, dug his nails into my poor bottom and rammed away as hard as he could. As he was about to come, I screamed:

'You are killin' me darlin'!' He lunged away and with a great 'whoa' spent himself. I pretended I had come and was exhausted. He looked like St. George who had slain his first dragon. He turned very gentle: 'Did I hurt you, dear? Do forgive me.' Hurt me? My foot! I replied in my most tired voice; 'No, darling, you did not hurt me. You just did me in. It was wonderful. Thank you, thank you, thank you.' George Atkins looked as if his salary had been doubled and he had scored a century at a cricket match. He lay beside me tapping his chest as if it were full of gold medals. I began to play with his nipples till they became hard. I kissed his paunch and stuck my nose in his navel. I could see his member was in a sorry state of dejection. I ran my fingers in his fuzzy red pubic hair and gently played with his whatnot. It began to stir like a snake in a snake charmer's basket. Then I applied my tongue to it till it was fully revived. It was quite a size. I came over him and took him between my thighs. I wanted him to have a night he would remember as long as he lived. 'I expect it's the Indian in you which makes you such a superb lover,' he said crossing his arms behind my back. I didn't like that and told him so 'No Georgie dearie,' I told him, 'there is nothing Indian about yours sincerely. I am as pucca as you: one hundred per cent British and proud of it. Now promise me one thing. You must get Alec a job some place up country. God promise?' I kissed him and wiggled my middle on him. I looked directly into his eyes and asked: 'Do I have your word?' He tried to look away, but I held his head in my hands. 'Promise! I'll make it worth your while,' I assured him. 'I will do my best,' he replied. That was enough. I glued my mouth to his, ran my tongue in his mouth and worked on him till both of us were like two animals: biting, clawing, drawing blood. We almost killed each other in the final act. This time it was, as they say in an attorney's office, 'Signed, sealed and delivered.' His *syce* drove me home at 3 a.m.

The next morning I nagged Alec and made him call on Mr Atkins. (I told him that I had spoken to someone who had spoken to Mr Atkins). My only fear was that Atkins might want to keep me in Cal. But you know what men are! Within a week he fixed Alec with a job in Delhi. I went to his bungalow to thank him. This time there were no candles, no champagne, no supper. He just fucked me.

That's how we came to be in Delhi in the spring of 1856. We rented a large double-storeyed house in Daryaganj where most of the European civilians lived. Our bungalow had a spacious compound and quarters for our *ayahs, khansama, masalchi, abdars, bhishties, syce, jamadars* and other servants. It was like a fortress with high walls and a massive iron gate. On the eastern side of our bungalow was the city wall with the river Jamna running below it.

In November I had my third child, another girl. We had her christened at St. James Church in Kashmiri Gate. I chose the name for her: Georgina. (I sent Mr Atkins a card announcing the birth and the name of our girl). Fifteen days later we had a party to celebrate Georgina's arrival. Just everyone who was anyone in Delhi was invited. More than fifty ladies and gentlemen responded. The Resident, Mr Theophilus Metcalfe, who was the *burra* sahib dropped in for a few minutes. Mr Beresford, the manager of the bank in the main bazaar, Chandni Chowk, and his wife came with their children. Captain Douglas, commander of the guard at the Red Fort came with Mr Simon Fraser, the Commissioner. Because of the baby I could not drink or dance. Everyone else had a wonderful time.

We did not ask any natives. Nevertheless many sent us presents. Amongst them was a lovely brocade piece from Begum Zeenat Mahal, the favourite wife of the old king Bahadur Shah.

Mr Metcalfe took me aside and asked me for a favour. He said that he wanted someone to keep in touch with the harems of the *nawabs* to know what their begums were saying. I do not know how he guessed that I could understand Hindustani. Since he spoke to me personally, I promised to do anything I could after I had weaned my baby.

Winters in Delhi are very pleasant. By December it is cold enough to have a log fire. There is frost on the ground in the mornings; the days are bright and warm. I made my place real comfy and kept an open house for Europeans. Captain Douglas and his young subalterns became regular visitors. I served them hot rum punch with cloves and nutmeg which they loved.

241

On Christmas eve, we went to the carol service at St. James Church. Next morning, our verandah was full of baskets of fruit and flowers sent by my husband's native subordinates for the *bara din*. In the afternoon, Mr Metcalfe was at home to the European community. We toasted Her Majesty the Queen on the lawns of his mansion beyond Kashmiri Gate. That evening we had a few bachelors join us round our Christmas tree. Everyone got very drunk: Alec was quite blotto and had to be put to bed. The men flirted with me — mind you nothing very serious! Just a lot of Christmassy kissin' and cuddlin'.

On Boxing Day Alec went out with Captain Douglas for *shikar*. They brought back two blackbucks, four geese and almost fifty partridges. We sent legs of venison and a brace of partridges to our friends.

We organized a grand feast on New Year's eve. Mr Metcalfe again did us the honour of a short visit. Once more he took me aside and reminded me of my promise to find out what the native women were saying. He sounded very eager about it. I assured him I would get down to the job.

The real fun began after Mr Metcalfe had left. Alec passed out and had to be put to bed. One of the subalterns almost raped me within a yard of where Alec was lying drunk. That stupid, besotted husband of mine kept egging him on, 'Take the bloody bitch..go on...' Such was life in Delhi!

After the season's festivities were over I sent letters of thanks to the wives of the natives who had sent us gifts on Georgina's birth and the *bara din*. Some begums came to call and protested that letters were not necessary between members of the same family. ('I a member of a native family! Really!') Natives are given to this kind of exaggeration. I was 'sister' to everyone. Their children called me *mausi*. Fawning and flattering you to your face but always ready with a dagger to plunge in your back!

*

It was some time in the April of 1857. I remember it had turned very, very warm. We had *bhishties* splashing water on the *khas* curtains we hung on the doors. No one dared to stir out in the afternoon. Even the nights were unpleasant. We slept on our roof and had a relay of *pankhawallas* to fan us throughout the night. One day Begum Zeenat Mahal sent us a trayload of watermelons and mangoes from her estate in Talkatora. I gave a handsome tip to the bearers and informed Mr Metcalfe about it. He sent me word that I should join the party of European ladies who had also received baskets of fruit and who were calling on Zeenat Mahal to thank her.

I took my two older girls with me in the phaeton sent by Mr Beresford, the banker. Captain Douglas received us at Lahore Gate. It was a memsahibs' afternoon. There was old Mrs Flemming, wife of Sergeant Flemming and her daughter, Mrs Scully, and a few others. Captain Douglas passed us on to Basant Ali Khan, a fat eunuch who was the head of the harem guard. He escorted us through the Meena Bazaar and endless corridors with rooms on either side occupied by the *salateen* members of the royal household. A scruffier, smellier lot would be hard to find anywhere in the world. Their quarters were worse than those of my servants; the women were poorer dressed than my *ayahs*. We were conducted to the queen's reception room which overlooked the river.

We were seated on *divans* overlaid with Persian carpets and bolsters covered with brocade to rest our backs. Carpets in the heat of summer! But there are natives for you! Every visitor had two women standing behind her waving huge fans. They sprinkled us with rose and *kewra* water. A female herald announced: 'Her Majesty, the Queen of Hindustan, Empress of the Universe, diadem of the age.' Natives love high-sounding titles. In came the queen. She certainly was a beauty! Large almond-shaped eyes, olive complexion and jet black hair. She was exquisitely dressed in her native chemise and *garara* with a gossamer-thin *dupatta* flung over her head. We stood up to greet her. She shook each of us by the hand, said 'good-afternoon' in English and patted my children on their cheeks. My girls curtsied to her. Trays of fruit and sweetmeats were passed around. She pressed us to taste them. Although she knew a little English, she spoke in Persian or Hindustani. Most of us had picked up a few words in Hindustani, so we got along quite well. When we ran out of words we giggled or laughed.

There was much coming and going of begums and their daughters all very curious to see the memsahibs and talk to them. Men were not allowed in the *zenana* apartments but Prince Jawan Bakht, the queen's only son, a sallow-skinned youth of sixteen who had recently married his cousin, was allowed in with his wife.

The queen had presents for all of us. We also had presents for her and her daughter-in-law. My girls received a silk chemise, a *salwar* and a gold bangle each. In return I gave the queen a bottle of Yardley's lavender water and her daughter-in-law, a lady's watch. They were very happy with the gifts.

The party broke up into small groups. I joined a group with Jawan Bakht and his wife. The boy had not been taught how to behave in the company of ladies. He kept chewing *betel*-leaf and spitting the horrible, bloody phlegm into a silver spittoon which a eunuch carried everywhere he went. And like common natives he kept scratching his privates. He also had the nasty habit of whispering in the ears of his cronies. At times he made remarks in Persian which he thought we could not understand. Since I had tried to speak to him he directed his evil eyes and tongue towards me. He recited a couplet in Persian to his wife:

> *Expect not faithfulness from nightingales*
> *Who sing every moment to another rose.*

The silly girl covered her face with her hands and went into fits of laughter. As his eyes were fixed on me, I suspected the couplet was about me. While his mother was talking to some of the ladies, he again said in Persian: 'An arrow in the side of a young damsel is better than an old man.' His wife re-doubled her laughter. This only encouraged the lout to go on:

> *When she saw something in her husband's hand*
> *Something limp, hanging like the lower lip of a hungry*
> *man...*
> *My ministrations will rouse one asleep but not a corpse.*

I was really *gussa*. 'What is this *buk buk* your husband is saying?' I demanded of his wife. Jawan Bakht tried to be very clever. It did not occur to the fool that I could understand Persian. 'Aldwell memsahib, this is poetry in praise of youth and beauty,' he replied with a smirk on his face. 'You have no cause to be angry. Regarding an angry woman, the same poet, the peerless Saadi, has said...' And he quoted in Persian:

A woman who rises unsatisfied from her bed
Will quarrel and contend with her man;
An old man who cannot rise without the aid of a stick
How can his own stick rise?

'I know exactly what it means,' I cut him short in Persian. 'You should be ashamed of yourself. Shall I tell your mother what you have been saying?' You should have seen the fellow's face! Yellow as a dry banana-leaf. And squirming like a worm on the hook. His mother turned to me and asked: 'What are you two quarrelling about?' 'You ask your son, Your Majesty,' I replied.

I left Jawan Bakht's group and went across the room to speak to one of the girls who had been trying to catch my eye. She wanted to try out the words of English she had learnt. Jawan Bakht also quickly turned away and began to talk to Mrs Scully. I don't know what he said to her but she suddenly stood up and spoke to Mrs Flemming: 'Mother do you hear what this young rascal is saying? He says that he will soon have the English under his feet, after that he will kill all Hindus.' Mrs Flemming was old and very blunt.

'Did you say that, Jawan Bakht?' she demanded angrily.

The queen looked very angrily at her son. Jawan Bakht grinned like a monkey with red teeth. 'I was only joking,' he replied.

'What kind of jokes have you been learning lately?' asked Mrs Flemming. 'First you are rude to a lady (meaning me) and then to the English race! If there is any trouble in Hindustan, you will be the first to have your head taken off your shoulders.'

'*La haul valla quwwat!*' chanted the maidservants. Queen Zeenat Mahal's face was flushed with embarrassment. Everyone knew that she had been knocking at the doors of the sahibs wanting them to proclaim Jawan Bakht as the next king of

Delhi. And there he was pouring cold water on her hopes. 'What kind of ill-mannered talk is this? You must apologize at once,' she said very firmly.

'*Amma Jan!*' whined the lout, 'I was only saying that there are rumours afloat that the Persians are going to invade Hindustan. And like Nadir Shah a hundred years ago,they will massacre the infidels. *Amma Jan,* you know very well that I would give my life to protect the lives of the European ladies of Delhi.'

That just proved what I had been saying about these natives—blatant liars from head to foot! Anyway I had something for Mr Metcalfe.

The reception came to an end. Zeenat Mahal sent for the tray of *betel* leaves and gave us one each with her own hands. I can't stand *betels* any more than other Europeans, but court etiquette required us to accept. So we stuffed the leaves in our mouths, *salaamed* the queen and left.

I told my hubby about the party in the palace. He was not surprised. He said he had overheard natives talking of a Persian or a Russian invasion and even seen posters on the walls of the Jamia Masjid saying that the invasion would take place that summer. He said that these rumours had been going on since the day Lord Canning had become Viceroy. When walking up to take the oath of office His Lordship's foot had caught in the carpet and he had stumbled. The natives were saying that this was a sign from Allah that Canning's government would likewise stumble and fall. Alec said that most natives believed that British rule would end on the hundredth anniversary of the Battle of Plassey, which was to be some time in June. 'All these bloody niggers can do is to *yak yak,*' he assured me. 'Let them try and we will stick a greased pole up their dirty black bums.' Alec had been using that kind of language ever since he had gone *phut.*

Alec called on Mr Metcalfe and told him what I had picked up at the palace and what he had heard in the bazaar. Mr Metcalfe thanked Alec and asked him to request me to keep in touch with the ladies of the harem of Mirza Abdullah, one of the many grandsons of the king.

Mirza Abdullah lived in Daryaganj. He was a follower of a

fellow called Hassan Askari who lived in the street behind our house. This Hassan Askari was known to have the king's ear. The king's daughter who had died two years ago had been his mistress. Mirza Abdullah's sister had called on me many times. I really had no intention of returning her calls. But after what Mr Metcalfe had said to my hubby I felt I should do my bit for the Old Country.

One afternoon I dropped in at Mirza Abdullah's house. My, how flattered these natives are when a European lady calls on them! And how flustered! The women were so excited and out of breath that they could hardly talk. And they were all very eager to tell me of the rumours about invasions and risings. 'You can't stop tongues from wagging, can you?' said Mirza's senior begum. 'There are as many rumours as there are people.' I asked her about Hassan Askari. 'He's a man of Allah,' replied the begum. 'But he is not of our faith. He is a Shia and we are Sunnis. We have nothing to do with him.'

I knew this was a lie. The tailor who did odd jobs for me also worked for Mirza Abdullah's family. He had told me that he often saw Hassan Askari in Mirza Sahib's house. As I said before, you can never trust natives. They learn to lie from the day they learn to speak. They think it's more clever to tell a lie than tell the truth.

Alec went to report on my visit to Mirza Abdullah's house to Mr Metcalfe. When he returned he told me of mysterious fires in the cantonments and strange people running about with *chappaties*. That the wily blacks were plotting against us we were sure, but we did not realize how soon these double-faced traitors would stab us in the back. How well I recall the day it happened!

Our usual practice before we retired was to spend the evening on the roof-top (unless there was a dust-storm blowing) where we had our sundowner and our dinner. Then as I've said, we'd have the *bhishties* sprinkle water and servants lay out the beds. At first I had mine alongside Alec's. But when he had eaten hot curry, he used to get very windy and make things unpleasant. So I had his bed removed to a distance so that we were not disturbed by his farting. On the roof-top the nights were cool and the early morning breeze very pleasant.

The betrayal began one morning in the month of Ramadan when Muslims fast from sunrise to sunset. I remember being woken by the muezzin's call for prayer. It was still very dark but I could not sleep because there were many mosques in Daryaganj and one muezzin followed another. Our Muslim servants were making a racket cooking and gobbling their day's meal. Just as the dawn appeared above the jungle across the river, a cannon was fired from the Royal Mosque. The explosion woke Alec and the children. The *khansama* brought up our *chota hazri*.

My girls were soon romping about on the roof, taking their time over their tumblers of milk. Alec and I were having our tea when we saw a fat Bania come with his brass jug and squat down near the wall: these natives can never resist a wall. Alec always had a catapult and a trayful of pebbles brought up with his morning tea. Before the Bania could relieve himself, Alec sent a pebble flying towards him. It hit the brass jug, *ping*. The Bania quickly stood up to adjust his *dhoti*. 'Bugger off you black bastard!' yelled Alec. And so the poor fellow did. We had a big laugh. Then along came a man carrying a wicker cage with a partridge in it. Another partridge ran a few yards behind calling *teetur, teetur, teetur*. Alec raised his *bundook* — he always had his *bundook* by his bedside to shoot geese or duck coming overhead from the river — aimed it at the partridge and said 'Bang! I'd like to get that fat one; make a nice partridge pie, what!' He used to aim his *bundook* at the partridge every morning and say the same thing. The day had begun like any other day.

The sun came up bloody red and bloody hot. With the sun came the flies. Alec and the children went downstairs. I was near the staircase when I noticed a cloud of dust on the other side of the river. I stopped to see what it was: It was a party of horsemen galloping over the boat bridge, firing their carbines. 'Alec, Alec,' I shouted, 'Come up and see!' By the time Alec came back to the roof-top the horsemen had disappeared behind the fort. But another party followed. This lot rode along the wall towards Daryaganj. They saw us standing on the roof and yelled '*Maar dalo saley firangi ko* — kill the bloody foreigners.' They were in the Company's uniforms.

We ran downstairs and had the gates of our bungalow shut.

The Last Emperor

There is a saying that when a sinner goes on fast Allah makes the day longer. So it seemed to us during the month of Ramadan of the year 1273 of our Prophet (Allah's blessings on Him), corresponding to May 1857 of the era of Jesus the Healer (on Whom be peace). We did our best to observe the injunctions of Islam; but the flesh is weak and often bends the will to its satisfaction. And that year the holy month of fasting fell during the mango season. The best time to enjoy mangoes is between mid-morning and the afternoon. This was forbidden. So be it. If Allah wished to test our faith, we who are King would abjure the fruit which is king among the fruits of our land.

Of late it had been our habit to rise a watch before sunrise and sit on the balcony overlooking the river. We had issued instructions that no one was to disturb us till we had said our *fajar* prayer. This gave us three to four hours to be alone with ourselves. We used these hours for contemplation. We liked to sit wrapped in darkness and in silence; we liked to watch the light of the waning moon reflected in the Jamna; on moonless nights we liked to gaze into the black heaven with its myriad stars; we liked seeing the silvery brilliance of the morning star fade into the paling sky. We liked to see the sun come up noisily with the screaming of *koels*. The cool morning breeze never failed to rouse the melancholic muse of poetry in our breast. Sometimes we would light the taper and pen a couplet or two; at other moments we would allow the lines of a *ghazal* to turn into song in our mind. And there were mornings when we scanned lines sent to us by Zauq or Mirza Ghalib or one of the other poets of our city.

We cherished these hours of peace and repose because we felt closer to our Maker then than at any other time; they prepared us for the unpleasant realities that pressed upon us during the day. When the world is itself draped in the mantle of night, the mirror of the mind is like the sky in which thoughts twinkle like stars; it is the best time to commune with one's inner self and realize how insignificant one is even though he calls himself King of Kings and Emperor of Hindustan.

After these hours of solitude we repaired to Moti Masjid built by our illustrious ancestor, Alamgir Aurangzeb (may Allah rest his soul in paradise). In the snow-cool atmosphere of this marble mosque we paid homage to our Maker (who gave silver to the stars and the moon, the fire and light to the sun) and His Messenger (Allah's blessings upon Him).

In the holy month of Ramadan this routine was somewhat altered. Kitchen fires were lit in the early hours so that people could feed before dawn appeared over the eastern horizon. During Ramadan we spent these early hours on a couch in the Diwan-i-Khas telling the beads of our rosary and repeating the ninety-nine names of Allah. Our morning meal was brought to us. We ate it alone. Our beloved Queen, Zeenat Mahal, sent us a *betel*-leaf rolled by her own hands. We chewed *betel*, smoked our *hookah* and watched the stream of the Jamna change its hues under the ordinance of the heavens. As the cannon roared over Lahori Gate to proclaim the beginning of the fast, our *hookah*-bearer removed the pipe from our presence.

*

To the best of our recollection this is exactly what took place on the morning of Monday 11 May 1857, the 16th of Ramadan. The night before, our royal consort Begum Zeenat Mahal and we had spent some time strolling on the balcony. She made some remark on the reflection of the moon in the river for the moon was full and the sky clear. And when we complained of the oppressiveness of the weather, she replied that it took the searing heat of the desert winds to give mangoes their delicious flavour, the jasmine and the *maulsari* their fragrance. She untied from her hair a chaplet made of these flowers and presented it to us as proof. We inhaled their perfume and when we held it back for her she said: 'Keep it beside your pillow. It will remind Your Majesty of your servant Zeenat.' Since knowledge of women is forbidden during Ramadan we had accepted this floral token. Its fragrance had filled our dreams; when we woke, the morning star and the morning breeze both reminded us of our beloved.

On the 11th of May we were a little late in our ablutions and prayers—nevertheless we beheld the dawn come over the

Jamna. We saw the fires lit by the melon-growers across the river grow pale under the light of the rising sun and our soldiers change guard on the boat-bridge. We had a light meal of partridge *pilaf*, followed by a couple of *Tsamar Bahisht* (paradise) mangoes which had just come in season. We also drank a tumbler full of ice-cooled milk spiked with saffron. This was followed by the usual *betel*-leaf and a few pulls at the *hookah*. After *fajar* prayer we returned to the Diwan-i-Khas. The royal physician, Hakeem Ahsanullah Khan, was ushered into our presence and permitted to feel our pulse. By the grace of the Almighty who alone determines the humours of the mortal frame, he pronounced us in good health. Then our slaves, the eunuch Basant Ali Khan and Vakil Ghulam Abbas, presented the accounts of the royal household. Our expenses were, as always, more than our income. We refused to look into them and waved the men away. We turned our back on the crowd of petitioners that had assembled and began to gaze at the scene along the Jamna.

The sun had risen. *Dhobis* were pounding their washing on slabs of stone while their women were spreading out washed garments on the sandbank to dry. Their children played in the sand. A line of labourers carrying baskets of melons was crossing the boat-bridge. It was like any other summer morning.

Suddenly there was tumult. We saw horsemen galloping across the boat-bridge firing their carbines in the air. The sentries on the bridge did not arrest their progress. The men galloped across the sand towards us and drew rein beneath the palace walls. 'Dohai! Dohai!' they screamed. 'Listen to our *faryad!*' Some shouted slogans: '*Badshah Salamat zindabad!*' We looked down over the parapet. The men wore uniforms of the East India Company. As soon as they saw us, they saluted and repeated: 'Long live the Emperor of Hindustan!' One shouted at the top of his voice: 'We have murdered the *firangis* in Meerut. The *nasara* (Christians) want to destroy our faith. We will rid the country of these vile infidels. We will make you Emperor of Hindustan!' Then they all shouted together: 'Long live the dynasty of the Mughals!'

'*La haul valla quwwat illah bi-illah hil ali yul aleem!* No fear, no power save Allah who is powerful and mighty!' We exclaimed.

'Who are these men?' we demanded of the eunuch Basant Ali Khan. He did not reply. He had a smirk on his black, bloated face. 'Inform Captain Douglas at once and see that they are not let inside the city,' we ordered.

Basant Ali Khan bowed and withdrew. Something in his manner told us that he was in no haste to carry out our command. We sent another messenger to the Captain. The soldiers from Meerut moved along the wall towards the harem apartments and began to yell: 'Long live the *Malika-i-Hind!*' More horsemen came galloping across the boat-bridge.

Captain Douglas who was officer-in-charge of the palace guards made his obeisance. He wanted to go down to speak to the men. We forbade him from endangering his life. We went to the balcony. We stood beside him to see that no one harmed him. 'What do you want?' he demanded of the men. 'What right do you have to disturb His Majesty in this way? Return to your regiments at once or you will be severely punished.' The men below stopped shouting and rode away to join their comrades assembled under the windows of our harem. Captain Douglas took leave to apprehend the mutinous gang.

We waited. We saw troops of soldiers wearing the uniform of the Company marching over the bridge. Mr Simon Fraser, who also lived in the fort, sent a messenger begging for a loan of palanquins to bring their ladies to the safety of our harem and permission to mount cannons on the gates of the fort. We ordered that these requests be complied with at once. But as fate would have it, the 'man' to whom we entrusted the execution of these orders was the eunuch Basant Ali Khan.

We waited. Messengers brought news of disturbances from different parts of the city. We pondered. Could we, whilst the fires of confusion were burning low, put them out by sprinkling on them the waters of stratagem? We issued orders that the mutineers should not be allowed to enter the city. We advised the sahibs going out of the city to remonstrate with them. No one paid heed to what we said.

An hour later we heard that the mutineers had been let into the city and had killed some Europeans in Daryaganj. Then we heard that the family of the manager of the bank who lived in Begum Samru's palace in Chandni Chowk had also been murdered. We became very concerned about the safety of the Europeans in the fort and enquired whether their ladies had been brought into our harem. It was then that we learnt that poor Captain Douglas, Mr Fraser and their ladies had been slain in their apartments.

Someone opened the gates of the fort to let in the mutineers. We were surrounded by a mob of soldiers which included many of our palace guards. They acclaimed us as their true monarch and the Emperor of Hindustan. 'Who calls us Emperor?' we protested. 'We are a *fakeer* prolonging our days on this wretched earth. We have no strength in our arms; our feeble voice is not heard beyond the walls of this fort.' But they would not listen. We were like a paper-boat set afloat on a mountain torrent.

All through that morning and afternoon soldiers kept streaming into our palace uninvited and unannounced. They did not bother with court etiquette. They pushed aside our servants, marched into the Diwan-i-Khas meant for special audience, grabbed our hands, kissed them and so extracted our blessings. Some presented us with silver coins; most of them only soiled our fingers with their lips.

It seemed like a dream compounded of episodes good and bad. And as sometimes happens we were violently roused from our dreams by an explosion which sounded like a thousand claps of thunder. The walls of our palace shook as in an earthquake. A few minutes later we were informed that English soldiers had set a torch to the powder magazine in Kashmiri Gate; several hundred of our subjects had been killed by the explosion. The whole city was in tumult.

Alice Aldwell *alias* Ayesha Bano Begum

I have never trusted the word of an Indian and I have been proved right every time. But as I said that afternoon we had no choice. I told my husband: 'Alec, let's not put all our eggs in one basket. You go with the others. I'll take the girls to Mirza Abdullah.' Alec agreed.

I dressed my girls in the native costumes that Begum Zeenat Mahal had given them. I borrowed a clean pair of *salwar-kameez* from my *ayah* and put on her dirty *burqa*. I sent for two palanquins. I put the two older girls in one and took the baby with me. One of our servants agreed to come with us. The flaps of the palanquins were lowered as they are when native women of rank travel in them.

Mirza Abdullah was, as I said before, grandson of the king. He lived in Urdu Bazaar close to the Royal Mosque. He had received many favours from my husband. His wife and sister had often called on me. 'You are our sister,' they used to say and called my children *betis*.

The crowd let us pass. We got to Urdu Bazaar without anyone questioning us. The ladies of the Mirza's household received us very kindly. His sister kissed my children and said that as long as she was alive she would not allow a single hair of their heads to be touched. I assured them that as soon as the trouble was over my husband would compensate them for their hospitality.

Urdu Bazaar was a Mohammedan locality. It had some bookstores and an assortment of shops—butchers, dyers, kite-makers, sweetmeat-vendors, *betel*-leaf-sellers. Behind these shops were the mansions of the rich *nawabs*. Although the approach to Mirza Abdullah's house was through a narrow lane, with a foul-smelling drain running alongside, the inside was very airy, with a large courtyard and verandahs. In the centre of the courtyard was a big *peepal* tree with boxes for Mirza's flocks of pouter pigeons. The verandahs were lined with potted palm and jasmine. On one side of the courtyard were the women's apartments where lived the Mirza's wives, mother, sister and a host of other female relatives and maidservants.

Mirza Abdullah was a bird fancier. On the roof of his house he had a loft where he kept his champion birds. He used to fly them round every afternoon directing them with a scarf and a whistle. He also owned partridges and fighting quails. Like other princes of royal blood, the Mirza had never grown up to be a man. Although he was in his thirties, he had never done a stroke of work. He lived on the allowance he received from the king. He was always in debt to the local Banias; his womenfolk were forever pawning their jewellery. None of this prevented him from taking more wives and going to brothels. He spent his afternoons challenging his neighbours at kite-flying or enticing their pigeons. In the evenings he took out his quails and partridges to fight other *nawabs'* quails and partridges. And if there was anything going on in the city, Mirza Abdullah was sure to be there.

Mirza Abdullah came home after dark. He was talking at the top of his voice. I could tell from his tone that he was boasting. He suddenly quietened down as someone told him of my presence in his house. He came into the *zenana* and greeted me with a familiarity he had never dared to assume before. 'Good-evening, memsahib,' he said in English, 'or rather, seeing the way Madam and her children are dressed, I should say *As-Salaam-Valai-kum.*'

The natives have a saying: a poor man's wife is everyone's sister-in-law. They think nothing of sleeping with their brothers' wives. I was certainly a poor sister-in-law to them. I accepted the pleasantry and replied very polite-like: '*Valai-kum-As-Salaam. Nawab* Sahib, it is very noble of you to allow us the shelter of your home for a few days. Allah will reward you for your kindness.'

'It is a great honour to have you here,' he continued in his bantering tone scratching his privates. 'But I would advise you to be in some place safer than Urdu Bazaar which is entirely Mohammedan,' he said. 'You know how Muslims feel about the *firangi* and the *nasara!*'

I could hardly believe he would use the word *firangi* for us and *nasara* for Indian Christians! There was no telling with these fellows.

'But now you look a true Mussalmani,' he went on. 'For your own safety all of you should learn the creed of Islam. I will send a *maulvi* to teach you. He will also escort you to my other house in Nai Sarak. You can leave your valuables here for safekeeping. Your slave will present himself tomorrow to see that you are comfortable.'

I decided to fall in with anything by which I could save my children's lives. When the *maulvi* came, I told him that my mother was a Kashmiri Mussalmani and that though I had been given away in marriage to a sahib, I had remained a Muslim. He had us repeat: 'La Illaha Lillillah, Mohammed Rasool Illah—there is one God and Mohammed is His Messenger.' He gave us Muslim names. From Alice I became Ayesha. The elder, Mary, became Maryam. The second, Fiona, became Fatima. Georgina became Jehanara. The *maulvi* was very pleased at having made three converts.

I left a bundle of silver rupees in safekeeping with Mirza Abdullah and took my leave of the women and set out for the *nawab's* other house. I took the girls in my palanquin. We were challenged many times but a word from the bearded *maulvi* was enough to let us through. We arrived at a *haveli* off Nai Sarak. The *maulvi* spoke to the caretaker who let us in.

With half an eye I could see that Mirza Abdullah used this place for his fun and games. The caretaker was a *hijda*. The room he showed us into had a wall-to-wall carpet covered over with white sheets. Bolsters were scattered about on it. There were large mirrors on the wall and a chandelier hanging from the roof. There was a dark anteroom with *charpoys* which was made over to us. The girls were worn out and fell asleep at once. I spent the night sitting beside them.

The next morning I sent my servant to Mirza Abdullah for the money I had left with him. He came back an hour later and said that Mirza Sahib denied having received anything from me. Furthermore he wanted us to get out of his house by the afternoon. The *hijda* promised to intercede on our behalf if I did as he told me. I agreed. I did not care what happened to me as long as my girls were safe.

In the afternoon the *hijda* came to help get me ready for the Nawab Sahib. He put henna paste on my palms and the soles of my feet. While the paste was drying he got *bhishties* to fill the bathtubs and poured cupfuls of rose-water in them. In the bathroom he undressed me. He ran his calloused hands over my body. He made me lie on the floor and spread out my thighs to shave my pubis. He inserted his dirty finger in me and made lewd gestures. While bathing me he squeezed my breasts. After drying my body with a dirty towel he rubbed gallnut powder on my privates: natives believe it tightens the muscles. To make sure that the powder had the desired result he made me lie down and applied his tongue. What these *hijdas* lack in the real stuff they make up for by doing lots of other things. This fellow worked himself into a frenzy. He stripped himself and thrust his stinking misshapen middle into my face screaming hoarsely, 'Kiss it, kiss it.' That was too much. I pushed him away. He slapped me. 'If you breathe a word to the Mirza,' he threatened, 'I'll slit the throats of your girls.'

He dressed me in embroidered silks. He put lamp black in my eyes and made me chew a foul-tasting, aromatic *betel*-leaf.

Confusion and shame together describe what I passed through that afternoon. I narrate what happened to me so that the world knows how rotten, villainous, treacherous, degraded and lecherous these Indians are! The entire nation deserves to be put against a wall and their carcasses thrown to pye-dogs!

Mirza Abdullah arrived with two of his cronies: their hair was oiled, eyes black with antimony, ears stuffed with swabs of scented cotton, mouths drooling the bloody phlegm of *betel*-leaf- juice. They wore thin muslin shirts and baggy pyjamas.

'*Wah! Wah!* Memsahib! How this dress becomes you,' shouted Mirza Abdullah as he introduced me to his friends. 'They are like my real brothers; nay, dearer to me than my real brothers!'

'You have shot a tasty piece of *shikar*,' said one of them.

'She looks ripe and experienced.'

Even in the circumstances in which I was that remark stung me.

'It's been my heart's greatest desire to make love to a white woman,' remarked the other. 'Mirza Sahib, I have to thank you for fulfilling my life's ambition.'

'You can only half thank me because only half of your desire will be fulfilled,' replied Mirza Abdullah. 'Alice *alias* Ayesha Begum is only half a memsahib; the other half is Kashmiri. No doubt you've disported yourself in many a Kashmiri vale!' The men roared with laughter and slapped each other's hand. This half-caste business I did not like at all.

Mirza Abdullah took me by the hand and made me recline on his bolster. The others sat facing us. The *hijda* brought a pitcher and poured out some evil-smelling liquid in four silver goblets. When he held out one to me, I shook my head. 'It is an unpardonable crime to drink during Ramadan,' I said.

'*Wah! Wah!*' exploded Mirza Abdullah. 'Yesterday's Mussalmani reads us sermons on Islam. Ayesha *bi*, during *jihad* everything is forgiven.' He gulped down the stuff in his goblet and repeated, 'During a *jihad* everything is allowed. Everything; you understand?' I understood. The men emptied their goblets; the *hijda* refilled them. Mirza Abdullah put a tumbler to my lips and commanded: 'Drink! Or I'll force it down your throat.' I knew what the blackguards meant to do to me. I decided I would be able to take it more easily if I were drunk. I took a sip and then gulped it down. It was spiced brandy; it burnt its way down my gullet into my belly.

'*Shabash*,' they cried in a chorus. 'Now the *mehfil* can get going.'

My goblet was refilled. The brandy loosened their tongues. One recited a poem of Saadi. Mirza Abdullah replied with lines from some court poets called Zauq and Ghalib. The third fellow quoted lines composed by the old king Bahadur Shah. Then they talked of the glories of Mughal rule and the wickedness of the English. 'As soon as the Company forces surrender,' said Mirza Abdullah, 'we will castrate all the *firangis* and take their women in our harems.' They laughed loudly at this joke.

Mirza Abdullah put his hand on my knee. He began to stroke and pinch my thighs. He touched my breasts and began to play with my nipples. His friends got up and asked: 'Have we Your Highness's permission to retire to the next room?' Abdullah nodded. They tottered out leaving the two of us reclining on the same bolster.

For some time Mirza Abdullah continued playing with my nipples. His other hand slipped round my waist. He undid the knot in the cord of his pyjama-trousers, took my hand and placed it on his middle. He was in a state of agitation. I picked up the goblet and drained it of its liquid fire. Now I did not care what anyone did to me. I thought it wiser to take the lead myself. I lay back and directed Mirza Abdullah into my person. A drunk man takes an age to come. At long last, when it seemed he was working himself up to a climax, Abdullah hollered out to his friends to see what he was doing. He dug his teeth into my cheeks as he shot his seed. As soon as he got up, his friends stripped me of the little clothing left on me and assaulted me.

I was like a piece of white meat fought over by two brown dogs: snarling, biting, clawing, shoving. So it went all through the long, long, sultry night. By the time one had finished, another had worked himself into a frenzy. And there was that *hijda* poking his fingers or tongue or whatever else he had. I was drenched with sweat and almost dead with exhaustion. By morning Abdullah and his friends were drained of all the poisonous semen in their vile bodies. They stumbled out singing and yelling obscenities. Only the *hijda* remained. I lay like a corpse while he tore me up like a dog tears carrion. He went on till the cannon announced the beginning of the day of abstinence. How much had passed between two risings of the sun!

I was woken up by Georgina's crying; 'Mummy, mummy, wake up!' The girls were in a state of shock. They had never before seen me like that—naked and bruised.

The only people who remained true to their salt were my servant Ali Ahmed and his wife. He realized what I had been through. At his own cost Ali Ahmed hired two palanquins and took us to his hovel. Very soon a large crowd collected. I heard voices shouting: 'Hand over that *firangi* woman.' Ali Ahmed's wife went out very boldly and scolded them: 'I am a Qureish of the tribe of the Prophet. The woman and the children who I shelter in my home are Muslims. You will first have to kill me and my husband before you can touch them. Is there anyone here who wants to have the blood of the Prophet on his hands? Come on, it is the holy month of Ramadan,' she challenged. The crowd melted away.

I did not want to endanger the lives of these poor folk. I asked Ali Ahmed to take a letter to the king and Queen Zeenat Mahal begging for help. I told them that I was born of a Muslim mother and had along with my two daughters recited the creed of Islam. I signed my name Ayesha Aldwell. I got no reply.

I wrote to many *nawabs*. Either they did not reply or sent notes regretting their inability to help. When all the rich and influential deserted us a poor man who owed us nothing came to our help. This was a tailor whose name I had never bothered to ask. He had stitched my daughters' frocks and got very fond of them. He came one morning with his cousin who was a sepoy. Although this cousin had gone over to the rebels he swore on the *Quran* that he would not let anyone harm us. We spent a day and night with the tailor's family. At sunset when the Muslims were at prayer we slipped out of the bazaar. The tailor and his sepoy cousin escorted our palanquins to the fort. We were taken over by the guards and produced before the king's son, Mirza Mughal. I then discovered that Mirza had intercepted the letters I had written to the king and Begum Zeenat Mahal. He ordered the guards to put us in the same underground dungeon as the other Europeans but to treat us as Muslims and not as *badzat nasara* (low-caste Christians).

On Wednesday, 13 May 1857, the family was re-united. Alec forgave me for what I had been through. He swore: 'I will split that bloody bastard Mirza Abdullah's bum in two.' But the English ladies were cold towards me. The favours that the guards showed towards us because I was a Mussalmani made them angry. They were given coarse *chappaties*, I was served meat-curry. Sometimes the guards would ask me and my children to eat with them.

The heat and the stench in the dungeon was terrible. There was no latrine and we had to relieve ourselves in a dark corner and with our own hands throw the slop out through a hole in the wall. And the insults we had to suffer! Every day crowds came to see us as if we were animals in a zoo and screamed the vilest abuse at us. One day Jawan Bakht came in and addressed me as *bhabi*. 'Mirza Abdullah is like my own brother,' he said with a smirk. 'So you become my *bhabi*, don't you?'

Then came Saturday, the 16th of May.

I knew something dreadful was going to happen. There were no *chappaties* for breakfast. 'You'll get plenty where you are going,' the sentries said. They reassured me that I need have no fear about myself or my children. A dozen sepoys came into the cell and ordered all the other men, women and children to march out. My girls ran to Alec and clung to his knees. The sepoys tore them away from their father and thrust them towards me. 'Don't let them take daddy,' they cried. I pleaded with the sepoys but they took no notice of me. Poor Alec was pushed along with the others. They bolted the door leaving my daughters, I and an old Mussalmani who had been caught helping Europeans in the dungeon.

I heard people shouting. Then a shot. Then children and women screaming. Then it became still. Absolutely still.

I am ashamed to confess that my first thoughts were: 'Now there is no one left to turn up their noses at me. Only Mirza Abdullah and his pals will talk about me. As soon as this is over, I will get Alec's pension. I will take my girls to England and start life again with no one making nasty talk about where I came from and who I was!' Then I cried a lot.

Bahadur Shah Zafar

Later in the afternoon some forty Europeans, men and women (there were possibly some children among them), their hands tied with ropes, were brought in our presence. A huge mob followed; the guards had difficulty in keeping it back. 'Dohai! Dohai!' they screamed. 'They've killed our men, we want justice. Hang these foreigners or hand them over to us.' The people wanted to avenge the lives lost in the explosion of the powder magazine. The white race had done many wrongs to us and our forefathers; but we refused to sanction vengeance on people who had nothing to do with the setting of fire to the powder magazine. We ordered the prisoners to be taken in our protective custody and lodged in an underground cellar of our harem.

The mob became very abusive; some men shouted slogans derogatory to our royal status. We ordered our Chamberlain to terminate the audience. He shouted 'Takhlia' and dropped the red curtain. The tumult continued for some time before saner people were able to persuade the hot-heads to bow to the wishes of their Emperor.'Khalq Khuda ki,mulk Badshah ka,hukum Jahan Panah ka—People belong to God, the country to the King, obey the law of One who gives shelter to the world,' they shouted as they departed. We ordered that food from the royal kitchen be sent to the European prisoners.

We said our afternoon maghreb prayer in Moti Masjid. We noticed that many strangers had lined themselves up behind us. We held our peace because we were in the house of God. But our mind was very disturbed; we were unable to ask Allah for guidance. When we came out of the mosque these people again began to shout slogans demanding the blood of the *firangi*. Some had the audacity to ask us to hand over the prisoners to them. Once again we refused to accede to their demands. We expressed our sympathy to those who had lost relatives in the explosion and advised them to submit to the will of God and bury their dead.

In the evening we learnt that the *khutba* had been read in our name in the Jamia Masjid. Our courtiers flattered us by extolling the greatness of our royal forefathers and our virtues. Thus did destiny launch our kite in tumultuous clouds without handing us the string with which we could control its movements.

We allowed ourselves to be seated on the silver throne which had been stacked away in the basement for over thirteen years. On this silver chair had sat our ancestors: Taimur and Babar; Humayun, Akbar, Jahangir, Shah Jahan, Alamgir Aurangzeb I, Bahadur Shah the First, Jahandar Shah Farrukhsiyar, Mohammed Shah, Alamgir II, Shah Alam and our revered father Akbar Shah the Second. We received homage from our subjects till the cannon boomed to announce the setting of the sun and we terminated the proceedings.

The crowd did not disperse. Many men spread their sheets on the stone and marble floors of our halls of audience to spend the night. Their horses filled their bellies with the flowers of our garden. Only the palaces alongside the river were left to us.

We asked to be left alone with our thoughts. We reclined on our couch in the Diwan-i-Khas and let our eyes rest on the ceiling. We remembered the days when it was encrusted with silver and gold leaf. Now even the plaster had peeled off in many places. We saw the marble columns and the empty sockets which once had been studded with ruby, amethyst, lapis lazuli and cornelian. Our gaze fell on the faded lettering proclaiming the glory of the days of our illustrious ancestor Shah Jahan: *Gar Firdaus bar roo-e-zaminast; Hameenasto, hameenasto, hameenast*—If on earth there be a place of bliss, it is this, it is this, it is this. A deep sigh rose from our breast; our eyes were dimmed with tears.

*

We were thus lost in our thoughts when our attention was

drawn by a polite cough. The chief lady-in-waiting bowed and said that her mistress, our Queen Zeenat Mahal, begged the privilege of our company to break the fast.

We dragged our weary feet towards our harem. Eunuchs and female heralds proclaimed our advent as we proceeded from one room to another. This time the very words we had been hearing for twenty-two years since we had been king seemed to have acquired a new meaning: 'Sirajuddin Khan, Mohammed Abu Zafar Bahadur Shah Ghazi, Shadow of God on Earth, Emperor of Hindustan.' We came to Begum Zeenat Mahal's apartment. The food was already laid on an embroidered table-cloth. Garlands of jasmine and *maulsari* hung from the chandeliers; cobs of *kewra* stood in vases in the corner. As we entered, maidservants bowed and backed out of the room. We took our seat on the carpet and rested our weary back on a bolster.

Begum Zeenat Mahal made her entrance. She was dressed as she was on the day seventeen years ago when we had brought her as a bride to our harem: in gold brocade with a white spider-web *dupatta* to cover the glossy black of her hooded-cobra curls. In it she wore the emerald-and-pearl clasp we had given her. Her large gazelle eyes sparkled with desire. She glided so gracefully towards us that although there were no bells on her feet our ears heard their musical tinkle. It seemed as if invisible hands had turned the knobs of lamps and made their tapers burn brighter. As Saadi said: 'A vision appeared in the night and by its appearance the darkness was illumined.' The tongue of eloquence could not describe her beauty.

'Has your slave permission to greet the Emperor of Hindustan?' She bowed low and *salaamed* us three times.

'*Subhan Allah!*' We exclaimed, taking in her beauty through our eyes. *Subhan Allah!* was all we had been able to say when we had first cast our eyes on her. She was then sixteen and we sixty-five. The seventeen summers that had ripened her beauty had also increased our appetite for her. We would rather have laid our head on her fleshy lap and let her run her fingers in our grey hair than eat the delicacies she had prepared for us. She must have read our mind. She asked us if we found the arrangements to our satisfaction. We quoted Saadi: 'I am hungry and opposite hungry and opposite to a table of food; I am like a lusty youth at the door of a *hamaam* full of females.' This brought the colour of pomegranates to her cheeks.

We noticed that Zeenat Mahal had prepared our favourite dishes: venison *kababs* with *nauratan* chutney made of nine condiments; roast wings of peacocks and quails; *kulfi* covered with gold leaf and garnished with slices of mango. She helped us wash our hands. She picked the food with her own fingers and placed it in our mouth. We could not recall when last she had shown such tenderness towards us. When the meal was finished she rolled a *betel*-leaf, mixing lime and catechu paste with scented tobacco, and placed it in our mouth.

While we were chewing the leaf, she asked us boldly whether she could have the privilege of sharing our couch for the night. We were a little taken aback. But it was not for nothing that it was said of our Mughal ancestors that they could take women till the last day of their lives. Though little else remained of our inheritance no one could deprive us of our ancestral blood. At the age of seventy we had run a *nilgai* across a boulder-strewn hillside and sliced its head off with our sword.

Allah had given our loins the same strength as He had bestowed on our arms. It was not the years but the holy law that set our head and heart at variance with each other. She read the conflict in our eyes. She assured us that the *shariat* provided for dispensation in times of stress, and since we had launched on a holy war, a little indiscretion would be forgiven us. In her sweet coquettish voice she recited Hafiz:

> *Do not sit one moment without your love or wine*
> *For these are days of celebration, roses and jasmine.*

So fragrant was the smell of her mouth, so great the warmth of invitation of her soft, fleshy hips that despite our eighty-two years, and the tumult of the long day, we banished fatigue from our limbs. We replied in the words of the very poet whose lines she had recited:

> *O how many vows of repentance are undone*
> *By the smile of wine and the tresses of a girl?*

264

We took a large spoonful of the aphrodisiac that Hakeem Ahsanullah had prepared for us. A little later we took our begum with the same passion with which we had consummated our first union. When we had finished our business, we again quoted Hafiz to convince her that we did not regret what we had accomplished:

> I do not restrain desire
> Until my desire is satisfied
> Or until my body touches hers,
> Or my soul from my body goes.
> When I am dead, open my tomb,
> You will see my heart on fire
> And my shroud in smoke.

Thus like young lovers we lay in each other's arms with nothing save the hairs of our bodies between us. We were roused from our slumbers by the firing of cannon. Zeenat Mahal opened her large almond-shaped eyes and was overcome with shyness. She quickly dressed and asked: 'Who is firing guns at this hour of the night?' She began to count the reports. 'One, two, three...twenty-one,' she said finally. 'A salute to the Emperor of Hindustan. Permit your maidservant to be the first to pay Your Majesty homage.' She bowed, salaamed thrice and glided out of the room.

We took our pen and put the final touches to a poem we had been composing for some weeks:

> In love it's not the loss of peace
> Or patience that I mourn.
> Love's sorrow has become my friend
> When other friends I have forsworn.

> 'Tis a thousand wonders that even now
> The cup-bearer brings not jug and wine,
> Knowing the days of pleasure, the rounds of mirth
> Not forever last upon this earth.

Of myself nothing did I know
But others' good and bad I knew
Then fell my eye upon my evil deeds
Remained none so evil in my view.

With the dazzling glory of the Sun
Today, after many days, she came.
All calm and patience did I lose
Not all her shyness did her restrain.

O Zafar! know him not as a man
However clever, wise, benign
Who in pleasures' pursuit forgets his God
In anger's passion wrath divine.

So was the candle of our hope lit in the gale of fortune. So did we launch our frail and ageing bark upon the stormy seas of Hindustan.

*

In youth the slumber that follows the night of love is oblivious of the progress of the sun. What use is it to the days that are past? We were roused by a gong striking the midnight hour. We rose from our beloved's couch with the weight of our years heavy in our limbs. We went to the mosque, performed our ablutions and said the *isha* prayer craving Allah's forgiveness for transgressing the rules of Ramadan.

We continued to sit in the mosque for some time. The moon was directly over our head. The marble courtyard was as cold as the snows of the Himalayas. We recalled that it was in the third week of Ramadan that the Almighty had summoned our Prophet (on Whom be peace) and charged him with His divine mission. We recited *sura* 96, the first that Allah transmitted to the world:

Recite: In the name of your Lord who created,
Created man from a clot.
Recite: And your Lord is most generous,
Who taught by the pen,

Taught man what he does not know.
No, but man is rebellious
Because he sees himself grown rich.
Indeed the return is to your Lord.

We had a strange feeling that Allah heard our prayer and forgave us. We left the mosque with a lighter heart and were able to get a few hours of restful sleep.

We were up before any of our servants had risen and went to the octagonal tower to spend some moments with ourselves. It was then that the enormity of the events that had taken place the day earlier came crowding into our mind. Had we acted rightly? Were we master of our destiny? Or a mere puppet in the hands of some wilful puppeteer?

We penned the following lines:

We are caught in the whirligig of time
Gone are sleep and life of ease
Death is certain, that we know
At dawn or dusk our life may cease.

The mirror of our mind was not clear. We were King only by title. We lived in a palace which was once said to be the most beautiful in the world; it was now a palace only in name. And even that was to be denied to our sons. We had been informed that on our demise (would that Allah send for us soon!) our family would be asked to quit the Red Fort. The *firangi* had given us only a drop out of the ocean of fortune that our great ancestors had bequeathed to us; we accepted that drop and called it a tribute. What other word can one use for what is owed to an emperor? But the *firangi* insisted it was a pension. An emperor a pensioner of his subjects!

One after another the great kingdoms of Hindustan (at one time all vassals of our great ancestors) were swallowed up by the *firangi*. He spared neither friend nor foe. Only a few months ago the great house of Oudh which had befriended the *firangi* was by the *firangi* deprived of its dominion. And before Oudh there were Nagpur and Jhansi and Satara and Tanjore and Murshidabad and Karnatak.

The holy book says: 'God does not love the oppressors.' No one could oppress the poor as did the *firangi* because he even interfered with matters of faith. For him religion made no distinction between clean and unclean flesh. He was allowed to eat both cows and pigs. But what right had he to order our Hindu and Muslim soldiers to put cartridges smeared with the fat of cows and pigs in their mouths? Did we need more to prove that he meant to despoil both Islam and Hinduism and make everyone Christian? His *padres* vilified the name of our Holy Prophet and the sacred *Quran*. What did a man live for except his faith and the honour of his name? What lived after a man died but his name? We put our trust in God. It is rightly said: 'What fear of the waves of the sea has he whose pilot is Noah!'

Then there was the vexing question of our succession. Our beloved Zeenat Mahal was anxious that Mirza Jawan Bakht, born of the conjunction of our groins, should be nominated in preference to the elder Mirza Dara Bakht. The Governor-General refused to take our advice. Allah in His divine wisdom took Shah Rukh then Mirza Dara Bakht as well. It was after we had lost these two sons that we gave in to Zeenat Mahal's pressure and forwarded the claim of Mirza Jawan Bakht. Once again the Governor-General brushed aside our advice and recognized another of our many sons, Mirza Fakhroo.

Fakhroo was bribed to sign an agreement whereby he would give up the Red Fort for a small pension. Then Allah sent for Mirza Fakhroo as well. After Allah deprived us of three of our sons, the *firangi* proclaimed his intention of depriving our successors of the fort and palace—and our successor, whoever it would be, of even the title of His Majesty. 'O Zafar, this rule is but for thy lifetime; after thee there will be no heir nor name to the kingdom for anyone to rule.' So eager was the *firangi* to shorten our sojourn on earth that once when we were ill he posted his own guard at the palace gates. We were constrained to write to the President: 'Honourable Sir, are we not to be accorded the privilege of dying in peace? Do you suspect our corpse will rise up in arms against you?'

Saadi had so rightly said: 'Ten *dervishes* may sleep under the same blanket but no country can hold two kings.' We have the same saying in Hindustani: 'A country can no more have two rulers than a scabbard hold two swords.' It had to be us or the *firangi*. This was clear to us.

We summoned a council of princes, noblemen and representatives of the sepoys. We advised them to reorganize the administration and draw up plans to expel the foreigners from our domains. The Council chose our elder son, Mirza Mughal, to be supreme Commander. Mirza Abu Bakr who was most eager to draw his sword was made a colonel.

After business was finished we sent for Hassan Askari. Askari was a *dervish* who, as it is said, had 'deeply plunged his head in the cowl of meditation and had been immersed in an ocean of vision.' He was possessed of eyes that could peer into the future. He lived in Daryaganj in the house of our lately departed daughter, Nawab Begum. While we awaited the *dervish* we ordered the daily papers to be read to us. The *Delhi Urdu News*, *Siraj-ul-Akhbar* and *Sadik-ul-Akhbar* had eyewitness accounts of the explosion of the arsenal at Kashmiri Gate with the names of the hundreds of martyrs who had fallen in the attempt to capture it. We asked if the English newspaper, *Delhi Gazette*, had written anything on the subject. Our newspaper reader informed us that there was no issue of the *Gazette* as its English staff had been slain and only one man, an American who had accepted Islam, had been spared. We heard all this without making any observation and dismissed the newspaper reader.

Hassan Askari was ushered in. We rose to receive him. He was a man of God. He had also petitioned Allah to take twenty years of his life and add them to ours. We seated him beside us on our couch and asked him what he felt about the storm that was blowing over our city. The *dervish* hoarded his words as a miser hoards gold. He shut his eyes and began telling the beads of his rosary. After a few minutes he raised his face to the ceiling, brushed his beard with both his hands and exclaimed: '*Shukr Allah! Shukr Allah!*' We became impatient and implored him: '*Dervish* Sahib, you who read the future in the book of destiny, tell us what fate has in store for us?'

The *dervish* pointed to the sky and replied, 'Only Allah knows the future. I am dust under the feet of the faithful.

Occasionally I have glimpses into the mirror of time.'

He fell silent again and resumed telling his beads. We entreated him again: 'In the name of Allah, look into the mirror of the future and loosen your tongue. Do not torture this poor man any more.'

At last the *dervish* spoke: 'Your Majesty may recall my dream of the flood engulfing everything save the throne of the Mughals.'

'Indeed we do!'

'At the time we had interpreted it as presaging the invasion of Hindustan by the Persians or the Russians. Now we know that the flood has risen from within Hindustan itself. It will drown the enemies of Your Majesty's dynasty. Only the peacock throne will be borne above the floods.' (Although the peacock throne had been taken away by Nadir Shah over a hundred years ago, our people continued to speak of the wooden stool covered with silver leaf which was now our throne as the peacock throne).

'*Ameen! Ameen!*' We exclaimed. 'Allah will surely fulfil the prophecy of those beloved of Him!'

We asked him of the prospect of the Persian army coming to our aid in the crusade against the *firangi*. He assured us that the armies of Islam were ever eager to measure swords with the Nazarene. The *dervish* told us of the birth of triplets to a Hindu woman in Hauz Qazi. The girls spoke immediately on birth. The first said: 'The coming year will be one of great calamities.' The second said: 'Those who will live will see.' The third said: 'If Hindus burn Holi in the present season they will escape all these evils. God alone is omniscient.' The Hindus, said *dervish* Askari, were burning Holi fire now instead of the usual time at the end of winter.

We thanked Hassan Askari and requested him to continue praying for us. We pressed a gold *mohur* in his hand, and before he could protest, walked away to our harem.

*

We were anxious to tell Zeenat of what the *dervish* had told us. She dismissed her visitors and maidservants. 'The *dervish*

Hassan Askari was here,' we said. We paused to heighten her sense of expectancy.

'And he told Your Majesty of his dream of the flood. And the Hindus lighting Holi fires. And the three girls who began talking as soon as they were born. Your slave should also be given a gold *mohur* for predicting the end of the Nazarene and the restoration of the Mughal dynasty,' Zeenat said.

How quickly news travelled round the palace! As if the walls had ears and the breeze tongues! Zeenat noticed the surprise in our eyes. 'Your Majesty, I have my own way of finding out what is written in the book of *kismet?*' she said, tapping her forehead. 'This is what the great Hafiz has forecast.' She opened a *Divan* of Hafiz to a page she had marked with a silk tassel and read:

> In green heaven's fields I saw the sickle of the new moon
> Remembered by sowing and by harvest,
> And said: O Kismet, you sleep and the sun blossoms
> The reply: Do not be as hopeless as the past.

She repeated the last line: 'Do not be as hopeless as the past.' It pleased us to see her happy and we kissed her cheeks. She blushed. 'What, in broad daylight ! Has Your Majesty no shame?'

'You speak of shame? Shame is my renown,' we replied quoting Hafiz.

During the first two days following the uprising we really felt as if we were Emperor of Hindustan and the *firangi* had taken his caravan out of our domains. But by the third day the veil of illusion that had clouded our vision was lifted. Our son Mirza Mughal had usurped all the functions of a ruler. People went to him for orders. Even our personal servants like the eunuch Basant Ali Khan paid court to the prince.

Prince Mirza Mughal incited the rabble of the city against the Europeans we had taken into protective custody. We argued with him and warned him against lending a ear to 'men' like Basant Ali Khan. But it was to no avail. Three days later—we believe it was Saturday the 16th of May—they dragged the prisoners out of the dungeon and slit the throats of thirty-nine of them including women and children as if they were sheep being sacrificed on Bakr-Id. The royal fountain in front of our palace was full of the blood and corpses 'of these innocent people. We sought refuge in our harem. Zeenat Mahal buried her head in our lap and wept like a child. We could not silence the shrieks of the victims from assailing our ears. And at night the howling of jackals on the riverbank sounded like women wailing at a funeral.

When we reprimanded Mirza Mughal and that impudent, emasculated Basant Ali Khan, they had the audacity to ask us whether we were on the side of the *jihadis* or the infidels. They insinuated that Begum Zeenat Mahal's father and our physician, Ahsanullah Khan, were in the pay of the *firangi*.

We listened to these calumnies with the expression of one whose ears register no sound. But thereafter our heart was divided. Sometimes we hoped for a speedy victory and the restoration of our empire; at others we wished that the sahibs would make peace with us, recognize us and our heirs as kings of Hindustan and administer the country in our name. In either case we prayed for peace so that we could spend the remaining years of our life in prayer and quiet meditation in some secluded hermitage.

On the evening of Sunday, the 24th May, the new moon was sighted. Our eyes could not discern it because of the dust in the air but Zeenat Mahal pointed to the red sky above the setting sun and assured us that it was there, shining like a silver poniard. The next day we rode on our favourite elephant Maula Baksh through the bazaars and joined our subjects for the afternoon prayer at the Royal Mosque. On our way back we showered coins on the crowds of beggars that milled about the feet of our elephant. By the time we approached Lahori Gate the sun had set. The walls of our palace were lit with oil-lamps. We turned round and saw the whole city including the Jamia Masjid twinkling with lights. Rockets shot their way into the sky and exploded in multicoloured stars. Cannons fired a twenty-one gun salute in our honour.

Id-ul-Fitr has always been a day of rejoicing. The knot of restraint which binds the faithful during the month of Ramadan is loosened. We shut the eye of censure to let people enjoy themselves. But our sons did not know how to take their pleasure without causing hurt to others. At midnight we were roused by the *darogha* who begged us to help him restrain one who had broken into the house of a rich Hindu merchant of Dariba. Another was picked up naked and drunk in the *hijda* quarters of Lal Kuan. A third was embroiled in a fracas in a house of ill-fame in Daryaganj run by a princess of royal blood. So low had the house of Taimur and Babar fallen!

Next morning we sent for our boys and let the tongue of reprimand lash their ears. They heard with their heads bowed. From their bloodshot eyes and waxen complexions we could see that their silence was more occasioned by ill-humour of the body than repentance of the heart.

The men who had taken over the reins of government were like novices on unbroken horses. They knew how to squander but not how to earn. They could not be bothered with accounts and let the treasury become empty. There were so many who wanted to fight in the *jihad*. But no one bothered to train them. They were sent into battle armed with pick-axes, spears and knives against trained men armed with muskets. Five days after Id-ul-Fitr there was an engagement across the river at Ghaziabad. Victory went to the *firangi;* martyrdom to our Ghazis. The same story was repeated a few days later at Badli-ki-Sarai on the Grand Trunk Road.

Dervish Hassan Askari told us that these reverses were Allah's warning to us to be better prepared. Our astrologers also predicted that the *firangi's* rule would end on the 23rd of June which was the hundredth anniversary of the Battle of Plassey. Our Ghazis went out in their thousands and fell upon the enemy who had massed his troops outside the city wall at Sabzi Mandi. Once again Allah granted our Ghazis the houris of paradise but gave the *firangi* and his Sikh and Gorkha hirelings the pleasure of victory.

The reverses at Sabzi Mandi plunged the city in gloom. People lost faith in their commanders. Everyone accused everyone else of treachery and being in the pay of the *firangi*. The hot winds blowing from the desert tried people's patience. Suddenly merchants began to hide their wares. There was no grain or fodder in the market. The poor were driven to desperation. Many turned to thieving and robbery. We did not know what the outcome would be. Then a strange man appeared in Delhi.

Nihal Singh

All my life I had been hearing of Dilli. When I was a child *Mai* told me of Aurangzeb, King of Dilli, who had cut off the head of our Guru. She called him Auranga and spat whenever she used his name. I also learnt to *thoo* on Auranga's name. When I was older, *Bapu* told me of the exploits of our ancestors who looted Dilli and brought back saddles full of gold and silver. And of Sardar Baghel Singh who built a gurdwara on the very spot where our Guru had been martyred. When I joined the Punjab police, my friends said 'If you haven't seen Dilli you have seen nothing.' In Dilli, they said, you could get everything; young whores with small mango-shaped bosoms, boys with rounded pumpkin bottoms; and if you did not have money to pay for a woman or a boy, you could have a *hijda* for a couple of pice—and he (she or it) could give you more fun than either. I prayed that something would take me to Dilli.

The Guru who knows the secrets of our hearts answered my prayer. One day when I was home on leave two men came to our village. One went round beating a drum asking everyone to assemble under the big *peepal* tree. The other fellow then told us that the Mussalmans had risen against Jan Company and put back a Mughal on the throne of Dilli. This Mughal was the grandson of the grandson of the same Auranga who had murdered our Guru. He said if we joined the army of Jan Company and captured Dilli all the gold and silver we could find would be ours. I asked the man to write an *arzi* to the police station asking for more leave, touched the feet of my *Mai* and my *Bapu* and took the road to Dilli.

There were two other boys from my village with me; Lehna and Natha. How hot it was! As if the whole world had been put inside a *tandoor* (oven). The dust blew into our eyes and nostrils and turned our black beards to khaki. We said to ourselves 'What is heat to Sikh Lions?' and rode through the burning afternoons. We washed ourselves at wells along the road, rested a little under the shades of *neem* trees and were off again. In two days we reached Ambala.

A big bald sahib with a face as red as a monkey's bottom came to inspect us. He had already a hundred Sikhs given by the Raja of Jind with him. He picked another hundred from villages on his route. I was in my police uniform and had my own horse, so he took me. He also took Lehna and Natha. Then he spoke to us in Poorabia language. I did not understand everything he said except that we were to fight Mussalmans and that our Guru had told Auranga that the sahibs would come from the side of the rising sun and with the help of the Sikhs overthrow his dynasty. Neither my *Mai* nor my *Bapu* had told me of this prophecy. However I said to myself, what the sahib says must be true because the sahibs are wise people. One morning at parade this sahib whose name I found out later was Hodson, walked down the line poking his finger into the boys' chests and bellies and feeling their arms. He did the same to me. He looked me up and down from my turban to my shoes. I was taller and bigger than all the boys on the line.

'What is your name?' he asked.

'Nihal Singh.'

'Nihal Singha,' he says exactly like a *pukka* Punjabi, 'Nihal Singha, you will be my orderly.' Hodson Sahib was like that. He never asked anyone anything. He just gave orders.

The boys were burnt up with jealousy. They slapped me on my back and said *Shabash*! *Vadhaaee*! (congratulations!). But when my back was turned they called me the sahib's *chamcha* (spoon). I did not care. I liked Hodson Sahib. Hodson Sahib liked me. And even though my wage was no more than that of the other sowars, even Sardar Man Singh who was our *subedar* always addressed me politely as *Bhai* Nihal Singhji.

We were given new uniforms; red turbans, khaki shirts, red cummerbunds and khaki breeches: red-khaki, red-khaki. Other sahibs began to call us flamingoes. We were given a new matchlock which could fire very rapidly and had a long knife at its nozzle. We also carried lances.

After a few days of drilling we were on the royal road to Dilli. At Karnal *gora* companies came down from the hills to join us. The *goras* could not stand the sun and the hot winds. So we rode by night and spent the days sleeping under shades of trees. We went through Gharaunda, Samalkha, Raee. These towns had turned against Jan Company. They did not dare to make the slightest *choon* before us. We reached the outskirts of Dilli in the pitch dark of the night. We were directed to our tents. The sahibs' *bandobast* was very good.

We had ridden twenty miles through a very hot and still night. The men were tired and fell asleep without taking off their cummerbunds or boots. I was excited and could not shut my eyes. There were twelve men snoring and farting in the tent. So I came out, washed myself and found a flat stone to lie on. I loosened my long hair and let the breeze cool me while I gazed at the sky full of bright stars. I must have dozed off because when I opened my eyes the stars were less bright and the sky had turned grey. My heart grew bigger and bigger till it was as big as the world I beheld. I recalled the words Guru Nanak spoke to his disciple: 'Look brother Mardana, the miracle of the Lord!'

'Wah! *Bhai wah*!' I exclaimed to myself. 'The great Guru has certainly raised a wonderful city.' On my left from where the sun was coming up there was a river as broad as the Sutlej. It went behind the grey wall of the city. This wall was very high and very long. It ran from the river bank right across to the sunset side as far as I could see and was lost behind clusters of trees. It had many bastions and many gates. Behind this grey wall I could see another red wall of a big fort. And domes and minarets and tops of houses. I could not see any signs of battle; not even a sign of anyone living.

*

As the red rim of the sun comes over the river, a cannon fires—*badham*. Thousands of pigeons fly up and crows *kan kan*. I see hundreds of vultures sitting on tree-tops and clustered on carrion like bees on a beehive. Then I notice half-eaten corpses dangling from the branches. Vomit comes to my throat. I go inside my tent and stretch myself besides my companions. I am very tired.

The bugle calls. We are up. I get myself a mug of tea and look round to see how our camp is laid. We are on a high ridge of red rocks. On top of the Ridge is a big house which the cook says belongs to a Maratha named Hindu Rao. It is beyond the reach of enemy guns so the sahib officers occupy this house. *Gora paltans* are encamped on the higher parts of the ridge which are also beyond range. We blacks are closer to the city wall. There are Pathans, Biloches and Punjabi Mussalmans. 'What are these Mussalmans doing here?' I ask the cook. 'They will fight the Hindus on the rebel side,' he says. 'And these Gorkhas?' I ask him. 'They will fight anyone the sahib tells them to fight,' he replies. 'A Gorkha's skull is made of iron and its inside is stuffed with cowdung. If the sahib says shoot your father, he will shoot his father and mother.' It is wonderful how the sahibs keep us natives separated from each other. The Guru has given them great wisdom. Also courage. As Hodson Sahib says, 'One white man is as good as ten blacks.'

It is high noon. Sun right above our heads. I am snoring peacefully under the shade of a *neem* tree when somebody shakes me violently. '*Oi*, Nihalia, haven't you heard the bugle? Do you want to be murdered in your sleep?' I jump up and wrap my turban round my head. What do I see? Sahibs peering through their telescopes. I look the way they are looking. What do I see? From the extreme right end of the city called Sabzi Mandi enemy cavalry is riding out towards us. Behind the cavalry are troopers on foot. They are in uniforms of the Jan Company. While I am still looking they start letting off fire-works from the city wall as if somebody is getting married. *Bhanh, bhanh* says the cannon; *shanh, shanh* go cannon balls. They crash on the ridge knocking down our tents and killing our horses. You have to admit these villains have good aim. They also know lots of tricks. Just as we get into our saddles, their drums begin to beat and they charge into our flank yelling '*Har Har Mahadev...Ali, Ali, Ali.*' Hodson Sahib draws his sword and yells '*Hamla!*' We ride full gallop to meet them. As soon as we are within range they fire their muskets at us, wheel, and ride away. While we are counting our dead and wounded their snipers start shooting at our sahibs. One fellow yells at me: 'O

Sardarji, why are you selling your life to the *firangi sooer*? Come over to our side. You'll get more rupees.'

They kill many of our men. We kill some of theirs too. But they do not get any of our boys alive; we capture about thirty of them.

We search their dead and find plenty of gold and silver coins in their belts. We hack off the ears and fingers of those who have rings.

Hodson Sahib lines up the captives under a tree. He orders them to go down on their knees. He loads his carbine and aims it at an old grey beard. 'How long have you eaten the salt of the Company?' he asks.

The grey beard clasps his hand and pleads: '*Kasoor hua* (I've been at fault). Forgive us!'

Others do the same, '*Huzoor*, forgive us,' they whine. 'Take all we have, but don't kill us.' They take off their belts and empty out coins, rings and other trinkets.

Hodson Sahib doesn't even look at the things. 'What regiment were you?' he asks the grey beard.

'The 26th. We served the sahib in many battles. We will fight for you again wherever you send us.' He grabs Hodson Sahib's foot. Hodson Sahib kicks him with the other foot. 'Who is your commander?'

'Mirza Mughal....Sahib, don't kill us. We will tell you all we know.'

'How many are you?'

They vie with each other in giving names of their regiments. There are 10,000 or more on the other side. Hodson Sahib knows all he wants to know. He cocks his carbine, jams it into the old man's chest and fires. 'Take this you *namak haram*!' The grey beard rolls over with a loud cry '*Ya Allah*!'

'Hack off the heads of these *namak harams* and feed their carcasses to the jackals,' he orders.

The prisoners become like living corpses. We take off their belts. Our sweepers pull off their uniforms and boots. We march them naked down the ridge. We line them and tell them to kneel with their heads bent. They whine, urinate, defecate. We hack off their heads with our *kirpans*. It is like slaughtering goats for the Guru's kitchen. Only a man's neck is thicker than a goat's and cannot always be severed at one *jhatka* (stroke).

Hodson Sahib gives us an extra ration of rum.

*

Two of our *risallah* had been badly wounded. I went to see them in the camp-hospital. They were lying under a *keekar* tree; there was no room inside for natives. The doctors were busy looking after *goras*, many of whom had cholera, dysentry or shivering fever. Some had just melted like wax under the heat of the sun. I sat with the boys and pressed their legs. Hodson Sahib brought a doctor who threw a packet of ointment on the ground and said: 'Spread this on your injuries and report back for duty in two days.'

In the afternoon I went to see Hodson Sahib. He was in his tent writing something. 'Sahib must be very tired. Shall I take off Sahib's boots?' He did not open his mouth but turned in his chair. I sat on the ground, unstrapped his *putties* and massaged his legs. He stopped writing and turned to me.

'Good fighting today, eh?'

'Sahib, they have killed a lot of our men,' I replied.

The Sahib looked at his paper. 'Seventeen dead, twenty-five injured, twenty horses dead or destroyed.'

I had seen many more than seventeen dead. I understood. The Sahib was only counting the *goras*. 'It takes more than an army of jackals to fight the English,' he said. 'This was their big *hamla*. We have broken their backs,' he explained: 'Today is the 23rd day of June. It is the hundredth anniversary of the Battle of Plassey when the English defeated the Mussalmans. They believed that after hundred years, it would be their turn to win. It takes more than a pack of jackals to beat the *sahiblog*,' he said again.

I pulled off his boots. 'The English are very *bahadur*,' I said as I pressed his feet.

'The best fighters in the world.'

I nodded my head. 'Sikhs are also very *bahadur*. One Sikh is equal to 1,25,000 others.'

Hodson Sahib didn't like that. He ran his hand over his bald head and asked 'What happened at Mudki and Pherushahr and Sabraon and Multan and Chillianwala and Gujarat?'

'Sahib, the Sikh army was betrayed by its officers.'

'That is what the defeated always say, we were let down by our commanders.'

Hodson Sahib had a very short temper; I did not want to get him *gussa* by arguing with him. I said in my mind: 'If the Sikhs were led by good generals instead of traitors, they would have marched up to your London town and fucked your mothers.'

I took off his socks and rubbed the soles of his feet. He shut his eyes and began to *ghurr ghurr* like a cat. After a while he said '*Theek hai*. You can go.'

I saluted and left.

Next morning when I went to see how the boys who had been wounded were doing, I did not find them under the *keekar* tree. I went to the hospital. They were not there either. A sweeper told me that they had died at night and their bodies had been taken away to be cremated.

*

These Dilliwallas would not let us breathe. At midnight when we were fast asleep they would start firing their cannons at us. On the hottest afternoon when we were dozing under the shades of trees they would creep up like thieves and go *thah thah* with their carbines. They sent emissaries to our camp. To the Mussalmans they sent Mussalmans with the *Quran* and begged them to *jihad* against the pig-eating *firangi*. To us Sikhs they sent Brahmins carrying Ganges water in brass-pots asking us to murder the cow-eating *maleechas*. They offered us hundred rupees for every *gora's* head and service with more pay. We remained true to our salt. We took the money they brought. Then we strung them up on *neem* trees.

The sahibs also employed spies. The chief was a one-eyed man called Rajab Ali. He came to our camp whenever he wanted and went back to the city. They said he had the ear of the king. And he did a lot of *phus phus* in Hodson Sahib's ear and took money from him.

The blacks liked Hodson Sahib but the *goras* did not care for him. I saw this when a *paltan* called the Guides arrived from Peshawar. Hodson Sahib had often talked of the times *'Jab ham Guides me tha...'* From the way he spoke, the Guides must have been the greatest warriors in the world. I didn't know why he left them. Only once he mentioned some 'hanky panky'. However as the Guides marched in and saw Hodson Sahib, the black men broke their ranks and ran up to embrace him. What a sight it was! Pathans, Biloches, Sikhs all embracing Hodson Sahib! The sahibs looked away as if they did not know him.

One day a *gora* asked me who I was.

'Hodson's Horse,' I replied coming to attention. He laughed, turned to the other *goras* and said, 'Hodson's arse.' They all laughed. I did not understand what made the sahibs laugh.

Even the *Jangi Lat* Wilson Sahib did not like Hodson Sahib. He would not allow him to attack Dilli till he got more troops. And Hodson Sahib's temper got worse as hot winds became hotter and dust-storms began to blow every afternoon.

One day early in July there was a storm the like of which I had never seen. Brown dust roasted by the sun was flung in fistfuls into our eyes and nostrils! After an hour the same dust turned cool. The day turned into night. The sky exploded with lightning and thunder. Then came the rain sweeping the dust and everything else before it. I ran out of the tent shouting to my friends: *'Oi,* Lehnia! The rains! *Oi* Nathia! You opium eater come out, the skies have burst!'

We threw off our turbans and uniforms and came out in our under-shorts. We let down our long hair and danced and sang. *'Oi,* if we only had a *mashooka* today we'd make the soles of her feet count the stars.'

The *goras* asked the natives what had happened to us. The Pathans shook their heads and smiled. The Dogras sniggered 'Sahib, these Sikhs have long hair. The heat gets them and they go crazy.' We yelled back at them, *'Oi,* your mothers and sisters also have long hair. They must feel the heat. Send them to us, we will cool the heat between their thighs.' That shut them up.

At dusk the trees were covered with fireflies. We caught them and stuck them in our beards till our beards sparkled. And we danced the *bhangra*.

It rained all through the night. It beat on our tent like a roar, sometimes like a faint echo from far away. No one could get much sleep.

I rose at dawn. The sky was full of grey and black clouds. Everything looked washed and green. I heard a peacock call *paon paon*. There were three — one cock and two hens on the parapet of Hindu Rao's mansion. The cock raised its tail and made it into a fan full of green-blue eyes. I put my head inside the tent and yelled: 'Get up you opium eaters! A peacock's dancing!'

'Let the peacock sleep with its mother,' replied Lehna gruffly as he turned over. Two men came out to see the wondrous sight.

A peacock dancing on a house-top with black clouds rolling behind is a sight worth a hundred thousand rupees. What beauty the Guru has given this bird! The peacock arched its neck backwards as proud as a young prince vaunting his manliness. It took two steps forward, two steps backwards. Its brown under-wings panted like an impatient lover out of breath. Its feathers quivered with delight.

Thah.

Down came the peacock tumbling over the wall.

Thah Thah.

The two peahens also tumbled down on the ground.

'Hoi, we've got all three!' cried the *goras*.

I sat down on the wet ground and wept. These were the peacock-killing mother-fuckers we were fighting for! What do these white *bunderlogs* know of the rains? Their women do not have black hair to remind them of dark monsoon skies. Nor do they have large-rounded bosoms which would remind them of billowing white clouds. Their girls do not know how to make swings on mango trees and sing songs to the monsoon. Have you ever heard *goralog* sing? I heard them in their church at Ambala: the mems screaming *hee, hee, hoo, hoo*; men braying *bhaw bhaw* like donkeys. How could they appreciate the *ragas* of rain and the dancing of peacocks? When all the world around was green and beautiful these *goras* thought only of killing. When I got up to give Hodson Sahib his morning mug

282

of *chai* he said 'Now is the time to strike! Get the men ready for battle.'

*

Heavy cannons are-hauled out by elephants. Camels and oxen are yoked to lighter guns. The ground is slippery. So we go barefoot. Only Hodson Sahib is on horseback. The rain slows down to a drizzle. The rocky ridge is all right, but near Sabzi Mandi we are knee-deep in slush. An elephant slithers and falls on its side with a great splash. Its mahout leaps clear but the cannon rolls over and its nozzle is stuck in the ground. The elephant manages to get on its feet and meekly raises one of its front legs to let the mahout clambar up. It takes twenty men to get the cannon back on its wheels. A slithering elephant is funny enough, a slithering camel is even funnier. It tries to sit on its bottom and gets its long legs entangled. The camel gets very *gussa* if you laugh at him.

We push on through the drizzle—slithering and falling as we go. It takes us two hours to cover a mile-and-a-half to get to Sabzi Mandi. We get there without attracting the enemy's attention. He is enjoying the first day of the monsoon drinking *bhang* with his *mashooka*.

The rain stops. Patches of blue appear in the sky. Soon the sky over Dilli city is full of multicoloured kites. They battle in the air and as one has its string snapped it wafts down in majestic sweeps. We hear boys yelling '*Bo kata*'. I see men waving scarves and whistling while flocks of black, white and brown pigeons wheel in the sky. From some house in Sabzi Mandi comes the jingle of dancers' bells and the beating of *tabla* drums. It seems as if everyone in Dilli has given himself up to merry-making.

'*Bhoom, bhoom, bhoom*' echo our cannons far away near Kashmiri Gate. Kites are quickly pulled down. Pigeons return to their lofts. Sound of singing and dancing dies out. '*Bhoom, bhoom, bhoom,*' reply the rebels' guns from the bastions near Kashmiri Gate and Mori Gate. Our trick has worked. While guns are hurling abuse at each other around Kashmiri and Mori Gates, we surround an area of Sabzi Mandi including a bazaar and a garden with a big house in its centre. The bugle sounds: *'Hamla!'* Our cannon fires into the bazaar. Then we go in on the double—shooting at any face that appears at a window, bayonetting anyone—male, female or child that comes in our way. Only from the big house in the garden is our fire returned. We take cover behind the trees. Every time any one of our party tries to get closer, he is shot. We bring up our cannon. The first ball makes a hole in a wall; the second, another. A part of the ceiling comes crashing down. We fire a volley into the house, fix bayonets and charge. There is no one to face us. We do not take chances. We surround the house and tiptoe in single file. I lead one party through a big room and up a broad staircase. And what do I see? I'll give you a thousand chances and you will not be able to guess right. A woman! There she stands on the top of the stairs with eyes bright as stars and a diamond glistening in her nose. And what do you think she is doing? Waving her sword at me.

'*Oi*, Nathia!' I shout to Natha Singh who is following me. 'Look what I've found!'

Natha Singh comes alongside and stares at the woman. '*Balley, balley!*' he exclaims. He shouts to the others. The staircase is full of Sikh soldiers armed with muskets and here is this woman waving an old *talwar* at us. She is no yesterday's chicken either. At least forty, flabby and pale as these city women are. Her white hair is dyed red with henna. Her teeth stained with *betel*. Her big bosom sags beneath her thin muslin shirt.

'*Bibi*, do you use that to pick your teeth?' asks Natha pointing to her sword. Then he goes up boldly and takes the sword out of her hand. '*Bibi*, why do you want to kill us with this?' he asks. 'It is easier to do so with your eyes.'

'Don't jest with her; she is the age of your mother,' I tell Natha.

'*Bhai*, I am a renowned mother-fucker,' replies Natha.

We have a hearty laugh.

Hodson Sahib rides up and we stop laughing. Natha drags the woman down the stairs and flings her at the feet of the Sahib's horse. The woman stands up and asks: 'Do you want to shoot me?' Not a tremor in her voice.

Hodson Sahib is taken aback. '*Aurat!*' he exclaims.

He guesses what she does for a living. 'Are you a prostitute? What were you doing in this house?'

'I am a *jihadin*,' she explains. 'I was helping my brothers to fight the *badzat nasara*.'

Hodson Sahib knows Hindustani well enough to know what *badzat nasara* means. To please the Sahib I stick my bayonet behind the woman's back and warn her: 'If you don't keep a rein on your tongue, you'll see the other end of this bayonet come out of your navel.'

The shameless wretch doesn't even shudder.

'Nihal Singh, take her to the camp for questioning. Then you can send her to the paradise she is so anxious to go to.'

We march the woman in front of us. If she slows down, I give her a smack on her buttocks; once I slip my finger in her tail. We have lots of fun on the way.

'*Bhai*, tonight we'll polish our weapons,' says Natha.

'Good woman! You cool our hot carbines and we'll cool a bullet in your body,' says Lehna.

The woman doesn't say a word. She doesn't even bother to look at us.

I take her to the Sahib's tent. He has just put off his helmet and unbuckled his sword. Without saying a word, Hodson Sahib turns round and slaps her hard across her face. He is not very big but he is very strong. The woman reels and falls on the floor. She begins to cry. 'If you want to kill me, kill me. Why do you torture me?' she whines.

Hodson Sahib sits down in his chair. He takes out his notebook and pencil from his desk. 'Name?'

'Anwar Bai.

'Where do you live?'

'Chawri Bazaar.'

'Who is commanding your troops?'

'Bakht Khan, the Bareilly General who took over two days ago.'

'Who made a *namak haram subedar* into a General?' demands the Sahib angrily. 'How many soldiers are there in Sabzi Mandi?'

'I do not know. I was sent there today to keep guard. Normally I stay in the women's barracks.'

'Women's barracks?'

'*Ji huzoor*! There are some women *jihadins*. Some like me are with the soldiers; others work in the hospital, or cook food for the troops.'

'What were you doing in that house?'

'I have already told the Sahib, I was with the guard. I gave up the profession two months ago when I joined the *jihad*. I hope Allah will forgive my sins.'

Hodson Sahib becomes very *gussa*. 'You call murder of innocent women and children a holy war?'

The woman does not reply. Hodson Sahib roars. 'Speak! Is this how you bloody Mussalmans fight a bloody *jihad*?'

This woman is not only without shame, she is also without fear. You know what she says in reply? 'Sahib, I have seen your people thrust their swords into women's bellies. With my own eyes I have seen children tossed in the air and spiked on bayonets.'

Hodson Sahib goes red in the face. I have never seen him in such a rage before. He cannot even speak. The woman goes on as if she did not care what anyone did to her:' And Sahib, now with your own hands you are going to spill the blood of a woman.'

She's a cunning whore. She wants to find out what the Sahib intends to do to her. Sahib remains silent for some time. He becomes cool again. He says to me: 'When a woman bears arms she has no right to expect to be treated any different from any other soldier. Take her away. I do not wish to hear anything more about her.'

I grab the woman by the arm and take her out.

The sun is about to set. It will soon be dark. I will have her first as I am the Sahib's orderly. Then I will have some sleep and let the others take their turns. Then I will have her a second time; then a third time. In the early hours, I will take her to the dump and shoot her. We have a saying: first quench your thirst, then spit in the well.

I bring the woman to our tent. The men are munching their *chappaties*. They resume their bawdy jests: '*Makhan pher*! What about it! Will you let us or shall we take you to the police lock-up?'

'*Oi, oi*, let her be, she is an old *buddhi*...'

'I bet her oven is still warm. We can bake our loaves before putting it out.'

'*Oi*, she's a whore. She must have run an army kitchen on her oven...I bet many regiments have passed between her thighs.'

'Nihalia,' says one of the youngsters, 'you scrub your weapon in her first, then we can also get rid of our surplus of semen.'

The woman pretends to be deaf. She turns to me and says, 'Sardarji, if I have your permission, I would like to say my evening prayer. Then you can do what you like with me.' She says this as coolly as if she were asking me to cook her an aubergine.

There is a chorus of approval. 'Nihalia, let her pray to her Allah. If it lightens her heart, she will lighten ours.'

'All right,' I reply. 'But make it quick—*phuta phut*.' I join the others over our ration of rum.

The whore spreads her *dupatta* on the muddy ground and sits down on her knees with her face towards the setting sun. The diamond in her nose sparkles.

'Who's going to get her nose-ring?' asks Natha.

No one answers. 'She's also got gold in her ears and on her arms,' says Lehna. 'Let Nihal Singh sell them and we can share the money.'

The whore stands up. Her eyes are closed, her lips keep moving. She bends down. Through her muslin shirt I can see her breasts hanging down like over-ripe marrows.

She goes down on her knees, presses her forehead on the ground a few times. Then she sits back on her heels and holds the palms of her hands in front of her as if she is reading a book. Her face glows. We stop making jokes about her. Her eyes fill with tears; they run down her cheeks and on to her muslin shirt. We stop talking. Her lips stop moving. She runs the palms of her hands across her tear-stained face. She turns her face first to the right and then to the left. I know Mussalmans do this to bless people on either side; we are on her right side. She takes out a rosary from her shirt-pocket and tells the beads. By now it is almost dark. She puts the rosary round her neck and stands up. 'Sardar Sahib, I am ready.'

No one answers. No one even looks up at her. After a while I say, 'Come inside.' She walks into the tent. I throw down the flap of the tent behind me. 'Sit down.' I thrust three *chappaties* and the lentils into her hands. 'Eat.'

'Sardarji, why do you take this trouble if you are going to shoot me?' she asks casually.

'Eat! We will talk afterwards.'

She eats a few morsels. I give her my water bottle. She drinks a lot of water. It is quite dark now. I pick up my carbine and order her to get out of the other end of the tent; the nozzle of my gun almost touches her spine.

Sentries challenge me. I give the pass word and explain, 'A prisoner to be shot.' We pass the dump heap; the stench is horrible. The woman covers her nostrils with her *dupatta*. We come within musket shot of Sabzi Mandi where we captured her. 'Can you find your way from here?'

She turns round and faces me. 'May Allah keep you... May Allah give you and your children long life...May Allah...'

I put my carbine on the ground and touch her feet. 'Forgive us for the way we treated you...forgive us for the hard words we used...you are like our mother.'

'Allah is the forgiver of all sins. If Allah can forgive mine, He will surely forgive yours.'

She is lost in the dark. I hear the *shap, shap* of her slippers in the mud. Then nothing. I hear a rebel sentry challenge some-one.

I raise my carbine to the sky and fire a shot.

Bahadur Shah Zafar

Bakht Khan was as big and as black as a rain-cloud. His eyes flashed like lightning; his speech was coarse like thunder. He came to Delhi just about the time everyone was praying for rain. Bakht Khan knew nothing of court etiquette. But as soon as he made his obeisance and thrust a couple of rupees into our hands we knew that Allah had answered our prayer. We presented him with a robe of honour. When he reappeared we addressed him as General Bakht Khan.

'*Badshah Salamat*,' he replied in the rustic accent of Bihar. 'I am no *jurnail-vurnail*. I am only a *subedar*. But I have ten thousand Ghazis with me. And we ask for nothing more than the honour to shed our blood for Your Majesty.'

It had been reported to us that Bakht Khan had been acclaimed by our troops and citizens both Muslim and Hindu. 'Bakht Khan, we make you General and Commander-in-Chief of our forces,' we said to him. 'May Allah crown your sword with victory!'

'*Arre Bhai, Badshah*,' he said without decorum. 'Your name is *Japhar*, isn't it? *Japhar* means victory, doesn't it? You will be *Japhar*. Anyone can take any bet with me,' he said putting out his hand in challenge.

With Bakht Khan came the monsoon. A short spring came to the autumn of our garden. For a while we let Bakht Khan take over affairs of war. We spent our days in the monsoon pavilions, Sawan-Bhadon, that we had raised in Hayat Baksh Garden behind Moti Masjid. Between these two pavilions was a large reservoir in the centre of which was another stone pavilion which looked as if it were afloat on the water. We had a small boat to take our guests to it. Our subjects named it after us, Zafar Mahal. Here we used to hold symposia of poets, entertained our friends with song and dance. That year we organized a small *mushaira* in honour of Taj Mahal Begum, younger sister of Zeenat, whom she had persuaded to join our harem. With Zeenat's consent we did honour to her virgin sister and had her share our couch for several nights.

For some days we did not hear the sound of guns; only the growling of black clouds, the pitter-patter of raindrops and the jingle of dancers' bells beating time to *tabla* drums. We spent the mornings flying our pigeons.

Then came the Flower-Sellers' festival. We took our beloved Zeenat Mahal and Mirza Jawan Bakht with us to pay homage to the tomb of Qutubuddin Bakhtiyar Kaki at Mehrauli.

We rode on our favourite elephant Maula Baksh out of Lahori Gate and down Chandni Chowk. We alighted at Ballimaran to pay our respects to our spiritual mentor, Kale Khan Sahib. At the mosque of Begum Fatehpuri we turned left to Lal Kuan where Asad Quli Khan (Zeenat Mahal's father) presented *nazar* and a basket of mangoes. We passed on through the prostitutes' quarters in Qazi-ka-Hauz. These ladies sprinkled flowers on us from their balconies.

We went out of the city through Ajmeri Gate. We went past the village of Paharganj and Raisina. At the observatory of Raja Man Singh known as Jantar Mantar, the gardeners of Talkatora orchards, which we had gifted to Zeenat Mahal, presented us with another basket of mangoes. We made a brief halt at the mausoleum of Safdar Jang to inspect the mosque and the *madrasa*. Our next halt was at Yusuf Sarai where we sampled the mangoes presented to us and took our siesta. When we rose the noon was well advanced and the southern horizon was heavily overcast with rain-clouds. Our mahout quickened the pace of Maula Baksh.

When we arrived at Mehrauli it began to rain. We were welcomed by the citizens who had been awaiting our arrival for many hours. They formed a procession led by parties of singers and dancers. We proceeded slowly through Mehrauli's narrow streets. People showered us with flowers, the heavens showered us with rain. When we arrived at our residence, Jahaz Mahal, fireworks were let off. The waters of Shamsi Talab already pocked by the falling rain burned bright crimson and blue and gold as cracker after cracker exploded in the sky and its embers came streaming down into the pool. *Wallah!* What a beautiful world it was! We slept to the sound of the rain beating on our roof and the gurgle of running water.

*

Next morning the sky was clear. We said our *fajar* prayer at the Auliya Masjid. This little mosque had been hallowed by Khwaja Muinuddin Chishti of Ajmer, Fariduddin Ganj-i-Shakar of Pak Pattan and innumerable other saints who had performed *chillas* (forty days of prayer and fasting) in its cells. After the morning prayer we went to the tomb of Qutubuddin Sahib Bakhtiyar Kaki and said a *fateha* at the graves of many of our kinsmen who were buried in the precincts.

Begum Zeenat who was with us was not allowed near the tomb of the saint. She presented a canopy made of roses and jasmines which was hung over the tomb. Then we watched divers leap eighty feet into a well in the courtyard and rewarded them suitably. We spent the rest of the day riding through the innumerable ruins that surrounded Mehrauli. First we went to the Qutub Minar and the Quwwat-ul-Islam mosque. We said *fatehas* over the tombs of Alauddin Khilji, Altamash and Imam Zamin. Then we rode past the house of Metcalfe Sahib to the mosque of Kamali the poet. The tomb of Emperor Balban was in a state of neglect. We ordered its repair.

We spent the evening in Jahaz Mahal. On the other side of the Shamsi Talab there were umbrella-shaped pavilions. We ordered a party of *shehnai* players to perform in them. The notes of the *shehnai* floated softly over the waters raising ripples as they came towards us. With the slow movement of the *alap*, clouds in the sky began to take bulbous shapes. As the melody went into the next movement, the *gat*, a gentle breeze began to blow. The clouds began to roll over faster as if keeping pace with the *tabla*. What improvization! We heard thunder and lightning and the hissing of the wind. And behold the sky was overcast! It became dark, lamps were lit. And as the *shehnai* moved into its finale in fast tempo, it began to pour. It is truly said that a great master can move the heavens to shed tears and the tapers to light themselves and burn in anguish and ecstasy! We heard the *Raga Megh Malhar* (melody of the rains) and then *Deepak* (melody of the lamps). And we were like one in a daze.

Thus we spent three days free of care. We visited monuments, listened to music and watched Kathak dancers. Sometimes we simply rested our head on a bolster and gazed at the clouds.

When we returned to Delhi, the state of affairs was, to use Saadi's expression, entangled like the hair of Negroes. The enemy had received reinforcements and siege trains. Our army was short of everything: powder, arms, provisions. Mirza

Mughal and Bakht Khan aimed barbed shafts of speech at each other. There were many incidents between the citizens and the soldiers. The citizens taunted the soldiers for their cowardliness, soldiers taunted the merchants for trading with the enemy. Most of our soldiers were Muslims; most merchants, Hindu. And Bakr-Id was approaching. Mirza Mughal and some of the Muslim *omarah* were in favour of taking away the Hindus' property, because the Hindus favoured the *firangi*.

Bakht Khan was against this policy. We lent our support to him. We forbade the slaughter of cows and ourselves set an example by sacrificing a camel. Bakr-Id passed off peacefully.

Two days after the festival the hand of Satan touched the powder magazine. Vast quantities of gunpowder was lost. Many people were killed and their houses destroyed. The *firangi* took full advantage of this misfortune. He circulated forged letters insinuating that our trusted adviser Hakeem Ahsanullah and our Queen Consort Zeenat Mahal had a hand in the explosion of the magazine. The mob set fire to Ahsanullah's house. We sent our bodyguard to rescue him and his family. The rabble had the temerity to force its way into the Diwan-i-Khas and make vile accusations of treachery against us. Our firmness saved the situation. We swore that if anyone was found in possession of the *hakeem's* property we would have his belly ripped open.

> *Mine enemies assembled in force on all sides*
> *O Ali! All powerful, for God's sake!*
> *Thou hast sent an unseen army to my aid*
> *It is from Thee I supplicate victory in my prayers.*

*

Foul vapours of suspicion continued to float over Delhi. We came to the conclusion that fate itself had loaded the dice against us and we could not win. Delhi was doomed. Prudence dictated that we should try to salvage whatever we could. We sent a secret emissary to Wilson Sahib, commander of the enemy troops, that if our life and those of Zeenat Mahal and our children were guaranteed and our pension restored to us, we would contrive to have the city gates thrown open to his troops. He did not have the courtesy to send us a reply.

We waited for the last grain of sand to run down the hourglass. It took only seven days to do so. On 14 September the *firangi* and his allies, Pathans, Punjabi Mussalmans, Sikhs, Dogras and Gorkhas launched their attack on Delhi. The entire northern side of the wall from Kabul Gate to the river was subjected to incessant bombardment. Cannon balls fell in the Red Fort. Homes of some of the *salateen* were wrecked.

General Bakht Khan fought back valiantly. He was everywhere; at Sabzi Mandi in the morning, at Mori Gate in the afternoon, at Kashmiri Gate in the evening. After sunset he came to the palace to report. The enemy forced his way into the city. The citizens fought them in every street. Even women and children hurled stones on the heads of the assailants. Although age had made our bones brittle we mounted our Arab horse Hamdam and went out to encourage our troops. But Allah willed that we would be taught a lesson in humility.

On 21 September Bakht Khan told us that Delhi was lost. He asked us to accompany him towards Oudh so that we could continue the battle. We asked him to forgive us; our eighty-two years weighed heavily on our frame. As the venerable Saadi had said: 'We thought proper to sit down in the mansion of retirement, fold up the skirt of association, wash our tablet of heedless sayings and no more indulge in senseless prattle.'

People began to leave the city. We also decided to go. At first we thought of going to Mehrauli where we could be closer to the sacred dust of Khwaja Qutubuddin Bakhtiyar Kaki. But Mirza Elahi Baksh (father-in-law of our late heir apparent Mirza Fakhroo) advised us to seek shelter in the mausoleum of our ancestor Emperor Humayun. Mehrauli, he told us, could not be defended; the mausoleum on the other hand was like a fortress and would be in a position to negotiate with the sahib. We accepted his advice.

The hand of fate struck the drum of departure. Our heart was heavy. We bade farewell to Maula Baksh and Hamdam who had been our companions from the days of our youth. We released all the pigeons in our pigeon lofts and told them to spread the news of our wretchedness. Our palanquins took the Agra Road. Our harem, *salateen* and servants followed in our train. All along the route we passed hundreds of people on bullock carts, *ekkas*, mules and on foot. When we arrived at Arab-ki-Sarai we saw that the gardens around the mausoleum were crammed with people. All our sons, grandsons, nephews, nieces along with their families and relatives were there. That night we rested our weary head at the foot of the grave of our ancestor Emperor Humayun.

Early next morning while people lay like corpses in their shrouds (the nights had turned chilly) we threaded our way to the tomb of Nizamuddin Auliya. No heralds proclaimed the advent of the Badshah Ghazi, the Shadow of God on Earth, the Emperor of Hindustan. After prayer we sat at the foot of Auliya's tomb and told the beads of our rosary. We said the *fateha* at the tombs of our father, Akbar Shah II, our brother, Mirza Jahangir, Begum Jahanara and the poet Ameer Khusrau. It occurred to us that we too would be soon sleeping among them. We recited the prayer of the *dervish*: 'O Lord, have mercy upon the wicked, because Thou hast already had mercy upon good men by creating them good.' We returned to the mausoleum fully prepared for the fate Allah had ordained for us.

Nihal Singh

Thereafter it rained every day. The Jamna rose and the flood swept away the boat-bridge. This was lucky for us as the rebels used to get most of their men and supplies from across the river. There was not too much fighting during the rains—an occasional skirmish in Qudsia Garden or the guns barking at each other.

The rain stopped as suddenly as it had started. More *goras* joined our camp. They brought big guns and gunpowder sticks. Two Sahibs, Nicholson and Taylor who were said to be great fighters, came to lead the attack on Dilli. Banias who came to sell us provisions told us that in the city the price of 'red pepper' was going up and the price of 'black pepper' going down day by day. That one-eyed Rajab Ali started coming every day and doing a lot of whispering in Hodson Sahib's ear. One evening as I was massaging the Sahib's feet I asked him: 'Sahib, what does this one-eyed man *phus phus* in your ear?' At first Hodson Sahib looked very *gussa* and said, 'So you try to listen?' I replied, 'No Sahib. If I listened in I would not be asking you.' Then Hodson Sahib told me: 'The old badshah says if we spare his life and give him his pension he will throw open the gates of Dilli.'

'And what do you say?' I asked.

'I say, first throw open the gate, then we will talk.'

Hearing this kind of talk I thought the *hamla* would begin any day. But nothing happened. More than two thousand *goras* were in hospital; every day a few died vomitting or shitting blood. Other *goras* complained of not getting enough rum and made pictures on the walls of Hindu Rao's mansion showing officers drinking and fucking. How could such people go into battle! Wilson Sahib Bahadur kept saying 'Tomorrow.... tomorrow.' And that fellow Bakht Khan, *subedar* or General or whatever he was, kept attacking our camp, killing our men and our horses.

*

Whatever else you may say of the *goras*, when it comes to fighting they fight like no other race on earth. Nicholson Sahib, for example, is as big as the demon Ravan with a beard as long as our Gurus' (some fools called themselves Nikalsainis, even said he was one of our Gurus reborn). He is so strong that with one blow he could fell an ox. Our own Hodson Sahib, who though he has no hair on his head or chin nor is as big as Nicholson, is as brave as a lion. Nicholson and Hodson Sahib become very restless. 'What kind of *Jangi Lat* is this Wilson Sahib Bahadur when all he can say is "Tomorrow, tomorrow"?' they ask. The two of them go to Wilson Sahib and say, 'We must start the battle now.' Just at that time the one-eyed Rajab Ali brings information that Bakht Khan is taking a large army to Najafgarh and Rohtak to attack *gora paltans* coming from the Punjab. So Wilson Sahib Bahadur says to Nicholson, 'If you are so anxious to fight, go to Najafgarh.' To Hodson Sahib he says: 'If you are also eager to fight, you go to Rohtak.'

Next evening we ride out to Rohtak. We are five hundred sowars and ten *gora* officers. We ride through the night and halt a mile short of Rohtak in the early hours of the morning. We have our *chai* and feed our horses. When the sun comes up, we are ready for battle. Half-an-hour later, the town gates open and out pours a stream of horsemen armed with muskets and swords. They charge towards us.

Hodson Sahib orders us to retreat. We gallop back half-a-mile. The fellows think we are running away. They chase us yelling '*Ali, Ali.*' When they are almost on us Hodson Sahib gives the command: 'Turn about and at them.' We wheel round. We unsling our carbines and fire a volley. Fifty of them topple down. Then we charge them with our lances. They break ranks and scatter. Only a handful are manful enough to face us. I see with my own eyes how my Sahib really loves fighting. He draws his *talwar*, gallops up to one of the fellows and challenges him to single-handed combat. The fellow slashes, lunges and backs away. The Sahib parries his blows. 'Try again—is this all you've learnt about swordsmanship?' shouts my Sahib. When the other has had his try, my Sahib strikes one blow that cuts the fellow in two halves. Then he takes on another. Then a third one. *Wah! Wah!* Hodson Sahib, *Wah! Wah!* You are one in a hundred thousand!

We slay over three hundred of the enemy for the loss of only two.

By the evening we are back on the Ridge. So is Nicholson Sahib. He gave that Bareilly General, Bakht Khan, such a thrashing at Najafgarh that he ran back whimpering like a dog with its tail between its legs.

Now Wilson Sahib Bahadur has no excuse to say 'Tomorrow.' The *gora paltan* from the Punjab marches in with all the guns we need. They are hauled into position and start firing. Within a few hours the city wall looks as if it has had an attack of small-pox. It has to be blown up before we can launch the big attack. This is left to our Mazhabi Sikhs. What courage the great Guru has given these poor Mazhabis! They go out one night with bags of gunpowder. Just as they are nearing the wall, rebel snipers spot them. Its too late to run back so one fellow charges forward with the bag in his arms. *Thah!* He falls. Two other run up pick up the charge and carry it a few steps forward. *Thah! Thah!* Both are killed. A third Mazhabi runs up, picks up the bundle and takes it still closer to the wall. In this way forty brave sons of the Guru lay down their lives. But it is the ambrosial hour of the dawn and the great Guru blesses their task with success. The charge is placed beneath the wall and fired: *Bharam!* The loudest *bharam* you can have ever heard! The earth trembles. A section of the wall comes crashing down. The breach is wide enough to let five pairs of oxen with ploughs pass through.

The sahibs do not tell us when we are to launch the big *hamla*. They *git mit* with each other. If anyone of us blacks comes near them, they use bad words like *belady* or *daym* or *foken* and stop talking. They are getting very short tempered.

It is the first week in the month of Assu (September). Early one morning our batteries open up: *puttack, puttack*. Stones fly like fluffs of cotton from a carder's bow. It goes on all day and continues till midnight. At midnight we are roused and told that the big *hamla* is to take place before sunrise.

Our army is divided into five columns which will start the attack at the same time all along the city wall stretching from the river to Sabzi Mandi. We get a double ration of rum. We are promised six months' additional wage if we take Dilli.

The night is as black as a Negro's face. When I stretch my arm, I cannot see my hand. No one is allowed to speak. We take off our shoes and stealthily move to our positions. We are facing Kashmiri Gate. As the grey dawn appears, cannons begin to roar. The rebels seem to have sensed our moves. They let go at us. It is like the end of a *tamasha* with both sides firing away with everything they have. This goes on for about one hour. Then the guns fall silent. What an awful silence! Sweat pours down my forehead. I gulp down my rum. Then a huge explosion. Stones fly into the air. A pillar of dust and smoke rises from Kashmiri Gate. The gate has been blown up. Our *subedar*, Man Singh draws his *kirpan* and yells: *'Boley So Nihal.'* We draw our *kirpans* and yell back: *'Sat Sri Akal.'* We rush forward into Dilli city.

Rebel drums begin to beat—*dug-a-dug-dug, dug-a-dug-dug*.
They let loose a hail of bullets at us and meet us boldly shouting:
'*Ali, Ali, Ali*' or '*Har Har Mahadev*.' Who said they had no fight
left in them! But we have more guns, more carbines, more men.
So we press on over the bodies of the dead and dying. We leap
over the earthworks. That one-eyed bastard Rajab Ali had lied
about the rebels when he said they would lay down their arms.
They come on us like a swarm of hornets without any care for
their lives. Their women and children yell filthy abuse at us.
They call us the *firangi's* bootlickers and hurl rocks on our
heads. (If that whore—what was her name?—is caught again it
would be the end of my life).

The battle rages through the morning and into the afternoon.
By the evening we have taken the bazaars stretching from the
Kashmiri to the Mori Gates. We are tired and thirsty. In
Kashmiri Gate there are many liquor shops. We break in and
drink whatever we can find. The *goras* get drunk. All night they
sing *ho, ho, ho* in praise of a bottle of rum. We ransack houses,
take gold and coins from the dead. We drive cows and buffaloes tethered in homes out of the city wall for safe-keeping with
our Mazhabis. Wilson Sahib Bahadur is very *gussa* and has all
the remaining liquor spilt into the moat and orders anyone
found looting to be shot. Who is to shoot whom? Sahibs say
they will appoint prize agents to divide the loot. We say *accha*.

Next morning the battle is resumed. We have to fight our
way into every street and every lane. Everywhere we see
women in veils and little boys helping the rebels. The *goras* say
the rebels killed their memsahibs and children, so they kill
every woman or child that comes their way.

It takes four days of fighting in the bazaars before the gates
of the Red Fort are thrown open to us. We march in through
Lahori Gate with our bands playing. There is no one in the Red
Fort except a blind woman and an old cripple. *Goras* make sport
of them with their bayonets; one plunges his weapon from the
front, another from the behind to see if they can meet in the
middle of their victim's body. They have a good laugh.

The British flag is hoisted. We present arms. The *goras* sing
a song praying for long life to their Queen. A salute of twenty-
one guns is fired in Her Majesty's honour. The *goras* are housed

in the palace. We are ordered to encamp in the open beyond the moat.

*

The next day we drive the rebels out of Chandni Chowk and the bazaars surrounding the great mosque Jamia Masjid. There are no singing girls in Chawri Bazaar, no whores in Qazi-ka-Hauz, no *hijdas* in Lal Kuan. But we get plenty of gold and silver, cows and buffaloes. We blow up many old palaces and set fire to many streets. The *goras* want to blow up the Royal Mosque, but Wilson Sahib Bahadur says: 'No, it will anger the Pathans, Biloches and Punjabi Mussalmans on our side.' The sahibs are wise.

The mosque is allotted to the Sikh *risallahs*. The space under the domes is for the men! To the long verandahs on the sides we tether our horses. There are two cisterns in the middle of the vast courtyard. One we use to bathe ourselves; the other to bathe our horses.

I climb up a minaret to have a look at Dilli. I feel like a king looking down on his kingdom. Palaces, houses, mosques and bazaars, smoke rising from many places which we set on fire. I look towards the south. What do I see? A stream of humanity pouring out of the city gates. I am still wondering where all these people are making for when I hear *thah*. A chip of the parapet flies into my beard. Some bastard is trying to kill me. The shot is from the direction of Chawri Bazaar. Now what would a chap be doing in the whores' quarter when all the whores have fled? I am not frightened. I don't take cover. I open my trouser buttons and show him what I have.

That evening I tell Hodson, 'Sahib, they are taking away everything. We will get nothing but our big thumbs.' He runs his hand over his bald head and thinks over the matter. Then he goes to Wilson Sahib Bahadur and gets permission to attack the city from the southern end.

Two days later, Hodson's Horse rides round the city walls. We have a great game of tent pegging. Only it is not blocks of wood we stick our lances into, but people trying to run away from us. Those who escape our lances we shoot with our carbines. We re-enter the city through Dilli Gate, ride through Daryaganj and up the steps of the Jamia Masjid. After the great ride and the grand *shikar* of humans we wash our lances in the mosque-cistern. The water becomes so red that even the horses refuse to come near it.

Bahadur Shah Zafar

We waited for two days. On the third morning a *gora* with a posse of fifty Sikh cavalry arrived at the gates. Their emissary was Rajab Ali, the one-eyed sycophant who had so often prostrated himself before us and begged the privilege of kissing our feet. He informed us that Mirza Elahi Baksh had promised Wilson Sahib Bahadur, the commander of the English army, to have us arrested. A Major Hodson had been authorized to execute the warrant. Our ears refused to believe that Hakeem Ahsanullah had also gone over to the enemy and was making an inventory of our properties. It is rightly said the smoother the skin of the serpent the more venom it has in its fangs.

We had no words left for anyone. The loathsome, one-eyed bastard, Rajab Ali, assured us that if we went with him our lives would be spared. What was our life worth at eighty-two? But we had to think of Zeenat Mahal and Jawan Bakht. Then there was our elder son, Mirza Mughal. He urged us to spit in the face of Rajab Ali. 'We will make *kababs* of this *gora* and his bearded *Sikhra boorchas!*' he boasted.

We listened to the contentious debate for an hour. We did not speak our mind but sent for Begum Zeenat Mahal and our son Jawan Bakht. We took them with us and descended the steps of the mausoleum. Mirza Mughal and his soldiers continued to shout. We became deaf to all advice save what Allah gave us. We told Mirza Mughal and our other sons to see how the sahibs treated us and then decide on their own course of action. We embraced them, little realizing that this would be the last time for us to be doing so. We bade farewell to our relatives and servants. They kissed our hands and wept.

Our palanquins were borne out of the gate of the mausoleum to where our captors awaited us. Before stepping out we recited the Throne verse ten times, ten times the Messenger Believes, and ten times Say He Is God. We raised our hands to the heavens and intoned: 'Allah! We commit Thy Servant Bahadur Shah Zafar to Thee. Watch over us.' We approached the sahib in command of the Sikh cavalry and enquired whether he was Hodson Sahib Bahadur. He nodded his head. We asked him if he would be good enough to repeat the assurance that our life and those of our Queen and son would be spared. He nodded his head again. We presented the famous *Zulfiqar* given by the Persian conqueror Nadir Shah to our ancestors to the sahib. Our son presented his sword. We were ordered into our palanquins. We were prisoners of the *firangi*.

*

It look us a whole day to get back to Delhi. We could hear the shouting of the crowd and many times our palanquins were halted. By the afternoon the tumult died down. When we finally entered Delhi Darwaza it was *Shahr-i-Khamoshan* (a silent city). We could hear no sounds except those made by the horses of the escorting cavalry. At the Lahori Gate Hodson Sahib handed us over to a troop of *goras*.

In the past whenever we entered the fort, cannons were fired to announce our arrival and the band played at the Naqqar Khana. This time all we heard was our name mispronounced 'Baddur Sha' as one *gora* soldier passed us on to the next. Our palanquins were borne through the Meena Bazaar. We were lodged in the subterranean rooms where a few months earlier we had given shelter to the European families before they were butchered by the mob. The doors were bolted from the outside and an armed guard placed at the gate. We were cut off from the world from everything save evil tidings.

The bow of fate loosened a hundred poisoned shafts into our body. As a limb numbed by poverty of blood feels not the prick of the thorn so was our mind numbed against sorrow.

Nihal Singh

It took seven days flushing out rebels from the hideouts before we could say Dilli had become the property of Jan Company. All that was left were empty houses and corpses. And dogs, cats and rats to eat them. After a few days the Hindus were allowed to return and open their shops. Mussalmans who tried to pass off as Hindus paid with their lives. We made them take off their clothes. We poked their cocks with our bayonets and asked: 'How did this fellow get his top chopped off?' The blood would drain out of their faces and they would start urinating. We knew they had come back for buried silver or gold. So we would march them to their homes, take whatever we could find and turn them over to the sahib judge. He would ask them a few questions and order them to be hanged. They would be brought to the *kotwali* in the centre of Chandni Chowk where our Guru had been executed by Auranga. A dozen gallows had been erected. In the evening after having had their dinner the sahibs would ride up to the place. *Khidmatgars* would lay out chairs and sofas for them and *abdars* fill their glasses with brandy and port and light their cheroots. And the *tamasha* would begin. In batches of six the wretches would be hauled up their hands tied behind them and nooses would be put round their necks. The sahibs would give the signal by clenching their fists with their thumbs pointing down and the planks would be pulled away. The sahibs would lay bets on which one would last longest. It was easy to tell who would die first—the one who struggled most, strangled himself quickest. Their eyes would pop out, blood pour out of their nostrils. Some died quickly; others had to have their legs stretched to finish them off. The sahibs enjoyed themselves laughing and joking, drinking and gambling.

*

Hodson Sahib never wastes his time on this kind of *tamasha*. His mind is on bigger game. One day he goes to Wilson Sahib Bahadur and says 'Let me go and capture the King of Dilli.' The *Jangi Lat* replies 'Accha, but I don't want to loose any more *goras.'* Hodson Sahib says 'I will take my Sikhs.' He then tells me, 'Nihal Singha, pick up fifty of your bravest boys and be ready in the morning for the big *shikar.'*

It is the 21st of September. The weather has changed. The nights are getting cool and the dew falls like the drizzle of rain. I pick fifty boys including Natha and Lehna and tell them to sleep round the pulpit of the mosque. I rouse them while it is still dark. We swallow a couple of *chappaties* and drink a mug of tea. We get into our uniforms and ride down the steps of the mosque. Hodson Sahib arrives with two Mussalmans riding behind him. One is that same one-eyed Rajab Ali. The other is dressed like a *nawab*: a big fur cap and a coat of gold kinkob. My Sahib addresses him politely as 'Mirza Sahib'. (I later discover his name was Mirza Elahi Baksh and that he was the father-in-law of the king's eldest son who had died some time ago).

The Mirza says something in the ear of Hodson Sahib and takes his leave. We proceed *clip clop, clip clop* through Faiz Bazaar and out of Dilli Gate. Hodson Sahib rides in front holding his unsheathed sabre on his shoulder. The one-eyed Rajab Ali follows behind him. I am behind the one-eyed fellow leading my fifty sowars. We carry our lances in our hands; our loaded carbines are slung behind our backs. We have two *kirpans* each—one attached to the saddle and the other to our belts. By the time the sun rises we are on the royal road to Agra. On either side of the road are many ancient ruins. They are full of people. The men are armed with guns and swords. But no one dares come near us or say a word.

The one-eyed Rajab Ali rides up alongside the Sahib and tells him about the buildings. Hodson Sahib is not interested, but this fellow keeps talking. 'That Sahib is a Buddhist pillar on top of the palace of Firoze Shah,' he says. I ask you what can a Buddhist pillar be doing on top of a Mussalman king's palace? We pass very high walls of an ancient fort. The one-eyed chap says: 'This sir, is the Purana Qila—the old fort—said to have been first built by the Aryans and was known as Indraprastha. Inside there is a mosque of Sher Shah Suri and the library of Emperor Humayun.' Who is to tell the Sahib that there cannot be a mosque inside a Hindu fort! I keep quiet as Hodson Sahib is paying no attention to the one-eyed *tuttoo*. By the time the sun is a spear high we arrive at the gate of a very large building with very high walls. All I can see of the inside is a huge white marble dome. This the one-eyed fellow says is the tomb of Humayun Badshah. The old king and his family are hiding inside.

The one-eyed fellow continues to babble. 'And this, Sahib Bahadur, is the tomb of Isa Khan and beyond that where the crowd is was once known as Arab-ki-Sarai. Beyond that you can see the red dome of the tomb of Abdul Rahim Khan-i-Khanan, one of the great ministers of Emperor Akbar. And these buildings behind you belong to the mausoleum of His Holiness Shaikh Nizamuddin Auliya. Many kings and queens and princes of royal blood have their graves close to the tomb of the saint.'

Hodson Sahib becomes very impatient. 'Yes, yes, Rajab Ali, another time you can tell me all about these ruddy monuments! We have more important work on hand. So get on with it *juldi*— I haven't the whole day to waste!'

Hodson Sahib and the one-eyed fellow dismount. I also dismount to take the reins of their horses. The one-eyed fellow slaps the big gate with the palm of his hand. 'Who's there?' demands a voice from the other side.

'Maulvi Rajab Ali, emissary of the Company Bahadur. I have an urgent message for His Majesty.'

After a while a small door in a corner of the gate opens. A sentry sticks out his head and sings! 'His Majesty Bahadur Shah Ghazi, Emperor of Hindustan, King of Kings, Shadow of God on Earth, commands the presence of Maulvi Rajab Ali Vakil of the Company Bahadur. Maulvi Rajab Ali may enter.'

'*Wah bhai wah!*' I say to myself. 'You hide like a rat in a hole but call yourself King of Kings!'

Rajab Ali disappears inside the little door which is shut behind him.

Hodson Sahib spits on the ground. He begins to pace up and down in front of the gate. He does not speak a word to anyone or even bother to look up at the crowd that is looking down at us from the walls. So many people and not a *choon*! The silence of thousands of people frightens me. All I can hear is horses champing at their bits, neighing, farting and urinating. And crows cawing. Then I hear voices of men quarrelling with each other. And a loud call: 'Narai Taqbir!' And a roar of hundreds of voices yelling 'Allah-o-Akbar.'

More yelling: 'Mar dalo firangi ko (kill the firangi).'

What can fifty Sikhs and one gora do against thousands? They will make mincemeat of us. But wah, wah Hodson Sahib! No one can be like you! He continues to pace up and down pretending he hasn't heard a sound.

Another hour. My mouth is dry: my tunic is wet with cold sweat. Voices on the other side come nearer and nearer. Hodson Sahib remounts. I tie the one-eyed fellow's horse to a tree and get into my own saddle. Hodson Sahib takes his pistol out of the holster and cocks it. I clutch my lance. Slowly the huge gates draw backwards. Three palanquins, one behind the other and a mob of wild looking men flourishing swords and carbines. Some women wailing surround the palanquins. They see Hodson Sahib and his Sikh sowars and turn to stone. The one-eyed Rajab Ali comes up to the Sahib and waggles his head. He goes back to the second palanquin and says something to someone. An old man steps out. He is tall, very thin and bent with age. He has a white, trimmed beard. He wears a big fur cap and a long fur-lined coat trailing down to his feet. He hobbles up to the Sahib, looks up and asks: 'Have I the honour of addressing Hodson Sahib Bahadur?'

'Yes, I am Major Hodson. You Bahadur Shah?'

'That is the name by which this unfortunate man is known. Hodson Sahib Bahadur, do I have your word that our life, the life of our Queen Zeenat Mahal and that of our son Prince Jawan Bakht will be spared?'

'Yes, Wilson Sahib Bahadur, the Jangi Lat has promised you your lives.' There is a murmur in the crowd.

Hodson Sahib holds up his pistol and shouts at the top of his voice, 'Listen you people! If anyone of you make an attempt to interfere, I will shoot the three people in these palanquins like dogs. Understand!'

What audacity! The crowd shrinks back. The old king ungirds his sword and holds it aloft with his shaking hands. Hodson Sahib dismounts, takes the sword and hands it to me. What a sword! Green jade and gold handle studded with precious stones! Then the badshah's son, a young chap named Jawan Bakht, steps out from the last palanquin and also hands his sword to the Sahib who passes it on to me. Another beauty! Gold, diamonds and rubies! Hodson Sahib orders the three palanquins to be brought out. Fifty sowars in front, then one palanquin, then my Sahib and I. Behind us the huge mob. We don't look back lest they think we are frightened of being shot in our backs. I have shivers going up and down my spine and more cold sweat on my body. But Hodson Sahib! Not a trace of fear on his red face! We pass along the battlements of the old fort with crowd still trudging behind us. Thousands of rebel sepoys come out of the old Indraprastha fort. We ignore them and go along at the pace set by the palanquin-bearers. Another half-a-*kos* and the crowd begins to drop off. And soon we are just fifty Sikh sowars and Hodson Sahib. And we are taking with us as prisoner the Emperor of Hindustan, his queen and their son. It is a miracle of the great Guru!

Instead of going through Delhi Gate we turn sharp left towards the side where the sun is setting and ride past Turkman and Ajmeri Gates. Then we turn right into Kabuli Gate to enter the city. Hodson Sahib wants everyone in Dilli to know that we have their King, Queen and son as our prisoner. But the streets are deserted. Only dogs tearing up corpses pause to look up. Vultures shuffle away a few paces to let us pass. In front of the *kotwali*, six corpses are still dangling from the scaffolds with crows pecking on them. As we pass the gurdwara where our ninth Guru was martyred by Auranga, we unsheath our *kirpans* and dip them in salute. I raise the Sikh battle cry 'Boley So Nihal!' The sowars shout back 'Sat Sri Akal.'

It is still daylight when we draw up outside the Red Fort. 'Who's there?' demands a *gora* sentry.

'Major Hodson to deliver up prisoners Bahadur Shah ex-King of Delhi, his wife Zeenat Mahal and their son Jawan Bakht.'

The gate opens. Hodson Sahib and the one-eyed Rajab Ali go in with the palanquins.

We ride back to Jamia Masjid.

We slaughter twenty goats. And while they are roasting we drink a lot of rum. We get very **drunk** and begin to sing. Lehna starts off with a song about a little old man who wanted to copulate with a she-camel. Lehna knows a lot of songs about this *budha baba*. But my *kismet*! The Sahib's *syce* comes and says I am wanted in the Red Fort. I am very high on rum but I follow him.

I ride to the Sahib's quarter. When I enter the Sahib is examining the two swords he has been given that morning. Under the light of the lantern the stones in the handle sparkle like stars. What craftsmanship! The Sahib tells me that one bears the name of Emperor Jahangir and the other of the Persian invader Nadir Shah. He is not very happy. 'That's all I got from Wilson Sahib Bahadur,' he says. 'Not even a *shabash*. I wish I had killed the old badshah and his puppy.'

'Sahib, if you had given me the slightest hint, I would have severed their heads from their bodies.'

'I know, I know,' he replies impatiently. 'I would have done it myself. But the white man's word has to be honoured. Now it will be different. I have permission to get the king's other sons and nephews. They are the *badmashes* who murdered the memsahibs and their little *babalogs*. Wilson Sahib says, "Do what you like but don't let me be bothered with them." Tell *Subedar* Man Singh to be ready with a hundred sowars at the same time tomorrow. This may be dangerous work. There'll be plenty of rum when this is over.'

*

Next morning I had real trouble getting the men ready in time. *Subedar* Man Singh had to shout at them. But Hodson Sahib arrived with another *gora*, Macdowell Sahib, and the one-eyed Rajab Ali. We were in our saddles lined up in front of the mosque. The two sahibs rode in front with Rajab Ali and myself directly behind them. (I was on his blind side so we did not even have to exchange glances). Behind us were our two *subedars* and then the hundred Sikh sowars with the ends of their turbans fluttering in the morning breeze and their spears glittering in the light of the morning sun. Rajab Ali didn't try his *buk buk* about the ancient buildings of Dilli on me.

We arrived at the northern gate of Humayun's mausoleum. And as soon as we arrived, a crowd began to collect around us. Some came from Arab-ki-Sarai, next door, some from Nizamuddin. The roofs and walls of buildings were soon full of people. Many men were armed with carbines.

*

Once more Rajab Ali goes in. Once more we hear yells of 'Allah-o-Akbar'. We can hear them coming nearer and nearer the gate. Slowly the gates open. A cart appears, drawn by two humped oxen, with three men sitting huddled on it and the one-eyed Rajab Ali standing by the wheel. Behind the cart a mob of sullen-faced, evil-looking men armed with carbines and swords. The sahibs mount their horses and ride up to the cart. Hodson Sahib commands: 'Rajab Ali, identify the three prisoners.'

Rajab Ali puts his hand on one: 'Mirza Mughal Bahadur.'

The man steps out of the cart and with trembling hands offers his sword. Macdowell Sahib takes his sword.

'Mirza Abu Bakr,' says Rajab Ali putting his hand on another. This man also steps out and hands his sword to Macdowell Sahib.

'Mirza Khizr Sultan.'

The third man follows the example of the other two. All three go back and huddle on the ox cart. The crowd watches the scene. You can see some people are getting very agitated. The burr-burr of anger becomes a roar. As the cart moves forward, the mob surges behind it.

Hodson Sahib turns round his horse, draws his sword and holds it aloft. 'Halt,' he orders. The mob halts and falls silent. Hodson Sahib orders fifty sowars to go ahead with the cart. He and Macdowell Sahib ride up to the mob. The mob withdraws step by step till it is back in the mausoleum gate. Hodson Sahib shouts at the top of his voice, 'Lay down your arms.'

Another miracle of the Guru! They throw down their swords and muskets on the ground. It takes us two hours to collect them and load them on carts. Never in my life have I known hours like these! And never in my life have I known a man like Hodson Sahib Bahadur! He, as I am always saying, is one of a hundred thousand!

We ride at a smart canter to catch up with our party. There are gangs of armed men all along the road. The gangs become bigger and bigger as we approach the city. We plough our way through and join our party escorting the prisoners. All round us and upto the city walls is this armed mob shouting.'*Allah-o-Akbar*' and brandishing swords at us. I pray to my Guru and promise to offer one rupee four annas at the Chandni Chowk gurdwara if my life is spared. The Guru hears my prayer. Hodson Sahib gallops up to the cart carrying the prisoners and orders it to halt. The *burr-burr* dies down. We are passing through a gate about half-a-mile from the city. On our right is the grey-black ruin of a Mussalman palace with that Buddhist column the one-eyed Rajab Ali was talking about; for the rest it is just a sea of heads, naked sabres and carbines. The sun is about to set. Hodson Sahib raises his hands and turns about in his saddle to speak to everyone. 'Listen you people of Dilli,' he roars. The people of Dilli listen. 'These three men in our custody are murderers. These butchers have the blood of many inno-cent women and children on their hands. You will now witness the justice of the Company Bahadur. Stand back, see, and remember.'

The crowd falls back. Our sowars form a ring around the ox cart. 'Get down all three of you and take off your clothes,' orders Hodson Sahib.

The three men obey. Their faces are yellow. Their hands tremble as they remove their shirts. 'Everything,' orders Hodson Sahib again.

Their knees shake as they slip down their pantaloon-type pyjamas. These Mussalmans not only cut the ends of their cock, they also shave their pubic hair. I have never seen sadder looking penises hanging their circumcized heads as if in shame!

'You Abu Bakr, step out in front,' orders Hodson Sahib.

A heavily built man of about thirty-five comes up a few faltering steps. He covers his nakedness with his hands.

'Nihal Singh, take that thing off this man's arm,' he orders pointing to a charm tied round Abu Bakr's arm.

I wrench off the amulet and put it in my pocket.

'Hand me your carbine.'

I give my carbine to the Sahib.

'Sahib, *mat maro*—don't kill,' wails Abu Bakr, clasping his hands in prayer.

Hodson Sahib aims at his chest. *Thah.* Abu Bakr cries *'Hai Allah'* and collapses in a pool of blood.

The crowd is struck dumb with terror. Not one person moves. The other two prisoners are more dead than alive when Hodson Sahib shoots them through their heads.

We have three naked corpses sprawled in the dust; blood gushing from their wounds, saliva oozing from their gaping mouths, eyes turning to grey marbles. The thousands of armed men who watched the executions look as dead as the three lying at our feet.

Subedar Man Singh raises his *kirpan* and shouts: *'Jo Boley So Nihal.'* We draw our kirpans and reply: *'Sat Sri Akal.'*

The corpses are loaded on the cart. We resume our ride back to the city. The crowd melts before us as the mist melts before the rays of the sun. We ride through Daryaganj. At Chandni Chowk we wheel left till we come to our gurdwara. We throw the three corpses on the steps of the gurdwara. We return to the Jamia Masjid to drink rum and eat goat's meat. Lehna sings of the little old man who wanted to copulate with a she-camel.

Next morning I go to congratulate my Sahib for his great courage. I enter his room and salute. He is writing a letter (he writes a letter to his memsahib every day). 'Well Nihal Singh!' he says as if nothing had happened. When I don't reply he asks, 'What do you want?'

'Sahib, I came to pay my respects and congratulate you for your great *bahaduri.'*

He nods his head and goes on writing, as if I am not there. I stand where I am not knowing what next to do. Then I ask: 'Does Sahib require me for anything?'

He puts his letter inside an envelope, seals it and hands it to me. *'Dak.'*

I take the letter. Suddenly he looks a little happier. 'Ask *Subedar* Man Singh to tell the sowars that the Sahib is very *khush.* Give them as much rum as they like. No more work for some time.' After a pause he asks: 'What are they saying in the camp?'

'Sahib, each time your name is uttered people say "Wah! Wah!"'

He is pleased. Then I asked him of a story I had heard just

before I left Jamia Masjid. 'Sahib, is it true that the heads of the three men you shot were cut off and presented to the old king? What did he say?'

Hodson Sahib's expression changes. He looks me in the eye. 'Nihal Singh, where did you pick up that gossip?'

'Sahib...People are saying...'

'Listen,' he cuts me short. 'The sahibs are a civilized people; they are not like the natives of Hindustan. They do not cut off people's heads and present them on trays to their relatives. The Company Bahadur is just—strong but just. Understand!'

'*Jee huzoor*,' I reply. I salute the Sahib and return to Jamia Masjid.

Bahadur Shah Zafar

A messenger was let into our dungeon to break the news of the deaths of our kinsmen and supporters. Our two sons, Mirza Mughal and Mirza Khizr, and grandson Mirza Abu Bakr were shot dead. We made no protest but only sent a petition that whatever was recovered by the sale of our property be expended on giving a proper burial to the dead. The bodies of Mirza Mughal, Abu Bakr and Khizr Sultan were interred in the mausoleum of Emperor Humayun. The *nawabs* of Jhajjar and Farrukhnagar who were hanged were buried in their family graveyards adjoining the tomb of Hazrat Qutubuddin Bakhtiyar Kaki at Mehrauli. The Raja Bahadur of Ballabhgarh, who was also hanged, being a Hindu was cremated at Nigambodh Ghat on the Jamna. Of the fate of our other sons and nephews and grandsons who were also executed we could not get any details save that their bodies were buried either at Nizamuddin or at Mehrauli. Amongst the thousands shot or hanged by the sahibs was our friend and poet Shaikh Imam Baksh 'Sabhai' and his two sons. No one knows what they did with their bodies.

An autumnal gale had blown through the garden that was once our kingdom. It uprooted every tree. We lost our peace of mind. We lost the will to live. As a captive bird beats its wings against the bars of its cage, we banged our head against the walls of our dungeon and lamented our fate. There was a time when the world seemed like a flower garden where the afternoon sun warmed the buds to unlock their treasure chest. The same world now exuded the stench of a hundred thousand rotting corpses. Here was a city bathed in the day by the sun, by the moon by night; here was a city in which lived women as beauteous as the houris of paradise. Who despoiled this city? Where has he taken away the loot? This was Delhi, the queen of all the cities of the world, now a ruined desolation. 'O Zafar, what calamity has come to pass? Or is it that thy own youth hath fled?'

It would take an ink-well full of tears to write of the way we were treated. At all hours people peered through the windows to gaze at us as if we were some kind of animal. The gates of our dungeon would be suddenly thrown open for parties of sahibs. Our womenfolk hid their faces against the wall. We had to stand up and *salaam* every white man and woman. They taunted us: 'You wanted to become Emperor of India, did you?' Sometimes a young *gora* imitated the bleating of a goat. '*Budha* man where are your young wives?' he would ask. And all of them would laugh. We accepted the insults as the will of Allah.

Our request for pen and paper was refused. We saved pieces of charcoal from our *hookah* and used the walls of our dungeon as our slate. We spent our time in prayer and in composing poetry.

In our younger days we had composed a verse on a lover's complaint at being imprisoned and tormented by his beloved. These lines which had become very popular ran somewhat as follows:

> *Why should our beloved jailer not torment us?*
> *May God not place anyone at anyone else's mercy.*

How appropriate were these lines when the jailer was not the beloved but an enemy!

The worth of the white man's plighted word was soon made clear to us. He called us savages because our troops had killed white women and children. People who knew swore that we had done our best to prevent these killings. The sahibs refused to believe us. For the three dozen of their own killed they slew more than a thousand times three dozen. Despite solemn assurances conveyed to us by Rajab Ali, that one-eyed product of evil seed, that bootlicking bastard, we were put up for trial. The sahibs were our accusers, our attorneys and our judges. They lined up men who had eaten our salt—Hakeem Ahsanullah, the *dervish* Hassan Askari, Rajab Ali, Ghulam Abbas, Mukund Lal—to repeat parrot-wise what they had been told to say.

It grieves us to record that amongst those who turned their tongues against us was the half-caste, Ayesha Aldwell. We had risked our own life to save the life of this woman and her three daughters. This Ayesha's mother had taken a *gora* husband. Ayesha had been brought up as a Mussalmani. But as she inherited a lighter skin from her father and from him learnt to *git mit* in English she passed off as a white woman and married an old *gora*. We could not save her husband. But as she recited verses from the holy *Quran* and made her daughters repeat the *kalima*, we were able to intercede on her behalf. We had hoped she would testify to all that we had done for her. She proved false to both faiths, the Muslim and the Christian. May Allah punish her!

Allah was our only witness. No mortal dared to open his mouth in our favour. They pronounced us guilty on all charges levelled against us. We were sentenced to be exiled from the land our ancestors had conquered and ruled for three hundred years. We would rather they had sentenced us to die and let our bones mingle in the sacred dust of Delhi.

Fourteen begums and our son Jawan Bakht agreed to share the misfortune of our exile. Later many of them changed their mind and on one pretext or another deserted us before we crossed the boundaries of Hindustan. Our beloved Zeenat Mahal stayed by our side. She remained our companion in the camel-litter of misery and our comrade in the closest of affection. We were reminded of the words our Holy Prophet used for his wife Khadijah: 'When I was poor she enriched me; when all the world abandoned me, she comforted me; when I was called a liar, she believed in me.'

On our journey we composed the following lines:

My beloved tormented me so much
We were forced to leave our native land;
As drops wax from the burning taper
So as we quit the circle of life
Fell tears from our eyes.
The gardener forbade us sporting in his garden,
With laughter we came,
With wailing we parted.

17

Bhagmati

Bhagmati is very disappointed with me. 'All these Punjabis came to Delhi without a penny in their pockets. And look at them now! They own the whole city. They have made palaces for themselves. They live on *tandoori* chicken and drink whisky. They take their fat wives out to eat the Delhi air in imported motor cars. And look at you! The same little flat, the same *khat-khatee* old motor every part of which makes a noise except its horn. Why even those fellows who came from your village only a few years ago own half of New Delhi and live like *krorepaties*. What do you get out of killing flies on paper all day long? You haven't bought me a sari or a bangle for many years.'

When Bhagmati is in this nagging mood, it is best to say nothing. But sometimes even my silence provokes her to go on and on. 'Why don't you say something? Why don't you do something? You are just getting old sitting and farting in your armchair all day long.'

That stings. I explode. 'Shut up! You get your fucking and get paid for it. What more do you want?'

'Not much of that either these days,' she retorts sarcastically looking into my eyes. 'As for the payment, even that Budhoo Singh outside asks me everytime I leave — "What did he give you for your *pan-beedi*?" That's all I can buy from the money you give me. It's no use getting angry with me. Truth hurts but I am saying it for your own good. I say do some *dhanda* like contracting business, exporting readymade garments. You will make a lot more money than scribbling pieces for newspapers and taking memsahibs to see the Qutub Minar.'

There is some truth in what she says. But how can I at my age start a new *dhanda* of which I know nothing. And where will I find the money to do so? I relapse into silence: silence and sulking are the best defences against this kind of onslaught.

I pick up a book and pretend to read. I wish she would go away and leave me alone. I am beginning to tire of Bhagmati as I am of Delhi. One of these days when I have enough money I will buy myself a one-way air ticket to London or New York and slip out of Delhi at midnight without telling Bhagmati.

She takes the book out of my hand and sits down on the floor in front of me. She places her hands on my knees and continues, 'You are becoming irritable these days. You get *gussa* with me whenever I say anything to you. You never used to lose your temper with me. What is happening to you?'

A sigh of resignation escapes my lips. I don't reply because I know what she is saying is right. She begins to press my legs with both her hands. It is very pleasant and sensuous. I know I have lost the battle. Where will I find another woman like Bhagmati who will abase herself to soothe my temper? She puts my legs in her lap and rubs the soles of my feet. She is a skilled masseuse. She knows I am beginning to enjoy a good massage more than sex. Sometimes I can't get roused till she has rubbed oil in my scalp and vigorously massaged the dandruff itch out of it with her stubby, sturdy fingers. Next to my scalp it is my feet which respond to her ministrations. If I don't fall off to sleep I end up by sleeping with the masseuse. My frayed nerves are soothed. My temper dissolves. I no longer want to buy myself an air ticket to go abroad to get away from Bhagmati and Delhi. I told you—once you are in their clutches there is no escape.

18

The Builders

We had two colour prints on the walls of our *deorhi* which was both the entrance to our home and waiting-room for male visitors. One above the wooden platform on which my father sat reclining on a bolster was of Queen Victoria. On the wall facing the Queen was Guru Nanak. Every morning after my mother had said her morning prayers, while churning the earthen pitcher of buttermilk, she would light two joss-sticks and stick one each in the frames of the pictures and make obeisances to them: first to the Guru, then to the Empress. And every evening, after he had recited his evening prayer and the invocation, my father would stand in front of the Queen with the palms of his hands joined together and say loudly: 'Lord, bless our Malika! Long may she rule over us! And bless us, her subjects! May we forever remain loyal and contented!'

When Queen Victoria died in 1901, we had a non-stop reading of the Holy *Granth* lasting two days and nights and prayed that her soul find a resting place beside the lotus feet of our Guru. When her son, Edward, was crowned king we sent plates of sweets to families with whom we maintained *bhai chaara* (fraternal relationship). Nine years later when Emperor Edward died, we again had a non-stop reading of the *Granth*. And a few days later when George V was proclaimed Emperor of Hindustan we celebrated the occasion by sending out sweets. Our family was as devoted to the Gurus as it was faithful to our English rulers whose salt it ate.

When the ship bearing King George and Queen Mary docked in Bombay on 2 December 1911 my father and I reached Delhi by train. He wanted to have the *darshan* of our rulers and explore possibilities of getting building contracts. He had been in the building business for some years. He had bored tunnels and laid railtrack between Kalka and the summer capital, Simla, but was lately of the opinion that there was more money in building houses than in drilling holes in mountains. He forced me to give up studies before I could take the final school-leaving examination. 'Education is for making money,' he said. 'For making money all you need to know is how to add, subtract, multiply, calculate simple and compound interest. You have learnt all that. The rest is *aaltoo faltoo* (dispensable rubbish).' When I protested that I wanted to learn how to speak English like Englishmen, he lost his temper and called me a *bharooah* (pimp) which was his favourite term of abuse. When he realized he had hurt my feelings, he added very gently that English gentlemen did not like Indians who spoke English like them and much preferred Indians who spoke *tutti-phutti* (broken English).

It did not take much to make my father lose his temper and lay about with his walking-stick. When he decided that at fourteen I had learnt all there was to learn, I had to leave school and join his contracting business. When I was seventeen, he decided I was old enough to get married and chose a thirteen-year-old girl from a neighbouring village to be my wife. Before she was eighteen (and I twenty-two) she had borne me two sons. Then my father decided that I should leave my wife and sons in the village and accompany him to Delhi to seek our fortunes.

I had never seen a city as grand as Delhi. At the time it looked bigger and grander because more than five hundred rajas and maharajas were encamped there with their retinues. Also hundreds of thousands of common people from distant provinces had come to see Their Majesties. It took us three days to find accommodation. We rented two rooms on the first floor of an old building behind a bioscope close to Dufferin Bridge under which passed trains running between Delhi and Punjab, Delhi and Rajputana, Delhi and Central India.

We bought *charpoys*, tables and chairs before we went to see the preparations for the *darbar*. A city of 40,000 tents called

Kingsway Camp had gone up on the northern side of the city stretching over twenty-five square miles from the river Jamna in the east to beyond the Shalimar Gardens in the west. All day long there were rehearsals with regimental bands marching up and down; caparisoned elephants being made to kneel and raise their trunks in salute; maharajas and their sons being lined up and told how to bow before the King and Queen. Every minute of the programme was gone over many times with the Viceroy, Lord Hardinge, his Vicereine and their Chief Adviser, Malcolm Hailey, riding around on horseback checking everything in detail. They said that over 90,000 rats had been killed in the previous month to make sure that nothing disturbed the proceedings of the *darbar*.

On the morning of 2 December 1911 the alarm clock which regulated my father's life went off at 4 a.m. It was bitterly cold. My teeth chattered while I washed my face in icy cold water. After a quick repast of stale *chappaties* left over from the previous evening gulped down with tumblers of steaming-hot, over-sweetened tea we set out in the pitch dark. We had to cross over Dufferin Bridge well before Their Majesties train was to pass under it on its way to Delhi railway station as the railtrack passing through Delhi including the bridge was later to be cordoned off by the police as a precaution against the designs of evildoers.

We had to walk almost three miles with crowds milling around us before we reached our destination. The roads near Kingsway Camp were brightly lit. By the time the streetlights were switched off we were in our places. A very bright sun came up on the huge open square. At one end of the square was a platform covered with a red carpet with two 'thrones' placed under a canopy. On all the other sides of the square were rows of chairs at different levels. There must have been over 3,00,000 people in these enclosures. I asked myself where in India you could see such an orderly, well-behaved crowd except in Delhi! White soldiers were directing people to their allotted seats; no one dared to question them. No shouting. No squabbling. And military bands playing all the time; as one brass band ended, bagpipes began to whine; when they ended another roll of drums and the clash of cymbals.

Suddenly the bands fell silent. From the distance we heard the thunder of cannons firing a twenty-one gun salute. Their Majesties had arrived at Delhi railway station.

An hour or so later we heard the roar of crowds from the city side come nearer and nearer towards us and sensed that the royal procession was on its way. A long line of elephants came lumbering down with bells clanging. Then came regimental bands followed by infantry, cavalry, more bands and more elephants. I trained my eye on every passing *howdah* to see if I could recognize Their Majesties from pictures I had seen. After all the elephants had gone by, I asked my father, 'Where are the King and the Queen?' He had also failed to spot them. 'That's the *Laat Sahib*,' he said pointing to a tall man on horseback. 'And that small gentleman riding on the white horse alongside Lord Hardinge is the King,' said a man sitting next to my father. I was disappointed. He should have been seated on an elephant. Besides the tall Viceroy, the king looked like a pink dwarf with a beard. I am sure few people realized that the king had ridden past them till they saw him and his queen walk up to their thrones. Then everyone stood up as massed bands struck up the National Anthem 'God Save The King'.

From where we sat we could not hear any of the speeches. Though the white soldiers could frighten Indians into staying in their places, no power on earth can stop Indians from talking all the time. *Yeh dekh! Voh dekh!* (See this! See that!)— everyone kept telling everyone else. All at once there was an uproar. A *shamiana* was on fire and people began to run. Tommies hollered at the top of their voices: 'Sit down, sit down.' No one cared: everyone valued his life above everything else. My father and I ran with the crowd and were out of the camp in a few minutes. We did not pause for breath till we were back in our apartment.

I had read about the disloyal activities of mischiefmakers in Bengal and Maharashtra. Perhaps they were behind this conflagration. In the bazaars people were making wild guesses about who started it, how many had been killed, how narrowly Their Majesties had escaped. And the heads that would roll because of the fiasco. Surely the wrath of the *sarkar* would fall on the city and it would order parts of it to be burnt down! It was only in the evening that we learnt from special bulletins issued by the local papers that the fire had been caused by a short circuit and had been put down immediately without any loss of life. The bulletins also mentioned two momentous decisions taken by the government: the partition of Bengal made six years ago was to be revoked and the capital of India would be shifted from Calcutta to Delhi.

The partition of Bengal by Lord Curzon in 1905 had angered Hindus who felt that it was designed to further divide Hindus and Muslims and create a Muslim state in East Bengal. Young Bengali Hindus and Maharashtrians and some misguided Sikhs vowed to undo the partition and destroy British rule. In Bengal bombs were thrown at English officers and some were murdered. In Gujarat an attempt was made on the life of Lord Minto who had succeeded Curzon as Viceroy. A Punjabi boy studying in London shot and killed Wylie. The English being wise realized that the partition of Bengal had caused too much heart-burning and decided to revoke it in the hope that it would put an end to terrorism. For a while it did. But it also created an impression that the English could be frightened with bombs and pistols. Indian nationalists said it was wrong to think that the white race was superior to the brown. If a yellow race of dwarfs like the Japanese could defeat the mighty empire of the white Tsars of Russia surely a nation of hundred-and-fifty million Indians could make mincemeat of the handful of Englishmen in India! They said if all Indians were to stand alongside and urinate in a tank there would be enough urine to drown the English population of India.

The transfer of the capital to Delhi was widely welcomed—the only exceptions were Europeans with businesses in Calcutta. They suspected that Lord Hardinge was behind the move and started a campaign to have him dismissed. They said that the letters H.M.G. no longer stood for 'His Majesty's Government' but for 'Hardinge Must Go'. Their efforts came to nothing. Delhi had always been the capital of Hindustan. It was closer to the heart of the country. Before Hardinge there were Viceroys who had given clear hints that they regarded

Delhi as India's most important city. In 1877 it was in Delhi that Lord Lytton had read the proclamation recognizing Queen Victoria as Empress of Hindustan. Likewise in 1903 it was in Delhi that Lord Curzon had held the *darbar* in honour of the coronation of King Edward VII.

Having made the proclamation there was no question of the king going back on it. Three days after inaugurating the *darbar* Their Majesties laid the foundation stone of the new capital at Kingsway Camp. The next day they left for Nepal to shoot tigers before returning to England.

My father was a man of foresight and had a knack of making money. He was also very tight-fisted and haggled over the prices of peanuts, onions and potatoes. 'Money saved is money earned,' he often said. 'Put a rupee in the bank today and let it accumulate compound interest — *sood dar sood.* Sitting in the bank without doing anything in a hundred years that one rupee will become one lakh rupees.' Although he could not speak English he could get round English officials and get them to do what he wanted. Whenever he went to call on them he wore his big white turban, a black coat and a gold-brocaded sash running from his left shoulder to his waist. He bought the best fruit available in the market and presented them to the sahibs saying they were from his orchard. We had no orchard. The only fruit that grew in our native village, Hadali, were date-palms. He told me, 'Never try to give sahibs cash or jewellery; they will abuse you and will kick you out. But fruit is *daali* — an acceptable gift.' He was open-handed with his tips to the sahibs' *chaprassies* and clerks. 'This is not *baksheesh*,' he explained to me later, 'but sound investment.' It was true. The sahibs' orders in his favour were never lost in officials' files but immediately attended to.

As soon as the *darbar* tents were struck, plans for building the new capital were taken in hand. Malcolm Hailey was made Commissioner and put in charge of the capital project. My father had met Hailey when he had visited our district town, Shahpur. He took me along when he went to pay his respects to the Commissioner. We bought oranges, apples and Kandahari pomegranates then available in Fatehpuri Bazaar and had several baskets nicely wrapped in pink tissue-paper and silver thread. One basket was presented to the sahib's personal assistant and the contents of another distributed amongst the orderlies. It was the personal assistant who reminded Hailey that my father had met him earlier and brought the pick of fruit from his orchard. Hailey who must have known that there were no fruit grown around Shahpur nevertheless graciously accepted them. He asked my father in Punjabi if there was anything he could do for him. My father introduced me to him 'as your own son,' and mentioned the experience we had in building. Hailey put down our names and address on a piece of paper and said, 'You will hear from me if anything comes up.'

Since we had nothing to do except wait for Hailey's letter my father decided to call on other officials — bank managers, property owners and heads of Delhi's leading families. 'You never know when one of them may prove useful. One must keep up with everyone who matters,' he said very wisely. We also saw the Red Fort and the Royal Mosque and went round Sikh gurdwaras. These last were poorly maintained as there were not many Sikhs in Delhi and none of them very rich. Even on Sunday evenings the congregation at Sees Ganj did not exceed a hundred men and women. Everyone we introduced ourselves to as newcomers asked us if we had seen the Qutub Minar. They said it was the highest tower in the world and from its top storey you could see the countryside with its ruins for miles around. 'One day we will hire a *tonga* and go to the Qutub,' my father said to me. By then I had started having dreams of my own. I replied, 'I will go to the Qutub driving my own motor car.' At the time no more than a dozen of the richest Indian families of Delhi owned cars. I could see my father was pleased with my ambition and self-assurance. Nevertheless, he laughed and snubbed me: '*Bharooah!* learn to earn before you talk of buying a motor car. You know how much one costs?'

He let me buy a bicycle — a beautiful, dark-green Raleigh made in England. It did not take me long to learn to ride it. The Raleigh cycle was to be my Rolls-Royce and my Daimler for the next fifteen years.

Give it to the English, when they say they will do

something for you, you can be sure it will be done. A month after we had called on Hailey, we got a note asking us to report at his office.

There were a lot of English officers present. He simply introduced us to the Chief Engineer of the Central Public Works Department (CPWD). Without bothering to reply to our greetings, the Chief Engineer said: 'You can start with roads and clerks' quarters. I'll see your work first and then we can think of other things. See the Superintending Engineer tomorrow morning.'

My father went straight to the CPWD office to find out who was who. From a clerk my father got the names and addresses of every one who worked there from the SE down to his *chaprassies*. On the way back we stopped at the telegraph office. I drafted a telegram to my younger brother who was looking after our property in the village to send a few reliable men who could organize labour and keep accounts.

The next morning before going to the office of the SE we called at his residence with the usual baskets of fruit 'from our orchards'. We gave handsome tips to his *chaprassies*. The SE did not see us; his chief orderly told us that the sahib never received Indians in his home. To this day I do not know whether the fruit ever reached him or was eaten up by his *chaprassies*.

We went on to the CPWD office. A few minutes later the SE drove up and sent for us. It was easier than I expected. He gave us a map of the roads to be laid round the temporary Secretariat building on Alipur Road. No tenders were invited. We were asked to submit in two days an estimate of the cost and the time it would take us to complete the work. We spent the afternoon working out the costs of hiring labour, stone, cement, sand and transportation. It came to a couple of lakhs of rupees. The next day my father handed over the estimate to the overseer with a thousand rupee note for him. The following day the overseer came to see us. He had scaled down our estimates very marginally still leaving us a handsome margin of profit. My father gave him another thousand rupee note and a bottle of Scotch. They embraced each other to cement an on-going business partnership. That became the pattern of our working life. Every Indian who had anything to do with our building contracts was given his cut in advance. Most Anglo-Indian officials also expected money or whisky. English officials who knew what was going on never accepted anything beyond baskets of fruit with a bottle or two of whisky thrown in on *bara din*.

It did not take me long to catch on to the business. We sent agents to hire Baagree labourers from Rajputana. This was not difficult as that desert land always suffered from drought and famines. They were happy to get half-a-rupee per day (less for women) and break stones, dig, mix mortar and cement from sunrise to sunset. Every evening they trooped back to their hovels with their women singing all the way. We who made money spent our time counting it and were miserable if other contractors were making more than us.

In April 1912 Edwin Lutyens, the architect approved by the king, and a team of town builders, came to Delhi to inspect the site of the new capital. They went by horseback around Kingsway Camp, the Ridge and along the river Jamna from above Majnoon Ka Tilla to Okhla. They went over the area several times again on elephants before deciding that Kingsway would not do because it was low-lying, too close to the river and swampy. They spent another fifteen days riding around villages between Paharganj and Mehrauli and from the Jamna behind Purana Qila to the Ridge before deciding that the most suitable site for the new city would be round village Malcha and that the Viceregal palace and the Secretariats should be built on Raisina Hill. Lord Hardinge who had earlier chosen the Kingsway Camp site agreed with them. It did not bother them that Their Majesties had laid the foundation stone at Kingsway. There was nothing sacred about the site, they said. The same foundation stone could be re-laid elsewhere.

And so it was. Hailey sent for my father (by now my father had become his most reliable contractor) and told him that he was to remove the foundation stone from Kingsway to its new site at Malcha. Not a word of this was to be breathed to anyone. He drove in his own car to the tomb of Safdar Jang and then took us on foot to a spot near Malcha where the stone was to be replanted. There was a barbed wire fence round the spot with a couple of armed policemen on guard.

Taking out the foundation stone and planting it in its new site was the first job my father entrusted to me to do all on my own. I was thrilled. First, I had a pit dug for the stone. Then I hired a bullock cart and selected half-a-dozen labourers for the job. We were given four policemen as our escort. Finally, one evening in May I rode my bicycle alongside the bullock cart loaded with labourers and policemen and reached Kingsway Camp an hour after sunset. I had the stone dug out and placed on a bed of straw spread in the cart. I covered it up with tarpaulin. We then proceeded on our journey led by a man carrying a petromax lamp. I walked with the rest of the party behind the cart. We looked like a funeral procession. It was a long distance to traverse as we had to skirt round the city. We reached Malcha after midnight. It took us another hour to fix the stone in the pit with mortar. I gave the labourers a rupee each as a reward. By the time I reached home it was daylight. My father interrupted his morning prayer to ask me how it had gone. I gave him the details. When I told him I had given the labourers an extra rupee, he called me a *bharooah*.

We were now making enough money to live in better quarters. (However, as we were used to going out in the open to relieve ourselves we found going to a dirty, smelly lavatory very constipating).

We did not get any contracts for the building of the temporary Secretariat which was almost entirely taken over by the CPWD and decided to move out to the site where the new city was destined to come up. With the labourers and the building materials available to us, it didn't take us a month to put up a couple of rooms, kitchen and courtyard. This was close to an old flour mill. Following our example other Sikh contractors also built shacks alongside ours on what later came to be known as the Old Mill Road. Although we came from different parts of the Punjab and belonged to different castes, we soon became like members of one family.

Lutyens prepared a plan of the layout of the new city and where he meant to locate the Viceregal palace and the

Secretariats. I heard that in his original plan Lutyens had wanted to dam the Jamna behind Humayun's tomb and make a huge ornamental lake extending from the Red Fort to Purana Qila with a lakeside drive and waterways running through the city. This was not approved because of the enormous cost. Lutyens also wanted to drive a road from the Viceregal palace to the Jamia Masjid piercing the old Mughal city wall and the bazaars. This was also turned down. The rest was approved by the Viceroy as well as King George whom Lutyens met on his return to England. Lutyens got an old colleague, Herbert Baker, to share the work with him. In addition to the general layout of the city, Lutyens assigned to himself the Viceregal palace and the War Memorial Arch; Baker designed the Secretariats and the Parliament. The rest of the work was equally divided between them. They had known each other for many years. Baker had chosen Lutyens to be his co-architect for buildings in South Africa. Lutyens was returning the compliment by choosing Baker as his partner in the building of New Delhi. Everyone thought they were good friends. But envy of Lutyens's genius and popularity with royalty and the Vicereine soured Baker's mind.

Lutyens was a man of vision. Although neither he nor Baker had too great an opinion of our old palaces, mosques and temples, they agreed to give an Indian touch to their designs. What impressed me most about Lutyens was that even before roads were laid, he ordered trees to be planted along the proposed routes. A huge nursery was set up to raise the right kind of saplings. Lutyens wanted slow-growing but massive, long-living trees like banyans, *neems* and tamarinds. The official horticulturist imported some exotic trees like the Sausage and the African Tulip tree from East Africa. Lutyens talked of designing a city which would meet the needs of its citizens for two hundred years and forecast that one day the English would leave India and let Indians manage their own affairs. I am not sure whether he was like some crazy Englishmen who sided with Indian nationalists, but his wife was known to do so. It was rumoured that she had run away to Madras and was having an affair with a Hindu boy who had been proclaimed a messiah. All I can say is that though I saw Lutyens many times in his office and bungalow I never saw his wife. Also, the English didn't like talking about Mrs Lutyens.

Our first summer in Delhi made us decide that we would make our home there. It was less hot than our desert village and the rainy season was very pleasant. Above all, we were making more money than we had dreamed of. By the autumn we had added more rooms to our home, hired a gardener and a couple of servants. My mother, wife and sons joined us. So did many other families from our village whom we employed as clerks, labour managers and storekeepers. Thereafter we only went back to the village to attend the marriages of relations or the funerals of people we knew.

Exactly a year after the royal *darbar* there was another. This time it was in honour of the Viceroy and Vicereine formally taking up residence in Delhi. Elaborate arrangements were made for their reception at Delhi railway station and the Red Fort. They were to be taken in procession on elephantback through the municipal gardens and Chandni Chowk to the Red Fort. As in the year before, there were many rehearsals and great precautions were taken to see that no untoward incident marred the solemnity of the occasion. Hailey who was in charge of the arrangements apprehended mischief and had Cleveland of the CID inspect every home and shop that lay on the route to make sure there were no terrorists lurking about. Armed policemen were posted on the roof-tops of Chandni Chowk. I felt that these precautions were overdone because till then I had not met a single Dilliwalla who had anything to say against the English.

As on the royal *darbar* so on the day of the Viceregal *darbar* we got up at 4 a.m. This was quite unnecessary as the Viceroy and Vicereine were not due to arrive till the afternoon. But such was the excitement and anxiety to find a place from where we could watch the procession that we were eager to get there well ahead of time. The morning of 23 December 1912 was cold and clear without a cloud in the blue sky. By the time the sun came up every flower and blade of grass was washed clean by the dew. It was as perfect a start of a day as I had seen since I had come to Delhi.

We set out from the house at 11 a.m. We hired four *tongas* to take us, our servants, our clerks and their families. Hundreds of labourers and their women kept pace with us as crowds on the road made the going very slow. We dismissed the *tongas* at Ajmeri Gate and walked through the prostitutes' Chawri Bazaar, Nai Sarak and were in front of the Clock Tower a little after noon. Crowds had already started collecting there. We went down Chandni Chowk to Gurdwara Sees Ganj. The caretakers had been instructed to let in only Sikhs on that day. So we had a balcony facing the Fountain on the other side of Chandni Chowk all to ourselves.

The firing of cannons informed us of the arrival of the Viceregal train. At the railway station, the Hardinges were received by some maharajas; at the municipal buildings an address of welcome was presented to them on behalf of the citizens of Delhi. As the police band which led the procession marched past below us, we knew that the reception at the municipality was over and the Hardinges were on their way. The police band was followed by Highlanders playing bagpipes, Sikh cavalry and other troops. I could not see very far towards the Clock Tower but I saw the line of elephants slowly lumbering towards us. There were over a dozen of them. The Viceroy and the Vicereine were on the eighth, the biggest in India called Gajumat, which had been loaned to him for the occasion by the Raja of Faridkot.

Suddenly the procession came to a halt. A lot of people started yelling at the top of their voices. I am sure I heard a loud bang but I was not sure if it was a cracker or a bomb. The four elephants in the front row stopped some yards away from us. I saw men running away from Chandni Chowk into the side-streets. Those on the roof-tops had disappeared. Some men running down the street on the Clock Tower side were shouting: '*Bhago, bhago* (run, run).' Other words I caught were 'bomb' and '*maar dala* (killed).' Had somebody thrown a bomb at the Viceroy's elephant and killed the Viceroy, his Vicereine and their attendants?

We were stunned. We did not know which way to turn. If the Viceroy had been killed we knew what would follow. Just a few yards on the left side of the gurdwara separated by a police station was the Sunehri Masjid. It was from this mosque that Nadir Shah had ordered the massacre of the citizens of Delhi because someone had fired on him. The sahibs were slow to anger but once their temper was roused their wrath could be terrible. After suppressing the Sepoy Mutiny in 1857, they had hanged hundreds of people in this very Chandni Chowk and blown up a whole bazaar with its shops and mansions in front of the Royal Mosque. We shut the gates of the gurdwara and collected round the *Granth Sahib* to listen to recitations of the Guru's words. The city awaited its fate.

We waited till it was dark before we slipped out of the gurdwara. There were no *tongas* or *ekkas* available and we had to walk home in the dark through deserted streets. My father kept muttering, '*Wah Guru! Wah Guru!*' all the way.

I could not get much sleep that night. What would happen if the Viceroy had been killed? Would they still go ahead with building a new Delhi? After this experience would the English ever trust any Indian?

It was from the morning paper that we learnt the truth of what had transpired. A bomb had been hurled from the roof of a bank building. It had killed the Viceroy's umbrella-bearer, and grievously wounded the Viceroy who had been immediately taken to hospital by car. The Viceroy's personal servant had also been injured. The Vicereine and another servant on the same elephant were unhurt. The ceremony at the Red Fort had taken place nonetheless with Mr Fleetwood Wilson reading the proclamation on behalf of the Viceroy.

Lord Hardinge who till then had thought of little else but the new city lost interest in the project. It took him a long time to recover from his injuries. He became impatient with Lutyens's grandiose plans and began to turn to Herbert Baker for advice. The Vicereine who did her best to keep up her husband's enthusiasm took Lutyens's side. Then she fell ill and had to be taken back to England for a major operation. She died soon after surgery. By then the papers were full of rumours of a war breaking out in Europe. Who would think of building a city while fighting a war? If England lost there would be no New Delhi.

In August 1914 England declared war on Germany. Lord Hardinge read the proclamation on behalf of India. Malcolm Hailey sent for my father. His note said that he should bring me with him. He was very friendly and very clear in his message. 'Sujan Singh (that being father's name) you know India is at war with Germany. We will need a lot of fighting men to go to the front. You come from a region which has some of the best soldiers in the country. You go back to Hadali and recruit men for the army. You will be well rewarded.'

My father assured Hailey that he would do his very best and pray to God that England would be victorious.

We divided the work between us. I looked after the business in Delhi. My father toured villages in district Shahpur. He did not have much difficulty in raising recruits as there were lots of young lads with nothing to do. They were mostly Baluch Muslims with relations serving in the army. He also managed to persuade some Sikhs to enlist. From our tiny hamlet, Hadali, with barely two hundred families living in it, he raised four hundred and thirty-seven men for war. He sent me their names so that I could show them to Hailey. I had no problem getting more contracts on very favourable terms. Hailey also promised to let us buy as much land in New Delhi as we could afford as the government wanted private people to share the burden of building the new city by opening shops, restaurants, hotels and cinemas.

While the war was on, no major construction work could be undertaken. The Viceroy devoted his energies towards winning the war. He travelled all over India and the Middle East. His mind was also distracted by tragedies that occurred in his family. After his wife's death, his elder son was mortally wounded in a battle in France. Three of his ADCs were killed within a few months.

The war that the British had expected to win in a few months dragged on and on. They were not as invincible as we had come to believe. Although thousands of our men were fighting on their side, we Indians being what we are, we secretly enjoyed the reverses suffered by them. Whenever the topic of war came up, someone or the other would always quote an Urdu poet: 'The English are victorious but it is the Germans who capture territory.'

Lord Hardinge was persuaded to stay on for another six months after his tenure as Viceroy was over. Lord Chelmsford who succeeded him as Viceroy showed even less interest in the capital project than his predecessor had in his later days. It was also known that Lutyens and Baker had fallen out and did not speak to each other. It was difficult to believe that two of the best-known architects of the world could get so worked up over trivial matters like the comparative levels of the Viceregal palace and the Secretariats and the incline of the road running through the Secretariats to the palace. Lutyens wanted the palace to be on a higher level and the gradient of the road at such an angle that the palace could be seen from a long distance. Baker wanted both buildings to be on the same level with the road rising gently so that the palace came into view when you were halfway up the incline. The matter was put to Hardinge who sided with Baker. It was again put to Chelmsford who took the easier line of agreeing with his predecessor. To me (I was taking private tution in English), it seemed a good example of making a mountain of a mole hill. All that Lutyens wanted was a foot-and-a half change in the angle of the approach road. They called it 'the battle of the gradient'. It was also an example of building castles in the air as even the foundations of the buildings had not been dug.

The longer the war dragged on the more restive Indian politicians became. They were Banias and lawyers who had not raised their little fingers to help our fighting men but were the loudest in demanding more self-government which would give them greater privileges. Chelmsford being a weak man gave in. He wrote to his government in London that more power should be entrusted to Indians. A thirty-eight-year-old Jew, Edwin Montagu, came to India in November 1917 to study the situation. He stayed nearly six months. Between the two they prepared an elaborate scheme of reforms which came to be known as dyarchy. In the provinces more departments would be administered by elected members; in the centre three of the Viceroy's six councillors would be Indians. The princes were to have a chamber of their own. All this was to await the successful termination of the war.

The war suddenly came to an end in November 1918. It was the time to reap the harvest of rewards promised to us. We did better than we had hoped for. We were granted large tracts of land in the canal colonies of the Punjab. I was given the choice of plots I wanted to buy in New Delhi. When tenders were invited for the main buildings, I bagged the South Block of the Secretariat, the War Memorial Arch and many clerks' quarters. My father, who was by now an older and a mellower man, was honoured with the title of Sardar Sahib. While he was still alive, I became virtually the head of the family. I let my younger brother look after our lands and properties in the Punjab and devoted myself wholly to building work and making money to realize my ambition of having my own car to drive to the Qutub Minar.

The end of four years of war did not bring peace to India. We had more peace during the war and more turmoil when the war ended. I saw some of it with my own eyes because I had been made an honorary magistrate and was often summoned by the Deputy Commissioner to be present with the police when there was trouble in the city.

A new leader appeared on the scene, Gandhi. He even got Muslims to join Hindus in anti-government agitations. At this time there was a lot of misery caused by an influenza epidemic which killed millions of people and famine caused by a succession of poor harvests. On top of all this Gandhi demanded that since the war was over, the government must give up powers it had assumed for the prosecution of the war. Even more mischievous was his supporting Muslims in their demand that the victorious British keep their hands off the Turkish empire of the Caliph. What did Turkey or the Caliphate mean to Hindus or Sikhs who together formed over eighty per cent of the population of India? But the trick worked. I saw Hindus and Muslims drinking water from the same water booths, marching through the bazaars arm in arm chanting *Hindu-Muslim Bhai-bhai*—Hindus and Muslims are brothers. Muslims invited a Hindu, Shradhanand, to address their Friday congregation in the Royal Mosque. The government quite rightly forbade Gandhi from entering Delhi. The fellow then tried to go to the Punjab where trouble was brewing in many towns and cities including Lahore and Amritsar. This encouraged the Amir of Afghanistan, Shah Amanullah, to plan on invading India. The government dealt with the situation with an iron hand. For three weeks I was on duty almost the entire day and night helping the police disperse agitated mobs. In Amritsar General Dyer fired on an illegal assembly at Jallianwala Bagh killing over three hundred and fifty people and wounding over a thousand. The province was placed under martial law. Mischiefmakers were flogged in public, their properties were confiscated and their leaders exiled. As for Amanullah, before he could mount an invasion, he was toppled from his throne. 1919 and 1920 were certainly very bad years for India. But they were the beginning of the realization of my dreams.

Nothing deterred the government from going ahead with building the new city. A narrow gauge rail-line was laid from village Badarpur, twenty miles south of Delhi, ending in what is today Connaught Circus. It was named the Imperial Delhi Railway. It was meant to transport red gravel, sandstone and rubble to the building site. Two huge sheds were raised under which stone-cutting machines were installed; thousands of stone-cutters were hired to chisel stone and marble to required shapes. Over 50,000 men and women from Bangardesh were employed as labourers. My own staff consisted of over fifty *munshis* and accountants and a labour force of over 3000. While politicians did their *buk buk* in their legislatures, often criticizing the capital project as a criminal waste of money, we went ahead raising a new city the like of which India had not known.

By the winter of 1920 the situation had taken a turn for the better. I had my family (by then consisting of my wife, three sons and a daughter) living with me in Delhi though my father had decided to go back and live on the land with my younger brother. Although I could afford to buy a car I was uncertain of my father's reaction—he was dead-set against such wasteful extravagance. Instead I bought a four-wheeled victoria and a horse to take my children to school in Daryaganj and then take me round the different building sites. I seldom got back before 10 p.m. Sometimes after a day's work I would go and visit my friends where I would take a whisky or two and listen to *mujras* performed by prostitutes from Chawri Bazaar. I would never have dared to do this if my father had been living with me in Delhi.

I built myself a double-storeyed house in Jantar Mantar Road where half-a-dozen other Sikh contractors had also built their houses. Although I was earning more than them, they spent more on themselves than I. One of them who had got the contract for the supply of stone and marble built himself a palatial mansion of stone and marble bigger than any private residence in Delhi. Another whose father had been a dacoit and was not doing half as well as I, acquired two cars.

One summer I received a telegram from my brother saying that father had been taken ill and I should come over as soon as I could. At the time they were living in Mian Channun where my brother was running a cotton ginning factory and had over two hundred squares of land. He had persuaded the railway authorities to name the nearest railway station after my father as Kot Sujan Singh. I arrived in Mian Channun just in time. It almost seemed as if my father had been waiting to see me before taking his leave from the world. No sooner I went to his bedside, he began to question me about the business. He was short of breath but refused to listen to the doctor who kept insisting he should not strain himself. He broke down and cried that he was leaving my brother and I an uncleared debt of one lakh rupees. We assured him that if that bothered him either of us could wipe it out within one minute by writing a cheque in favour of his creditors as between us we had assets of about one hundred lakhs. 'That may be so,' he replied amid gasps, 'but before leaving the world a person should balance his account by repaying every loan he has taken.' He began to cry because he was very weak. We cried because he was crying. Then he asked everyone save my mother and brother to leave the room. 'I want you two brothers to make me a promise in the presence of your mother that you will stick together and share everything no matter what profits or losses the other incurs.' We brothers embraced each other and bowed over his chest to let him put his arms over us. Being a man of the world he added, 'And if you ever decide to partition the family property you will do it amicably without anyone in the world knowing about it. If you have any dispute, you will accept your mother's verdict without question.' My mother who had been pressing his feet all this time broke down and began to wail. 'Don't talk of leaving me. The doctors say you will be all right. The great Guru will give you good health.'

The doctors gave him different medicines but the Guru closed his account book. Half-an-hour later he sat up and looked around as if he wanted something. He opened his mouth very wide as if he was yawning and with a gasp sank back on his pillow and stopped breathing. My mother closed his eyes with her hands and wailed the lament for the dead: 'My light is the name of the one Lord; its oil is sorrow.'

The news quickly spread to the town. Within an hour it seemed as if the entire population of Sikhs, Hindus and Muslims had come to share our grief. Professional women mourners came in groups beating their breasts and singing litanies in praise of the departed. That afternoon his cortege decorated with coloured strips of paper and balloons was led by the town band followed by over 2000 mourners. Mothers made their children walk under the bier so that they could live as long as he. In our family it was customary not to mourn the death of an old person but celebrate it as release from the world's bondage. My father was sixty-five when he died.

I stayed with my brother for the ten days of mourning and then returned to Delhi with my wife and children. A few months later my wife bore our last child, a son. And a few months after that I bought a secondhand car, an Oldsmobile, from an English engineer who was due to return to England in a few weeks. Since he had helped me secure contracts, I gave him the price of a new car for his old one. He more than compensated me by passing all my inflated bills.

I did not know how to drive. I hired a Muslim chauffeur who had a teaching licence to teach me as he drove me to work. I stuck to my resolve that I would drive myself to the Qutub Minar in my own car.

It took me a month to learn how to drive. Being an honorary magistrate I got a driving licence without having to pass a driving test. The great day came. I told my family that we would have a picnic at the Qutub Minar the following Sunday. My wife made great preparations and filled baskets of *parathas* stuffed with potatoes and fruits. There was enough to feed twenty people. When I took the wheel, we were nearly a dozen in the car. The driver cranked the handle (there were no self-starters those days) and the automobile throbbed into life. My wife and children and maidservant crammed into the rear seat. My head clerk and chauffeur were in the front with me. Four servants, (two on either side) stood on the footboards of the car. We started off with a loud cry of *'Sat Sri Akal'*. One servant standing beside me blew the bulb horn all the way. We passed by Safdar Jang tomb and hundreds of other ancient buildings, strewn about the wilderness near Yusuf Sarai and Hauz Khas. And suddenly the Qutub Minar came into view and everyone shouted, 'Look there's the Qutub Minar!'

While the servants spread *durries* in the gardens and laid out the food, we went up the Minar, climbed all its steps and looked down at the ruins lying below us. I came down and walked round the mosque and tried to embrace the Iron Pillar standing in its midst. I did not know much history, the names of the builders or the things based on the place. My elder son told us about the first Muslim city of Delhi, of Qutubuddin, Altamash and Alauddin. I was pleased he had learnt so much in so short a time at school.

We ate our potato-stuffed *parathas*. The children went round looking at the monuments. I lay on my back on the *durri* gazing at the Minar which seemed to sway as wisps of clouds blew past it. I wondered how much the contractors had made out of the job. It was obvious they had stolen a lot of stone and marble from older buildings. Did they pass it off as new? Did they have to bribe architects and overseers to get their bills passed? How was it that without cement or concrete they had been able to make buildings last a thousand years? Would the buildings I was making last five hundred years? Would anyone know I had made them? Or would they only be known as the handiwork of Lutyens and Baker and the Viceroys in whose times they were begun or ended. Somehow these thoughts did not depress me because for me it was a day on which one of my ambitions had been fulfilled. I had driven to the Qutub in my own car. Soon I would be able to buy a new car every year. I was well on the way to becoming a rich man, a millionaire. What more could anyone aspire to in life?

In January 1921, the king's uncle, the Duke of Connaught, came to visit New Delhi. At this time Delhi did not look like an inhabited city. All it had were a few bungalows along broad avenues lined by young trees. The Viceregal palace, the two Secretariats and the War Memorial Arch were well behind schedule. Nevertheless the Viceroy was anxious to commemorate the Duke's visit in some permanent way. So he was asked to lay the foundation stone of the new legislative building which included the Princes Chamber and was to be located close to the Secretariats. It was also announced that New Delhi's main shopping centre half-a-mile northwards of the Secretariat would be named Connaught Place. At the time there was only a circular road without a single building. I was among the contractors presented by the Viceroy to the Duke. The Viceroy had been informed that I had bought more land in the future city centre than anyone else. So he told the Duke in front of me, 'This man is going to build the first shopping arcade, cinemas and restaurants in the shopping centre to be named after Your Grace.' Till then I had no idea what I was going to do with the land. There were not enough people in New Delhi for it to have shops or restaurants. But I knew that so broad a hint dropped by no less a person than the Viceroy was a command which had to be obeyed. As if to encourage me, at the king's next birthday, I was given the title of Sardar Sahib.

A few words about the contractors' families. We came from different parts of the Punjab and had not heard of each other till we met in Delhi. I was the only one of them who had been to school and had picked up some English; the others were a rustic lot and few could not even write their names in any language. It made no difference. We were Sikhs and began to look upon each other as members of one clan. There were a few Sikh engineers and overseers as well. Although they kept their distance from us and extracted their percentages for passing our bills, they felt a part of us. In times of tension (such as times when Hindu-Muslim riots broke out in the city) we guarded each others' homes. If any of our boys got into trouble with the police we exerted joint pressure to get him out. One afternoon when an eighteen-year-old daughter of a Sikh engineer eloped with her Muslim music teacher, her father alerted the community. We posted our men on every road going out of Delhi and on all platforms of the railway station. Before nightfall the couple were nabbed in a car heading for the Jamna bridge. The girl was handed over to her father to be dealt with as he deemed fit. The Muslim boy was given a thrashing he would not easily forget. To forestall his reporting the incident to the police and claiming the girl had been converted to Islam and had married him as well as getting his fellow Muslims to take up his cause, we told him that we had already lodged a report charging him with abduction and rape. The fellow decided to get out of Delhi as fast as he could.

Sudden wealth creates its own problems. We were far too busy making money to be able to keep our eyes on how our sons spent it. We also derived some pleasure in spoiling our boys. When I say we, I really mean the others, because I was very strict with my sons. While others gave their sons cars to drive about in, I gave my two elder boys bicycles. As a result while my sons went through school and college, theirs went to the bottle and the prostitutes of Chawri Bazaar. The eldest son of one who was a most devout Sikh acquired a veritable harem of women from different parts of India and sired dozens of children through them. Another who had five sons was lucky in having one who was sober who helped him with his building contracts. The others just had a good time going for *shikar*, having nautch parties and getting drunk. One of them became the most notorious whoremonger of Delhi. He used to boast that he had three different women every day and before he died he would fuck every prostitute in the city. Nobody knew how far he got in achieving his ambition but one night after he had finished with his third assignment for the day he got into a brawl with some Muslims at a *panwalla's* shop. One man struck him with an ice pick which pierced his chin upto his mouth. He grabbed his assailant by the scruff of his hair (he was very strongly built) and marched him to the police station. Then he went to the emergency ward of a hospital and had his wound stitched and bandaged. Having done this he walked to his home which was four miles from the hospital. Before going to bed he felt blood oozing out of the bandage and went to the bathroom to wash it off. As he bent into a tub full of water he collapsed into it. His servant found him dead with his head in a tub full of blood. His father did not shed a tear. When I went to condole with him he said without any emotion: 'He died a dog's death. He asked for it.'

My lifestyle changed. I began to wear European clothes. On formal occasions I wore a black frock-coat, grey striped trousers and spats on my shoes. I was amongst the select few Indians allowed membership in the Gymkhana Club. I never learnt to dance and sensed that Englishmen did not like Indians dancing with their women unless they brought their wives to dance with them. My wife, despite my attempts to get her to learn English from an Anglo-Indian woman, failed to pick up more than a few words and would even confuse 'good-morning' with 'good-bye'. As for dancing, she would have sunk into the ballroom floor if asked to fox-trot. I went to the Gymkhana Club once every week to keep up appearances. I offered drinks to English members who cared to accept them. They seldom returned the hospitality. For relaxation I sought the company of Indians. I felt more at home with my Muslim and Hindu friends than with Sikhs. A Muslim engineer had Delhi's most famous singer as his mistress. I found her a flat to live in and was often invited to listen to her singing. Another Hindu friend had the prettiest Muslim girl as his concubine. We often met in her apartment for drinks and a chat. As far as possible I avoided going to parties in the prostitutes' quarter.

Lord Chelmsford was succeeded by a sixty-year-old, Lord Reading, as Viceroy. He had no *picchha* (breeding) being the son of a fruit-seller and a deck-hand on a ship. Being a Jew, he had brains. Also being a Jew he wanted to prove he was more British than the English. When he arrived in India in 1921 there was an agitation amongst the Sikhs to liberate their gurdwaras from hereditary priests. Gandhi and his Congresswallas were also demanding self-rule and the Muslim Moplahs of Malabar had risen against Hindu money-lenders. Reading first invited Gandhi over for a cup of tea to be able to size him up. A few months later he jailed him as well as the two Nehrus, Motilal and his son, Jawaharlal. All of them had called for a boycott of the visit of the Prince of Wales. (Incidentally with the Prince came the last Viceroy of India, Lord Mountbatten, who became engaged to Edwina Ashley at a party given by Reading). He sent the army to Malabar to crush the Moplahs. Reading was that kind of man: he only befriended Indian politicians to know their minds. However, he couldn't do much to stem the Congress tide. The party swept the polls in the 1923 elections and Motilal Nehru became its main spokesman in the Central Assembly.

Reading was more interested in Indian politics than in the building of New Delhi. Nevertheless, it was during his tenure that the city began to take shape. The Viceregal palace was completed and only needed furniture and fittings. The two Secretariats were in the last stages of completion; the Legislative Assembly building was completed; so were a large number of bungalows and clerks' quarters. I had built a block of shops with apartments above them and was well on the way to giving New Delhi its first cinema house, restaurants and department stores.

A sense of urgency was given to the building operations with the arrival of the new Viceroy, the forty-five-year-old Lord Irwin. Since he had only one arm, he was known amongst Indians as the *tunda laat*. Being very religious minded, he was also known as the padre. We were told that all the work on the Viceregal palace and the two Secretariats had to be completed by a certain date as the new Viceroy intended to inaugurate the new city. Work went on round the clock in three shifts.

With the Viceroy being so friendly with nationalist leaders we felt that Englishmen and Indians would work hand-in-hand as partners. The real trouble was that the nationalists were split into many factions: some were willing to cooperate with the English; others wanted to drive them out of India, by force if necessary. I was witness to one such attempt.

One morning in April 1929, having obtained a pass, I was seated in the visitors' gallery of the Central Assembly. It promised to be a very lively debate as the Congress party was to open up with all its guns against the passage of the Public Safety Bill introduced earlier by the government to combat terrorism. I was looking down into the hall to see if I could recognize any of the members from their pictures I had seen in the papers. I did not take any notice of the others in the gallery except two young men who took seats on my right. They wore no coat or tie and looked like boys from college. The debate was not as exciting as I had expected. There were a lot of long-winded orations which I could not hear distinctly. I had brought a newspaper with me and began to scan its headlines. Suddenly I heard a loud explosion. I looked up and saw the two young men who had been sitting next to me firing shots at the members. Smoke was rising from the hall and everyone was running towards the doors or taking shelter behind the benches. The visitors' gallery was empty; only I remained seated where I was with the boys shooting into the pit of the assembly. They took no notice of me. I saw one of the boys slapping his gun with his hand. It had jammed or run out of ammunition Then policemen with pistols in their hands surrounded us. 'Hands up,' ordered an Anglo-Indian sergeant. We put up our hands. The boys smiled at me before handing over their weapons. Since I was an honorary magistrate the policemen recognized me and escorted me out of the building.

What those boys wanted to achieve by killing legislators was beyond me. I knew they would hang for it. (They did for the murder of an Anglo-Indian sergeant committed earlier. Bhagat Singh, Sukh Dev and Rajguru were hanged on 23 March 1931). What I found more appalling was the attitude of the Congress leaders who talked of non-violence in one breath and condoned political killings in the other. Even padre Irwin was disappointed at their reaction. In a statement he said, 'To condemn a crime in one breath and in the next to seek excuse for it by laying blame on those against whom it is directed, is no true condemnation.'

I was out of step with the times. I believed that British rule was good for India; we Indians never had nor ever would be able to run an administration which was just and fair to all communities. But there was no one who seemed to agree with my views. My old mother who had at one time lit incense in front of a picture of Queen Victoria now spent her time praying and spinning her *charkha* and once gave me a bundle of yarn she had spun to be presented to Gandhi. Two of my elder sons when they went to buy material for their school uniform came back with *khadi* (handspun, hand-woven cloth) because Gandhi had proclaimed a boycott of British fabrics. I knew that behind my back my Sikh employees called me a *jholi chook* (one who stretched his apron for alms). Many a time when I was on duty with the police to prevent a riot, the mob yelled *todi-baccha* (son of a toady) and beat their breasts shouting *hai, hai*. I persisted in my belief that the English would stay in India as rulers in my lifetime. I had eaten their salt and was not going to betray them.

Lord Irwin did his best to accommodate the nationalists. At his instance a commission headed by Sir John Simon which included Attlee visited India in 1923. The nationalists organized massive demonstrations against the commission wherever it went. Irwin arranged for Round Table Conferences in London to discuss giving India Dominion Status. The nationalists boycotted the first one and sent only Gandhi to the second. They launched one civil disobedience movement after another bringing the country to near anarchy. They talked of *satyagraha* (truthfulness) and *ahimsa* (non-violence) but gloated over bombings and political murders. The worst example of this was the way they treated a god-fearing man like Irwin. The date for the inauguration of New Delhi had been fixed. Lady Dorothy, the Vicereine, had sent for Lutyens to help her choose the right kind of furnishings, curtains and decor for the Viceregal palace and the kind of flowers to plant in the Mughal gardens. All was ready by the end of August 1931. On 23 December 1931 the Irwins came by train for the inaugural ceremony. I was amongst the dignitaries chosen to receive them on the ceremonial platform of New Delhi railway station. As the train slowed down on its approach to the station, a bomb planted on the track went off.

Fortunately it missed the Viceroy's carriage and blew up the one behind it. The Viceroy and the Vicereine looked completely unperturbed and went through the ceremony as if nothing had happened. Ironically it was this Viceroy, Lord Irwin, who had given his heart to India and who chose the words inscribed on the Jaipur column facing his residence:

> *In thought faith*
> *In word wisdom*
> *In deed courage*
> *In life service*
> *—So may India be great.*

My rewards came in the form of titles—Sardar Bahadur, then C.B.E. then a knighthood and nomination to the Council of States. I am not sure what Indian nationalists said about them behind my back, but after every award, they turned up in their hundreds to felicitate me with garlands. By now I was regarded as the main builder of New Delhi and often referred to as owner of half of the new city (which was untrue). I was by then living in a large double-storeyed house on Queensway which I had named as I had my earlier house on Jantar Mantar Road, *Baikunth* (paradise). Top nationalist leaders readily accepted my hospitality. There were times when Sapru, Jayakar and C. Rajagopalachari stayed with me. Gandhi who stayed in Birla House across the road from my new house on the one side and Jinnah who had a house on the other would walk over to discuss political problems while strolling in my rose-garden.

*

Now that I am an old man and have seen all there is worth seeing in life and India being ruled by Indians the new generation asks me tauntingly, 'What did you get out of a lifetime of licking the boots of the British?'

I am not a man of great learning nor have I read many history books. What I say in reply comes from the heart based on what I have seen with my own eyes, experienced of my

own countrymen and the few Englishmen I have known. I
have seen the city I helped to build and which Lutyens
designed for two centuries become ruined in twenty years.
We built magnificent buildings which will last for many
centuries; they build shapeless, multi-storeyed offices and
jerry-houses wherever there is open space and have
smothered hundreds of ancient monuments behind bazaars
and markets. We laid wide roads; they make narrow lanes on
which two cars cannot pass each other. We planted slow-
growing, long-living trees which will give shade to our great-
grandchildren and their great-grandchildren. They plant
quick-growing *gul mohars* and laburnums which blossom for
a fortnight or two and yield neither fruit nor shade. All they
want is something to show in the shortest possible time. They
have no sense of the past or the future. As for licking British
boots, I tell them that if I was given the choice of being born
in any period of Indian history I liked, I would not choose the
Hindu or the Muslim—not even in the short period of Sikh
dominance in the north—but the British. I would re-live my
days as a builder-contractor under the British Raj.

'Have you no pride in being an Indian?' they sneer. 'Have
you no sense of shame praising alien rulers who exploited and
humiliated us for over a hundred years? Have you forgotten
what they did to your forefathers after the First War of
Independence of 1857? Have you in your generosity forgiven
them the massacre of innocents at Jallianwala Bagh in 1919?
And the hangings, tortures and imprisonment of thousands
upon thousands of freedom fighters?'

'No, I have not forgotten any of this,' I reply as calmly as I
can. 'Nor have I forgotten what Indians have done to each
other. I can show some of their handiwork in Delhi. Ever seen
the Quwwat-ul-Islam next to the Qutub Minar? Twenty-
seven Jain and Hindu temples demolished to build one large
mosque! Faces and limbs of gods and goddesses hacked off.
Tell me of one place of worship, Hindu, Muslim or Sikh which
the English destroyed? Remember Babar raising pyramids of
Rajput skulls, the general massacres of citizens ordered by
Taimur, Nadir Shah and Abdali! No one was spared, neither
the aged nor the new born, nor their mothers. Tell me of a

single instance of a massacre ordered by the English. Not even after the murders of their women and children in Delhi, Lucknow and Cawnpore after your so-called First War of Independence did they touch your women or children. They hanged a few people, levelled some bazaars to the ground. That was all.'

'That was not all,' they yell back at me. 'They treated us like dogs—worse than dogs because they are dog-worshippers. They called us niggers, had their 'Europeans only' clubs, 'For Europeans and Anglo-Indians only' compartments in railway trains. There was one law for the white man another for the black.'

I shout back at them: 'There was no justice in India till the British came. There will be no justice in India after their impact has worn off. They gave you freedom to do your *buk buk* against them and only took action when you preached violence. Can you think of another race besides the British who would have put up with your Gandhis and Nehrus preaching sedition against them? If they had been Germans, French, Russians, Italians, Chinese or Japanese, they would strung up your Congresswallas on the branches of the nearest trees.'

'If they had tried that their lease would have been shorter. Our freedom fighters would have booted them out during one or the other of the world wars when they were neck deep in trouble in Europe.'

'Freedom fighters my foot!' I shout back. 'Hired yellers of slogans who spent more comfortable time in jails than in their own hovels. And now want to be compensated with life pensions. Don't talk to me about freedom fighters. They make me sick.'

'You have been brainwashed,' they tell me. They tell me of the great progress India has made since the British were thrown out—'More advance in ten years of independence than in a hundred years of British rule. We produce all the food we need because of the dams and canals we have built. We produce the best textiles in the world; we produce our own cars, aeroplanes, tanks and guns; we can make nuclear bombs, send satellites into space, pick up nodules from the ocean bed; the Indian tri-colour flies in the wastes of Antarctica. Don't you feel a sense of pride in your country's achievements?'

'Indeed I do. Also a sense of foreboding. We are amongst the poorest of the poor, the most ignorant of ignoramuses of the world. We breed like rabbits. Soon we will be more than we can feed, clothe, or shelter. Then we will resume fighting each other like dogs on a dung heap. We are also the corruptest of the corrupt. Everyone from the Prime Minister down to the poorest-paid police constable has his price. And we are more prone to violence than the most violent races of the world. What we saw in the summer and autumn of 1947 when we slew each other like goats unveiled our real nature. You will see much worse in the years to come. Hindus, Muslims, Christians, Sikhs, Buddhists will go on killing each other in greater numbers. Your Gandhi and his *ahimsa* are as dead as .... as dead as .... Whatever the dead bird is called.'

'Dodo.'

'That's right! Dead as the dodo.'

'So are people like you. The last of your tribe will go with you. India is a great nation, that is the truth. And you may or may not know that our national motto is truth will forever be triumphant—*Satyamev Jayate*.

19

Bhagmati

Bhagmati's great passion other than me (as I like to think) is mangoes. It's been a good year for mangoes but a bad one for the monsoons. That often happens in Delhi. The first crop of mangoes start coming in from Tamil Nadu some time in April. Fat, pulpy stuff without any character. In May the much-fancied Alfonsos from Maharashtra make their appearance in Delhi's markets. Delicious but murderously expensive. More so since Delhi's foreign community cultivated a taste for mangoes. I only get to taste Alfonsos when some industrialist or minister of government sends me a crate. I send a few to my neighbours in the hope they will return the gift when mangoes from Uttar Pradesh start coming in. These days I have to scout around for more and more mangoes for the way Bhagmati tucks in I wouldn't get to eat any. Without as much as a by your leave she will eat three or four at a time, suck their kernels with great relish till there's nothing left on them. She ends her feasting with a loud belch, washes her hands and face—then proceeds to tie up whatever fruit remains on the table in the folds of her sari to take home. 'I know you haven't paid for them,' she tells me. 'My poor family hasn't tasted a mango this season,' she says as she leaves.

Nothing in the world of fruit compares with Dussehris, Langdas and Ratauls from the orchards of Uttar Pradesh. Of the nearly thousand varieties of mangoes, these are the three I relish the most. Unfortunately they also happen to be Bhagmati's favourites. During the mango season her visits are more frequent. When she comes she makes a meal of my mangoes and takes away what she can't eat. She says they are good for her digestion, the best thing to take for constipation.

She is not bothered about putting on weight.

As I said we've had a poor monsoon. In the first week of June I heard the monsoon bird calling. Rain should have followed within a few days. There is news of heavy downpours in other parts of India. The Bombay and Calcutta streets are under water, and floods are devastating Assam. But not a drop in Delhi through June and July. A few miserable showers in August. The bloody songbird of the clouds, the *meghapapeeha*, hasn't been heard of for the last three months. 'There will be famine,' prophesies Bhagmati tucking into her fifth Langda, 'people will die of hunger in the streets of Delhi.' Then she adds philosophically 'No matter. People are always dying in this wretched city. If it is not hunger, then it is by cholera, plague, small-pox, murder, suicide. Or old age.'

20

The Dispossessed

What brought us to New Delhi can be briefly recounted. We lived in a hamlet in the midst of a vast desert. On our east ran the river Jhelum; in the north was a line of barren hills which yielded nothing except rock salt. The rest was sand dunes as far as the eye could see. Hadali had about two hundred families of which at least a hundred-and-sixty were Mussalman and the remaining Hindu or Sikh. Mussalmans owned the desert and strings of camels. They grew a few blades of wheat and some vegetables near their wells or gathered dates from date-palm trees that grew in the waste. They sent their sons to the army or the police. These sons sent home their earnings, and when they retired, came back to settle in Hadali. We Hindus and Sikhs were tradesmen and money-lenders. We lent money to the Mussalmans. And when they did not return our money with the interest we made them pay it off by serving us. We bought rock salt from the Range and had these fellows take it on their camels to distant cities like Lahore, Amritsar, Ludhiana and Jalandhar. We sold the salt and brought back tea, sugar, spices and silks to sell in our desert villages.

We Hindus and Sikhs lived in brick-built houses and had buffaloes in our courtyards. The Mussalmans lived in mud-huts and looked after our cattle in exchange for a pot of milk a day. We looked down upon them because they were poor. They looked down upon us because we were few and not as big-built as they. Even their women were taller and stronger than our men. They could pull up large full buckets from the well as if they were thimbles. They could carry four pitchers full of water, two on the head and one under each armpit without the least bother. And their men were over six feet tall and made as of whipcord. We were scared of them.

I will tell you of the incident which compelled us to leave Hadali. It took place sometime in the last week of August 1947.

For some months we had been hearing stories of Mussalmans killing Hindus and Sikhs in Rawalpindi and Lahore. We heard that Hindus and Sikhs were fleeing eastwards where there were not many Mussalmans. Then we heard that the Mussalmans had got a country of their own called Pakistan and Hadali was in Pakistan. Some of our elders suggested leaving Hadali and joining other Hindus and Sikhs who were going to Hindustan. But we had money owing to us, we had our brick-houses and buffaloes in our courtyards. So we decided to stay on till we got our money back and had sold our properties.

I, Ram Rakha, was then sixteen years old. I had a sister, Lachmi, a year younger than I. She had been betrothed to a second cousin since she was born. (This was not uncommon amongst us! Pregnant women often agreed to betroth their children to be born if they were of different sex). My parents felt that it was unwise to keep a fifteen-year-old unmarried girl in the house. The date of marriage was fixed. As was the custom in our village, *bhaaji* (sweets) were sent to most families in the village including those of the Mussalmans. A fortnight before the day fixed for the wedding, the groom's father needing money to feed his guests asked one of his debtors to pay up. And when the fellow said he hadn't any money, the groom's father filed a suit against him. No one had done this before.

The Mussalmans returned our *bhaaji*. This too had never happened before.

We went ahead with the preparations for the wedding. According to custom, my sister spent the last week before her wedding indoors wearing the same dirty clothes. On the seventh day women of the family bathed her, dyed her palms with henna and slipped ivory bracelets on her arms. They sang songs to the beat of the drum. In the evening Lachmi and her girl-friends went out together to relieve themselves. They were sitting on their haunches defecating and babbling away, when a gang of young Mussalmans surrounded them. The girls were so frightened that they could not even scream for help. The thugs had no difficulty in recognizing Lachmi. A lad picked her up, threw her across his saddle and rode off into the desert.

My father was like one possessed of the Devil. He screamed and tore his hair. He went about the village lanes calling the Mussalmans sons of pigs. He ran thirteen miles over the sand dunes to a police station and lodged a report. He gave wads of rupee notes to the inspector. Next day, he came back with the police with warrants of arrest against the boys he suspected of being Lachmi's abductors. Two days later we went to a magistrate's court. The accused were brought in handcuffs. The rascals twisted their moustaches and made lewd gestures at us. One of them said loudly, 'Let me get back to Hadali and if I don't split the bottoms of all these *kafirs*, my name isn't Turrabaz Khan.'

Their lawyer said that my father's complaint was false as my sister had of her own accord gone away with the boy she loved. He asked Turrabaz Khan to stand up. Then Lachmi was produced. She was wearing a *burqa* so she could not meet our eyes. 'Yes,' she said, 'I love Turrabaz Khan and went to him of my own will. I have become a Mussalman and have married him. I do not wish to return to my parents' home.'

The inspector and the police were Mussalmans. The accused and their lawyer were Mussalmans. Our lawyer was a Mussalman. (All the Hindu lawyers had fled to India). The magistrate was also a Mussalman. He dismissed my father's complaint and ordered the accused to be released forthwith. They went out of the courtroom jumping for joy.

We begged for protection. The magistrate sent for the Mussalmans and said, 'You've got what you wanted. Leave the miserable *kafirs* alone.' The inspector took more money from us to escort us back to Hadali. Constables were posted outside our homes for our safety. They also took money from us.

How could we continue to live in Hadali with one of our own flesh and blood being ravished a few doors away? Our womenfolk said they felt unsafe; when they came back from the well, the Mussalmans would wait for them and expose themselves. We complained to the policemen but they did nothing. One evening when a dust-storm was blowing we packed our utensils and quilts, loaded them on our buffaloes and cleared out of Hadali.

We travelled all night and day with hot sand blowing in our faces. We came to Sargodha and found the encampment where thousands of Hindus and Sikhs were waiting to go to India. Our buffaloes were taken away. For many days we lived on stale bread and pickles. Then soldiers came and put us in their trucks. They drove us to Lahore. We passed long lines of people on foot and in bullock carts. Those going our way were Sikhs and Hindus. Those coming from the opposite direction were Mussalmans. We saw many Sikhs lying dead on the road with their long hair scattered about and their bearded faces covered with flies. We crossed the Indo-Pakistan border. There were many more corpses along the road. From the shape of their penises I could tell they were Mussalmans. There were lots of women and children among the dead.

We were sent to a camp in Kurukshetra where more than 70,000 refugees were living in tents. For many days we did nothing except stand in lines for rations and talk to everyone we met. My mother cried all the time calling my sister's name. Then officers came and told us that we must go and look for work. 'What kind of work?' my father asked them. 'We were money-lenders. We have no money to lend.' However he sent a postcard to a Sikh whom he had known as a boy in Hadali. This Sikh was said to have made a lot of money as a building-contractor and had been living in Delhi for many years. Two days later we got his reply asking us to come over. We took the train to Delhi.

In the train my father talked of the days when he and this Sikh had played together on the sand dunes around Hadali. The closer we got to Delhi, the more my father's childhood memories came back to him. I was sure that as soon as they met, my father and the Sikh would fall into each other's arms.

We had to walk six miles from the railway station carrying our utensils and quilts on our heads. With great difficulty we found the Sikh's house. My father asked us to wait at the gate while he went in to find out. He had hardly gone ten paces when an enormous dog charged at him. My father ran back. The dog ripped off a piece of his shirt before he was able to get back to us. A man in khaki uniform came out of the house and demanded angrily what we wanted. My father asked very humbly whether this was the house of so-and-so. 'Yes,' growled the man, 'state your business.' My father showed him the Sikh's letter. 'Wait here,' ordered the man in khaki. The dog stood baring its teeth at us.

The man came back, shooed away the dog and beckoned us to follow him. We picked up our belongings and followed the man. It was a large, two-storeyed house with a big garden. The Sikh and his wife were in the verandah having tea.

'So you've come, Sain Ditta!' said the Sikh sipping his tea. My father put down the load on his head and touched the Sikh's feet. My mother slumped on the floor, laid her head on the Sikh lady's knees and began to wail. 'What will you make by wailing? What's happened has happened,' said the lady and told the man in uniform to take us to the kitchen and give us something to eat.

We were told to make ourselves comfortable in a garage. Half of the garage was used to store trunks and crates. The other half was to be our home. We slept on the floor like people who have had a death in the family.

This is how we began our new life in New Delhi.

*

My parents were quicker in getting used to the new surroundings than I. My father was given the job of night-watchman. He had to walk round the house all night with a hurricane lantern in one hand, a stave in the other and yell 'Khabardar ho' at every corner. He made friends with the big dog which had torn his shirt. The dog kept him company. My father learnt to answer to 'Oi' and say 'Jee' to the Sikh who had once been his best friend. My mother swept the floors and pressed the feet of the Sikh's wife.

What hurt me very much was the way my parents changed towards me—their only remaining child. I knew the reason. They had spent all their money. My mother's gold bangles and ear-rings had to be sold as my father's wages were not enough to feed the three of us. If I asked for another *chappati*, my mother would ask, 'Have you a belly or a well?' My father started calling me *mushtanda* (lout) and *nikhatoo* (idler). One day both turned on me and told me to go out and look for work. So I was thrown out into the strange world of this strange city.

Where was I to start? My father told me to go to peoples' houses and ask if they wanted a servant. Delhi was full of Punjabi refugees looking for work. Every house I went to had a man at the gate who asked me my business. When I told him, he would order me to move on. I got to know Delhi, both the old city and the new; the big buildings where big officials went to work in their big motor cars and clerks went on their bicycles. I got to know all the bazaars and what was sold where. But I found no work. My father got very harsh with me. My mother had to shield me from his temper. I began to come back after dark and slip into the garage when my father was doing his rounds. My mother would then give me food and press my legs till I fell asleep.

I often dreamt of Hadali with its stretch of treeless expanse and the sands on which I used to play on moonlit nights. I dreamt of the tall Mussalman women with pitchers on their heads, the black points of their nipples showing beneath their wet muslin shirts and the joy of being crushed between their legs. Sometimes the dreams turned into nightmares. I saw these Mussalman men menace me with their penises the size of randy donkeys. I would start moaning. My mother would shake me up, take me in her arms and rock me back to sleep.

My father stopped talking to me. My mother tried to make up for his behaviour. She would ask me what I had seen. 'Why don't you take your mother with you some time?' she would say.

One Tuesday she took permission of her mistress to come with me. I showed her the government Secretariats and the Parliament House. She gasped with wonder as if she was a little girl. She asked me all sorts of questions; I made up all sorts of answers. She made me feel very important. She took my hand when she got nervous of buses and motor cars; she made me feel like a strong, grown-up man. I took her to the Birla temple. She prayed to Shiva and Parbati and Ganesh; to Vishnu and Lakshmi; to Krishna and Radha, and then to Rama and Sita and all the other gods and goddesses. She prayed for Lachmi. She waved a copper paisa round my head and gave it to the *pandit*. She asked him to smear my forehead with sacred ash and bless me so I could get a job.

From the Birla temple we went to the Hanuman temple. There was a large crowd and lots of stalls of sweetmeats, toys, balloons and bangles. Here too my mother gave a paisa to the *pandit* and prayed to Hanumanji to get me a job. We went round the stalls. She gave me some paise to buy her glass bangles and slip them on her arms.

By the time we left the temple, the sun had set and the sky was like a grey giant about to go to bed. The trees in Connaught Circus were full of chattering mynahs and parakeets. Once more my mother took my hand. We watched well-dressed ladies and gentlemen buying things and driving away in their beautiful motor cars. By the time we got home, it was dark. My father was out with his stave and lantern yelling 'Khabardar ho.' Although she was very tired, she warmed the food for me. When I lay down, she took my head in her lap and rubbed oil in my scalp. The last words she said before I fell asleep were: 'Surely, one of the gods will hear my prayer and get you a job!'

The gods heard my mother's prayer and the very next morning I got a job. Where do you think I found it? In a house just across the road. That is a story by itself.

The house in which we lived faced a roundabout from which many roads branched off. Across one road was the house of Jinnah Sahib who made Pakistan. Before running away to Pakistan, this cow-eating Jinnah sold the house to a rich Hindu who made it the headquarters of the Cow Protection Society. On the other side across the road facing our garage was an even bigger house belonging to Seth Birla, nephew of the man who had built the temple. This Birla was said to be the richest man in India. There was always a crowd at his gate and lots of policemen. At first I thought that these people were looking for jobs like I was and that there would be no point in my joining them. And I was frightened of policemen. I had heard songs and speeches coming over the loudspeaker and was told that Mahatma Gandhi lived there and anyone could go in to have his *darshan*.

The next morning I went to have Gandhiji's *darshan*. Nobody stopped me. There were many people including white sahibs and memsahibs sitting on the lawn. In the front there was a platform with a microphone. I sat down in a corner. A party of young men came and sat near me.

A few minutes later the Mahatma arrived leaning on a woman's shoulder. Everyone stood up. Some people shouted, *'Mahatma Gandhi ki jai.'* The young men sitting near me shouted, *'Bharat Mata ki jai* (Long Live Mother India).' Mahatma Gandhi sat down on the platform and shut his eyes. A party of men and women began to chant:

> *Raghupati Raghav Raja Ram*
> *Patitpavan Sita Ram.*

I had never heard this song before. It sounded very nice. Then they sang:

> *Ishwar Allah Terey Nam*
> *Sab Ko Sammati Dey Bhagwan.*

That also sounded nice. A young man sitting near me muttered: 'Not *Ishwar Allah* but *Mohammed Allah Terey Nam.'*

When the hymn ended, a bearded Mussalman came and sat beside the Mahatma. He opened a book and drew the microphone towards his beard. He began to intone something. The young men beside me began to shout: 'Shut up...the Mussalmans have ravished our mothers and sisters...we will not allow the *Quran* to be read in our country anymore.' They jumped up and began yelling, *'Bharat Mata ki jai.'*

The Mahatma drew the microphone towards him and in a

toothless, frog-croaking voice said, 'Brothers and sisters, I will continue to respect all religions. If you do not agree with me, do not come to my prayer meetings. If you cause interruption, I will pray alone. Go back to your homes and ponder if it is right that our independence should end in this way, in the killing of brother by brother.' He stood up, said *namaskar* and went away.

Before I knew what was happening, the police surrounded us. I was pushed along and forced to get into a van along with the other boys. They continued to shout '*Bharat Mata ki jai*,' till there was no one to hear them.

The officer-in-charge who was sitting with the driver turned back and said, '*Mahatma Buddhoo* (stupid) *ki jai*!' The young men laughed. The constables and the van-driver also laughed. 'Sub-inspector sahib, don't take us too far,' said one of the young men.

'Wherever you like! But please do not go back to Birla House,' he said joining the palms of his hands, 'otherwise they will slit my throat.'

'Just let us off near the Birla temple; we have no more programmes for the day,' the young man assured him.

We were dropped at the Birla temple. It was then that one of the boys noticed me '*Arre*! Who are you? What troop are you?' he asked. 'I know no troop-shoop,' I replied and explained that I was a refugee and had been arrested by mistake. They had a big laugh. 'Why don't you join us?' another boy asked, 'Or are you one of the Old Man's Mussalman-loving disciples?' I told them that my sister had been abducted in Pakistan; how could I be a Mussalman-lover? 'You are a big, strong Punjabi,' said a fellow who appeared to be their leader. 'You should be like a true Kshatriya fighting for the Hindu *dharma*.' He patted me on my back and felt my muscles. No one had ever called me big and strong before.

They asked me what I did. I told them I did nothing. 'Then come and join the Sangha,' said their leader. 'You can work in the office and eat in our canteen.' I did not know anything about this Sangha but I went along with them. I signed a piece of paper and was given a number (only the leader knew the names of the boys, the rest of us were known by numbers). I was to dust the office furniture and sit outside the door to see that no one who did not know the password for the day came in. I was given a uniform and five rupees as an advance against my salary.

This Sangha which I joined had a long Sanskrit name. Every time I said *Rashtureeya*, the boys laughed. Every time I said *Savayam*, they laughed. So I simply called the Sangha by its English initials RSS.

I gave the five rupee note to my mother. She was very happy. She made some *halva*, gave some to the Sikh and his lady and their servants. She even gave a palmful to the dog. My father stopped taunting me.

I used to leave home early in the morning and dust the furniture. Then I got into my uniform and lined up with the boys. Our leader hoisted the saffron flag of the Sangha. We saluted it by holding our hands across our chests. This was followed by an hour of drill and wrestling. We were taught how to fight with sticks. They told us we would soon have guns and be taught to shoot. In the afternoon we had lectures on Hindu *dharma* and history. They told us of the greatness of Aryavrata, the land of the Aryans. They told us how the Mussalmans had come and destroyed our temples and massacred millions of innocent Hindus, abducted and raped Hindu women; how thousands of these noble Hindu women had burnt themselves on funeral pyres rather than be dishonoured by the Mussalmans. They exhorted us to fight for our *dharma*, cleanse Bharat of the unclean *maleechas*, Mussalmans as well Christians, who were also foreigners and ate our sacred cow-mother.

What right had the Mussalmans to be in Delhi or anywhere else in India when they had driven us, Hindus and Sikhs, out of their Pakistan? Why could we not take away their women and property as they had taken ours and send them packing to Pakistan or *gehennum*? Such questions were put to us every day.

One day the chief sent for me. 'Are you number 840?' I came to attention and saluted. 'Is it correct that your sister was abducted in Pakistan?' I replied *'Jee haan.'* 'Are you going to do nothing about it? How long will you keep sitting with one hand on the other?' I did not know what he wanted me to do. I replied, 'Sir, 840 can make a present of his life. He has nothing else to offer.' The chief smiled, 'We Hindus only know how to give our lives, not how to take the lives of others! It must change. Are you prepared to lead an attack on the Muslims of Delhi? Remember what they have done to your sister!'

Blood rushed into my face. I again sprang to attention, saluted and said, 'Number 840 is ready to lay—ready for any sacrifice.'

The chief had a paper in front of him. He read out some numbers. 'These boys will be with you. When you are ready for action, you will report to me. I shall see that the police do not come in your way.'

I saluted and left the room.

The real problem was to find out who was Muslim and who was not. As soon as the Mussalmans of Delhi heard what had happened in Karnal and Ambala and Amritsar and Jalandhar, they burnt their red fez caps and furry Jinnah *topees* and started wearing Gandhi caps instead. They shaved off their beards, gave up wearing *sherwani* coats, loose pyjamas and learnt to tie *dhotis* round their waists. Their women stopped wearing *burqas* when they went out and started to put red dots on their foreheads and say *namaste*. The only way we could tell if the fellow was a Mussalman was to see if his penis was circumcized. How could we stop everyone and say 'Show me your cock?' We could not go into action without careful planning and preparation. We began by marking Muslim homes and shops with swastikas. Muslim *goondas* got to know of this and put swastika marks on Hindu shops and homes. We changed our plans and decided to attack a few well-known stores owned by Muslims and watch the results. There was a big one in Connaught Circus in the centre of New Delhi. The chief approved of the plan and suggested a date for its execution.

As the day came closer I began to get nervous. I wanted all the Mussalmans to be dead but I was frightened of killing one. I wanted to run away from Delhi. There was no one I could talk to about the things going on in my mind. If I confided in my mother she was sure to kick up a fuss and tell my father or the Sikh lady.

The evening before we were to go into action I went home early. My mother was in the garage shelling peas for the Sikh's kitchen and talking to the dog which was often with her. I laid down on my mattress.'*Vey Shambia*!' (his name was Simba), you have not seen my Lachmi, have you? Well, if these evil Mussalmans had not taken her, she would have been here with us. You would have seen her married. You would have seen the fireworks and heard the band. But her *kismet*!' She slapped her forehead with both her hands and began to cry: '*Hai Lachmi*! *Hai beti*! Where are you! May the accursed Mussalmans who took you go to hell.' The dog came to her, sniffed in her ears and began to whine. My mother put her arms round its neck and hugged it. This was too much for me. 'Why do you cry mother?' I asked her. 'I will teach these Mussalmans a lesson for what they have done to our Lachmi.' After that I could not back out, could I?

I slept very poorly but was up before dawn when the jeep came to pick me up. The other boys were already at the headquarters. We said a short prayer, had tea and biscuits and were driven to Connaught Circus. I posted the boys at positions I had selected earlier and showed them the exact spot where the jeep would await us after we had done the job. We compared the time on the watches that had been given to us and I told them to look out for my signal. I had a sharp-pointed steel rod tucked inside the sleeve of my shirt.

I strolled along leisurely in the inner colonnade of the Circus. I saw shop-owners arrive, mumble prayers and unlock their shops. The Muslim store we had selected was still shut but four attendants were waiting outside. I passed by them. Despite their Gandhi caps, I could tell from their speech that they were Muslims. I had hardly gone a few paces when I saw a car mount the pavement opposite the store and pull up under a tree. One of the boys who recognized the owner dropped a small cane he was carrying to indicate 'this is our man'. I took my position behind a pillar in the colonnade. The man put up the window-panes, locked the car, tried the handles and then sauntered across the road. He was a paunchy man about forty years old. He was dressed like a fashionable Delhiwalla: muslin *kurta* with gold embroidery down the middle; white, baggy trousers stiff with starch. He carried a silver *betel*-leaf-case in one hand, a tin of cigarettes and a matchbox in the other. A half-smoked cigarette dangled from his lower lip. He walked like a pregnant woman. The boys emerged from their places: three from one side, three from the other. I awaited my quarry. As he crossed the road and stepped into the colonnade, I came up behind him. The attendants bowed and said: '*As-Salaam-Valai-kum.*' He nodded his head. He handed over his *betel*-case to one of the attendants and put his hand into his pocket to get the keys. I drew the steel rod from my sleeve and lunged it in the middle of his back. '*Hai Allah!*' he screamed as he fell back on me. His eyes were wide with terror. I pulled out the rod and let him drop to the pavement. I blew my whistle. The boys fell upon the attendants. '*Bachao* (help); police; *mat maro* (don't kill),' they screamed. No one came to their help. Within a matter of seconds five Mussalmans lay on the pavement in puddles of blood groaning and writhing. We smashed the plate glass of the store-windows and rushed in. It was a shoe-store with other kinds of leather goods: bags, belts and wallets. I picked two large suitcases and stuffed them with whatever I could lay my hands on. I cleaned up the owner's table which had a small radio set, a silver calendar and some fountain pens. By then many other people — *chowkidars*, peons, students were in the store taking whatever they could find. We took our haul to the jeep. By that time, the whole of Connaught Circus was in turmoil. Hindus and Sikhs began attacking Muslims and looting their shops. Police vans went around in circles, constables ran about blowing their whistles. We had no difficulty in getting away.

My hands and knees shook as if I had fever. My heart thumped against my chest — *dhug, dhug, dhug.* I could not talk. When we reached the headquarters I lay down on a *charpoy*. They gave me a mug of tea and two aspirin tablets. I put a cushion on my face to blot out the scene I had enacted. It was of no use. I saw the whites of the eyes of that

Mussalman I had murdered. My ear-drum resounded with the scream, 'Hai Allah.' It went on and on and on till I was exhausted. I was not able to stand on my feet till the afternoon. Then I had a bath and felt better. I examined the things I had stolen. I put aside some things to take home and put the rest back in the other suitcase. I took the things to Sadar Bazaar. Since many Muslim shops had been looted I could not get very much. Nevertheless I came back with more than a hundred-and-fifty rupees. The radio alone fetched me a hundred.

On my way home I bought a flashlight for my father and a coloured muslin *dupatta* for my mother. I also bought some fruit and a small tin of clarified butter. I waited till it was dark so that no one in the Sikh's house would see me come in with my big, new suitcase. I went straight into the garage. My mother was baking *chappaties* on an earthen stove.

I told my mother that I had spent my month's wages to get these things. I spread the *dupatta* on her shoulder. She hugged me and cried. She heard my father's footsteps and ran out to get him. She was so excited that all she could say was 'Vekh, vekh (See, see).' I took the lantern from my father's hand and gave him the flashlight. He was like a child with a new toy. He pressed the button and played the beam on the walls of the garage. They tried out the shoes, patted the wallets and the suitcase. They were very happy.

I could not sleep. I was afraid of shutting my eyes. I was frightened of the ghost of the man I had killed. He kept on crying, 'Hai Allah' in my ears. I waited for the crunch of my father's footsteps on the gravel and his cry, 'Khabardar ho!' to reassure me that I was safe. I began to shiver and moan. I pretended I was having a nightmare. My mother woke up and asked me what was wrong. I moaned louder. She came over and took my head in her lap. I put my arms round her waist and feigned sleep. She rubbed my back. After a while she lay down beside me. My shivering stopped. I felt warm and safe and unafraid. I tightened my arms round her bosom, put my right leg over her and drew her closer to me. Then I fell asleep.

*

The morning after the killing I complain that my bowels are loose and stay at home for the next five days. In any case I could not have gone out because riots have broken out in different parts of the city. The Muslims are being flushed out, their properties are being looted, their shops and businesses are being taken over and their homes occupied. They are fleeing in the hundreds of thousands to Pakistan. Those that remain are herded into the Purana Qila and the big mosques. The first battle for Delhi has been won. But much more remains to be done. We have to fight these Mussalman-loving Hindus like Gandhi and Nehru, drive out the remaining Muslims to Pakistan and wipe out all traces of Islam from our Bharatvarsha.

Gandhi is our enemy number one. He says: 'Get out of the mosques and Muslims' homes.' I want to ask him: '*Oi*, Old Man if we got out of their mosques and homes, where are we to live? On the pavements? It does not behove you who lives in Seth Birla's palace to talk like this.'

Nehru is our enemy number two. He calls us *goondas*. I want to ask him: '*Oi* Pandit, where was your police and your army when Mussalman *goondas* were slitting our throats?'

Sardar Patel is our friend. 'They are not thieves and dacoits but love their country,' he says. Only to please Gandhi and Nehru he adds that we are 'misguided'. The police are also our friends. And why not? Most of the new police are refugees from the Punjab. They know the truth about the Mussalmans and are not beguiled by the Gandhi-Nehru *bakvas*.

One day the Sangha chief says to me 'We must know what this Gandhi fellow is up to. Number 840 you will attend the Old Man's meetings and report what he says and who comes to see him.'

I am given money to buy a white Gandhi cap, a thick, handspun *khaddar* shirt and trousers and a woollen shawl. I start going to Birla House in the early hours. I take down the names of people who come to the meeting. I make note of all the *buk buk* I hear about Hindus and Mussalmans being brothers.

I learn to imitate Gandhi's voice. When I report what I have heard I use the same toothless, gummy Gujarati-Hindi: 'I am waiting for the direction of the inner voice...straining my ear to catch the whispering of the inner voice and waiting for its command.' Everyone roars with laughter. I can also imitate his gestures. I sit cross-legged, wrap the shawl over my head and continue: 'I am in a furnace. There is a raging fire all around. We are trampling humanity underfoot...I am groping for light. 'I strike a match to show how. 'I can as yet only catch faint rays of it.' I bring the match close to my nose. 'When I see in full blaze the *dosti* (friendship) of Delhi then it will really become *dili* (rooted) in the heart.' They double over their bellies. The boys rename me Gandhiji Maharaj. They say that if the Old Fellow had been a member of our Sangha he would not have got a more appropriate number than mine. 840 is twice 420 which is the section of the penal code defining fraud—and Gandhi is a double fraud.

The Sangha chief tells us that we should gird up our loins because soon war will break out between India and Pakistan. We must finish Pakistan once and for all and plant the saffron flag of Hindu *dharma* on the Khyber Pass.

Our chief is right. Pakistani tribesmen invade Kashmir. Every day we expect India to declare war on Pakistan. But Gandhi goes on croaking about peace and love. As if that is not bad enough he says India owes Pakistan a lot of money and must pay up at once.

Gandhi fasts every Monday. That day he also keeps his mouth shut. Instead he grins at everyone who comes to see him and scribbles notes on bits of paper.

Monday morning, January 1948. It is very cold and since it is the Old Man's day of silence, instead of going to Birla House, I stay snugly wrapped in my quilt till the sun is up. Then I bask in the sunshine and feel good. I have a mug of tea and a stale *chappati*, then saunter across to Birla House. Old Gandhi is in the garden soaking in the sun and scribbling something. His secretary Dr. Susheila Nayar is seated on the grass by his chair taking charge of scraps of paper he hands to her. I like Susheilaji. She is fair and buxom, her hair is curly and she has dimples in her cheeks. Although she is much older than me, I would like to make love to her. She reads something the Old Fellow has written, jumps up as if a wasp has stung her on her big buttocks. She runs and tells her brother, her brother tells someone else who tells someone else till everyone knows about it. A meeting is summoned and Susheilaji reads out a statement on behalf of the Old Man. Tomorrow, when he opens his mouth, he will begin a fast to death.

I can't remember everything that was said but it was about two kinds of fasting ! You may fast if you are fat; or you may fast if you have done wrong to someone and want to punish yourself. The Old Man wants to fast because we have done wrong to the Mussalmans. He says he's been feeling impotent of late. He's been brooding over it for three days and knows that if he fasts he will become potent again. He says, 'No man, if he is pure, has anything more precious to give than his life. I hope and pray that I have that purity in me to justify the step. God sent this fast. He alone will end it, if and when He wills.' Whatever he says about God, it is clear he doesn't want to die. He says if there is a re-union of hearts between Hindus, Sikhs and Mussalmans he may change his mind and start eating again.

I take a taxi to the headquarters.

They have heard the news over the radio. 'Let the Old Man die; Hindu *dharma* is eternal,' says the chief. 'But we must watch the situation very carefully.' 'You,' he says pointing to me, 'you must remain on duty at Birla House and report everything immediately. Take a taxi if you have to.' (Thank you for that! Six to seven rupees for me for the next few days, I calculate). 'We must organize demonstrations to counteract the mischief of these Gandhi followers.'

I get back to Birla House.

The crowd is bigger than ever. The regulars strut about looking very important; besides them there are lots of others including whites and some Negroes as well. Though it is still Monday, Gandhi is yakking away. I push through the crowd and get nearer him. Lots of chaps scribbling in their notebooks. Lots of questions to flatter the Old Man to show how concerned they are.

His son, Dev Das, is also there and the two go at each other. The son calls the father impotent. The father calls the son's thinking impotent and superficial. Then tells him to mind his own business. You can see the father and son don't like each other. Gandhi does not like any of his three sons.

'I claim that God has inspired this fast,' repeats the old humbug many times to many people. 'No human agency has ever been known to thwart nor will it ever thwart Divine Will.'

I do not think this is worth reporting so I go home to get a good night's sleep.

Next morning there are more policemen and soldiers about Birla House than ever before. And more newspaper chaps. And Nehru and Patel and Maulana Azad and Sheikh Abdullah of Kashmir. I gather they are planning demonstrations in Gandhi's favour. I rush to the headquarters, make my report and am back in Birla House.

There is a prayer meeting at 11.30 a.m. It begins with the Old Man's (and my) favourite hymn:

> He who feels the pain of others
> Is truly a man of God.

Susheilaji sings something in English. I don't like the way she imitates white women's *whoo, whoo, whoo*. Then comes the hymn about God being both Ishwar and Allah. The Old Man speaks into the microphone. He tells the Muslims he is fasting for them. He tells the Hindus and Sikhs he is fasting for them. He tells the Kashmiris he is fasting for Kashmir. And he tells God he is fasting because God told him to fast. Even now he is on lime and orange-juice.

In the evening our chief sends three busloads of refugees to Birla House. They march up from one end of the road chanting 'Khoon ka badla khoon sey lengey (We will avenge blood with blood).' Nehru looks up but says nothing. They chant: 'Gandhi Budha murdabad (Death to Old Gandhi).' Nehru becomes like one possessed of the jinn. He rushes towards them flailing his arms. 'Who dares to say Gandhi murdabad?' he demands. 'Let him who dares repeat those words in my presence. He will have to kill me first.' He vents his temper, glowering at everyone. Then he drives off in his limousine, followed by a jeepload of armed policemen.

I slip into Gandhi's room. He is lying on a *charpoy*, wrapped up in a shawl with only his bald head and face showing under the light of the table-lamp. The room is full of people. He asks, 'What are they shouting about?' Susheilaji replies 'Gandhi *murdabad!*' and brushes a tear off her cheek.

Gandhi says, '*Ram, Ram, Ram*' and hides his face under his shawl. So passes another day.

The next morning the Old Man is brought out on a *charpoy* so that the crowd can see him. The crowd shouts '*Mahatma Gandhi ki jai.*' He joins the palms of his hands and bares his gums. He doesn't look like a man who has not eaten anything for two days.

The entire government of India is now on the lawns of Birla House. Pandit Nehru and his ministers sit on chairs round a table. They decide to give Pakistan thirty-five crore rupees so it can buy guns and bullets to kill Hindus. They go to Gandhi and say: 'We have done what you wanted us to do, now will you give up your fast?' He shakes his head and replies, 'No, not yet. I want much more. My sole guide, even dictator, is God, the infallible and omnipotent.'

*

The Ganga has begun to flow in the opposite direction — upstream from the sea towards its source in the mountains. That is the only way I can describe what is happening. Three days ago we were driving the Muslims out of Delhi and everyone was with us. Now the Muslims are coming back to Delhi and everyone seems to be against us. People who looted Muslims' shops come to Birla House to give up their loot; men bring women they abducted to Birla House and ask them (the women) to forgive them in front of Gandhi. Men who spilled Muslim blood cut their own hands and with their own blood sign petitions asking Gandhi to give up his fast. Everyone is going Gandhi-mad. An old sahib, who has been editor of an English paper, starts to fast and says if Gandhi dies, he will also die. How can anyone fight this kind of madness?

The chief wants me to be at Birla House all the time because something big is to happen. He has given me his residence telephone number so I can ring him at night. As soon as the sun goes down it turns very cold. I curl up on a sofa in the verandah. I have my pullover and coat, warm socks and a shawl over me; yet I shiver so much that I cannot keep my teeth from chattering. The Old Man rises at 3.30 a.m. The sky is black and full of stars. Lights are switched on. Hymns are followed by silent meditation. The old fellow gets to work. I can see him under the light of his table-lamp picking up one letter after another and mumbling something which a fellow takes down on a piece of paper. This goes on for some hours. Then the Old Man has his Bengali lesson. What is the point of learning a new language if he really means to die? By then the sun is up and the sunshine streams into the verandah. I stop shivering. I try to get a little sleep. But there is so much jabbering around me that I have to get up. The doctors are examining the Old Man. They give him orange-juice and waggle their heads. The Old Man joins the palms of his hands and sends them away. You take it from me it is all a put-up show, a *tamasha*.

The Old Man is his own doctor. He takes no medicines or injections or anything. 'The name of Rama is my nature cure,' he says. It is taken down on paper by a dozen scribes. It is, as I said before, a put-up *tamasha*.

Hymns, recitations from the *Ramayana*, the *Gita*, the *Quran* and the *Granth* go on all day. And all day there is a continuous stream of people with the sorrows of the world on their long-drawn, stupid faces. Nehru is in tears. He says if Gandhi dies, India's soul will die with him. Maulana Azad is in tears (later in the day he blabbers to 1,00,000 people for one hour. He loves his own voice).

In the evening the Lord Sahib Viceroy Mountbatten, his Lady Sahiba and Missy Baba come to Birla House. The Old Man makes some joke about his fast bringing the mountain to Mohammed. The tall handsome Maharaja of Patiala comes and says he saved thousands of Muslims. The Old Man does not believe him. The Nawab of Malerkotla comes and says he saved the lives of thousands of Sikhs and Hindus by threatening to kill ten Muslims for each Sikh or Hindu killed. The Old Man believes him.

Everyone in Delhi has turned a Mussalman-lover. A procession of 1,00,000 come to Birla House chanting:

Hindu, Muslim, Sikh, Isaee
Bharat mein hain bhai-bhai

They yell '*Mahatma Gandhi ki jai*.' Hotels, cafes, shops close down. It is like a big holiday. I tell you it is Delhi's biggest *tamasha* of all time.

On the sixth day of his fast, the Old Man complains he can't piddle. I would like to ask him: 'What happened to all the orange and lime-juice you drank?' He babbles as if only half-awake. The radio says he is dying. Thousands turn up as if their real fathers were dying. They tell him that they have been fasting with him — their fathers, mothers, wives and children too. They submit petitions saying they will not molest Muslims; they will get out of mosques and Muslims' homes, even welcome Muslims returning from Pakistan.

They bring Muslims from wherever they can find them, put garlands round their necks and parade with them in the streets. They force tea and lemonades and sweets down the Muslims' throats. They form Peace Committees. The chief says if everyone is going mad, we should also pretend to be mad. The RSS puts its name down on the Peace Committee. The Old Fox is only waiting for this. As soon as he hears that the RSS has joined the Peace Committee he agrees to give up his fast.

It is Sunday, 18 January. It is also the birthday of Guru Gobind Singh the last of the Sikhs' ten Gurus. The Mussalmans had killed his father, his sons, thousands of his followers and then murdered him. We had planned to celebrate the day by driving every remaining Muslim out of Delhi. Our chief had said, 'Once we start it, the Sikhs are sure to join us.' But as I said, the Ganga is flowing the wrong way. There are hundreds of thousands of Sikhs at Gurdwara Rikabganj where the Guru's father's body was cremated a hundred-and-seventy-two years ago. Amongst them are hundreds of Mussalmans paying homage to the Sikhs' holy book. The Old Fox says it is an auspicious day and since he's got what he wanted he is going to break his fast. At 12.45 a.m. he takes a glass of orange-juice from the hands of the goatee-bearded Maulana Azad, says *Ram Ram* and drinks it up. The hypocrite! So the work we have done over the months, the blood we have spilled undone by the Old Man in six days!

You can see how he enjoys his victory! Nehru comes running to congratulate him. He replies: 'Live long and continue to be the Jawahar (jewel) of India.' He has the sahib editor rung up to give up his fast because the battle has been won. In the afternoon, Mussalman women draped in their tent-like *burqas* arrive in shoals and say, 'We've been fasting with you.' The old fellow grins. 'Oh, have you? Let me see your faces. No woman veils her face before her father. I am your *Bapu*.' The *burqa* flaps are thrown back. The old lecher has a good look at the sallow-faced Mussalmanis. 'This shows what real love can do,' he says very pleased with himself.

He rubs more salt in our wounds. He tells us Hindus and Sikhs to read the *Quran*.

In the afternoon the sky clouds over and it begins to rain. The gods in heaven shed tears at the fate of Bharat.

*

I don't remember who started it but the boys are saying that the gods desire human sacrifice before they will restore *dharma* to its rightful place. The chief says that such honour is reserved for a *Karmayogi* who the *Gita* says must act without expectation of reward. What reward can anyone expect for such sacrifice except the gallows? However none of the Delhi boys is considered good enough for the task. One tried and failed.

It is two days after Gandhi has given up his fast. The prayer meeting is over. The Old Fox is at his usual *buk buk* about loving everyone including those who hate you and poke your mothers and sisters. There is a loud *puttaakha*. It must be the fart of a passing motor car, I say to myself. But there is smoke and Gandhi *chelas* running about as if Hanumanji has set fire to their tails. 'Listen! Listen everybody!' screams Gandhi. 'If we panic like this over nothing, what shall be our plight if something really happens?'

No one listens to the Old Man. They run as fast as they can. I run too, out of Birla House, get into a taxi and tell the driver to take me *phuta phut* to the headquarters. When I tell them about what happened, all the chief says is '*Buss*, that's all?'

He orders that all the papers in the office should be burnt immediately and he orders me to return to Birla House and not budge until summoned. 'More is yet to come. Victory to the Hindu *dharma*,' he intones.

*

Gandhi talks a lot about his 'inner voice' and God telling him everything. But he does not know anything about the explosion. He thinks it was the police at target practice. As a matter of fact it was one of our boys aiming at a target which happened to be the Old Man himself. He is a Hindu refugee from the Punjab. His name is Madan Lal Pahwa. The police had thrown him out of a mosque in which he had been staying since he had come out of Pakistan. Pahwa threw a bomb. He had another with him when a policeman caught him.

The next day Gandhi says that Pahwa probably looks upon him (Gandhi) as an enemy of Hinduism and himself as an instrument sent by God for his removal. He requests the police not to harass Pahwa but to convert him to 'right thinking'. I want to tell the Old Fellow there is no 'perhaps' about it. He *is* the enemy number one of the Hindus.

*

Gandhi wants to be different from everyone else. On 26 January everyone goes to see the great parade. Gandhi says he does not like parades and stays in Birla House. I take the day off and take my parents to see it. It is a wonderful *tamasha*! Thousands of soldiers come down the slope between the Secretariat left-righting; hundreds of tanks, guns, armoured cars follow and rumble through India Gate. They salute Nehru. Nehru salutes them. Airplanes streak across leaving trails of coloured smoke in the sky. Then Nehru tells us that India is the land of Gandhi; India does not believe in tanks, guns, armoured cars or airplanes but in *ahimsa*.

Gandhi does not like a military *tamasha* because he has his own special kind of *tamasha*. The next day he announces he is going to the tomb of Qutubuddin Bakhtiyar Kaki near the Qutub Minar in Mehrauli. It is this Kaki fellow's death anniversary. Kaki had come to India some 600 years ago and converted many Hindus to Islam. Hindu refugees from Multan drove away the Mussalmans and settled in Mehrauli. They broke the marble screen around Kaki's grave. But when they hear Gandhi is coming they line the road and shout '*Hindu-Muslim bhai-bhai*' and serve tea to the Muslims. I am so angry that I want to yell: 'Bastards! Have you forgotten how your mothers were raped in Multan?'

Gandhi bows to Kaki's tomb. The Mussalmans ask him, 'Repeat our *fateha*.' Gandhi raises his hands, recites: 'In the name of Allah, The Beneficent, The Merciful.' That makes him a Mussalman, does it not? If a Hindu were to kill him he would be reducing the population of the enemies of Hinduism by one.

Gandhi asks the Muslims to forgive the Hindus and Sikhs for breaking the marble screen. He tells them he has heard some very good news. One-hundred-and-thirty Hindus and Sikhs have been massacred by Mussalmans at Parachinar near Peshawar in Pakistan. He says it is good news because the Hindus and Sikhs showed 'non-violent courage'. I say *shabash*! Do you need any more evidence of Gandhi being our greatest enemy?

A man who has escaped a massacre of Hindus and Sikhs at Gujarat railway station tells the Old Fellow: 'You have done enough harm. You have ruined us utterly. You ought now to leave us at once and retire to the Himalayas.'

'I cannot retire at anybody's orders,' replies the Old Man. 'I have put myself under God's sole command.'

'No,' insists the refugee. 'It is through us that God speaks to you. Our minds are crazed with grief.'

'My grief is not less than yours,' replies the great hypocrite.

How could you put sense into the skull of a man who keeps saying, 'I am right, everyone else is wrong. Muslims are right, Hindus and Sikhs in the wrong.'

It is Friday. The date, the 30th of January. The day, the month and the year (1948) are printed on my mind like my name Ram Rakha is tattooed on my right arm.

I am sleeping on the sofa I have been using for the last many days. It feels like the coldest night of the year. The lights are switched on at 3 a.m. I get up. I slap my arms across my chest, jump up and down to get the ice out of my limbs. I go and defecate in the dry water drain outside the house. I wash my bottom at a hydrant in the garden and rinse my hands with mud. I tuck them under my armpits to prevent them from freezing. I go to see what the Old Man is up to. I say *namaskar*. He looks through his glasses and smiles at me. He drinks a glass of hot water spiked with honey and lime-juice. Then another glass of orange-juice. He tells people that he will live to be a hundred-and-twenty-six. That's all he knows of God's ways.

Before the sky turns grey he goes through his routine of hymns, recitations from holy books and meditation. With the sun come the crowds. It is a regular *mela*. Morning turns to afternoon. The crowd becomes bigger. Sardar Patel arrives with his daughter Maniben. He has a scowl on his face. She is pale, thin as a stick and looks as if she has never known a man or how to laugh. They spend a long time arguing about something with the Old Man. Gandhi who is never late is ten minutes behind time.

When the Old Man comes out for his afternoon meeting he seems very happy. And why not! He has one arm resting on one girl, the other on another. Both girls are young and pretty. He jokes with them. His jokes are very silly. One girl gives him a carrot. 'So you are giving me cattle-food!' says he. Everyone laughs.

He pulls out his watch from the fold of his *dhoti*. 'I am late by ten minutes. I hate being late. I like to be at the prayer punctually at the stroke of five,' he says.

I edge up closer to him. I like being close to him because I get into the pictures in the newspapers and show them to my mother. People stand up to greet him. Someone shouts '*Bolo, bolo*'; others respond '*Mahatma Gandhi ki jai*'. The Old Man grins and says *namaskar*.

And then everything happens so quickly that I have to go over it again and again to make sure I really saw it happen. A stout, young fellow muscles his way through the crowd, pushes aside a girl who tries to stop him, bends down as if to touch Gandhi's feet, draws a revolver from the fold of his *dhoti* and before anyone can guess what he is up to pumps three bullets into the Old Man, *thah, thah, thah.*

Gandhi's hands remain joined as if he is bidding *namaskar* to the world. He says, *Ram, Ram.* Then he crumples down in a pool of his own blood.

A fit of madness comes over me. I jump on the man and bring him down. I tear the hair off his scalp; I bash his head on the ground and call him all kinds of names: mother-fucker, dog, bastard, son of a pig. A policeman grips me by the neck, pushes me aside and grabs the fellow. There is a lot of confusion. I jostle my way out of the crowd and run away. I start crying — running and crying, crying and running. I sit down on the pavement and slap my forehead with my hands and yell *hai, hai, hai.* A crowd of people gather round me. They ask me very kindly: 'Son, why are you crying?' I look up at them through my tears and reply: 'My *bapu* is dead.' They make clucking sounds of sympathy. One says, 'You must be brave. You must stand by your mother. You must carry on whatever work your *bapu* was doing.' Then he becomes more serious and asks, 'How did your *bapu* die? Was he very ill?'

'No, he wasn't ill at all, I killed him with my own hands, I killed him.' Then I slap my forehead and yell, '*Hai, hai,* I murdered my *bapu.*'

Bhagmati

Budh Singh is very angry with Gandhi and his *dhoti-topee* gang as he describes the Mahatma's followers. They want the British out of India. Budh Singh wants them to stay. He is setting up a British Retention League. He has invited H.M. the King of England to become its chief patron. He has nominated me as honorary treasurer and designated my apartment as the headquarters of BRL. He has started a signature campaign and proposes to send a scroll of a million Indian names protesting the transfer of power from the King to the *dhoti-topeewallas*.

So far he has only succeeded in persuading Bhagmati. She can't write so he's made her affix her thumb impression against which he has inscribed her name, sex and profession. Bhagmati—Sex: neutral *Hijda* ; Profession: prostitute. Proudly he displays the scroll to me and asks me to be the second signatory. I try to reason with him. I tell him all the events he wants changed took place a long time ago and there is nothing he can do about them. He looks at me as though I am mad so I decide to adopt his line of thinking and try and deflect him using an argument he will understand. I say: 'The British themselves want to leave India. Didn't you read in the papers that they will give Muslims their Pakistan and go away on the 15th of August?'

'That is all *buk buk*,' he retorts with disdain. 'This Lord Mountbatten is a Gandhi *chela*. I have written to Buckingham Palace about his mischief.'

'He is related to the king. His nephew is married to the king's daughter.'

'It is the traitor within who brings down the castle.'

'Don't you want India to be free?'

Budh Singh hasn't given the problem much thought. He mumbles in his beard; 'What freedom? Freedom for what? Loot, kill. Everyone talk freedom, freedom—don't know what freedom means.'

The doorbell saves me from Budh Singh. 'Let me think over it,' I say and go to open the door. It is my friend the Sikh journalist. Before he can explain the aims and objects of the British Retention League to my visitor, I gently push Budh Singh out. 'Another time, after I've had time to think. One should not decide such important matters in a hurry.'

The Sikh journalist is a joker. He tells me an old joke as if it were the latest one. 'When Rama, Sita and Lakshmana were leaving Ayodhya for their fourteen year exile, the citizens came to see them off. At the city gate Sri Ramchandraji begged them to return to their homes: "Ladies and gentlemen, thus far but no further." The citizens obeyed his orders and went back. Fourteen years later when the exiles returned to Ayodhya they met a party sitting outside the city gates. "You did not give us permission to return to our homes," they said. "You only allowed the men and women to go back. We are neither because we are *hijdas*." Sri Ramchandraji was so overcome by their devotion that he blessed them: "In the year 1947 I grant you *hijdas* the empire of Hindustan."'

He bursts into loud laughter '*Ha, ha, ha.*' I join him '*Hi, hi, hi.*'

The doorbell rings again. It is Bhagmati. 'What is the big joke?' she asks me.

'You tell her,' replies my journalist friend, looking at his watch 'I must go to the Coffee House at 11 a.m.' And breezes out of the apartment.

'What was he saying?' demands Bhagmati as she flops on the sofa. How can I tell her?

*

After the rains come months of dew and mists. Every dawn when I set out for a game of tennis I have to wipe dew off the windscreen of my car. The duster turns soggy and black with soot. One morning I return home to see Budh Singh sitting on his haunches with his head between his knees. He looks up. His eyes are bloodshot. He glowers at me with murderous intent. 'What is the matter, Budh Singh?' I ask him in as kindly a tone as I can manage.

'My eyes have come,' he mumbles wiping them with the back of his hand.

'You should see a doctor.'

He takes no notice of my suggestion and puts his head back between his knees.

I go into my apartment. My cook is lying on the carpet and groaning. 'What is the matter?' I ask him.

'My body is breaking.'

I ring up the doctor. His home-clinic is in the neighbouring block. He comes over, takes one look at Budh Singh and pronounces, 'Conjunctivitis, everyone in Delhi is getting it.' He prescribes an ointment.

Then he asks the cook to open his mouth and say 'aah'. The cook opens his mouth and says 'Aah'. The doctor turns up his eyelids and peers into his eyes. He sticks a thermometer in his mouth. Temperature: 102 degrees. He asks him if he is having loose motions or vomitting. 'No,' replies the cook. 'My body is breaking.'

The doctor turns to me and says, 'It is not hepatitis or cholera; lots of it around in Delhi. It is probably malaria or dengue-fly fever or perhaps viral fever. Everyone in Delhi is down with something or the other. I'll have to examine samples of his blood, urine and faeces to make sure.'

He prescribes analgesic tablets for the cook, malaria preventive pills for me. I fork out one-hundred-and-fifty rupees for the visit. I go to the chemist, get the prescriptions and hand medicines to Budh Singh and the cook. I tell them to stay in their quarters. 'These diseases are very catching. Don't come back till you are well.'

I have the apartment all to myself. It would be nice if Bhagmati were to come over. We could have some nice conjunctivitis together. Probably the bitch has already contracted one or the other ailment from her diseased patrons.

378

After a cold shower, I make myself a mug of Ginseng tea and get down to the newspapers. First, I pick up *The Hindustan Times*—Delhi's worst paper with the largest circulation. I start with page four which is largely devoted to obituaries and in memoriams. In Delhi all demises are sad and untimely. When their time is up, Delhiwallas do not simply die, they go up to their heavenly abode with reassurances from the *Gita* that death is no more than a changing of garments: the body (which wears garments) perishes, but the soul does not as it is eternal. So good care is taken that their earthly remains are consumed by fire at Nigambodh Ghat or at other crematoria. Delhi's dead consume a sizeable forest of timber every day as they proceed on their onward journey. The only takers for the electric crematorium which costs less than a quarter of the expense of disposal by wood are the dead of the anglicized rich or the unclaimed bodies of beggars. The right bank of the Jamna from the Tibetan colony at Majnoon ka Tilla to Raj Ghat where Gandhi was cremated has been consecrated to *viharas*, temples, burning *ghats*, the electric crematorium and memorials for the famous: Nehru, Shastri, Charan Singh, Sanjay Gandhi, Indira Gandhi and the original Gandhi, Father of the Nation. The Jamna riverside has become the launching pad for the journey into the unknown.

Back to page four. A boxed item says Nigambodh Ghat has been inundated by the flood waters of the Jamna. People should take their loved ones elsewhere. Perhaps for the first time, the electric crematorium will be earning dividends. I have nothing much to do. So I decide to take a look before joining my cronies at the Coffee House. I go by Purana Qila to the Ring Road. I leave the regional Headquarters of the World Health Organization (WHO) on my left, the prime cause of Delhi's ill-health, the filtration plant, on my right. Its four chimneys belch smoke all round the clock and provide WHO brochures their best illustrations for environmental pollution. They shower Delhi with soot. Its filtered water gives Delhiwallas Delhi belly, hepatitis, cholera, dysentry and other intestinal disorders. From the top of the overbridge I catch a glimpse of the Jamna licking the lower road of the old iron bridge and rolling its muddy waters past Gandhi's *samadhi* and the Velodrome. At the roundabout near the bridge is a police barrier: the bridge is closed to vehicular traffic. I turn round and drive into the electric crematorium. Sweepers are busy sweeping the road and the hall. Three corpses of beggars are put on a wheel-barrow behind the building to await disposal when bookings have been taken care of. The clerk in the office looks at his wrist-watch and asks me, 'Has the body arrived? There are three bookings for the morning. I've fixed them an hour apart.'

I tell him, I am not a mourner, just a *tamashbeen* (a sightseer). He gives me a dirty look and says acidly, 'If you like this kind of *tamasha*, take my job.'

I get out of the crematorium just in time. Coming in from the other side is a hearse laden with wreaths followed by a long cavalcade of cars with military markings. Old soldiers also die.

The Coffee House is crowded. My journalist friend and our political adviser have their faces covered with their newspapers as if they are not on talking terms with each other. I join them, they put down their papers. 'Say brother, where have you been all these days?'

I tell them of the number of relations and friends down with viral fever and conjunctivitis. And my servants.

'You are lucky you haven't got AIDS,' says the Sikh journalist. 'Knowing what you are upto with all these foreign cunts, you'll be the first Delhiwalla to get it.'

'Thanks,' I reply, 'you look out for yourself. It's sods like you who get AIDS. Straight sex does no harm to anyone.'

'Do you have anything else besides sex on your minds?' reprimands the politician. 'Here in Delhi people are dying like flies and all you can think of is sodomy and fucking foreign women. Are you one bit concerned about the future of your city?'

'No,' we reply in a duet. 'As far as I am concerned it can go to hell,' I add. 'It is no longer the Delhi I grew up in and loved. You Punjabis who invaded us in 1947 have buggered it out of shape.'

'Be more serious,' he advises me. 'We had no choice in 1947 except coming to Delhi. It is the others coming in every day who are creating the problems. Do you know 70,000 pour into Delhi every year from all over India? As if Delhi is the nation's orphanage. Where are they to be found homes, schools, hospitals? Do you know thirteen lakh Delhiwallas shit in the open because there are no lavatories for them?'

'You start a movement restricting shitting to once a week,' suggests the journalist, 'I promise to put it on the wire services.'

'It's no use talking to fellows like you—absolute waste of precious time,' says the politician getting up. 'Mark my words, Delhi is a dying city. The more it has of people like you, the sooner it will die. For this prophecy; you pay for my coffee,' he says as he strides off.

*

Life has gone by faster than I thought possible. When was it that I found Bhagmati lying on the road under the noonday sun? How many times had we lain together? Countless. And in between while she had plied her trade, I coupled with scores of women from countries known only to the Secretariat of the United Nations. Today I can recall only a few names and faces. I am not ashamed of what I did but can do no more. Bhagmati does not seem to mind my diminishing appetite for her. Her visits have become rarer and rarer. From dropping in once in two or three months when she needed money, for the last three or four years she has visited me only on Diwali. She no longer talks of her *hijda* husband (perhaps he is dead) or of sex but of Ramji and of Hindu temples and Muslim *dargahs* she visits. (Despite the years she consorted with me she has never displayed more than a cursory interest in Sikhism; she has certainly never bothered to go inside a Sikh gurdwara). She says she would like to spend her remaining years on the banks of the Ganga at Hardwar or Varanasi. At times she also talks of going on Haj (or is it Umra?) to Mecca and Medina. 'If only I could tear myself away from the lanes and bazaars of Delhi,' she says. 'But I think I will die in Delhi.' Sometimes she adds 'I hope you will take my ashes and throw them in the Ganga.' At others she says, 'Buy a two-yard plot of land near the mausoleum of Hazrat Nizamuddin for my grave.' I tell her that I am likely to go before her and she should throw my body into the Jamna. Both of us know that we may not hear of the other's demise till months after it has taken place.

Budh Singh has turned very hostile. After the incidence of 'eve-teasing', he sank into deep melancholia. I took him to the mental ward of the Medical Institute. The doctor gave him some electric shocks which upset him very much. He was more upset at the doctor's suggestion that I should have him admitted to an asylum in Agra or Ranchi. Budh Singh snapped out of his melancholia and turned aggressive. He called the doctor a *bahinchod* and nearly hit me when I restrained him from hitting the doctor. He sits in front of my apartment and growls at me every time I come in or go out. He has made friends with the Bhai of the gurdwara behind my apartment and the two have devised ways of torturing me. The Bhai switches on his microphone at full blast at four in the morning and starts chanting prayers with the loudspeakers turned towards my bedroom. When I remonstrate with him, he tells me to mind my own business. Once when I reported him to the police, he told the sub-inspector that it was the wish of the *sangat* (congregation) and who was I to object? His only *sangat* was, and is, Budh Singh. When the sub-inspector left, the Bhai warned me that the next time I reported him to the police he would get Sant Bhindranwale's followers to put me on the right path. Budh Singh yelled: '*Sant Jarnail Singh Bhindranwale zindabad!*'

My cook-bearer went on his annual leave and never came back. I have to fend for myself. Living alone is not so hard as I thought it would be. Between an electric kettle and a toaster I make tea, boil eggs and eat toasted sandwiches. The Bhai's loudspeaker wakes me up at 4 a.m. I make myself a mug of tea and go into my study where the Bhai's unmelodious voice cannot pursue me. I switch on the BBC news at 4.30 a.m. Thereafter I can choose between the Bible Societies Service in Hindi or the morning service from the Golden Temple in Amritsar. I usually opt for the Golden Temple because I am familiar with the morning hymnal. Perhaps suppressed religiosity is rearing its head. Perhaps I will make my peace with the Great Guru as the time of confrontation with Truth draws near.

As the light comes on I go for a walk in Lodhi Park. Most of the walkers here know each other. Some deign to answer my *namaskar*. Back in my apartment I make myself another mug of tea and a couple of pieces of toast. I read the papers while the sweeper woman sweeps the floor. Then I do not know what to do. I cannot afford to run my rickety old car more than a couple of miles a day; but I have to drive it a little to keep the battery going. At times I run it to the Coffee House. It is not much fun to hear people say: 'This old man has been coming here for over fifty years.' I spend my afternoons at the India International Centre library of which I fortunately took a life membership in my more affluent days. Sometimes someone asks me to join him over a cup of tea. There is always some lecture, cinema show or dance-recital which I can attend free of charge. So pass the long evenings. On my way back to my apartment I buy *chop suey* or *seekh kabab* from a take-away joint in Khan Market. The only thing I really look forward to is whisky (now, alas, Indian stuff) which I sip listening to old tapes of *ghazals* of Mehdi Hassan or Iqbal Bano or Farida Khanum. I sleep badly. I am beset by nightmares. What will happen if I am taken ill? There is no one to look after me. It would be nice if I went one night in my sleep and next morning the sweeper girl found me dead in my bed. She could take everything she wanted from my flat: transistor radio, cassette player, watches, clocks, ball-point pens, cash and deposit them in her home before she came back and screamed that the old man was dead and would somebody do something about him. It wouldn't be too bad if a thug broke into my flat and did me in. It would save a lot of people a lot of trouble. And save me all the bother of finding a bed in a hospital and paying doctor's bills.

*

Days go by. I am less and less awake when I get out of bed and drag myself to my study. One morning I kicked the stool on which I keep my electric kettle. I was lucky—only a few drops of boiling water fell on my foot. At times I doze off listening to the *keertan* from the Golden Temple. It is becoming a bore. I listen to it because at that hour there is nothing better to tune into. Ever since that fellow Bhindranwale started spouting hateful words against Hindus from the precincts of the Golden Temple, something seems to have gone out of the *keertan*. The Bhai and Budh Singh call him a saint. I feel a lesser Sikh because I think he is a *bhoot* (incarnation of Satan).

On the first of June 1984 the morning service from the Golden Temple is somewhat erratic. I am not sure whether the *tabla* drums have been put too close to the microphone or it is something else. The beat sounds like gunfire. Papers say that the army has been ordered to get Bhindranwale dead or alive; perhaps it is trying to frighten him to surrender. Mrs Gandhi has been assuring the Sikhs that she will never order the army into the Temple. Sensible woman! She knows that mounting an invasion on the temple will turn it into a bloody battlefield. No Sikh will ever forgive her.

I read newspapers more carefully. And listen to the morning service more intently. The 3rd of June is the anniversary of the martyrdom of the builder of the temple. Thousands of pilgrims have come from distant villages to bathe in the sacred pool.

I can hear the hubbub of their voices behind the *keertan*. And the crying of babies roused from their slumbers. And their mothers bribing them with their breasts to keep silent. Roars of *Wah Gurus*! during the invocation include women's voices. Foolish people! What are they doing in the temple with Bhindranwale's men and the army trading shots! Curfew has been imposed on the city. The Punjab has been handed over to the army and sealed off from the rest of the world. On the morning of the 5th of June I hear gunfire more clearly than the *keertan*. The next morning there is silence. Papers carry triumphant headlines: 'Tanks of the Indian army blast Bhindranwale's stronghold.' The BBC says well over a thousand including Bhindranwale have been killed. The bullet-ridden corpses of women and infants-in-arms float in the sacred pool. What made Indira Gandhi do such a stupid thing?

384

A deep depression enters my soul. I ask myself over and over again, am I Sikh? I am certainly not the Bhindranwale brand nor the gurdwara Bhai brand. Bhindranwale was loonier than Budh Singh. I cannot remember when I last went to a gurdwara. I have not prayed in fifty years.

On the morning of the 6th of June I go to the gurdwara behind my apartment. There is quite a crowd. Many are in tears. Their tears bring tears to my eyes. I am one of them. At the end of the service, the Bhai makes a short, fiery speech. 'We Sikhs never forget or forgive. Remember what we did to the Afghans and to Massa Ranghar? We desecrated their mosques and cut off Massa's head. That's what some son of the Guru will do to these demons. You wait and see,' he says. Great boasters, these Sikhs! They live in the past and refuse to understand that in a civilized society you don't desecrate mosques or cut off people's heads.

The Bhai and most Sikhs seen on the road have taken to wearing black turbans. After a few days I also have a couple of my turbans dyed black. Yes, I am one of them.

Budh Singh has turned more rabid. Everytime a Hindu passes by my apartment he yells: 'Sant Bhindranwale zindabad.' They laugh at him. If he is too absorbed in himself, they provoke him: 'O son of Bhindranwale! Let's have the slogan again!'

So passes the hot summer. And the torrid months of rains and clouds we call the monsoon. September gives way to October. And comes the autumn season of festivals.

*

It is the last day of October. I am in low spirits. No reason whatsoever. Slept soundly. Long relieving fart while peeing. Pee no longer a powerful jet but an intermittent spray. Enlarged prostate. To be expected when you are seventy. A mug of hot Ginseng and bowels as clean as the inside of a gun barrel. News no worse than other days. Weather has changed for the better—neither too warm nor too cool. Fragrant *madhumalati* and hibiscus about the windows in full flower. Two chorizzias on the lawn covered in pink and white. Moonbeam hedge along the face like a green wall speckled with stars as in the milky way. Dew on the grass sparkling like diamonds in the early sun. What more can Allah do to assure me that He is up there in His heavenly abode and pleased with His handiwork?

My spirits refuse to lift. Read the headlines of papers and toss them in the grate. Stretch my legs on a *moorha* and doze off. Dream of Bhagmati. Since she has become a once-a-year visitor she makes up by often coming into my dreams. We haven't had sex for the last ten years but in my dreams she is still very bawdy and very lusty. I wake up with a start. Bell rings non-stop; thumping on the door. Bhagmati? I run up and open the door. It's Budh Singh. Eyes madder than ever; nostrils flared. He yells in my face sending a spray of spit from his beard to mine: 'Indira Gandhi shot dead! Long live Sant Jarnail Singhji Bhindranwale!'

Budh Singh is becoming impossible. I try to shut the door. He sticks out one foot and prevents me from doing so. 'You think Budh Singh mad? You think Budh Singh lie? Listen to radio BBC.' He turns about and marches off swinging his arms and yelling: '*Khalistan zindabad! Indira Gandhi murdabad! Sant Bhindranwale amar rahey.*' I switch on my transistor. All India Radio stations merrily play film music, programmes for farmers, youth of the land. Half-an-hour later I get the BBC. Indira Gandhi has been shot by her Sikh bodyguard and has been rushed to the All India Medical Institute. There will be no official statement on her condition till President Zail Singh and her son Rajiv Gandhi return to Delhi. Indira is unlikely to survive the volley of stengun fire and pistol shots pumped into her frail body etc. etc.

I sit in my chair. Head between hands. Dazed. Look blankly from bookshelves to ceiling, ceiling to bookshelves. The bell rings again. I tiptoe to the door and peer through the Judas hole. Not Budh Singh but the Bhai of the neighbouring gurdwara. I open the door. He dips his hand in a bowl he is carrying and takes out a palmful of flour pudding. '*Pershad*,' he says, 'the desecration of the Golden Temple has been avenged. The Sikh *Panth* has won a victory. Indira *kutti* (bitch) is dead.'

386

Without replying I slam the door in his face and return to my chair. Celebrating the murder of a frail, little woman! What have the Sikhs come down to? If only the stupid woman had owned up her mistake, gone to the Temple and said, 'My Sikh brothers and sisters I am sorry, I made a big mistake, forgive me,' they would have forgiven her. But to get one demented monk and his gang of armed goons she let the army slay a thousand innocent pilgrims: grey-beards, blackbeards, no beards, women and babies-in-arms. Blasted the Akal Takht, seat of Sikh spiritual and temporal authority. Let the army loot cash, utensils and burn down the archives. In short, to kill a rat, she pulled down the house. One crime follows another. One lie by a bigger lie. The entire country pays the price for these blunders and lies.

I fiddle with my transistor switching from All India Radio to the BBC, to the Voice of America to Radio Germany to Radio Moscow. AIR says she is still alive. The BBC and the Voice of America say she is dead. Moscow simply quotes Delhi. Hours pass. Not a soul on the lawn in front. Not a soul on the road facing the gurdwara. A few buses run by without their usual hooting, a few cyclists hurry homewards bent double over their handlebars as if facing a strong wind. An eerie quiet spreads like a pestilent fog.

The shadows lengthen. The newspaper boy shoves *The Evening News* under my door. Banner headlines: 'Indira Gandhi Shot by Her own Sikh Guards. One of them has been killed; the other badly wounded. At the All India Medical Institute teams of surgeons are taking out bullets and pumping in blood into Indira Gandhi's body and trying desperately to save her.' Stale news. By then most foreign radio stations are saying she died on the operating table. What now?

The bell rings. Followed by slapping on the door. I peep through the Judas hole. Some fat, old woman I cannot recognize in the dim hallway light. She bangs on the door with her fist. I open the door. It is Bhagmati. Sparse hair daubed with henna. No teeth. Squashed mouth. Hair-bristle about her chin. Is this the same Bhagmati I had lusted after most of my lustful years? *'Hai Laam! Hai Laam!'* she says with her toothless mouth. She holds her ears with her hands, sticks out her yellow tongue, '*Toba! Toba!* What I have seen with my own eyes, may no one ever behold! They are killing every Sikh they see on the road, burning their taxis, trucks, scooters. Connaught Place is on fire. They are looting every Sikh shop, office, hotel. And you are sitting here waiting for them to come and kill you! *Hain*? I am going to take you to Lal Kuan. Nobody will bend a hair on a *hijda's* head. *Chalo*,' she orders.

'Patience!' I tell her as I open the door to let her in. 'If they are killing every Sikh they find, how do you think we will get to Lal Kuan? It is best to stay where you are. The police is bound to stop it in time.'

'Police?' she asks contemptuously. 'Those *bahinchods* are with the mobs. "We give you thirty-six hours to finish every Sikh in the city," they tell them.' She sinks down on the sofa, covers her face with her hands and is convulsed with sobs. It is my turn to comfort her. I put my hand on her shoulder, 'It can't be all that bad. This is a civilized country,' I tell her.

She looks up with her tear-stained eyes. 'You want to see it with your own eyes? Come up on the roof and look.' She takes my hand and heaves herself up from the sofa. We climb up the four storeys of my apartment building and go on the roof. She points northwards towards Connaught Circus. The sky is aglow: not with electric lights but with flames. In the dusk I can see clouds of smoke rising from different points. I look around in other directions. There are bonfires and smoke on many roads. 'Sikhs' taxis and trucks,' Bhagmati informs me. The evening breeze wafts across the voice of crowds roaring in unison, '*Indira Gandhi zindabad* (long live Indira Gandhi).' '*Sikh hatyaron ko khatam karo* (finish the murderous Sikhs).' A mob is moving up the road towards my apartment. Bhagmati panics. '*Chalo, chalo*,' she screams. 'I'll cut your hair and beard quickly. Then we can get out safely. All they can burn will be your books. They are of no use to Dilliwallas.'

'Don't be silly,' I snap, 'Nobody is going to cut my hair or beard.' I follow her down the dark staircase back into my apartment. There is no time to unscrew my nameplate; I get an iron rod, stick it in the space behind the door and the plate and wrench it off. It breaks into two. 'Now no one will know who lives here.'

'You are a stupid Sikh!' she exclaims angrily. 'They will ask your neighbours. Do as I tell you. Let me cut your hair and beard and we can go to some hotel or something.'

'No,' I yell back stubbornly. 'Let them do their worst. I'll kill one or two before they get me.'

'And me. You stupid, old *budha bewakoof*! Will you ever get sense in your head?' I am not used to being abused by Bhagmati. My temper rises. Our argument is silenced by the mob yelling somewhere behind my back garden. We slip out into the dark garden and watch through the thick hibiscus hedge. The mob is composed of about fifty young boys armed with iron rods. Some have canisters of petrol in their hands. They surround the gurdwara and storm in. They drag out the Bhai and beat him up with their fists and rods. He cries at the top of his voice: '*Bachao! Bachao!* Police!' They shout back. 'Bhindranwale *key bacchey* (son of Bhindranwale)! Ask your father to save you now.' They bring out the *Granth*, its canopy, carpets and *durries*, heap them up in a pile and sprinkle petrol on it. One puts a match to it and the heap bursts into flame. The Bhai's hair is scattered over his bloodied face but he pleads, 'Do what you like to me but don't dishonour the holy book. *Rab da vaasta* (for God's sake).'

'Let the bastard go with his holy book,' shouts someone. They pour petrol over his hair, splash it on his beard and push him on the flaming pile. He shrinks and crumples into a flaming corpse. They yell triumphantly: '*Indira Gandhi amar rahey* (Indira Gandhi is immortal).'

My knees buckle under me and I sit down on the wet grass. I cannot hold my bladder. Bhagmati sits down beside me and massages my back. After a while she helps me stand up and whispers in my ears, 'Let's go indoors before they spot us.' I stay rooted to the ground and peer through the bush. I see a fellow reading something from a paper in his hand. He points to garages owned by Sikh mechanics. The mob moves to the garages. Cars lined outside for repairs are set on fire. Garage doors smashed open. People watch them from their balconies. Someone pleads, 'These cars belong to Hindus; the Sikh mechanics have fled. If you set fire to the garages, the whole building will catch fire. We are only Hindus, Muslims and Christians here. Why don't you go to the taxi-stand?'

That makes sense to the mob. It makes its way past the Bhai's funeral pyre towards the cab-rank. I can hear the exchange of abuse. The cab-drivers are defiant. I stagger to the other side of the garden with Bhagmati tugging at my arms and pleading with me to get back into the room. Six unarmed cabbies face an armed mob which has grown to over two hundred. Abuse changes to hurling of stones. A posse of armed constabulary watch the unequal combat without moving from their places. Stones smash into the cab-drivers kiosk and the window-panes of the cabs. The fellows nevertheless keep the mob at bay. A shot rings out and a driver crumples down beside his cab. The other five run away as fast as they can. Armed police form a ring round the cabs, take out wallets, transistors, cassette players. Then they let the mob set them on fire. The policemen direct the mob to Sikh shops in the market. They move away from my apartment. Bhagmati tells me to change my trousers. I feel ashamed of myself.

Pins and needles down my legs. Bhagmati stares vacantly at the wall without saying a word. I get out my last bottle of Scotch (which I had kept for an emergency) and pour out a stiff one. 'The best thing in times of trouble,' I announce to her.

'And nothing for your old *budhia* woman?' asks Bhagmati. 'I have never touched the stuff; but today give me poison or give me wine.' I pour her a generous portion and mix it with Campa Cola to sweeten its taste. She gulps it down as if it were a glass of buttermilk. A glow spreads over her wrinkled, toothless face. 'More,' she orders.

'Not so fast, you'll get sick.'

I help myself to a second, a third. She eyes me banefully while she shakes her empty glass. I take a fourth and give her another smaller one. 'Don't gulp it down; learn to drink like a lady.'

'Lady be buggered!' she replies. She is her old self. 'What's happened to that mad Sikh you had? What was his name? Buddhoo or something like that.'

'Budh Singh. He was around this morning. Raving like a lunatic. If these fellows lay their hands on him, they will make a *seekh kabab* of him. If he comes round, we must lock him up in a room.'

I empty a packet of cheese crackers on a plate and put it before her. 'This is all I have at home,' I tell her. She picks up one and feels its texture. 'How can I eat wooden biscuits? I have no teeth.' She soaks one in her Scotch and Cola till it turns soggy and pops it in her mouth. She eats up the entire packet without bothering to find out if there is anything left for me. In any case I have no appetite for food. I tell her to sleep in my bed while I sleep on the sofa. She accepts my offer and waddles into the bedroom. A few minutes later I hear her belch, snore and break wind.

I switch on my radio and tune it to foreign stations. All give detailed news about Indira Gandhi's assassination at the hands of her own Sikh bodyguards. And very briefly talk of anti-Sikh violence. Only Radio Pakistan talks of hundreds of Sikhs massacred and hundreds of gurdwaras burnt in Delhi. The telephone rings: 'Is that you?' it asks. 'Yes.' The caller proceeds to abuse me. 'Bloody bastard you murdered your mother.' I hit back. 'Bloody mother-fucker, bastard yourself. You murdered your Bapu Gandhi, who are you to *buk buk*?'

The abuse upsets me. The telephone rings again. This time it is someone very polite. 'Don't drink water out of your tap. It's been poisoned by the Sikhs.' He puts down his receiver.

A few minutes later another ring. 'Trainloads of dead Hindus massacred by Sikhs in the Punjab have arrived in Delhi. Hindus will avenge these killings.' Again the receiver is put down before I can say a word.

I sit and wait for the phone to ring again. It is dead. At midnight there is another hubbub. Slogans, yelling, people running from somewhere to somewhere. Everyone is awake. Another truckload of boys arrives. They burn another couple of cars and disappear. People peer through their windows to see the conflagration. Policemen armed with rifles stop by for a few minutes and then walk away.

Fatigue overtakes me and I doze off in my chair. I am woken up by the sound of shouting coming from the side of the gurdwara. I get up with a start and run out into the garden to see what is going on. It is early dawn but everyone seems to be on their balconies and windows looking at the gurdwara. Bhagmati comes heaving herself along as fast as she can and shouting at me.

'Get inside,' she screams. I ignore her and peep through the hedge.

I see Budh Singh in the gurdwara courtyard beside the smouldering ashes of the *Granth* and the Bhai. He has a *kirpan* in one hand and is whirling about like a dancing *dervish*, yelling abuse at a gang of young men armed with steel rods who have surrounded him. 'You *madarchods*, you *bahinchods*, may your seed be destroyed! You burn our holy book. May your *Vedas* and *Shastras* be burnt!'

The young gangsters play a cat and mouse game with him. They take turns prodding Budh Singh in the back with their rods. The old fellow is getting tired. He can't fight so many men. As he pauses for breath, an iron rod crashes on his shoulder and brings him down. His *kirpan* falls out of his hand. One fellow picks it up and pokes it in his bottom. Two lads pounce on him and pin his arms behind his back. One takes out a pair of scissors and begins to clip off Budh Singh's beard. Budh Singh spits in his face. The fellow slaps him on the face, catches him by his long hair and cuts off a hunk. They've had their fun. They get down to serious business. A boy gets a car tyre, fills its inside rim with petrol and lights it. It is a fiery garland. Two boys hold it over Budh Singh and slowly bring it down over his head to his shoulders. Budh Singh screams in agony as he crumples down to the ground. The boys laugh and give him the Sikh call of victory: '*Boley So Nihal! Sat Sri Akal.*'

THE COLLECTED NOVELS

Khushwant Singh

Witty, eloquent, outrageous, and always entertaining, Khushwant Singh has acquired an iconic status as a writer and journalist. This omnibus edition brings together three of his novels written over four decades.

Train to Pakistan, Khushwant Singh's first novel, published in 1954, brought him instant fame. A powerful and moving account of the tragedy of Partition, set in the small Indian frontier village of Mano Majra, it is also the touching love story of a Sikh dacoit and a Muslim girl.

I Shall Not Hear the Nightingale, his second novel, deals with the confict in a prosperous Sikh family living in Punjab in the mid-1940s. The father is a magistrate who works for the British, while the son dreams of glory as the leader of a terrorist group rebelling against foreign rule.

The best-selling *Delhi,* a vast, erotic, irreverent magnum opus centred on the Indian capital, is the third book in this anthology. The principal narrator of the saga, which extends over six hundred years, is an ageing reprobate who loves Delhi as much as he does the hijda-whore Bhagmati. As he travels through time, space and history to 'discover' his beloved city, we find it transformed and immortalized in our minds for ever.

Khushwant Singh's phenomenal success as a writer springs from a most unwriterly virtue: he writes for the reader, not for himself. He has the knack of seeming to speak directly to the reader, shrugging himself out of the confines of the printed page.
—Times of India

THE COMPANY OF WOMEN

Khushwant Singh

Recently separated from his nagging, ill-tempered wife of thirteen years, millionaire businessman Mohan Kumar decides to reinvent his life. Convinced that 'lust is the true foundation of love', he embarks on an audacious plan: he will advertise for paid lady companions to share his bed and his life. Thus begins his journey of easy, unbridled sexuality in the company of some remarkable women.

In *The Company of Women*, his first novel in ten years, Khushwant Singh, India's most widely read author, has produced an uninhibited, erotic and endlessly entertaining celebration of love, sex and passion.

'. . .the book is a triumph.'
—*Outlook*

' . . . the most erotic modern novel written by an Indian. . .'
—*India Abroad News Services*

NOT A NICE MAN TO KNOW
The Best of Khushwant Singh

In an essay in this anthology, Khushwant Singh claims that he is not a nice man to know. Whatever the truth of that assertion, there is little question about his skill as a witty, eloquent and entertaining writer. This book collects the best of over three decades of the author's prose—including his finest journalistic pieces, short stories, translations, jokes, plays as well as excerpts from his non-fiction books and novels. Taken together, the pieces in this selection (some of them never published before) show just why Khushwant Singh is the country's most widely read columnist and one of its most celebrated authors.

'Khushwant's greatest quality, and one which illuminates all his writings, is the ability to talk to the reader and not at him.'
—*Business Standard*

'(The book) is compelling re-reading not because it is memorable but because it is unforgettable.'
—*The Tribune*